AN INSIDE JOB

The crystal walls ⬚⬚⬚⬚⬚⬚⬚⬚⬚⬚⬚⬚⬚ up to the ruby quartz t⬚⬚⬚⬚⬚⬚⬚⬚⬚⬚⬚d. Her limbs shook; her ⬚⬚⬚⬚⬚⬚⬚⬚⬚o lifts along the sides. ⬚⬚⬚⬚⬚⬚⬚⬚⬚ eflecting a thousand versions of herself from angular fractures. The crystalline structures mesmerized Kivita into a state of bliss, as if she already dreamt in her cryopod.

In the center of the floor stood a three-foot amethystine altar. A round red gem the size of a child's fist hung suspended over it. Nothing visible held up the gem.

Kivita stilled. Three armored Aldaakian bodies lay around the altar. Through the narrow faceplates, the albino faces looked asleep. They might have been dead for a day or a decade. Part of her wanted to touch them, while another wanted to look away. Strange how heat created life as well as destroyed it, while cold drained life while preserving it.

Yeah. Now she sounded like a Sage.

The tingling in her brain increased. Shit, not another headache. Something tickled her throat, and Kivita's breath quaked in her lungs.

Reflected in one Aldaakian faceplate was a tall, hulking form.

She slowly turned.

Five Kith had entered the crystal tower. They stepped easily around the altar, th⬚⬚ ⬚⬚⬚⬚⬚⬚ ⬚⬚⬚ ⬚⬚⬚ mirroring the pulsing geode ligh⬚⬚ ⬚⬚⬚ ⬚⬚⬚⬚⬚ ⬚⬚ ⬚⬚⬚⬚ined her, and serrated bla⬚⬚ ⬚⬚⬚ protr⬚⬚ ⬚⬚⬚ their hands.

"Damn it." Her mouth ⬚⬚⬚⬚ ⬚⬚⬚⬚⬚⬚

INHERIT
THE STARS

Tony Peak

A ROC BOOK

ROC
Published by New American Library,
an imprint of Penguin Random House LLC
375 Hudson Street, New York, New York 10014

This book is an original publication of New American Library.

First Printing, November 2015

For more information about Penguin Random House, visit penguin.com.

ISBN 978-0-451-47653-1

Printed in the United States of America
10 9 8 7 6 5 4 3 2 1

Penguin
Random
House

To my son, Zander,
may you always find light in the darkness

ACKNOWLEDGMENTS

First I want to thank Diana Gill for helping an unknown author like me turn this into a real novel. Her professional guidance finally showed me how to "kill those darlings," and her enthusiasm for the project was second only to my own. Rebecca Brewer and Robin Catalano have my gratitude for their final edits, which added polish and clarity. The cover artist, Torstein Nordstrand, perfectly captured my characters and for that I am amazed and thankful. My key beta-readers deserve special mention for their patience and advice: Meredith Lopez, Ian Welke, and Gregory Clifford—they read multiple drafts, replied to my incessant e-mails, and tolerated my writing indulgences. I'd also like to credit all of the members from the Online Writing Workshop who reviewed my fledgling chapters, particularly Jon Paradise, whose critique proved insightful.

Finally, I'd like to thank my family, who forged me into the person who imagined this story (I've made it, Mom & Dad!), but especially my wife, Melody, who was brave enough to marry a writer who had little else but a hope and a dream.

1

Her oxygen canister was near empty. Numbness spread down her legs. Her footsteps slowed. Ancient vacuum frost floated in the zero-G, disturbed by her passage. Outside the viewport, three red supergiants throbbed with power. A frigid pulse stabbed her mind again and again. . . .

Kivita Vondir rubbed her forehead. Not even off the ship yet and those stupid dreams were still bothering her. Ever since salvaging near Xeh's Crown, the dreams had plagued her. With a hand poised over the airlock button, she forced herself not to wobble. She'd just woken up—that's all.

Every time she left cryostasis, though, the headaches worsened. The visions became more invasive: tall white exoskeletons. Unfamiliar star patterns. Horrified people trapped in green, gelatinous vats. Suffocating in that old Vim derelict. And that crazy, cold hammering in her skull.

She blinked away the visions and stumbled through *Terredyn Narbas*'s airlock. "Damned if I don't need a better line of work."

After a year in cryostasis, Haldon Prime's yellow sun strained her eyes. Every nerve itched; every bodily movement was stiff and dull. Recalling the dreams made her head throb further. Maybe she should stay aboard. Rest awhile.

Biting her lip, she glanced back into *Terredyn Narbas*'s interior. Her quarters were lit in a cool gray sheen. Ascali claw graffiti, placards of beefy males and busty women, and glue pen chits covered the bulkheads. She'd clean it up one of these days.

Rhyer, her father, had fixed up the old trawler and named it after some ancient queen. She'd bent Inheritor laws in keeping it, since no one could inherit technology from a deceased relative. Usually it all went to the prophets, to aid their ultimate goal of escaping the Cetturo Arm. Whatever.

Her favorite placard hung beside the hammock. It showed Kivita, eight years old, with Rhyer. The blue, green, and pink gas giant of Tejuit Seven loomed behind them through a viewport. That trip was the fondest memory of her father.

At seventeen she'd buried him here on Haldon Prime. Mention of radiation leaks still churned her stomach.

Lips tight, she cinched lead-lined, radiation-resistant leather chaps around her thighs, then adjusted her leather vest and black bodyglove. Aldaakian polyboots protected her feet. A shortsword dangled from her belt, since firearms were prohibited in Inheritor spaceports.

"Be right back, girl." Kivita patted *Terredyn Narbas*'s hull and stepped outside. A warm breeze stirred her jaw-length, red-blond hair. White clouds stretched over a shadow-blue sky. Sure, it was nice, but she wasn't a tourist. After salvaging from a debris field in a neighboring system, all she wanted was hot food, jiir juice . . . and maybe sex.

Kivita scanned over *Terredyn Narbas*, ensuring that no panels had loosened during reentry. The two-hundred-foot-long trawler resembled a Susuron hammerhead fish, with a gray-red, atmosphere-rusted hull. Her father's insignia, a sword with a flaring star, remained visible above the airlock.

The spaceport outside rumbled with activity. Some claimed it was the largest in the Cetturo Arm. Though Haldon Prime was her home world, Kivita seldom visited, except to trade salvage for much-needed supplies. *Terredyn Narbas* was her true home. A womb she could sleep in, live in. Even hide in, when the universe threatened to freeze her heart.

She swallowed and forced down the flutters in her chest. No way would he be here.

"Remember—there's jiir juice and sex out there." Kivita inserted a data chit into the soot-caked terminal at the pad's edge. The display showed the current date: Charter Year 11,409. A beep indicated her recovery memo had been accepted. Rolling her eyes, Kivita willed the metal door to slide open faster.

Outside, clay and stone walls separated each pad. Other oblong vessels dotted the spaceport. Salvagers from across Inheritor Space haggled with merchants, traded stories, or headed for brothels. A medical tent sold treatments for cryomaladies like stunted hair growth, perpetually chilled skin, loss of smell, or short-term memory loss. A dressed-stone bulwark segregated the spaceport from the local population. Kivita wished they'd just tear it down, but Inheritor prophets forbade commoners from socializing with outsiders.

Kivita remembered being a teenage farmhand before becoming a salvager, weeding crop rows, planting red-grain seeds until her father returned from a salvaging run. How long had it been since she'd smelled dirt on her hands instead of hydraulic oil? Sometimes she missed it.

Most of the time she missed Sar Redryll.

She'd been dreaming of him again, too. Black curly hair, green-speckled eyes. Had it really been two years? Six would have passed for him if he'd stayed on Gontalo. Whenever she dreamt of Sar, those unfamiliar stars also came to mind. Her head tingled, and she rubbed her temples. Damn headache.

Maybe she'd been in space too long. Alone and cold.

Scowling, Kivita left the pad. Spacers in worn fatigues sloshed through muddy thoroughfares hemmed in by metal-framed stalls. Bars and brothels dotted the area. A bald prophet in yellow robes handed out religious chits with a patronizing smile. Inheritor soldiers in red jumpsuits haunted every corner. A few looked at her, then whispered into their helmet mics.

She didn't remember this many soldiers here the last time. Odd.

One merchant sold Ascali prostitutes for twenty pounds of Freen iron ore. Short brown fur covered their athletic bodies; a long, straight mane of hair spilled from their heads. They originated from Sygma, an arboreal world where the blue-leaved jiir trees grew.

The prickling in her cranium returned. Kivita sighed and walked away. This tingling better not dampen her day. There was little else to look forward to during these visits. No family, and most childhood acquaintances were dead or worked the fields. If they were lucky.

"Vondir? Now, what have you brought back this time?" a merchant asked from a nearby stall. He scratched his gray beard and smiled.

Kivita grinned. "Not enough to retire yet, Marsque. You're looking well." Actually, he'd aged a few more years since the last time she'd seen him. She almost hadn't recognized him.

"Not near as well as you. You just dock, or have you been giving your business to some fancy Naxan vendor?" A hint of farmer drawl colored Marsque's Meh Sattan, the common tongue of the Arm.

"Just docked, smoothie. How've you been? Anything big happen while I was gone?"

"Nothing but a few more restrictions on goods from Tannocci Space. More trouble from the Thedes, and . . ." A shadow crossed Marsque's gaze; then he smiled again. "Ah, you know how it is here. More sermons, more rules. Got your data chit ready?"

She dug the chit from her vest pocket and handed it over. "That's sixteen tons of scrap from Q'Daor. Should contain some lead-lined bulkheads, like those in the old feudal ships."

"You hauled all that by yourself?" Marsque frowned. "You ever think about getting a partner to help out? Few salvagers go it alone anymore."

"No, thanks. How much, then?" Heat rose in Kivita's cheeks. He made it sound as if she liked being alone out there.

Marsque tapped his glue pen on the counter. "Lead-lined bulkheads, huh? I'll take your word for it. I've got Bellerion protein slabs, fresh Susuron water, and even some jiir liquor from Sygma."

Merchants on Inheritor worlds traded in necessities or luxuries, never advanced tech. Only salvagers could barter for cryotech and energy dumps, because of their special status. An engine overhaul and a hull reseal would be nice, but she'd need at least a hundred tons of salvage to cover it.

"I've also got plush furniture from Haldon Six and handmade thermal blankets. New cosmetics, like the dark stuff they wear around their eyes on Soleno Four. Course, you're still too pretty to be wearing that." Marsque winked at her.

"Slow down, smoothie. What I need is some pseudo-adrine, oxygen canisters, and new scrubbers for my air intakes on *Terredyn Narbas*. Oh, and a new mist ionizer."

"I'll even throw in a skinsuit from Susuron. I know you always liked that world, even when you were a wee thing." Marsque jotted down the items in glue pen on Kivita's computer chit. With the chit's data linked to the spaceport's computers, she wouldn't be cleared to leave the spaceport until she paid for the transaction.

Kivita recalled walking these same merchant stalls with her father, staring agog at rare items from other worlds or listening to salvager tales of prehuman derelicts. The prophets considered such tales heretical.

"Don't pay heed to those Inheritor prophets, Kiv," her father had once said. *"You'll find something special out there someday. Just gotta keep looking for it."*

Back then, Marsque had been near her physical age now, twenty-one. Kivita had spent an additional twenty-three years altogether in cryosleep, traveling throughout the Cetturo Arm. She swallowed with a dry throat.

"Here you go." Marsque handed her the chit.

Kivita grinned. "And here you go, smoothie." She kissed his cheek.

Marsque blushed. "Go on—get out of here. I'll have that order sent to your ship."

"See you later." Kivita didn't tell her old friend how long she'd be gone. Years might pass, depending on the distance to her next contract. Marsque might be retired or even dead when she returned. Maybe she should've asked about his family or bought him a drink. More and more, her only social links were business transactions between light jumps.

Sar had warned her that the salvager's life went nowhere. What did he know? Ever since childhood Kivita had yearned to see the stars, other worlds. Maybe even discover an antique feudal colony ship or an intact Vim starship.

She shoved the chit back into her vest pocket and stomped along the dingy aisles. Sar was wrong. The things and places she'd seen out there were worth the sacrifice. They had to be.

The next stall contained Inheritor paraphernalia: icons of yellow suns, dogma pamphlets, sandstone pendants, or red tunics with a small yellow star sewn on the shoulder. Only the prophets themselves could wear solid yellow, representing the Vim's beneficial stars.

"Have you opened your eyes to the light of the Vim?" a young prophet asked. "Remember that your sins must be forgiven before you can join the Vim in the galactic Core. Remember that only the righteous may inherit their knowledge!"

Kivita hurried toward the nearest spacer bar. Religion was boring, the Vim were extinct, and she didn't care about sins or the hereafter. Each cryosleep was already an afterlife between the stars. Freezing herself just to see what lay out there in the void.

Something would turn up, though, once she got a drink and got laid. Kivita had survived everything this universe had thrown at her. Strutting along, she smiled at a few handsome spacers passing by.

Two Inheritor soldiers stood guard outside the bar entrance. One examined her credentials chit and motioned her inside. Aromas of jiir alcohol, slosh wine, and cerulean-mollusk vapors filled her nose. Various pilots, salvagers, and mercenaries mingled around three wooden counters. Many drank alcohol from ceramic cups, while others sniffed mollusk vapors through breath masks. All were human, with no Ascali or renegade Aldaakians present.

Cracked tiles clinked under Kivita's boots. Elbows, rumps, and all-too-eager hands brushed her while she navigated the crowd. A bubble troubadour performed in a dark corner in deep, warbling tones. The bubbles from his instrument floated through the air, reflecting the patrons back at her. Dim orange lamps lit everything in a nauseous glow.

She grinned. This was more like it.

"Wanna come to my ship?" a woman in a red skinsuit asked. A few scars and tattoos lined her curvy form.

Smirking, Kivita caressed the woman's blond braid. "Maybe. I think . . ."

The pain in her temples returned. Head swimming, Kivita glimpsed three soldiers watching her from across the bar. One whispered into his helmet mic.

"What are you thinking—hmm?" The woman brushed her thigh against Kivita's.

"I'm . . ." A shudder traveled up Kivita's back; then she cleared her throat. "I'm just looking for a drink."

The woman fingered Kivita's tresses. "Has it been long?"

"No, I . . ." Kivita ran her hand down the woman's

neck, then drew back as the soldiers came closer. Her entire skull ached. "Um, maybe later."

The woman gazed with disappointment; then she patted Kivita's bottom. "Come find me, you change your mind."

Other patrons stared at Kivita in lust, contempt, or jealousy. Two Sutaran bouncers, brawnier due to their high-G homeworld, watched her carefully. A salvager in a lubricant-stained jumpsuit tapped the seat beside him and licked his lips. Two women beckoned and offered her a filled glass, but Kivita nudged her way to the bar. Being one of the few salvagers to return from Xeh's Crown must have gilded her reputation. Great.

On her right, a young spacer gasped vapors from an air mask. A bearded man with two braided Dirr women gazed at her on the left. The soldiers milled around right behind her. Kivita pretended to adjust her vest, then bought a glass of jiir juice from the bar.

Video screens along the back wall showed Inheritor-state-owned news briefs, current barter standards on Haldon Prime, and a prophet giving a sermon. None paid the screens much attention. Kivita avoided looking at the salvager's dock roster. It didn't matter if he were in the Haldon system.

The bartender finally brought her juice. As she sipped the sweet blue liquid, Kivita studied the other patrons. Salvagers like her, seeking physical release, emotional contact—meaningless relationships with all the warmth of a cold hull. And three Inheritor jerks who stared at her too much.

Her temples flared again. Damn it, this weird headache was pissing her off. Kivita gulped the juice and headed for the door.

The walk back to her landing pad took forever. Dodging prophets; avoiding other spacers. Evading two more soldiers mumbling into handheld mics. Each step sucked her boots deeper into the muddy street. *Terredyn Narbas* was a prison as much as it was an escape, but she needed it right now. After a little sleep she'd come back, find that woman, and have a good time.

Upon reaching her ship, Kivita took a deep breath as her hand brushed the airlock doors. The headache leveled off into a regular, tingling throb.

Strange stars shifted in her mind, same as they had since salvaging that datacore at Xeh's Crown. After each dream, the stars became clearer, brighter. Kivita grunted and tried to think of something else.

The stars refused to disappear. They blinked in her mind, as if communicating with her.

"Kivita Vondir?" a male voice called.

She turned around. Four Inheritor soldiers dressed in red polyarmor approached the pad. Each carried a kinetic rifle.

"Yeah?" she replied, tense but flashing a smile. Perhaps they wanted to parade her before the farmers, like Inheritors often did. Salvagers had been folk heroes even in Kivita's childhood.

The lead soldier didn't smile back. "We will escort you to the Rector's Compound. His Holiness has requested your presence for an audience."

"Yeah? Then lead on." She kept silent as the soldiers flanked her, but Kivita's breathing quickened. The Rector was the Inheritors' religious and political leader. Billions of people lived under his rule, and he had selected her for an audience?

Shit.

2

The soldiers led Kivita through reinforced doors. A metallic odor erased the stench of the spaceport's streets. Kivita paused and stared.

Outside the stone wall surrounding the spaceport, wooden arches swept between towering glass polymer buildings. Quartz lanterns shimmered. Yellow Inheritor banners fluttered from engraved columns. All decor bore representations of bright suns and faceless deities: the Vim and their healthy, yellow stars of promise.

"Do not tarry," the lead soldier said.

"Yeah, okay." She tried to sound tough and nonchalant, but her heart thudded. Spacers rarely received permission to enter the city proper. Much less meet the Rector himself.

Kivita stilled her wonder and walked into Fifth Heaven, the capital. Just inside the doors stood twenty more soldiers, eyeing her with calm disdain. Behind them a wooden-rail barricade kept dozens of peasants at bay. Men, women, and children dressed in coarse clothing gaped at her. As a child, she, too, had gawked at famous salvagers entering the city gates. Dreaming of being a salvager like her father.

More admiring grins greeted her as they journeyed onto quiet, clean streets. Citizens wore cloth garments cut in classic Inheritor style: high necklines and obscuring brown cloaks, and long skirts for women. Beggars lined the stone wall outside the spaceport, while factory workers huddled near trolley platforms, awaiting a ride.

Nothing had changed. The scene could have been plucked from her childhood.

Beyond the city walls stood farmers' sod hovels, surrounded by miles of cultivated fields. Whenever Rhyer had been away on a salvage contract, Kivita had resided in such housing. Gray-white exhaust plumes rose in the distance from factory smokestacks.

As they passed two beggar boys, the pair looked up at Kivita. She drew a protein slab from her pouch and handed it to them. Both grinned, their eyes wide. Small dirty fingers touched hers.

One soldier snatched the slab and pushed the boys away. Kivita forced down her anger and kept walking. Maybe that was one of the newer rules Marsque had mentioned. Poor kids. What else had changed?

The soldiers escorted her onto the trolley platform. Kivita stepped into the narrow, rail-driven vehicle. Cramped seats, silent passengers, and a loose handrail made the journey even worse.

For all Fifth Heaven's beauty, its ambience of torpid stasis suffocated Kivita. Citizens gave soldier patrols a wide berth. Children stayed close to their parents on the sidewalks. Kivita hated the quiet. After a year in cryo, she wanted activity.

Her heart beat faster as they passed Judgment Square, where heretics were executed. Ahead, a domelike structure reflected the sun: the Rector's Compound. Yellow banners large enough to cover her ship flapped in the wind. Thirty-foot sculptures of late prophets encircled the Compound.

The trolley slid to a stop. One of the soldiers prodded her. As she exited the vehicle, forty more soldiers surrounded her. Kivita tried to control her rapid breaths.

After climbing the Compound's sandstone steps, the soldiers herded Kivita into a long, high-arched corridor. Yellow-hued windows allowed in brilliant golden sunlight. Statues on sandstone daises depicted Inheritor heroes. Prophets in yellow robes and shaved heads walked past. The scent of overcleaned ventilation ducts stung Kivita's nose, made her eyes water. Her scalp tingled.

"Rector Dunaar Thev awaits you." The lead soldier opened a large wooden door on the right. Inside, crimson and orange drapes hung from sandstone walls. A forty-foot statue of Arcuri, the first Rector, stood in idealized sandstone repose. A round skylight focused the sun on a granite dais. Dozens of minor prophets lined an aisle fashioned from pure quartz. Thirty Proselytes guarded the dais, their faces hidden by black veils.

Kivita tried to stand as tall as a queen. She'd faced worse things.

"All acknowledge the presence of His Holiness, Rector Dunaar Thev of the Inheritors!" a voice called out.

A man in sparkling yellow robes rose from a quartz throne carved in the shape of a four-rayed sun. The thick, cloying smell of Bellerion lotus clogged her nostrils.

"Thank you for answering my summons, Kivita Vondir. The Vim has blessed you with substantial finds, I hope?" The cultured voice seemed to emanate from the skylight, as if the Vim themselves spoke to her.

Kivita squinted. "Yes, Rector."

"You are uncomfortable, my child. Allow me to remove my robes of office before we continue."

An Ascali female ascended the dais and removed the glittering garment. Underneath, Dunaar wore the yellow robes of an Inheritor prophet, with a ruby quartz chest plate. His bald, jowly features and kind brown eyes belied the security around him.

"The Vim artifacts you recovered from Xeh's Crown solidified your status as one of our greatest salvagers," Dunaar said. "Why, the commoners whisper your name as much as they do Arcuri's."

Kivita glanced at the Proselytes, the Rector's personal guard. What else had they been whispering? "Thank you, Rector."

Dunaar rubbed his face with ring-studded fingers. "The Inheritor religion gives people hope, but they need a sign. There are no more habitable worlds within reach of current engine technology. Many of the Arm's suns are rapidly aging, which no scientist can explain. All humans in the Cetturo Arm must escape to the galactic Core, where the Vim awaits us. I want you to help me usher in the sign they need."

Scents of baked bread made her stomach growl in postcryostasis hunger. "I'm only a salvager, Rector."

"A salvager the Vim has chosen." Dunaar arched an eyebrow.

"I just collect the Vim's junk floating in the outer systems." As soon as she said the words, Kivita's heart plummeted into her stomach. Sar had always claimed no filter existed between her brain and her mouth.

Her words brought murmurs and glares from everyone. Kivita stiffened and fought down labored breaths.

Maybe she should have been more tactful, but an extinct race didn't decide her fate. She alone controlled it.

Dunaar stepped down from the dais. "It is a salvager's holy mission to return all finds to the Inheritors, as per the Charter. What hope will anyone have if we don't control the flow of technology? The human factions—Tannocci, Naxan, Sutaran, and others—would fight wars again. Those blasphemous Aldaakians would conquer every habitable system in the Arm. Technology would be used to make us lazy, sinful. But you have just arrived, my child. Cryostasis often makes one hungry."

A door on Kivita's right opened. A female Ascali in translucent clothing entered, carrying a food tray. Steam rose from a bowl of stew. A platter of oiled bread rolls lay beside a rack of sugar-powdered sky celery. Even as her stomach growled again, Kivita shook her head.

"Forgive me, Rector. But how often is a salvager invited into your Compound and offered a meal?" She glanced at the waiting Ascali. The female was tall and muscular, with a mane of dark, silky hair and a body covered in short auburn fur. Russet-colored eyes studied Kivita from a lovely face.

Dunaar paced around Kivita. "Realizing your well-deserved reputation, I have selected you for a special salvage."

"Go on." Kivita stood still, though the food demanded her attention.

"Have you ever traveled to Vstrunn?"

Kivita blinked as all hunger sensations faded. Vstrunn was a small, high-G world covered in sharp crystal formations. Rumors claimed the Kith inhabited it. Their claws could shred polyarmor; their strength could snap a Sutaran like a twig. Those crazy tales of an ancient treasure buried on the planet had circulated well before Kivita's birth.

"The Wraith Star system is twelve light years from here, Rector. I've got phased fusion energy dumps on *Terredyn Narbas*, but you'll still have to wait eight years. Four there; four back." Kivita crossed her arms.

"You will be well compensated." Dunaar took a bread roll from the tray and ate it in small bites.

"That's a long trip just for crystals or gems." Kivita's head tingled again.

"Previous salvagers discovered a Vim datacore on Vstrunn. I have learned the Aldaakians are interested in the planet. The datacore would be the only reason. Of course, only holy prophets can access the technology of the sainted ancients, so the Aldaakians cannot retrieve it."

"Then why would they want it?" Kivita asked, trying to keep sarcasm from her voice. Few spacers believed the prophets could read the datacores. No doubt they used some old Vim computer to do it.

"They patrol the system to hamper us."

"So I won't be the first salvager you've sent, then." Kivita took two rolls and a celery stalk from the tray. The warm bread melted in her mouth. Snapping the celery between her teeth released cool, sweet juices. The tingling in her head stopped.

"That is why we need your ... skills. The Kith guard the fabled Juxj Star, a red gem. Since the Vim stored their data in stone and crystal, this gem must be the datacore. If you bring the Juxj Star back to me, I shall guarantee the payment of six fusion energy dumps, an upgrade of your ship's systems, and as much food and water your ship will hold." Dunaar licked oil from his fingers.

Kivita stopped chewing. A single energy dump could propel *Terredyn Narbas* for fifty light years. With six fresh ones, an improved nav system, and a cargo bay filled with foodstuffs, she could quit salvaging and just explore. Chart more of the Cetturo Arm, then retire on Susuron's beaches later on. No more weird dreams.

"What about the Aldaakians?" Kivita asked. "If they couldn't take the gem . . ."

"As I said, their race cannot access Vim vaults or datacores," Dunaar said. "Besides, they probably searched for the Juxj Star with an entire assault team. You will be alone."

Kivita wanted to say no. Vstrunn was a spacer's graveyard, and Aldaakians always shot first then demanded answers later. With six new energy dumps, though, she could travel the space lanes for a long time. Long enough until she found something out there to fill the void inside herself.

"Maybe." Kivita finished the sky celery and pretended to study a topaz wall mosaic.

"That is as good as a positive from a salvager." Sweat beads appeared on Dunaar's shaved head. "I will have the Juxj Star's coordinates sent to your ship."

Kivita's body flushed with heat. "I said maybe, Rector."

Two Proselytes stepped toward her, but Dunaar held up a hand. "Think of what you will see out there, my child. Think of the knowledge you will be bringing back to us."

The strange stars from her dreams twinkled again in her mind, like beacons in her subconscious.

"I need a few hours before I go. I've got cargo on board *Terredyn Narbas* that's already been sold." Her words came out too quick, too eager.

"Of course. As a show of good faith, my soldiers will bring extra supplies to your ship. The Vim's healthy yellow stars shall burn bright for us all, my child. With the Juxj Star, humanity might finally learn how to leave the Arm."

Kivita took a deep breath and smiled. "Then we have a contract, Rector."

Dunaar touched his forehead and swept the hand toward Kivita in a blessing gesture. "May the Vim light your path, Kivita Vondir, as yours will soon light it for all."

After taking three more bread rolls, she brushed past Proselytes and prophets, who stared at her in edgy silence. As Kivita entered the corridor, sunlight from the windows shone on her. She took her time, enjoying the warm rays.

Eight cold years awaited her.

Dunaar waited while the Ascali servant draped the glittering robe back over him. Kivita had been easy to convince. No surprise. Salvagers cared only for profit, but few braved the Cetturo Arm's star systems for Vim relics. The Inheritors needed to forge their own fate while commanding everyone else's. The Vim had chosen him to do so.

"That is all, Zhara. You are dismissed." A single sweat bead trickled down his cheek, but he refused to wipe it off before all these minor prophets.

The Ascali bowed and exited the chamber. Dunaar smiled at Zhara's feral sexuality, though not out of lust. When it came to her, patience had gained him much so far. He turned to the gathered prophets. "My brothers, I must meditate on our coming journey. May the Vim bless you."

As the Proselytes herded the others from the chamber, Dunaar pressed a button on the throne's armrest. "Bring her in."

A panel opened through the topaz wall mosaic, and two Proselytes entered with a thin, dark-haired woman. Though she possessed full lips and large green eyes, years of torture and malnutrition had left her skeletal and scarred.

"Bredine Ov," Dunaar said. "You sensed Kivita's abilities?"

Bredine looked up at him and shivered in her evergreen bodyglove. "Rector, Rector. Hmm? Kivita tingled. Yes, tingled." Her broken Meh Sattan had an archaic lilt.

"Then she is a Savant after all." Dunaar frowned. The bread rolls had been coated with ionized butter to prevent Kivita from sensing Bredine's probing. Kivita had no idea of her talent, then.

Savants were humans who could decipher the information within a datacore. Knowledge stored in stone and crystal, accessed via electrical pulses from a human brain. Data gained from these holiest of objects had given the Inheritors power over the old human feudal worlds, but some populations still regarded starships as magic. The primitive fools needed guidance.

Dunaar knew the Vim would open all eyes in the end. The means mattered little.

"Rector? Rector? Kivita tingled." Bredine's gaze kept darting to the food tray.

Caressing the throne's quartz armrest, Dunaar studied Bredine through narrowed eyes. Upon touching a datacore, a Savant could recite the stored information, but remembered little of it afterward. The Inheritors corralled all known Savants; such individuals, if loosed, constituted a threat to Inheritor power. The more people who could spread knowledge, the more chances it would be used for sin.

He'd continued the tradition of testing young adults throughout Inheritor Space. Savant ability, which remained undetectable in childhood, matured with age. Thus all Inheritor adults underwent brain-pulse analyzer scans. Few Savants escaped notice.

Except, until her last contract, Kivita Vondir.

"Has *Arcuri's Glory* been readied for our journey?" Dunaar asked.

"The crew and soldiers are boarding now, Rector," a Proselyte replied.

Dunaar had sent six separate teams to Vstrunn. Each had consisted of Inheritor soldiers, a trusted Proselyte, and a captive Savant. Each had met with failure, but Kivita's salvager abilities might gain her the Juxj Star. Resulting action from Aldaakian patrols near Vstrunn would gain him the war he needed. Those pale-skinned infidels must be eliminated before humanity could leave the Cetturo Arm safely. He thought of all the poor, ignorant Inheritor children he would thus save. The next human generation was his charge, and he its savior.

"And *Frevyx* is still in this system?" Dunaar asked.

"Yes, Rector. That trawler's beacon is still broadcasting from orbit," the Proselyte said.

"Prepare the holo display. I think Sar Redryll will accept my proposition. Bring Zhara, and get the other Savants ready. Feed them a little. Here's her meal." Dunaar grimaced at Bredine and tossed the half-eaten roll to the floor. What a travesty that the Vim had selected trash like her to decipher their secrets.

3

Sar reclined in *Frevyx*'s pilot chair as the trawler orbited Haldon Prime. The pink, yellow, and turquoise emanations from the Sanctuary Nebula dusted the bridge in similar hues. If only everything could be so enchanting. His gray bodyglove bore mud stains from Fifth Heaven's spaceport, and he still smelled those nasty mollusk vapors. Though he'd sold most of his salvage to the Inheritors, a few rare items remained for his allies. It gnawed at him to support a regime he despised, even if just for cover.

Cheseia entered the bridge and rubbed his shoulder. "Cease the pouting. It certainly mars your face."

"Thanks." Sar swiveled the chair around. Short brown fur covered Cheseia's tall Ascali frame. Dark, silky tresses, held in place with a jiir headband, spilled over her shoulders. The blue glasslike leaves contrasted with her russet gaze.

"The Thede cell in this system wasn't completely destroyed. It will assuredly rise again." Cheseia touched his cheek and smiled.

"This might be easier if the kinetic pistols we'd stashed on Haldon Six hadn't been found," Sar said.

"If the insurgency keeps getting beaten down in this system—"

A beep from the computer console interrupted him. He frowned at the text crossing the screen. "Looks like the Inheritors want to hire me again. You make contact with our agents planetside before we left?"

Before she could answer, the console's holo display flickered. A figure in glittering robes appeared. Beautiful Ascali women in skimpy gowns and veils sat at the person's feet. Sar rubbed his jaw to hide his grimace.

"May the Vim bless you, Sar Redryll," Dunaar Thev's hologram said. "Please forgive my intrusion, Sar Redryll, but since you operate under the Inheritor Charter, my message is warranted. I see you appreciate beauty around you, as well."

Cheseia crossed her arms and stiffened. Guess she hated slavery as much as he did.

"What services do you require, Rector?" Sar kept his face neutral, though he gripped the chair's armrests.

"I have received word that one of your rivals, Kivita Vondir, has taken an Aldaakian contract. Those albino meddlers have asked her to find the Juxj Star on Vstrunn. Records show that you have ventured to that planet. I ask you to do so again, my child."

Kivita working for the Aldaakians sounded far-fetched; she'd always been an Inheritor salvager. Going after what most regarded as a spacer's legend made the idea even stranger. Crazy girl was in over her head, as usual.

Dunaar's robe made Sar squint. "You want me to find it first."

"Of course, my child."

"*Frevyx* isn't armed." He maintained eye contact

with Dunaar and leaned back in the chair. Let the bastard beg.

"You will not be required to engage humanity's shared enemies."

Sar said nothing. Cheseia's hurried breathing became audible.

Dunaar's brow creased. "I realize the danger you will be facing, but the Aldaakians must not—"

"Ten polysuits, three energy dumps, and two gravity fluxers," Sar said, though he needed none of the items. The Thedes did.

Dunaar's hologram smiled. "I will add an extra energy dump, should you bring Vondir back, as well. I fear she must be tried for heresy, aiding the Vim's enemies like this. So, you accept my offer?"

Sar nodded once. "You have a contract, Rector Thev. Setting coordinates for Wraith Star now."

"May the Vim guide you, Sar Redryll. I shall await your return." The holo display deactivated as Dunaar smiled wider. What an asshole.

A cold ball formed in Sar's stomach. Anybody but Kivita. Her hurt, hazel stare still greeted him every time he entered cryostasis. There was no way she could survive Vstrunn. The fool girl had gotten into something larger than herself.

"You agreed quickly, Sar. Very quickly." Cheseia gripped his shoulder. "But you certainly made the right choice."

Sar gazed out *Frevyx*'s viewport. Kivita would resist his intrusion, maybe even fight. He'd spared Kivita the hard, secretive life he now led. In doing so, he'd cheated them both.

"Kiv probably has the same engines on that old

trawler," Sar said. "We'll reach Vstrunn right after she does. Navon might get angry with us, going after the Juxj Star, but this is something the Thedes need to investigate. Dunaar's been sending too many ships that way the past few years."

He shut the viewport, which protected the eyes of passengers during light jumps. Sar had met more than one old spacer who'd gone blind from staring out an open viewport while making a jump. On the console screen, the planet's coordinates glowed in purple-blue lettering. His last visit there had been a nightmare of high-gravity, sharp crystals, and the awful sense of being watched.

Cheseia whistled a low note and smoothed his hair. "Navon would definitely want us to investigate. What really troubles your heart?"

"Nothing. Been a while since I've been to Vstrunn— that's all." Sar selected the coordinates and rose. "Cryopods are waiting." He stripped from his bodyglove.

Cheseia frowned. "This woman surely cannot endanger what I have built with you, Sar. All that the Thedes have worked relentlessly for, all we have shared—"

"I'm fine. My fling with her was two years ago. Out here, that might as well be an eternity." Sar exited the bridge and walked down *Frevyx*'s central corridor. A galley, toilet room, storage lockers, and two airlocks waited on either side of him. Navy blue bulkheads enclosed him as memories drifted through his mind.

The taste of Kivita's lips when they'd met in her airlock over Gontalo. Her mischievous hazel eyes. Those shocks of straight red-blond hair. Sar had told Kivita to do something else with her life rather than salvage. To do something different from what he'd done for so many years. He'd warned her he served a higher cause.

On the wall, Caitrynn's placard drew his attention like a magnet to his heart. The gaze of his dead sister, killed during the Inheritor conquest of Freen, their homeworld. Her husband and children had been massacred along with her. The cold ball in Sar's gut ground into icy hatred.

He'd abandoned Kivita to dedicate himself to the Thede cause: dispersing knowledge to the uneducated, and aiding insurgents against Inheritor aggression. That wasn't enough anymore. Sar wanted a rebellion, a reckoning. Knowledge meant little if humanity remained a slave to those prophets.

Once, he'd gone after the Juxj Star, too, but for profit. If the Thedes could access the gem, the secrets they could learn . . . and the advantage it might give them against the Inheritors.

"You both definitely had the same eyes," Cheseia murmured, looking at Caitrynn's image.

He'd not informed Kivita of his mutation. Growing up in Freen's toxic mines had left green speckles in his brown eyes, plus occasional lesions on his feet and hands. Any children fathered by him would share these abnormalities, maybe worse. Sar had told Kivita space radiation had sterilized him. The bottle of green spermicide pills in the medicine cabinet revealed his lie.

"Sar?" Cheseia fingered one of his black curls. He turned away and continued through the ship.

En route to the cryopods, Sar passed through his clean-swept quarters. A linen hammock hung over a heating vent. Pots bolted to the floor contained white and maroon hibiscus flowers. Sugar reeds from Bellerion rested in a square vat, and a jiir sapling grew from a spherical wall dish. More and more he took pieces from each world with him, to beautify the cold one he lived in.

He'd kept no reminders of her.

Sar entered the cryopod chamber and eased himself into one of three pods. Cheseia hesitated before his pod.

"You have mostly forgotten her?" Unblinking, she stripped naked.

Sar opened his mouth, but the words refused to come out. Cheseia had been his lover since her assignment to him as a field agent. A bond born of space travel, through a lifestyle of perpetual caution. Not love.

"You have especially forgotten her?" Cheseia whispered, removing her headband. Her raw physical beauty should turn him on. Instead it chilled him further, like he already lay in cryo.

"What?" His voice sounded harsher than he'd meant, and he held up a hand as she frowned. "Sorry. This isn't easy for me."

Cheseia leaned into his pod and kissed his lips. "Eventually it will be. You will definitely forget about her after this mission. Yes, thankfully so." She stepped back, and the cryopod hatch closed.

Sar cursed himself as the familiar cryo chill flooded his extremities. Though Sar didn't want to hurt Cheseia, he also didn't want old feelings for Kivita swamping his emotions for the coming mission.

He needed that gem. Not her.

Dunaar's soldiers waited while Kivita's autoloader lifted the bonus food crates into her ship. Its six steel arms slid on a rail along the cargo hold's ceiling. None of the soldiers spoke. Not that she wanted them to. One stared at her breasts too much, and another checked the magazine in his rifle too often.

Turning away, Kivita watched Haldon Prime's sunset. Soon the sky would be filled with stars and far-off nebulae. As a child she'd tried pointing out the systems she planned to visit. No matter what happened to her, an undying wonder of the stars would always keep her young inside.

The autoloader creaked, its task complete. Without a word, the soldiers left.

"Yeah, same to you." Kivita shut the doors and locked down *Terredyn Narbas*. She removed her clothing and shoved it all into a storage locker.

Damn it. Vstrunn would test her. Maybe even kill her. But she could never see enough new planets, even the cratered, desolate ones. Worse, each new discovery left her hungry for more. And she'd been starving for a long time.

After stripping to her two-piece underwear, she pulled a jump rope and dumbbells from a locker. If she didn't exercise regularly, Kivita's muscles would atrophy due to gravity fluctuations. Worse, she'd menstruated only once while on Gontalo, and feared she might be succumbing to a cryomalady.

Lifting the dumbbells, Kivita pumped her biceps, triceps, and deltoids with perfect form. Muscles clenched and relaxed, each repetition searing her body. After squatting until her quadriceps and calves burned, Kivita snatched the jump rope. Soon her forearms quivered as she twirled the rope and jumped from the balls of her feet.

Covered in sweat, she headed for the shower pod.

With the new mist ionizer from Marsque, the device scrubbed her pores deeper, wasting less water.

Kivita put on fresh underwear and entered the bridge as night stole over Haldon Prime. Thousands of pinpoints still beckoned to her. Red and yellow effulgence radiated from the Vim Wall, a massive nebula bordering the Cetturo Arm. The blue sliver of Haldon Three and the brilliant orange crescent of Haldon Two lit up the darkness in plum shades.

Gripping the manuals, she initialized *Terredyn Narbas*'s engines. The nav computer offered guidance aids, but Kivita ignored them and lifted the craft from the landing pad. She preferred to control the ship as much as possible, holding fate in her own hands.

As the ship ascended through the atmosphere, the bridge's flashing running lights reminded her of the dreams. The brief moment she'd touched a datacore from Xeh's Crown had filled her mind with star coordinates. Glimpses of those odd creatures in stark white exoskeletons, or visions of spectacular nebula not existing inside the Cetturo Arm.

Once in orbit, Kivita keyed in the coordinates for the Wraith Star system. Twelve light years. She'd never traveled farther than six in one jump.

With space's vacuum chill evaporating heat from the ship, Kivita hurried to her cryopod. Her steps lightened as *Terredyn Narbas* eased into zero-G for the journey. The ship vibrated slightly for a moment, then gave off a regular hum above its normal operating sounds.

She now traveled at three times the speed of light.

Sliding into the cryopod, Kivita wondered how many people she'd seen on Haldon Prime would still be alive when she returned. A salvager's life amounted to spaceport flings and salvaging runs, then dreamlike epochs in cryostasis.

Again, Kivita was alone.

Jaw tight, she mashed the pod's stasis button. The transparent cover hissed as it sealed. The usual cold sensations numbed her toes, fingers, and back. As the spreading cold eased her into wintry darkness, Kivita knew she'd find something out there to make it all worthwhile.

4

Inside the main chamber of *Arcuri's Glory*, Dunaar studied a hologram of mutated children on Freen. Bloated foreheads; boil-covered flesh. Until Inheritor control had been established, abysmal mining conditions had contaminated generations of pitiful offspring. Scowling, he changed the image. Gaunt Tahe citizens lay on lice-ridden cots. The population had been near starvation when the Inheritors liberated their world.

"May the Vim grant me the means to show them mercy." A coil tightened around Dunaar's heart. Mercy often had to be brutal, since tenderness invited sloth and sin. Only the righteous could show them the way.

After Kivita played her role.

Dunaar turned away from more holos of people the Inheritors had saved from their own ignorance. The Thedes enlightened peasants, consequences be damned. One insurgent enclave on Tahe had constructed a fusion reactor without fully understanding its operation. Dunaar had been forced to cleanse the area. The irradiated victims would have infected the rest of the inhabitants.

Moisture rolled down his cheek. Dunaar wiped it away, wishing it were tears instead of perspiration. His sweating malady and thyroid disorder had been inflicted in his youth—exposure to a radioactive Thede bomb on Haldon Six. Years spent in Fifth Heaven's Golden Seminary as a neophyte, then a prophet, had taught Dunaar that only the Vim could deliver harmony.

But now the Aldaakians threatened that stability, demanding the Inheritors hand over Vim technology so they might find the ancients. Dunaar would never let that happen.

Everything was pressing against him. Populations were growing, and all habitable planets with arable land had been developed. All the unexplored stars within reach were red-giant systems containing dead worlds, and, like he'd told Kivita, the stars were aging far too quickly. Xeh's Crown, just seven light years away, had been predicted to supernova in twenty years. The Cetturo Arm held no future for humanity.

He had to find the Vim soon, before everything his people had striven and died for was gone.

Dunaar walked into the adjacent chamber. The adjoining hall's sandstone tiles, quartz lamps, and topaz trim all signified the Vim's yellow stars of promise. He smiled. So much weight aboard a ship indicated power: the power to generate enough force to lift such a craft from a planet, then send it across the cosmos. Power granted by the Vim, through the technology they'd left behind for the faithful.

In the next chamber, dim yellow lamps lit a circular area a hundred feet in circumference. A few dozen cryopods lined the walls. Each held the preserved body of a previous Rector. Dunaar paused before one pod in particular. Through its semitransparent hatch, a thin face stared back at him, the eyelids closed.

"Guide me, Arcuri. Your vision may yet save us all." Dunaar touched his head and gesticulated. The sainted Arcuri had founded the Inheritors—the humans in the Cetturo Arm who would inherit what the Vim had left for them.

The ship's intercom rattled a speaker in the corridor outside. "Rector, they have arrived."

Dunaar entered the antechamber, where Zhara waited with his other female servants. Because of his Oath of Propagation, he enjoyed the company of the finest slave girls; his holy genes would flower on future worlds.

His children had possessed the same disorders he'd been cursed with. So far, three dozen monstrosities had been euthanized before seeing their first month. The clones, which he kept aboard, frozen from public view, hadn't fared much better.

"You were fed well, my child?" Dunaar caressed Zhara's furred cheek.

"Yes, Rector." Her melodious voice stole the air from the room. So beautiful, even if she was little more than a beast. Though Ascali and human unions produced no issue, Dunaar needed Zhara in his collection. The payoff would be immense.

What he also needed were more Savants. Bredine had never produced a child. That willful tramp hampered the creation of children that might possess her talent. And every time, the half-witted bitch had to be beaten just to spread her legs.

Minutes later, Dunaar entered the bridge. Captain Ilurred Stiego snapped to attention. The pilot, navigator, and security officers straightened at their stations. The nav computer displayed holographic simulations of *Ar-*

curi's Glory and another craft. The other loomed four times larger than Dunaar's flagship. Through the viewport, the gray-green hull of a Sarrhdtuu vessel blotted out the stars.

"Docking is complete, Rector," Stiego said. A tall, thin man, he wore red Inheritor naval livery. A holo monocle rested in his left eye.

"Inform our allies we are ready to board, Captain." Dunaar exited the bridge and descended a short flight of steps onto the supply deck. Few had ever seen a Sarrhdtuu, let alone entered their ships. The Sarrhdtuu claimed no worlds or systems in the Arm; many believed they resided only aboard their starships.

Eight Proselytes armed with blades and kinetic pistols waited at the secondary airlock. After a few moments, the safety light switched from red to green, and the airlock slid open. The momentary churning in his stomach from gravity fluctuation passed.

Dunaar stepped into a dimly illuminated chamber. Moist, leathery coils sat in several piles. Knobs and curled protrusions stuck from the bulkheads. The mildewed stench typical of all Sarrhdtuu craft made Dunaar take shallow breaths.

Something clicked above them, and a boom lowered on fleshlike stalks. The mildew smell strengthened. A dais resting on coiled tentacles slithered into the chamber as the boom sprayed green jelly over it. Dunaar forced his face not to scrunch up as the mildew stench became so overpowering, his nostrils burned.

The jelly built up and morphed into a sleek humanoid torso, complete with a half-crescent head and two arms ending in coils. Four purple eyes opened and stared at Dunaar. Inside the transparent jelly body, organs pumped and liquids ran along thousands of veins. A puckered mouth hissed open.

"Prophet of Meh Sat. You have initiated our request?" The Sarrhdtuu's voice contained a heavy lisp.

"Indeed I have, Zhhl. I hope your operations have gone well?" Sweat dribbled down his nose and past his lips.

Zhhl writhed back and forth across the floor. "What of the rebels of Meh Sat? Luccan's progeny."

Dunaar smoothed his yellow robes. "There is a slight change I must discuss with you concerning our plot."

"Tell." Zhhl ceased writhing and morphed into a wall. The coils crawled along the surface as the jelly body adopted a thinner, longer shape.

"I have dispatched a Savant to take the Juxj Star on Vstrunn, as you suggested."

Zhhl hissed. "Kith, Prophet of Meh Sat."

Dunaar's pulse quickened. "True, but the one I hired is a salvager. She might evade the Kith; she survived an encounter with them near Xeh's Crown. My plan will be reported to the Thedes by Sar Redryll. I have no doubt they will attempt to intercept my salvager as soon as she has the gem. Once revealed, I shall track and eradicate the Thede leadership."

Zhhl's information about Redryll's Thede allegiance had come a year ago. Other sources had revealed his dalliance with Kivita, making him the perfect one to inadvertently reveal the location of his allies. The fool would no doubt usher her and the datacore to his Thede mongrels.

"Aldaakians." Zhhl split itself into three smaller beings and walked on the ceiling.

"They still patrol the Wraith Star system. Vim willing,

they will intercept my salvager. My ship will arrive and create an incident. I already have the appropriate news briefs prepared: an attack on Inheritor shipping to neighboring Tejuit. The Aldaakians will be blamed, and the Thedes will be implicated. I will declare all human worlds under Inheritor protection. That silly peace treaty the Tannocci worlds agreed to with the Aldaakians will be retracted."

Dunaar knew Sarrhdtuu and Aldaakians lacked the human Savant ability, though simple devices could detect its presence. Even if Kivita or the gem entered their custody, neither alien species would know how to use them. The Vim had chosen humans, and no one else, to share in their glory.

Morphing into one form again, Zhhl dropped down before Dunaar. It now stood over twenty feet tall. "Aldaakians must be defeated. They betrayed the Vim. Vengeance, Prophet of Meh Sat."

A sweat bead ran down Dunaar's chin. "Yes, we will avenge the sainted ones. Everything has been set, as we'd originally planned. Do I still have your cooperation?"

"Ships will be prepared after new war is declared on Aldaakians. One prize for Sarrhdtuu aid." Zhhl raised one coil.

"Yes?" Dunaar licked sweat from his lips, hoping Zhhl didn't ask for more human slaves. In their last dealings, Dunaar had depopulated three Bellerion towns just to sate Zhhl's demands.

"Require the salvager of the Xeh's Crown datacore. The one with tendrils of flame on her head."

Dunaar had to think for a moment. "You mean Kivita Vondir? She is the salvager I have sent to Vstrunn. The beacon you donated has been placed on her ship."

Sliding onto the boom, Zhhl morphed back into piles of coils. "Yes, Prophet of Meh Sat." The audience was over.

Dunaar hurried back to the airlock, trying to keep his expression neutral.

Why would Zhhl want a Savant, when no Sarrhdtuu had ever shown interest in a datacore?

5

Kivita snapped awake as something wet stung her tonsils and blistered her tongue. Lips numb, she tried to cough. A spasm wrenched her throat before she realized what was going on.

The cryopod's tube had splashed pseudoadrine into her mouth. Before she could blink, her gums absorbed the synthetic adrenaline into her bloodstream. Kivita's limbs jerked once; then energy blazed through her veins and ignited her muscles. Within seconds the sensations faded, leaving her cold but alert.

Beeps emitted from the cryopod's life-monitor readout, and a green light flashed. Great; she had woken in good health. She smoothed back her hair with trembling fingers. No matter how many times she underwent this same resurrection, Kivita always hated it.

Grunting, she rose as the cryopod's transparent cover opened. *Terredyn Narbas* hummed around her, dark and cold. Heating and life support had activated minutes before her awakening, but vacuum frost still covered the bulkheads. She shivered in her two-piece underwear.

"Damn." Kivita grabbed her black bodyglove and

slipped from the pod. *Terredyn Narbas*'s running lights and gravity activated fully. The cryopod closed with a sucking noise.

Kivita stretched, touched her toes, then did fifty jumping jacks. Burning sensations jolted her muscles again. Deep breaths cracked her chest. After a final stretch, she headed for the bridge. Blue-white lamps activated along the floor. Moments later she opened the bridge viewport.

Vstrunn dominated the vista as the trawler entered the planet's orbit. Wraith Star, a white dwarf sun, lit up the planet's crystallized surface in red, purple, and white twinkles. Gray cloud banks encircled the sphere. The planet was like the corpse of someone's dream, left to rot in the void.

She couldn't imagine a worse place to explore: more than twenty-thousand miles in diameter, with high-G and a seven-hour day—and nothing but hydrogen for an atmosphere.

Viewing the computer readout, Kivita snapped on her polyboots. No Aldaakian ships appeared on the scanner. Frowning, she studied Vstrunn's scintillating surface once more. High-G, combined with the jagged surface, would make for a dangerous landing.

"Yeah. Let's see what you got, you big lug of a planet." After eating a protein slab, she donned an envirosuit, then girded on her kinetic pistol with a ten-round magazine.

"I'm going to leave you up here, okay, girl? Be right back." She patted the bulkhead and stepped into the landing unit's cramped bay. She slid into a small planetary capsule and sealed the hatch behind her. Two small seats waited with frost-caked buckles and ripped cushions. A tiny console beeped to life. She buckled herself in and triggered the tandem beacon. When she needed to return, the capsule would lift off and reunite with *Terredyn Narbas*.

Before pressing the release button, she thought of her mother. Rhyer had claimed Kivita looked just like her. Hazel eyes, golden red hair. She caught her reflection in the console screen and swallowed.

"Here goes." As soon as she tapped the red button, Kivita's stomach churned and she gritted her teeth. One instant she gazed upon the landing unit's bulkhead; the next, Vstrunn rose below her in monstrous vastness.

Dark void filled reality on either side of the capsule. *Terredyn Narbas* grew smaller above her. The Wraith Star burned with a dying, impotent fury, casting everything in subdued tones. Vstrunn's hydrogen bands seemed to reach up and grab the capsule.

The computer beeped again. Two minutes until landing; each second a mini eternity of crushing acceleration and gut-wrenching free fall.

Vstrunn's outer atmosphere encircled the landing capsule. Yellow-gray mist obscured the viewport as turbulence shook the small craft. Kivita gripped the seat handles as vacuum frost came free and struck her suit. She squeezed her legs together, the sensation to urinate overwhelming. The protein slab she'd eaten jumped in her stomach, and Kivita bit her lip to keep from vomiting.

Stillness fell over the capsule. Cloud cover dissipated, revealing a landscape dotted with twisted spires, jagged plateaus, and mile-deep canyons. Kivita smiled despite her reentry travails. She'd never seen placards of Vstrunn; just heard rumors in spacer bars.

The white dwarf sun lit everything in ghostly repose. Violet, sapphire, and ruby quartz hues gleamed in sparkling glory. Coronas flared through thin crystal formations. Geodes the size of starships glittered with a thousand illuminated facets.

The sight took her breath. For a long moment, the capsule seemed to stop midair, as if to grant her a view from deepest fantasies dreamt worlds away.

Kivita grunted as the capsule's braking thrusters fired. A thick parachute deployed from the module above her. She braced herself.

The capsule jerked. Her helmet slammed against the seat. Frost crystals slid across her faceplate, but she blinked away the pain. Kivita started to cough, then choked as the capsule slammed into the surface. Her restraints squeezed the breath from her lungs as she jostled about. Crystal shrapnel smacked the viewport. Red warning lights flashed on the console.

"Shit," she breathed.

As Kivita unbuckled herself, each inhalation grew harder. Sweat crept down her brow by the time she rose and studied the console. It felt like giant hands were trying to press her down into the floor. She'd forgotten just how much high-G hampered her movements and strained her muscles.

The console beeped new messages across its screen. One thruster had been crushed, and the port-side bulkhead was cracked, but not breached. Kivita glanced out the viewport. The parachute lay in tatters on sharp stalagmite-like terrain forty yards away.

"Great. But we're otherwise okay, you piece of—"

A steam jet blew against her right arm. She jerked back. Within moments, the steam's moisture crackled into ice. The newly formed crystals clattered onto the capsule floor. Kivita fought the rising lump in her chest and studied the readout again. As long as the structure held and the crushed thruster didn't rupture, she could still take off.

Her canisters held nine hours of air.

Kivita took three deep breaths and turned on her wrist compass. The speaker inside her helmet beeped once. The tiny compass screen displayed a flashing arrow, indicating the direction of the trajectory given by Dunaar. The location of the Juxj Star.

"C'mon, five miles?" Under high-G, the distance would be grueling. She also wasn't sure what time of day she'd landed; she guessed four hours of light remained. After that, Vstrunn would really turn cold.

Kivita exited the capsule and stepped onto minuscule ruby shards, scorched black from her landing. She gazed around, getting her bearings.

Sapphire canyon walls rose at least one hundred feet above her, and a slope led into a large black crevice fifty feet on her right. Her landing had been fortunate. Hell, more than fortunate. Shivering, she tried not to guess the fissure's depth. As she walked from the capsule, her knees wobbled and her lungs compressed. Her heart thumped as if she'd been running.

"Six energy dumps," she whispered, then stepped onto a mesa covered in fine purple crystals. They crunched under her boots like glassware baubles.

Ahead, the landscape glittered and twinkled. Huge transparent crystal clusters filled the valley below the mesa. Hundreds of thin, brittle stalks rose dozens of feet into the air, and tiny flakes of frozen hydrogen dusted the landscape.

For an instant, the visions she'd seen since Xeh's Crown flooded her mind. Galactic arms filled with yellow, blue, and orange stars, rather than the dying red giants dominating the Cetturo Arm.

Kivita shook her head. This high-G must be playing tricks on her.

The compass beeped and the arrow flashed toward the crystalline grove below. Kivita took another deep breath and trudged on. She'd trained in high-G before, but as she climbed down the mesa wall, her muscles burned with exhaustion. Sweat ran in rivulets down her face. Her faceplate's defroster worked extra just to keep it from fogging over.

Soon she traveled through the grove she'd spotted from above. Her footsteps popped and cracked over crystals. Kivita avoided rubbing against the larger ones with her suit. One puncture, and she'd become a permanent resident. Twice she paused to catch her breath.

Something caught the sunlight behind a ruby geode formation. Kivita paused, then stiffened.

Two hundred feet away sat a squat Inheritor shuttle. Panels had been ripped off the outer hull, and three forms in envirosuits lay a short distance from the craft. Hydrogen frost had covered the faceplates.

A chill entered Kivita's chest. Her legs trembled as she staggered toward a skinny quartz formation.

"Six . . . energy . . . dumps . . ."

The impulse to steady herself against a crystal spire nagged her. Her lungs burned, working harder. Aeons passed as she crept through the grove, then into a massive arched tunnel, its ceiling forty feet above her. Luminescent sapphires glowed with mysterious inner fire.

Pausing, she recalled some of her father's tips. Don't

fight nature; work with it. Kivita stopped resisting the high-G so much and relaxed. Her breathing leveled off as she developed a walking and inhalation rhythm. There—she could do it. Dunaar hadn't hired just any spacer; he'd hired Kivita Vondir, and she could . . .

The compass indicated two miles to go. Damn.

She entered a second arched tunnel. The glow of ruby and violet geodes reflected off a familiar polished surface lying at her feet: Inheritor polyarmor. A cuirass, greaves, one boot. A kinetic rifle lay snapped in two, its magazine gutted. Dark crimson stains covered the surrounding crystals, and tufts of flesh lay in scattered piles.

Kivita's breaths came slow and painful as she drew her pistol. The shots could pierce polyarmor, but with only ten rounds, she'd have to make them count.

The compass beeped and the arrow stopped blinking. Kivita halted and swallowed.

Outside the tunnel, a tall square tower of sapphire and violet gems soared three hundred feet above her. A huge quartz stone with ruby veins rested atop it, catching the faint sunlight in pink motes. Other angular formations dotted the surrounding area, but she couldn't tell if they were built from the crystals or had been overgrown. Kivita wondered if any other buildings existed on Vstrunn, and who might have built them.

Who could have built anything on this planet?

The tower's presence defied her disbelief.

She scanned the area. Kith were hulking, seven-foot-tall creatures and rather ugly. Surely she'd spot one easily across this gorgeous landscape. Nothing disturbed Vstrunn's stillness. Gripping the pistol, Kivita walked on.

The tower doorway loomed before her like the mouth

of some legendary monster. She entered with cautious steps. Even if she found the Juxj Star right now, it would be night once she reached the landing capsule.

The tower's interior gleamed with luminescent crystal blocks cut in exact fittings. Kivita switched her wrist compass to indicate the distance from her capsule; she'd flee as soon as she found the gem. Once she stepped from a foyerlike room into a grand chamber, thoughts of leaving faded.

The crystal walls pulsed with inner light, reaching up to the ruby quartz three hundred feet above her head. Her limbs shook; her head tingled. No steps, no lifts along the sides. The walls were as slick as glass, reflecting a thousand versions of herself from angular fractures. The crystalline structures mesmerized Kivita into a state of bliss, as if she already dreamt in her cryopod.

In the center of the floor stood a three-foot, amethystine altar. A round red gem the size of a child's fist hung suspended over it. Nothing visible held up the gem.

Kivita stilled. Three armored Aldaakian bodies lay around the altar. Through the narrow faceplates, the albino faces looked asleep. They might have been dead for a day or a decade. Part of her wanted to touch them, while another wanted to look away. Strange how heat created life as well as destroyed it, while cold drained life while preserving it.

The tingling in her brain increased. Shit, not another headache. Something tickled her throat, and Kivita's breaths quaked in her lungs.

Reflected in one Aldaakian faceplate at her feet was a tall, hulking form.

She turned.

Five Kith had entered the crystal tower. They stepped

easily around the altar, their metallic gray flesh mirroring the pulsing geode lights. Triangular black eyes examined her, and serrated black claws protruded from their hands.

"Damn it." Her mouth went dry.

The Kith swept toward her, claws raised. The high-G rooted her in place while not affecting them.

Kivita's sight flashed with images of a spiral galactic arm filled with blue stars. Hands numb, she dropped the pistol. It clattered on the crystal floor. She closed her eyes and suppressed a whimper.

No. It would not end like this.

Spreading her arms, Kivita waited. No way she'd die in fear. With slow breaths, she calmed her nerves. In her mind, the vision of the spiral arm solidified. The name of an unknown star came to her lips.

Something cracked and broke at her feet. Kivita opened her eyes.

One of the Kith had stepped on her pistol. The creature lowered its head right before her faceplate, and the tower's glowing crystal lights danced in its black gaze. Kivita dared not look away or move. A patient intelligence waited in its eyes.

She licked her lips and tried to whisper. "What do you want?"

As one, all the Kith stepped back.

Swaying, Kivita gulped for air. Her knees, exhausted from high-G exertion, slammed into the floor. Both kneecaps flared in agony. With a groan, she pulled the emergency drawstring on her waist. The envirosuit's inner layer clamped her body in case the outer layer was torn.

The Kith didn't move. Her knees throbbing with

fresh bruises, Kivita braced herself against the amethyst altar. Why wouldn't the tingling in her head go away?

The entire tower hummed once. The vibration shook Kivita's whole person. Glowing geodes shone one bright ray on the altar, then darkened.

"What do you want from—?"

Her hands slid over smooth stone. The altar cracked open. She fell into its opening a few inches, and a churning red glow lit her faceplate.

The Juxj Star orbited her head.

With the altar chipping around her, Kivita fumbled to her feet. Her hands brushed the gem's surface. The tingling in her head magnified to a cerebral throb. Kivita lost her breath as her skin numbed and a chalky taste rose in her mouth. Her eyes filled with images far beyond anything she'd ever imagined.

Lush worlds covered in canopies of green vegetation, where multicolored birds chirped and made weblike nests from morning dew. A star encircled by gargantuan starships, siphoning off its energy. Ships packed with healthy, attractive people. They were free of disease, hunger, or war. Each person had plentiful heat, food, and water. Families had children, mammalian pets, and personal riches beyond what the Inheritor prophets possessed.

Kivita stood, the Juxj Star in hand, as coordinates filled her thoughts: *galactic clusters located a hundred light years outside the Cetturo Arm. Undiscovered yellow main-sequence stars. The whereabouts of Vim derelicts, capable of mining nebula gases to power impossible journeys. Aboard them were clinical, sterile chambers filled with cryopods and automated caretakers.*

The visions ended as she backed from the crumbling

altar. The Juxj Star glowed once and darkened to its normal luster. The Kith had vanished.

A low-toned beep from her envirosuit dispelled her blithe sensations.

She had only two hours of air left.

What? She must have stood in this damn tower for hours! Maybe something had cracked her canisters, and the lack of air was making her light-headed. The tingling in her head swelled to a sharp pain and disappeared. She moaned upon realizing she'd just been mouthing the strange coordinates from her mind.

Whatever this thing was, Dunaar could have it. Kivita put the Juxj Star into her side pouch and snapped it shut. She forced her legs to carry her from the tower and toward the arched tunnels. The wrist compass beeped again, as if mocking her doomed struggle to return.

6

"We are in the Wraith Star system and nearing Vstrunn now, Your Holiness," Stiego's voice blared from the intercom in Dunaar's quarters.

Dunaar waited as Zhara placed the glittering robe over his shoulders, while a minor prophet handed him the Scepter of Office. The slim gray stone datacore had been in Inheritor possession since Arcuri wrote the Charter. Never had the weight of his office been more palpable.

A Proselyte appeared in the doorway. "Rector, it's Bredine again."

"So?" Dunaar said. "Use a baton. There are more pressing matters."

The Proselyte inclined his head. "Rector, she claims she has detected a message. Through space."

Swallowing a rebuke, Dunaar stared at the man. "Message? Perhaps you have used the baton too much and addled her brain. Bring her to me."

"Rector, forgive me, but she is being held in Medical. Her screams upset the other Savants."

Dunaar walked past the Proselyte and down the hall. Servants trailed him across the red carpet to Medical.

Keeping a filthy Savant nearby made Dunaar's pulse race.

A feminine wail came from the ward.

"You should have gagged her." Grunting in annoyance, Dunaar threw open the door. Sterile smells stung his nose. Harsh white lamps lit a rectangular room containing medical cots and therapeutic machines.

"Kivita sends. Sends, sends!" Bredine screamed, writhing on the floor. "Vim. Vim message! From the wonderful tower. Rector, hmm? She sends it. Sends!"

Dunaar gestured at her. Two Proselytes hauled her up. The half-wit's struggles overturned wheeled trays filled with bandages and needles.

"Careful how you blaspheme the Vim. What message?" Dunaar pressed the Scepter against her neck.

"Kivita sends it for all. Vim message through void black. Hmm. Coordinates to hidden Vim. Wonderful tower was a beacon, sending, sending, and sending!"

Dunaar almost swatted her with the Scepter, but a notion tickled his thoughts. "Wait. We need—"

"Rector, *Terredyn Narbas* is now on our wideband scanners," Stiego's voice came over the hall intercom. "Calibrating main sensors to implanted Sarrhdtuu beacon."

Something in Bredine's green eyes sent a chill along his skin. Dunaar pushed the intercom button just inside Medical's entrance. "Captain, mark these coordinates and tell me where they lead."

He motioned, and the Proselytes brought Bredine to the speaker.

"Recite what you have received," Dunaar said.

She gaped up at him. He glanced at the Proselytes holding her. One of them slapped her cheek, and the other booted her in the back.

"Recite it."

Bredine spoke a short set of coordinates into the speaker. Not being a navigator, Dunaar made little sense of her gibberish.

Stiego's voice came back in a bullish tone. "That's only fifteen light years from Haldon, near the Terresin Expanse. Those calculations aren't Inheritor in origin, Rector."

Bredine had never led Dunaar, or previous Rectors, false. No Savant had received a message through space, either. Dunaar wondered why *Arcuri's Glory* hadn't detected the same signal.

"Vim are calling. Hmm. Narbas?" Bredine gasped, then sagged in the Proselytes' grip.

"Rector, an Aldaakian cruiser has been detected in the system!" Stiego called over the intercom. A general alarm echoed throughout *Arcuri's Glory*.

"Set an intercept course, Captain." Dunaar wiped sweat from his shaved head. Perhaps the Juxj Star held more secrets than he'd imagined. The quicker Kivita helped him eliminate the Vim's enemies, the faster he'd learn those secrets.

Fresh out of cryostasis, Sar jerked on his bodyglove, then snapped into his polycuirass and matching boots. Cheseia slipped into a bulky envirosuit. Outside *Frevyx*'s bridge viewport, Vstrunn's hydrogen cloud cover parted. The crystalline surface beckoned them with glimmers of light. Far ahead, a small dot representing *Terredyn Narbas* orbited the planet.

Sar sat down in the pilot's chair, reached for the mic, and hesitated.

"Will you truly hail her again?" Cheseia fastened the envirosuit's clamps around her wrists and ankles.

He gave her a sidelong glance. "Kiv would've responded by now. I bet she's planetside. I'm guessing she hasn't been here long."

No. She had been on Vstrunn too damn long.

The beacon scanner showed no other craft nearby, but with the instrument's light-minute delay, another vessel could enter the system's fringes without him knowing. They had to chance it. Sar gripped the manuals and steered *Frevyx* toward the planet.

Cheseia snapped on boots, donned insulated gloves, then examined the nav screen. "This Kivita Vondir is very brave, and certainly foolish. I have a signal from a landing capsule near the upper pole."

Sar keyed in the trajectory as she read it to him. "I don't like this. Any moment, an Aldaakian cruiser might enter the system." He buckled himself down as *Frevyx* neared Vstrunn's outer atmosphere.

She strapped into the navigator chair and tied her mane back with a leather thong. "You are definitely the best pilot I know. I am truly more worried about the Kith."

Hydrogen-cloud turbulence sent shudders along the ship. He kept his breathing calm, his eyes on the console. More turbulence nearly tugged control of the ship from him. One particular nasty patch jostled them in their seats, but in the next instant, *Frevyx* cleared it. Sar flew them between crystal spires hundreds of feet high, then down into a canyon three miles deep.

"Will she surely be happy to see you?" Cheseia asked, her russet eyes anxious.

"Doubt it. She won't turn down a rescue, though. Kiv's got a tongue more barbed than a slag-dust addict. Be patient with her."

Cheseia grunted and mashed her seat lock down.

Frevyx's scanner found the landing capsule beside the rim of a fissure six miles deep. Sar gave a mental curse at Kivita's recklessness.

He set *Frevyx* down on a mesa a hundred feet west of the capsule. Even through the hull, the crackling of scorched crystal was audible as his braking thrusters activated. Sar unbuckled himself and rose. From the viewport's perspective, he realized Kivita wasn't in, or anywhere near, the capsule.

He rushed to the storage lockers and put on an envirosuit.

Cheseia took up an envirohelmet. "I am absolutely stronger than you. Let me search for her."

"Stay here. Watch for Kith or anything else. Kiv shouldn't be far; she never was good in high-G. No radio messages, though. Any Aldaakians will pick it up before they detect our beacon."

After handing him the helmet, Cheseia grasped his arm. "Return within an hour, or I will surely search for you."

"That's not enough time for me to find her myself." Sar snapped on the helmet.

"You came for her, definitely not the gem." Cheseia squeezed his arm so hard, his suit sleeve creaked.

He touched her furred cheeks. "Told you where my heart lies. Kiv knew it, too."

Cheseia looked away, chest rising in heavy breaths.

Where did his heart lie? Shattered on Freen? Pierced over Gontalo, where he'd left Kiv? Or frozen out there in the cosmic darkness, where even he was afraid to look? He wasn't sure if the answer mattered anymore. All that mattered was his revolution against the hated yellow banner.

"Come back to me," Cheseia whispered, still not looking at him.

As the airlock opened, Sar smirked. The angry surprise on Kivita's face would be worth it.

Seul Jaah read a list of infant names on the flat-panel display inside *Aldaar*'s communal atrium. Like all Aldaakian women, she'd donated her ovary eggs to the Pediatric Ward. Seul had seen her baby daughter only once, right before the infant had been taken to receive her cryoports.

All Aldaakians received cryoports at birth: three in each arm, two in each leg, two in the chest, one in the stomach, and one behind the neck. Seul wondered how cold space would really feel without the ports regulating her bodily systems. How humans traveled through space without freezing to death amazed her.

Since ten light years separated her current post at Vstrunn from her homeworld, the girl would be the same age now. Seul would never know her. Aldaakian infants were tested and trained for future duties, like Shock Troopers, Archivers, pilots, or doctors. Loyalty was placed in the race, not individuals or relatives. She knew it was the right way.

Behind her, off-duty Troopers sat at a counter, enjoying protein slush and gelatin sticks. A spherical lamp gave the atrium a blue glow. Everyone wore the same blue-gray uniform, stood six feet tall, and had white-within-azure eyes.

Kael grinned up at her. As shuttle pilot for her squad, he remained out of cryostasis more than most. It'd long been Aldaakian custom to keep most personnel frozen until needed, in order to conserve resources. Looking him up and down, Seul didn't want to conserve anything when around him.

"Drop that smile and hand me some Touu berry gelatin." Seul sat beside Kael. Her cryoports relaxed despite her mock austerity.

"As you command, Captain Jaah. I am your servant." His hairless albino skin glistened from a recent mist bath. Seul still had two recreation debits before the next jump cycle. Maybe she'd spend one with him.

She scooted her hand closer to his on the counter. "You'd better be. I've been trying to get you promoted to Commander Vuul's bridge staff for three jump cycles now. You're wasted as a pilot."

"You keep trying to get rid of me. It won't work." Kael passed her a yellow Touu stick and smiled.

Seul took the stick and licked it. The Touu's sweet-and-sour flavor stuck to her tongue. "How much longer until you go back into cryostasis?"

"Six hours, during which I have to run diagnostics on all of *Aldaar*'s shuttles. Why?" Kael asked.

Regulations were lax concerning relationships in dry dock, but . . . being on an Aldaakian cruiser meant one was always on duty. No personal quarters; just a cryopod surrounded by other cryopods. A request for privacy would earn her a psychological evaluation. Overt interest in him would earn her a demerit.

"It's nothing." There had to be a hint, some clue she could give him. Seul could ask him to—

Aldaar's alarm blared through the atrium speaker.

"Do you think the Inheritors are trying to take the gem again?" Kael asked.

"Not if I can help it," Seul said.

While Kael rushed to the airlock bay, Seul headed for the bridge. Other Aldaakians manned battle stations or secured weapons from lockers. Sparse lamps lit the ship's narrow corridors, which were lined with cryopods. Cryogenic exhaust hissed from vents along the floor, tainting the air with a stale frost scent.

Seul entered the bridge as Commander Vuul rose from his seat. His cold white-within-azure stare measured her. She and seven other officers snapped to attention. The flight staff waited at their terminals, worry in their eyes.

Flat displays presented readouts of Vstrunn and its white dwarf sun. Wide trapezoidal viewports revealed the crystalline world and a field of dim stars.

One human craft orbited Vstrunn, while beacon signals emitted from two others on the planet's surface.

Seul's cryoports tingled with apprehension. For decades her people had assumed the Vim had left something on the planet. Something many had died for.

"New Inheritor forays on Vstrunn have produced an unpredictable result," Vuul said in a deep voice. "In the past, I deployed squads to investigate; each met with fierce Kith resistance, or were unable to enter the tower. Something is different this time. Captain Jaah, I want your squad to board the orbiting vessel and secure it."

"It is done, Commander Vuul." She inclined her head and touched her chest cryoports.

"The rest of you, activate your squads from cryostasis and remain on standby," Vuul said. "More human ships might arrive. I have sent word to my fellow commanders throughout the Cetturo Arm."

Everyone on the bridge stood rigid and silent. Seul's

heart beat faster, and her cryoports clenched. The Inheritors had never sent more than one ship before, and only in dire circumstances did an Aldaakian commander alert other fleets.

"May I inquire about the situation, Commander Vuul?" Seul asked.

"A signal has been sent from the planet's surface," Vuul said. "One our entire race has sought for centuries."

Seul's cryoports clamped shut in shock as she studied the flat display. The familiar radio wave all Archivers taught Aldaakian children about had finally been detected.

A Vim signal.

Ever since the Aldaakian exodus from the Khaasis system, Seul's ancestors had searched for their ancient allies, the Vim, to receive promised technology to defeat the Sarrhdtuu. Sarrhdtuu attacks had destroyed many Aldaakian worlds, atomized several armadas. Surviving fleets had sought refuge in the Cetturo Arm—yet their old enemies, and the xenophobic Inheritors, had greeted them.

Seul knew their Vim allies had been here long ago. Now they were returning to help them defeat the Sarrhdtuu.

"You all have your orders." Vuul turned and studied the display.

As Seul exited the bridge, a strange numbness permeated her body. Aldaakians had bred themselves and reshaped their society to survive Sarrhdtuu depredations. Everyone was trained to fight, and all resources had to be rationed. Cryostasis had offered an answer to many problems; individuals not needed simply slept in a cryopod, sometimes for years. Now, with the possibility of reuniting with the Vim, her race might find peace again.

Standing inside a locker, Seul waited as a full polysuit socketed itself into her cryoports. Slim rods turned and inserted into each cavity. Seul didn't even grimace anymore, having been long accustomed to the process. The armor converted perspiration into cryonic gas, which helped to maintain body temperature, while the inner layer clung to her body like a second skin. A helmet with a tinted faceplate snapped into place over her head.

Seul loathed meeting any humans on the enemy vessel. Their darker skin and body hair were grotesque, and she abhorred their lack of cleanliness. She'd met friendly ones in the merchant lanes around Tejuit, but their mangling of Meh Sattan had tortured her ears.

After shouldering a beam rifle, Seul joined her squad in the airlock bay. One by one they boarded an assault shuttle and locked their armor into standing positions within deployment tubes. Kael and a female navigator reclined in the cockpit's elasticized seats, system tubes protruding from their cryoports.

"Troopers loaded. Stand by." Kael gave Seul a slight smile.

The navigator disengaged the artificial gravity; then the shuttle exited *Aldaar* and sped toward the human vessel. Seul clenched her abdominal muscles to prevent nausea.

"Bring us alongside and magnetize our airlock with theirs," Seul said. "Point One, set your rifle to a fine cutting beam. Point Two, follow me with Flank Three and Four. Use your blades; no rifle fire. Auxiliaries Five through Eight, wait here for orders."

A pop, followed by a resounding clang, heralded the coupling of their airlock with the human one. Each Trooper's deployment tube released them as false gravity activated.

"The human beacon is sending out strong signals, Captain Jaah," Kael said. "Sarrhdtuu signals."

Seul frowned. "It could be advertising itself beyond this small star system. Perhaps we'll discover more information aboard. Point One, on my mark."

She stepped aside as the Trooper lowered his beam rifle. Once the shuttle's airlock slid open, the human vessel's own airlock doors greeted them. Small dents and tears pocked its surface.

"Mark." Seul drew her polymer shortsword.

Point One cut into the airlock with the rifle's concentrated green beam. In the small space between the ships, slag cooled and hardened as soon as it peeled away from the incision.

"Go." At Seul's command, Point One kicked aside the locking mechanism. The human doors slid open. Seul jumped through, sword raised. The other Troopers followed.

Bluish-white running lights activated along the floors. Seul's polyboots magnetized, and she clanked across the floor. Her squad discovered a hammock, some battered polyarmor, and placards of seminude humans. What ugly, hairy bodies. Ascali claw graffiti and glue-pen chits marked the walls. Grime coated the shadowed, unused corners. The bridge had only one seat and a gyro harness.

"Jaah to *Aldaar*: human vessel is secured, and could belong to a salvager. No one aboard. Kael, take the shuttle and scout Vstrunn's exosphere."

"Acknowledged, Captain Jaah," Kael's voice came back over her helmet speaker. The shuttle demagnetized from the airlock and flew just above Vstrunn's horizon. Seul released a tense breath.

"Squad, take positions flanking the airlock." Seul knelt in a firing position near the hammock. On the wall, the creased placard of a human man and a young human girl with golden red hair caught her attention. The girl's smile stirred Seul's heart.

She touched the picture, wondering what her own daughter looked like now. But everything she did contributed to the return of the Vim and the safety of all Aldaakian children. Seul kept telling herself that, though her heart swelled the longer she stared at the placard.

7

A jagged stalagmite ripped the left sleeve on Kivita's envirosuit. She caught her breath, but her lungs demanded more. The mesa where she'd landed loomed closer, but she was even nearer to asphyxiating. Her muscles ached as if she'd been beaten by a crazed Proselyte.

Crystal shards slid down a slope on her right. Kivita pulled herself up by grasping the stalagmite. It sliced through the palms of her gloves. The envirosuit's inner layer strangled her, guarding against chill and hydrogen seepage. Her faceplate fogged over as more carbon dioxide than oxygen floated around her cheeks.

A hulking shadow cast itself over her from the crest of the slope.

As the Wraith Star set over the horizon, it revealed a figure with bulges around its arms and legs, and a bubble-shaped head. The Kith had followed her after all. As she tried to focus on what to do, her scalp tingled.

Kivita flinched as coordinates for unknown systems in the Terresin Expanse flooded her mind. Ever since touching the Juxj Star, she'd no control over what entered her thoughts. No doubt her slow suffocation contributed to these hallucinations.

The figure stood over her and extended its arms. A final ray of sunset illuminated the face beneath the tinted faceplate: dark curls above a square, swarthy jaw. Kivita laughed, no longer caring that she wasted valuable air in doing so.

"Sar?" She laughed again, then choked as her lungs rejected the excess carbon dioxide.

Firm hands lifted Kivita to her feet, and she leaned, gasping, against the body. She wobbled toward the ground. A second set of hands caught her. The ruby, sapphire, and violet landscape tossed in her sight. Sometimes it blurred into the faces of people she'd known: her father, with his trimmed mustache and adventurous brown eyes. Marsque, who'd watched her grow up between her light-year journeys.

Sar, who'd made love to her in a sweaty, cramped hammock.

For a time it seemed she floated over Vstrunn. Crystal spires pierced the night sky, where thousands of faraway stars tempted her with a new flood of coordinates, light-year distances, and unnamed star systems. Up she went, closer to the sky, closer to the hydrogen gas bands high overhead. The mesa's flat surface dragged under her feet, and Kivita's flesh chilled, as if she rested in cryostasis. The faceplate fogged with hydrogen frost on the outside. Kivita wanted to laugh again, but her lungs constricted.

Something banged behind her. A humming filled her body. Her ears popped, making her groan. Fingers forced her mouth open; then a mask covered her face.

Strength surged in Kivita's limbs. Somebody thought they could steal her salvage? Her fist connected with something hard and smooth; then her foot kicked a slim object.

Voices roared in her ears. Her lungs expanded so much her chest hurt. Kivita sucked in delicious, fresh air. Clasping the mask with both hands, she breathed deep.

"Are you well, Sar?" a musical, feminine voice asked.

"I'll live. Told you to stay on *Frevyx*." Sar's Freen accent, with its overemphasis on the vowels, churned in her ears as if someone poured water into them.

"Humans are certainly stubborn," the female voice said.

Kivita's eyes snapped open, and she tried, muscles protesting, to sit up. All she managed was a graceless squirm on the floor. Navy blue bulkheads surrounded her. The scent of hibiscus and jiir plants replaced the stale carbon aromas she'd sniffed for hours. Normal gravity blessed her with a freedom she'd never thought to feel again.

An Ascali female leaned over her, studying Kivita with wide russet eyes. A luxurious dark brown mane flowed over the shoulders of her envirosuit. "Can you truly hear me, Kivita Vondir? No, certainly do not stop using the oxygen mask yet." Her Meh Sattan was more song than speech.

Kivita sucked in one last breath and cast the mask aside. "I'm . . . Oh, shit. I'm . . . fine now. But what—?" She stopped as Sar rose nearby, rubbing his right shin. Blood ran from his busted lip.

Her mouth went dry as heartbeats pounded against her shivering chest. Her stomach fluttered.

"You still have good aim with those hands and feet, sweetness." Sar removed his envirosuit. "Still need more high-G training."

His chastising tone kindled an eager fire within her. She wanted to kill him for so many reasons.

"Asshole." She rose to her knees. Every muscle in her

body burned, and her damp hair clung to both cheeks. The flutters in her stomach turned to icy nausea. "You saved me out there?"

"Lucky I got to you in time. Real stupid of you, Kiv." Sar didn't look at her, but his nostrils flared.

"I learned from the best, didn't I?" As her mind cleared, Kivita thought she recognized the Ascali from the Rector's Compound. "What the hell are you two doing here? Dunaar will be pissed."

The Ascali yanked Kivita to her feet and pushed her against the bulkhead. "I am Cheseia. Sar and I tracked you here to Vstrunn. I truly do not serve Dunaar. We mercifully rescued you, so truly show some respect!"

Sar frowned at Cheseia. "Set her down."

He and the Ascali shared a long, tense look. Finally, Cheseia's glower gave way to an apologetic sulk. Something passed between them. Kivita's nausea punched her in the gut. Oh, no way. This couldn't be happening. An intimacy lay between Sar and this Ascali. Furious heat rose in Kivita's cheeks.

"Yeah? Thanks. Now, why'd you trail me all the way out here?" A chill washed over her skin as Kivita shook off Cheseia's loosened grip. They knew about her mission! "I . . . didn't find the Juxj Star."

Sar hung up the suit, his gray bodyglove tight in all the right places. "Kiv, I see the bulge in your pouch." He tugged off her envirosuit.

"Hey, damn it!" Kivita couldn't protest much, since it took all her strength to remain standing. She did manage to wrest the pouch free.

Sar peeled the suit and its clinging inner layer down to her ankles. Her sweat-soaked bodyglove made her self-conscious in an instant.

"The crystal did not truly rupture the lining. That is most assuredly good. Did you see any Kith?" Cheseia asked, slipping from her envirosuit. Short brown fur covered her muscular curves, and only a breechcloth covered her crotch. Sar had always worked alone in the past, not with breathtaking, half-naked Ascali women.

Kivita kicked away the ruined suit and backed away from them. The pouch weighed her down as if she held a hundred pounds of copper. "At least five or six— Hell, I don't remember. Who hired you?"

Sar sighed. "Kiv, Rector Thev said you contracted for the Aldaakians. Said he wanted you returned safely. He must want the Juxj Star bad. Can't let the Inheritors have it for that reason alone."

"What the hell? The Rector contracted me, not the Aldaakians! If you try to rob me, you risk expulsion under the Inheritor Charter," Kivita said.

Cheseia's biceps flexed. "You must certainly bargain with us." Her eyes begged Kivita not to bargain.

"You'd be helping others, Kiv. Name your price." Sar crossed his arms.

"Same old story, huh?" Kivita gave a mock laugh. "Yeah, that's the kind of talk you gave me over Gontalo. Well, don't stick your nose into my life, asshole. This is my salvage."

"And you almost got yourself killed for it. I'll double whatever Dunaar offered."

Kivita eased toward the bridge. Maybe she could seal it off from them, then fly the ship herself—if she were quick enough. "The high-and-mighty Rector himself promised six fusion energy dumps and a nav upgrade. He already gave me a cargo bay filled with foodstuffs. No way you can top all that."

Shoving past Kivita, Cheseia blocked the path to the bridge. "Enough of her stalling. Sar, let us surely take the gem and quickly leave her ... in her ship."

Sar stretched his right leg where she'd kicked him. Neither of them made a threatening move, but Kivita knew they wouldn't let her take the Juxj Star back to Haldon Prime. Had Sar lowered himself to stealing other's salvages?

"No, Cheseia," Sar said. "Kiv, you really think Dunaar will pay that much? Soon as you return and hand it over, you'll be quartered in Judgment Square for heresy."

"Oh, and I should trust you?" Kivita tried to maintain her tough demeanor, but they had saved her life. It didn't mean they controlled it, though. "So, how much? Those secret allies you always whispered about got deep pockets?"

Cheseia's eyebrows rose. "You definitely never said you had mentioned that to her."

"Yeah, he's great at keeping secrets. Better get used to it." Kivita wanted to rub his face in something, anything. Anything to make him pay for how much she'd missed and wanted him since their parting.

Sar ran a hand through his sweaty curls. "We're wasting time. Aldaakians might be around, and Kith ready to pound that airlock in. We'll discuss this in orbit. Strap yourselves in." He sat in the pilot's seat and buckled his restraints.

"So, that's it? I'm not your prisoner, and I'm not—"

The throttle of *Frevyx*'s engines drowned out Kivita's words. Her jaw tensed and she glared at Cheseia. Oh, how she'd like to punch her.

Kivita buckled herself to a bench outside the bridge.

Though she felt foolish in doing so, she clutched the pouch to her chest. It was just a Vim datacore. Sar could have it if he trumped Dunaar's offer, but her reputation in Inheritor Space had grown. She needed it, had worked too hard for it.

She sure as hell didn't need him.

Cheseia sat beside her and strapped in. She pushed the mane from her face and held it back with a jiir leaf headdress. The blue glasslike leaves from Sygma reflected Kivita's haggard, pale face back at her.

"Sar said I should be extremely patient with you. Extremely." Cheseia studied Kivita like garbage she wanted to toss out the airlock.

"Yeah? That's sweet of you. Doing just what he says, like a good little girl. Sar? Dock with *Terredyn Narbas*. I mean it." Her voice didn't sound as tough as she wanted it to.

Frevyx shook as it lifted from Vstrunn's surface. The clicks and pops of burnt crystals singed by the ship's thrusters reached Kivita's ears. She breathed even easier than before, and downed a mixture Cheseia handed her. It tasted sweet but clung to her mouth.

"What's this?"

Cheseia grinned without humor. "Bellerion woodsnake milk. Sar claimed you would certainly need it after we rescued you."

Kivita pursed her lips to spit it out, but Cheseia's scornful stare made her finish it. "So, you live on board *Frevyx* with him, right? Thought nobody kept Ascali slaves since feudal times. Do you give him baths, too?"

She hated the words as soon as she spoke them. An awful, silent moment dragged by.

As she gripped Kivita's bench restraints, Cheseia's

nose almost touched hers. "You are thinking I am probably a beast? Less than you? I could crush you terribly, but I do not. Your prickly tongue makes you the beast."

Cold shame doused the jealousy, suspicion, and anger growing inside Kivita. A new wave of weakness made her go limp in her seat restraints. "Damn it, I didn't mean that. I just wasn't expecting . . . you know."

Cheseia released Kivita, her gaze far away. "You have surely been through much. We all have."

Kivita shot her a look. "Yeah. Lots of things seem strange right now."

Frevyx neared the fringes of the planet's atmosphere, and the cabin trembled with the last vestiges of turbulence. Sar remained cool and calm on the bridge. Kivita eyed his back, the way he sat composed and certain, how he gripped the manuals. Such a serious man, but she knew a heart beat deep inside him. Why should she care now, though?

"I do not wish enmity between us," Cheseia whispered. "It is not the Ascali way. What you hold in your hand may change the Cetturo Arm greatly. Ponder that deeply, before you choose profit over benevolence."

Kivita didn't look at Cheseia as the bridge viewport filled with stars. "Yeah. We'll see. Right now I just want to get back on *Terredyn Narbas*."

8

Frevyx shuddered from a slight gravity flux; Kivita's own ship must be close. She handed the milk canteen back to Cheseia and rolled her eyes. "What's the deal, Sar? You going to magnetize the airlocks or what?"

She unstrapped herself and stood. More strength had returned to her limbs, but she still yearned for a long norm sleep cycle. And to get away from Sar.

"You been doing business with the Sarrhdtuu, Kiv? Your beacon is sending out one hell of a signal." Sar's voice held a worried edge.

She tried to ignore Cheseia's scornful glance. "Of course not. It can't be that strong."

"But it is, sweetness." Did he have to call her that?

Kivita hurried into the bridge. It still smelled like him: faint sweat, freshly washed hair. Newer computer consoles and some sort of projector had been added since their time together. Of course he'd upgraded. He was Sar Redryll, the greatest salvager in the Cetturo Arm, right? Asshole.

Sar's console showed beacon readings beyond human norms. Such a signal would transmit on an interstellar scale, across the surrounding systems. Kivita's throat constricted. She had her prize and just wanted to leave. Waiting outside the bridge viewport, *Terredyn Narbas*'s lonely shape begged her to return.

"Picking up other ships," Sar said in a low voice. "Someone else has followed you." He stared at her, then turned the manuals. *Frevyx* neared her ship at docking speed.

Kivita's stomach quivered. "Shit, Sar. Hurry up! Get me aboard, and we'll cut from this system."

Cheseia grabbed a spike baton from the weapons locker. "Where will you go? Your beacon will be positively traceable."

"Just get me on *Terredyn Narbas*. No way someone else would come this far from Inheritor Space." Kivita shook sweat from her lank hair. Her mission grew more complicated and mysterious by the minute, matching a deeper fear.

Others wanted the gem. Maybe enough to kill for it.

Sar snorted. "We'd better leave now, with all of us on *Frevyx*."

"Like hell we will! I'm not leaving my ship." Kivita locked stares with Cheseia. The pause from the bridge made her tremble with anxious energy.

"Stand ready for the airlock, Kiv," Sar finally called from the bridge. "Better trust us. You know I'll track your trajectory, so there's no point in pulling some trick. Wait . . . Got several signals, closing. Cheseia, close the doors as soon as she leaves."

Frevyx hummed louder. Gravity relaxed for a second as both airlocks magnetized with each other. Kivita rose onto her tiptoes, ready to jump into her gyro harness and clear Vstrunn as soon as possible.

Cheseia approached the airlock's left side. "Truly, you must follow us. That gem is certainly important—"

"Yeah, yeah. Shut up for now, okay? We'll share jiir wine and trade stories about Sar later." Kivita studied her airlock across the short space between ships.

Invisible magnetic bands kept air and items inside during passage between ships. A still, lifeless void waited in that small space. On her own airlock doors, a fine line had been burned all around the inner opening. Slag pellets floated near the hull.

Kivita jerked back. "Sar! Someone's already boarded—" *Terredyn Narbas*'s airlock whooshed open.

"Disarm them!" a female voice shouted from Kivita's ship.

A thin green beam shot out and sliced through Cheseia's spike baton; then three figures in black polyarmor barged into *Frevyx*. A gauntleted fist slammed into Kivita's right shoulder, and she smacked into the bulkhead wall.

"Aldaakian Shock Troopers!" Cheseia brought the baton's lower half onto one's helmet. Shards of polyarmor and faceplate flew into the air. The Ascali ducked a shortsword swipe, then kicked the Aldaakian's chest. The Aldaakian tumbled back into *Terredyn Narbas*'s airlock.

"Surrender, Inheritor scum!" the same voice called.

Frevyx lurched. The magnetized airlocks disconnected by four feet. Two Aldaakians made for the bridge, swords drawn. *Frevyx* shook again, and gravity faded to zero-G within seconds. Everyone floated into the air, save for Kivita and another Aldaakian, whose polyboots magnetized to the floor with a clang.

Cheseia steadied herself on the airlock handhold and kicked another Aldaakian back into *Terredyn Narbas*. One tried to fire a rifle at Cheseia, but Kivita rammed the Aldaakian's shoulder with her own. The rifle's green beam went astray, melting a lamp socket in the ceiling.

"Check your fire—we need them alive! Point Two, rush the airlock with me!" the Aldaakian with the crushed face-plate shouted.

Two Aldaakians jumped from *Terredyn Narbas* and grabbed hold of *Frevyx*'s airlock rim. Sar peeped around the corner and fired a kinetic pistol. The shot echoed in the airlock chamber, blasting off an Aldaakian's hand at the wrist. The Aldaakian recoiled and drifted into the space between both ships.

"Kiv, close the airlock!" Sar ducked back into the bridge as two beam shots melted holes into the corner where he'd taken cover.

Kivita shoved with all her strength against the same Aldaakian, but he backhanded her. Scorching pain lit up her cheek and jaw. Scuffling, both of their polyboot sets loosened from the floor. The motion sent the Aldaakian spiraling toward Cheseia, and Kivita toward the airlock.

"Dammit, the airlock!" Sar called from the bridge. Another green beam struck the corner, ensuring he remained there.

Kivita floated before the airlock, her hand near the release lever. Kicking her feet out, she managed to move herself a few painful inches.

"Surrender!" The Aldaakian female with the broken faceplate swung a shortsword at Kivita. The blade grazed Kivita's left leg as her fingers brushed the lever.

Cheseia shoved the ruined baton into the other Aldaakian's faceplate. Green beams fired from *Terredyn Narbas*. One sheared off the life-support cover on the female Aldaakian's back.

A crack, then an earsplitting pop, reverberated in the airlock chamber. The release of oxygen and cryonic gas flung the female Aldaakian against Kivita.

Kivita bumped into the manual-release lever as a final beam fired from *Terredyn Narbas*. It singed a bulkhead, raining white-hot sparks on Kivita's back. Each nipped her flesh like a bee sting. An Aldaakian clinging to the airlock tried to reach inside, but the sliding doors crunched on his polygauntlet.

Gravity returned to normal on *Frevyx*. Kivita hit the floor on her right side, jarring her bones. The female Aldaakian, still loosing cryonic exhaust, landed on Kivita's legs. The cut on Kivita's leg flared, and she sucked in a breath.

Cheseia, still holding the baton handle, landed on her feet. The Aldaakian she'd been fighting crashed onto the floor, dead.

"Clear the doors!" Sar yelled.

Kivita glanced up. Three gauntleted fingers still wriggled in the sliding doors.

"Back." Cheseia aimed the dead Aldaakian's beam rifle. With a short zap, she melted away the armored fingers. The airlock closed.

Kivita lay in a stupor, the fire along her leg powering a new set of visions: *schematics on a geothermal harvester. Deep-space asteroid mining.* Technologies she'd never even heard of. She rubbed her forehead and tried to slide out from under the Aldaakian. Blurred colors swam in her vision.

Furred hands shook her back to reality. "Kivita, we must truly leave the system. Strap yourself . . . Sar, she is certainly wounded!"

Kivita sat up as realization stabbed her brain. *Terre-*

dyn Narbas had been taken! With effort, she pushed the limp Aldaakian off her legs. The sword graze burned hotter. The spark burns on her back simmered.

"No! Not without my ship! Damn it, Sar, don't you dare!" Weak legs propelled her into the bridge with a mind of their own.

Sar keyed in coordinates with flurried strokes, using his left hand. His right held the pistol — aimed straight at her. "No choice now. Strap yourself in."

"Don't you . . ." Kivita suppressed a whimper and had to lean against the corner. "I swear I . . ." Every word sapped energy, stole her breath. Their eyes lingered on each other's. The pistol in his grip didn't waver. Her knees did, and she sank to the floor.

Red and yellow warning lights flashed on Sar's console. Outside the viewport, *Terredyn Narbas* drifted away, with three Aldaakian bodies floating around it. Kivita collapsed, her eyes still on Sar's. He lowered the pistol and sighed. Was that sympathy in his face? He thought she was finished? She forced herself back to her feet, lips trembling with raw words.

Over the curvature of Vstrunn, three small shapes grew larger. More ships had arrived. Fear clawed a ragged pit into her heart.

"Damn you, Sar," she whispered before pain, exhaustion, and anxiety sent her into darkness.

Sar turned away from Kivita as she plunked against the bulkhead and slid to the floor. Did she think all this was his fault? The console's scanner beeped again. Three more shapes had entered beacon range, two large and one small. The latter was perhaps a shuttle. He keyed in jump coordinates of a last resort.

"Cheseia? Brace yourself back there." Leaning out from his chair, Sar tugged Kivita toward him, then lifted her onto his lap. She breathed heavily, eyes rolling back into her head. A cut ran across her left leg a few inches above the knee. A fresh bruise spread itself across her right cheek and jaw. Dozens of tiny holes on the back of her bodyglove smoldered.

She looked dirty, pitiful, vulnerable. A little stringy from too much exercise and not enough decent food. He gingerly touched her lips.

She was still more beautiful than he remembered.

He pressed the jump activation button, switching _Frevyx_'s engines to light-drive mode. The bridge viewports sealed shut, and the entire ship vibrated. A short jerk glued him and Kivita to the seat as gravity fluxed a few seconds. Sar's stomach knotted for a moment, then relaxed.

Vstrunn and the other ships were far behind them. He wondered for how long.

"Sar, hurry back here instantly," Cheseia called from the airlock chamber.

Sar rose and strapped Kivita into the chair. As his fingers wiped sweat from her brow, the image of a galactic arm filled with blue stars entered his mind. Sar had never seen it before. Touching her had never sent images into his thoughts before, either. He suppressed a shiver.

"Sar?"

He tore away from Kivita and hurried to the airlock. Scorch marks and dried slag pools marred his clean ship. Two Aldaakians in polyarmor lay on the floor, both of their faceplates busted open. One, a male, had a melted half baton shoved into the bridge of his nose. Polyarmor and glass shards crunched under Sar's boots as he halted over the other body.

Kneeling beside the prone figure, Cheseia looked up. "This one truly lives. She must have been their leader; she shouted orders to them after I roughly shattered her faceplate."

"And you?" Sar picked a glass shard from her silky mane.

She nodded. "I am truly well. Kivita was—"

"Grazed. We'll patch her up after taking care of this one." No point in saying anything to Cheseia about what he'd just saw. Besides, he didn't need an argument with her now about old feelings for Kiv.

The Aldaakian's albino face bore sharp cheekbones, a pert nose, and thin lips. She lacked hair, even eyebrows. Sar had heard Aldaakians bred away all hair follicles through a strict eugenics program.

"What do we actually do with her?" Cheseia shot him a narrow-eyed look. "I will not mercilessly kill her."

"Agreed. Time to ask her some questions."

They carried the dead Aldaakian into the second airlock. Sar sealed the inner door; they'd strip the armor and dispose of the body later. Cheseia poured bleach solvent over the blood pool where the body had lain.

Together, he and Cheseia unsnapped the polyarmor's locks, then pried it from the female's body with a suctioning noise. While she moaned, Sar bound the Aldaakian's wrists and ankles with flexi cables.

Underneath the armor, she wore a skintight, blue-gray uniform. Cryoports along her body sealed with a small hiss. Each cryoport was an inch in diameter, round, and rose above her smooth flesh half an inch. A flat stomach and toned musculature testified to rigorous conditioning.

"Perhaps the Aldaakians truthfully hired Kivita after all?"

Sar rubbed the stubble on his chin. "No, I believe what she said. Dunaar will—"

The Aldaakian awoke with a grunt. Sar and Cheseia stepped back.

"Stay." Sar aimed the pistol.

The Aldaakian said nothing, her white-within-azure eyes boring into them. Her cryoports shriveled, then widened.

"Name?" Sar asked. Aldaakians, like humans and Ascali in the Arm, spoke Meh Sattan. Inheritors claimed the Vim had taught it to everyone.

The Aldaakian glared at him.

"We definitely do not sell captives into slavery, like the Inheritors do," Cheseia said in low, smooth tones. She lifted the Aldaakian from the floor and carried her to the bench outside the bridge. "We truly will not harm you."

The Aldaakian still didn't reply, though her eyes softened.

Sighing, Sar ran a hand through his hair and holstered the pistol. "Ascali vocal tricks don't affect Aldaakians. Secure her. I'm going to give Kiv a thogen dose; then we need to enter cryo. Got an Aldaakian pod this one can use, if she behaves herself. And answers my questions."

He entered the storage room and thumbed through the medical cabinet. Slings, cloth bandages, cold packs, blue tape, crushed thogen barnacles, and other items came under his perusal. He sighed again, deeper.

"We surely saved her and the Juxj Star," Cheseia said from the doorway. "Stop unnecessarily blaming yourself."

"Do all Ascali read emotions as well as you, and at

the worst times?" He slammed the cabinet shut. "It's not just her wounds bothering me, Cheseia."

"Then we should certainly go to Navon and the other Thedes. You could easily key in a change of course."

Sar shook his head. "Anybody following us will trace our beacon signal, and then all we've worked for—it'd be destroyed. Navon will have to wait."

"You certainly do this to be spending more time with her." Cheseia turned and left.

Snatching a thogen bottle, Sar stalked back into the airlock chamber. Cheseia hefted the Aldaakian over her shoulder and headed toward the cryopod chamber, her eyes flat.

Sar blocked her path. "Kiv's too headstrong, too young. Too foolish to evade the Inheritors for long. We'll make her a better deal for the gem, and then we take the Juxj Star to Navon. Maybe I'll drop Kiv near Tejuit, well out of Inheritor Space."

"How did a human manage to send such a signal?" the Aldaakian blurted, then fell silent.

Sar faced the Aldaakian. "You want that Aldaakian cryopod for this trip, tell us your name. Your mission."

"You're not Inheritors?" The Aldaakian's accent lent her vowels a deeper sound.

Sar grimaced. "Hell, no. Now talk."

"I'm Captain Seul Jaah of the battle cruiser *Aldaar*, under orders from Commander Vuul. The ship I boarded was sending a Sarrhdtuu signal. I was deployed to investigate."

"Why was *Aldaar* in this system?" Sar asked.

"We were on patrol until a Vim signal emanated from a structure on the planet." Her words held a note of awe.

His frustration with Cheseia gave way to a strange

chill. Sar disbelieved the Inheritor's Vim religion, but since Kivita had found the Juxj Star and he'd touched her . . . No, Sar refused to think she could be a Savant. Dunaar would've killed instead of hired her.

"What's special about that?" Sar paced around the airlock chamber.

Seul looked at him as if he were a dullard. "Now the Vim will come and aid us. We are ready to rejoin them against the Sarrhdtuu and these maddened Inheritors. You must turn over whomever took that gem to me. My people need to prepare for the Vim's answer!"

Sar shared a frown with Cheseia. "The Inheritors are my enemy, too. But Kiv comes with us."

"Enemies? You killed some of my Troopers—"

"You attacked us first, remember?" Sar said.

While Seul glowered at him, Sar's mind churned. How had Kiv activated this so-called signal? He knew the prophets considered the Aldaakians heretics, but this was new to him. Could he convince the Aldaakians to join the Thedes against the Inheritors? He knew which planets to strike, which shipping lanes to cripple. The Aldaakians had battle fleets, legions of soldiers. Kivita might just be the catalyst he'd been searching for. It'd be hell convincing her.

"I have answered your questions," Seul said. "You'll need to unbind me so my cryoports will be in the correct placement to take full advantage of cryostasis."

"Maybe. Situate her, Cheseia, while I doctor Kiv." Sar walked into the bridge.

Kivita still moaned in the seat harness. Sar knelt and pressed two thogen powder capsules through her lips. The highly addictive painkiller would make her sleep for hours. He undid the harness and lifted her over his left shoulder.

In the cryopod chamber, Cheseia pointed a beam rifle at Seul and watched her enter the Aldaakian cryopod. Sockets extended from within the oval pod and inserted themselves into Seul's cryoports. She hadn't lied; Seul had to lie straight while all the sockets completed their insertions. Before the transparent hatch closed, Sar barred it with his hand.

"I don't have the resources to keep you under cryostasis forever, so mind yourself and your behavior. Might turn you back over to your kind soon as we can. We have a proposition you might like, about the Juxj Star."

Seul nodded, her stare blank. He let the hatch close, then laid Kivita in his usual cryopod.

"Where is *Frevyx* truly taking us?" Cheseia asked. "The Inheritors will surely be expecting Kivita's return."

Sar configured the pod's stasis time. "The Ecrol system." He put the pouch with the gem into the cryopod with Kivita.

Cheseia set the rifle aside. "In the Terresin Expanse? We must certainly rendezvous with Navon instead. And why is she truly in your pod?"

Sar met her eyes. "We have only three pods, and Ascali metabolism is higher than a human's. I have to share it with her. Will you stop being so damn jealous?"

"I will when you stop looking at her with truly joyed eyes." Cheseia lay down in the octagonal cryopod.

On his right, Seul had already closed her eyes. Aldaakians fell into cryostasis faster than any other race because of their cryoports. He wondered if they even had time to dream.

Sar frowned and slid in beside Kivita. She snored lightly, like old times. After the cryopod hatch cover snapped shut, *Frevyx*'s lights shut off and the gravity reduced to zero-G. Groaning, Kivita clutched the Juxj Star in both hands. She must have pulled it from the pouch in her sleep.

"Just what the hell did you do down there, Kiv?" he whispered.

She pursed her lips, and her breath blew over his face as his eyes closed.

9

Dunaar stood before the bridge viewport on *Arcuri's Glory*. In the distance, *Terredyn Narbas* flew into the Aldaakian cruiser's hangar. The infidels were making this easier than he'd hoped.

"All K-gun batteries are aimed and ready, Rector," Stiego said. The other bridge staff sat in silence, sweat running down their faces. Red emergency lamps soaked everything in crimson shades.

"Release the wreckage we brought," Dunaar said.

The forward cargo bay opened. With a burst of thruster jets, the remnants of three Inheritor craft spilled into space. Warped bulkheads and stiff, frozen corpses glided past the viewport.

"Rector, we have the Aldaakians' radio frequency." Stiego's right eye ticked as the bodies continued to float by.

Dunaar used his deeper oratory voice. "Aldaakian vessel, this is Rector Dunaar Thev of the Inheritors. How dare you attack this trio of ships! And now you capture a trawler that is under contract to me? Surrender in the name of the Vim, or suffer dire consequences."

The speaker on the console crackled.

Dunaar rapped the bulkhead with his Scepter. "Answer, or be fired upon—"

"I am Commander Vuul, captain of *Aldaar*," a cold voice broke in. "You are in violation of the Tannocci-Terresin Treaty. We have fired on no human ships. The unmanned trawler is outfitted with a Sarrhdtuu beacon. You have no claim here."

"I have the claim given to me by the holy Vim themselves." Dunaar lifted his index finger, and a security officer fired the starboard K-gun battery. Three kinetically charged sabot rounds hurtled toward the Aldaakian ship.

"One minute to target," the security officer said.

"Rector, we have *Frevyx*'s jump coordinates. Sar Redryll has headed into the Terresin Expanse itself." Stiego's holo monocle displayed a readout six inches from his face.

"Either that heathen Aldaakian commander is lying, or Kivita was taken by Redryll," Dunaar said.

"Thirty seconds," the security officer said.

Aldaar's black hull shimmered for a moment. A blur passed over the stars behind it; then the craft vanished. The three sabot rounds coursed through space on an eternal trajectory.

"Track that jump!" Stiego shouted as he ran toward the nav officer's console.

"They will have trailed *Frevyx*." Dunaar paced the bridge. If Bredine had been correct, Kivita had indeed found the Juxj Star.

The console beeped, and the security officer spoke up. "Rector, the Sarrhdtuu wish an audience."

Dunaar hesitated. He had not expected them so soon. "I will communicate with them in my quarters."

After leaving the bridge, Dunaar activated the holo

terminal in his chambers. Peasants couldn't view such advanced technology. Only the prophets and their chosen could bask in the Vim's former greatness and not be blinded.

Above the terminal, an image flickered and coalesced into a three-dimensional figure of Zhhl. Dunaar straightened his glittering outer robe.

"Prophet of Meh Sat, this frequency irritates my body." The Sarrhdtuu's voice sounded grainy through the speaker.

"My followers cannot be allowed to hear our conversation. I assure you, our plan is still intact."

The image went awry with static. "Kivita Vondir touched the jewels taken from Xeh's Crown. She has touched the Juxj Star, for we know the vault on the planet below is now empty. We must have her."

Dunaar frowned. "My scanners have picked up a strong signal. A Vim—"

"It is known, Prophet of Meh Sat. Kivita Vondir is our payment for any war with the Aldaakians. They will also desire her now." Zhhl's sibilant voice thickened.

"The Aldaakians have *Terredyn Narbas*." Dunaar gripped the Scepter in both hands. "It is more likely the Thedes have Kivita now; Sar Redryll's ship has left the system. You shall have her once we find them."

"The Thede ship has been predicted to arrive near an ally."

"Oh?" Dunaar tried to keep his voice indifferent. "Then it would seem you already have Kivita Vondir in your grasp." He gripped the Scepter harder. Zhhl wasn't telling him everything it knew.

"This ally has agreed to bring her to the Tejuit system, Prophet of Meh Sat," Zhhl said.

Dunaar grinned with all his teeth. "That is the very

system I have chosen to gather my fleets. The Aldaakians will have no idea what bears down upon them. You will have your own fleet there?"

Zhhl didn't reply, as the holographic image disappeared with squealing pops.

What was that jelly-filled monstrosity keeping to itself? Had he overlooked something about Kivita?

Dunaar informed Captain Stiego of their destination, then entered the chamber where former prophets resided. The sleeping faces all seemed to beseech him for another chance at rulership. He keyed in one pod's revival-code sequence. Only the current Rector could converse with the sainted frozen.

Cryofrost fell away and the pod opened. Inside, the wrinkled form of Rector Broujel stirred as a tube squirted pseudoadrine into his crusted mouth. A musty aroma of sweat and stale air drifted from the pod.

"I have need of your council, Rector Broujel." Dunaar waited while the old man righted himself and opened his eyes.

"By the Vim . . . such a dream." Broujel's weak voice had an old, feudal accent. "Who? . . ."

"I am the current Rector, Dunaar Thev. I have awakened you for a question."

Broujel's cough shook his frail liver-spotted body. The man must have been near death when frozen. Dunaar would live to see the Vim on his own two feet, not frozen in stasis like this.

"Ah . . . I remember you, Thev. You asked me about the . . . the moons near Tejuit Seven—"

"What do you know of Savants?" Dunaar said. "Ones who could transmit data over great distances?"

Broujel scowled and coughed. "The Omni-Savants?

Those were reined in and outlawed. All traces ... eradicated."

Dunaar leaned forward. "What makes these Omni-Savants so special?"

"Special?" Broujel entered a coughing fit. Dunaar winced as the older man's lungs rattled. "They are an abomination! An Omni absorbs datacore knowledge and can transmit it to others ... even through space. Their electrical brain pulses act as radio signals. Why, in my time, we executed at least three. I imprisoned all other Savants, one of them my own daughter ... bred through the ... Oath of Propagation ..."

As he leaned back, a shiver of fear sliced through Dunaar's heart. If Bredine was correct, then letting Kivita fall into Thede hands constituted a great strategic blunder.

"The Sarrhdtuu are searching for one," Dunaar said. "A human woman. They want her as payment, in exchange for their aid against—"

"It is sacrilege to barter Savants, Thev! All your ancestors have struggled for ..." Broujel coughed and spat up mucus. "You're making the same mistake Rector Cyanev did with that wretched Susuron queen, Terredyn Narbas. Her banner, a sword with a flaring star, blighted several Inheritor worlds before she kissed the executioner's blade...."

While Broujel coughed, Dunaar tried to breathe. Terredyn Narbas ... it was the name of Kivita's ship, and that symbol was on its outer hull ... her talent ...

Before the Thedes discovered such things, he needed to act with extreme haste. Zhhl must already know.... But were they not the Vim's allies? Sweat ran down Dunaar's face, stinging his eyes and lips.

"Why is this not in the records? As Rector, I should

know everything!" Dunaar raised the Scepter and loomed over Broujel.

"I told you . . . all traces were . . . destroyed. Only the prophets can be allowed to spread knowledge. Savants can be controlled, contained. Omni-Savants . . . cannot. The Narbas line would have destroyed us, had the queen lived. Why ask me this? What has happened?" Broujel tried to leave the cryopod, coughing anew.

"I thank you for your wisdom, Rector Broujel. May the Vim illuminate our paths." Dunaar slammed the pod shut and mashed the stasis button. Inside, Broujel banged against the transparent hatch with weakening strikes. The old man finally drifted into cryostasis, lips curled in frustration.

Zhhl wanting Kivita was even more suspicious—but Dunaar needed Sarrhdtuu firepower to tip the balance in his favor. Just one of their battleships could annihilate an entire fleet.

As Dunaar hurried into his private chamber, Zhara avoided his scowl. He motioned in two Proselytes from the corridor. "Watch this Ascali wench at all times. Do not let her out your sight."

The blue sun blinded Kivita, though the one-hundred-foot-tall viewport was tinted to full power. The star's brilliance bathed its orbiting planets with life-giving energy as well as refueling her ship. In the surrounding void, thousands of similar systems shone back at her.

"Khaasis." The star name she'd almost said on Vstrunn.

Something warm touched her left shoulder.

Kivita inhaled as the blue star and gigantic viewport became a huge chamber filled with rows of cryopods. She stood, dressed in a yellow insulated suit, on a catwalk above them. The sterile scent of bleach solvent stung her nose. Kivita tried to count the pods, but the rows extended into distant cryofog.

The warmth moved up her shoulder and lay across her neck.

Crushed debris floated around Kivita over a reddish-brown nebula. The wreckage extended for miles in all directions. Thrusters, bulkheads, rigid bodies. Her faceplate frosted over as her air ran out.

"No," she murmured. The warmth traveled up her neck and rested on her cheek.

Kivita tried to turn away as a white-tiled room surrounded her. The hum and whir of machinery droned in her ears. In transparent tubes around her, humanoid creatures floated in yellow-green ichor. Kivita neared one tube. The occupant looked human, but fine hair covered its body, like that of an Ascali.

Shivering, she groaned as her temples throbbed.

"Don't pay heed to those Inheritor prophets, Kiv," her father said as they stood outside Terredyn Narbas. *"You'll find something special out there someday. Just gotta keep looking for it." The yellow sun rose over Haldon Prime, warming Kivita's face. Rhyer Vondir towered over her, attired in his brown flight fatigues. His kind smile didn't dispel an eerie notion in her mind: Kivita had grown into a woman now; she almost told him so.*

Moaning, she scooted toward the source of warmth. It touched her knees, her breasts.

She turned to tell her father about this gem she'd found, but he was gone. Now the Vim derelict from Xeh's Crown filled her vision instead. Globs of dried green jelly littered the decks, and rows of stone columns housed Vim datacores. Hundred-foot-high viewports showed the tri-nary super–red giants outside in hellish shades. A band of Kith watched her.

"Sar!" she cried, hoping he'd be there to help her again.

Stinging liquid filled her mouth and she coughed. The warmth contracted around her; then someone cursed into her hair. Kivita forced her eyes open.

Sar's green-brown orbs stared right back, inches from her face.

A cryopod hatch opened above them as he retracted his arm from around her. The source of warmth now revealed, Kivita recoiled, her skin tingling. The Juxj Star lay between them. It glowed once and dulled.

"What in the . . . ?" Kivita wiped pseudoadrine from her lips. Sar rose beside her, still in his gray bodyglove.

"Easy, sweetness. You almost crushed me trying to snuggle close." He yawned and stretched his arms.

Kivita sat up and snatched the Juxj Star. "You were groping me like a spacer who's been in orbit too long." Not looking at him, she lurched from the cryopod. Her cheeks burned so much, she feared they'd ignite.

Cheseia exited the cryopod on her left, stretching her supple form. The Ascali's near nudity made her cheeks hotter, and Kivita checked her own body. Blue medical tape covered the cut on her left leg, and the burns on her back only stung now.

"Move aside." Cheseia took up the beam rifle and aimed it at the third cryopod.

On Kivita's right, a hatch opened and frost crystals puffed into the air. An Aldaakian female wearing a tight uniform exited and regarded them all with caution. She

stretched, then ran in place. Her defined, muscular lithe-
ness didn't jiggle as she exercised.

Sar pushed past Kivita and stood on the floor.
Frevyx's gravity had already activated, but the heating
system had yet to raise the temperature fast enough.
Though Kivita shivered, the Aldaakian seemed unaffected as she balanced on one foot and stretched again.

"Seems like you've got a harem here, Sar. Why
couldn't you have shared her pod?" She gestured at
Cheseia. "And what the hell is this one doing here?" She
pointed at the Aldaakian.

Sar glowered at Kivita, then looked at the Aldaakian.
"I'm setting you off where we're headed. Remember,
Seul—I have an offer to make you."

"Seul?" Kivita snorted. "So you're on first-name terms
with one who tried to kill us?"

Seul stopped stretching and looked straight at Kivita.
"Too many Aldaakians have died to retrieve that gem.
It's the right color. The shade of blood."

Cheseia hefted the rifle. "I will guard Seul. Surely a
check on our location might be advisable, rather than
this measly arguing?"

Sar muttered under his breath, then smirked at Kivita. "Better play nice, sweetness. Don't have too many
clothes on board that will fit you. Can't let you go out
like that." He exited the chamber.

"Damn him." Kivita shoved the Juxj Star into her
pouch. Why had Sar let her keep it? "So, where are we
supposed to be? You seem to be on the uptake more
than the rest of us, Cheseia."

The Ascali remained focused on Seul. "The Ecrol
system."

"Ecrol? But that means we were in cryo for another year! I have a contract with the Rector of the Inheritors himself!"

To hell with the Rector, too. As soon as she could, Kivita would escape and sell the Juxj Star to whomever. Sar didn't need to know that, though. Let him squirm afterward.

Sar neared the doorway, buckling on a polycuirass. Polygreaves and vambraces protected his shins and forearms. "Hate to end your whining, Kiv, but time's short. I found some things you can wear. They're in the toilet. You get first use of the mist ionizer."

"You certainly do reek." Cheseia grinned without humor.

Kivita stormed from the cryopod chamber. *Terredyn Narbas* had been stolen, maybe even towed to one of those cold Aldaakian worlds. Rector Thev might null her contract or even execute her, like Sar claimed. Aldaakian warships had appeared over Vstrunn, and Sar had offered to pay double for the gem.

Oh, but he hated to end her whining? What a jerk.

Once inside the toilet, Kivita shut the door. Like *Frevyx*'s other cabins, the walls, floor, and bathing pod were well maintained. A pile of clothes lay on the counter. Three full-length mirrors displayed an alter ego who made her frown: dirty hair, smudged face, ripped bodyglove.

"Shit the cryopod. I do stink."

Kivita stripped and entered the bathing pod. Collection vents opened above; drains below. Five sprinklers misted her with hot water, while three vaporizers extended from the ceiling. The mist became steam. Scrubbing herself with a pumice sponge, she sighed with relief.

So, options for escaping? Cheseia could fight, and so

could Sar. Seul was a prisoner, too, no matter what Sar mentioned about some offer. Maybe they could escape together.... Sar wouldn't be the only one to make the albino woman a proposal.

A gradual throb rose in her forehead.

Eyes closed, her thoughts shifted to a world with green soil. *Steam geysers shot hundreds of feet into an orange sky. She stood on an observation deck, holding a stone staff. Dozens of Kith worked below, arranging rock columns, metal spires, and crystal geodes into a square structure.*

"Huh . . . ?" Strength left her legs for a second, and she bumped into the pod wall. *In her mind, the square structure resembled the tower on Vstrunn. Millions of colors stabbed into her eyes from the glare of crystal spires. . . .*

The mist ionizer shut off as the vision left her mind.

Steadying herself against the pod's transparent wall, Kivita glanced at the pouch on the counter. A yearning for Sar to tell her what it all meant, for him to hold her again, overcame the thin wall around her heart. How easy it would be to call for him. She slumped to her knees and fought back tears.

"No," Kivita whispered. Strength welled in her heart. She set her jaw, wiped her eyes.

"Not this time, Sar Redryll. I told you you'd found something out there in me. You should never have let me go." She sniffed and exited the bathing pod.

Kivita smirked as she studied her clean nudity and fluffed tresses in the mirrors. There was no Ascali fur on her, but her legs were still nice, and those boring workouts kept her stomach flat. Yeah, let Sar gawk at what he'd been missing.

The smirk vanished as she examined the clothes he'd left her: a blue breechcloth, ply chaps, and a blue top that wouldn't extend past her navel. The copper-meld brassiere, complete with Tejuit love chains to be tied behind the neck, made her cheeks burn anew.

"Damn him," Kivita said.

At least she still had her polyboots.

Seul maintained a calm composure as Sar approached her with the flexi cables. "You'll not require those. My superior will have already docked me from the Effectives List."

"You'll be freed once we're planetside. I just want you to hear me out."

Seul doubted she could handle them both, and she couldn't pilot the ship even if she defeated all three. They'd treated her well, considering the circumstances. Perhaps her Troopers would be alive if she'd not fired first. She hoped Kael was safe.

"I am listening." She tried to keep her tone neutral.

"Good." Sar looped the flexi around her wrists anyway. Cheseia kept the beam rifle aimed on her.

"Is a human's word as strong as an Aldaakian's?" Seul asked. "Bring me no harm and release me after we disembark, and you've my word I won't cause strife."

"I still want these on your wrists," Sar replied. "Hold out your arms, close together."

Seul's cryoports squeezed, but she did as he asked. As soon as possible, she'd find a way to rejoin her race. Excitement over the Vim signal still left her awed. Everything she'd dreamt about could happen, and now she was a prisoner? Not for long.

After Sar finished trussing Seul's wrists, Cheseia

spoke. "Truly, why have Shock Troopers tried to take the Juxj Star? If it is a datacore, you surely cannot read it."

Despite her revulsion regarding the Ascali's hirsute body, Seul liked Cheseia's voice. It reminded her of the flutes human refugees played in the hive ships around Tejuit Seven.

"Datacores can be scanned by running electrical current through them, but little information is learned," Seul replied. "We try to keep datacores from the hands of our enemies."

Sar's eyes narrowed. "Never heard that before. Keep talking."

Seul's cryoports tightened as she struggled with their searching stares. "The ship I boarded was suspicious due to its Sarrhdtuu beacon."

"This wasn't just about Kiv's ship. What else?" Sar's hands remained on her wrists.

"The tower sent out a signal to wherever the Vim are now. My people have waited for this signal a long time." Seul struggled to keep her voice emotionless.

Sar released her, his eyes worried. "*Frevyx* never picked up such a signal."

"Human scanners lack the proper configuration, though the Sarrhdtuu will have also detected the signal. Now do you understand my mission? Do you regret the Aldaakian blood you've shed?" Seul's cryoports gave an audible snap.

Exchanging a look with Cheseia, Sar nodded. "I'm regretting lots of things here lately."

Seul studied Sar's swarthy face. Handsome, despite those nasty shocks of hair on his head. But something in his eyes spoke truth. "What is your offer?"

"The Inheritors are both our enemies," Sar replied.

"Whatever Dunaar wants that gem for means trouble for my friends and yours. Then you tell me about this Vim signal. Seems we have common cause here."

"You suggest an alliance?" Seul tried not to laugh. "What are your weapons? Where are your fleets? Words cannot defeat both Sarrhdtuu and Inheritor starships."

"Your people have the weapons, the ships. My people, the knowledge. You've been fighting the Inheritors a long time and you haven't won yet. My friends operate right under their noses." Sar arched an eyebrow.

She wanted to believe this human. Though the loss of her fellow Troopers still festered in her heart, Seul knew her people needed help to win this long, awful war. The quicker it ended, the closer she came to her daughter.

"Tell me more," Seul said.

"A friend of mine can read what's on that gem," Sar said. "I can't say any more right now, until I know you're committed."

He made no mention of the red-haired human. Did Sar plan to sell the woman or kill her? Seul had to be careful. "How do I prove this?"

Sar hesitated, his eyes prying into hers. "Pretend you're my prisoner once we debark."

Cheseia nudged Seul's arm. "Let us find you something to truly wear."

"My appearance is inappropriate?" Seul asked. Kael had always appreciated her form.

"You look too crisp for where we're going." Sar led her to the ship's storage lockers.

Though this ship was cleaner than the trawler her squad had boarded, Seul paid it little mind. Was *Aldaar* still in orbit over the crystal planet? Would Vuul follow this ship? She knew every decision would be weighed against the discovery of the Vim signal. Her own actions had to take that into consideration. If this gem's potential matched Sar's claims, her people's search would be over.

First, Seul had to hear the rest of Sar's offer. Trepidation dampened her elation for a moment. Her race's doom or glory might rest in the hands of that red-haired salvager, the one Sar called Kiv. No one else had been able to retrieve that gem.

Kiv would not get out of Seul's sight.

10

With Tejuit love chains jingling, Kivita entered *Frevyx*'s galley. Cheseia scowled at her and elbowed Sar. He spilled his water flask.

"Surely you have better garments than those?" Cheseia's biceps twitched.

Kivita wanted to glare back, but Sar's annoyed look and Cheseia's jealous one made her smirk and place her hands on her hips. "Yeah, guess I'm ready for a night on the spaceport in this getup."

Sar and Cheseia sat on stools behind a counter. Seul stood in a corner, wrists bound, wearing a farmer's smock. Food lockers and water drums filled another corner. A hot-wave disk and dry-disher lay beside the counter. Too bad her ship lacked such a nice galley. Damn Sar for his trappings, but he'd earned them.

If she sold the Juxj Star, *Terredyn Narbas* could have far better furnishings.

"What kind of disguise is this immorally supposed to be for her?" Cheseia asked Sar.

Kivita bit her lip to keep her smirk from erupting into a triumphant smile. "What—these old things that Sar dug from his Locker of Former Lovers? C'mon.

Like there's anyone in the Ecrol system to see me, anyway."

Sar rose and handed Kivita a carb stick. Did his eyes just wander down to her exposed midriff? "There is. Umiracan."

"You been sucking jiir wine? That haunted planet is an old granny trawler's tale." Kivita bit into the carbon stick. The taste of sour nuts, sweet tree taffy, and protein grit made her mouth water. She inhaled it in two bites.

"It definitely exists. Fortunately for us, Inheritor charting doesn't truly know its location." After Cheseia handed Seul a mug filled with blue slush, her eyes focused on the wall behind Kivita. Yeah, trying to dismiss her. She wanted to savor the Ascali's insecurity, but the genuine emotion in Cheseia's gaze blunted Kivita's mirth.

"There's pirates, though," Sar said. Kivita caught him ogling her again, but he averted his gaze. "Shekelor Thal himself rules Umiracan, last time I was here."

"The cruelest pirate in the Cetturo Arm? Are you crazy?" Kivita hesitated. "I didn't snore that loudly to deserve this."

They shared a grin. Old times flooded her mind. Gambling with pirates near Gontalo, or exploring the planet's northern ice cap. Holding each other in his hammock during norm sleep. Sharing salvage stories. Sharing each other.

Seul choked on her mug's contents. "This isn't the correct temperature for protein. It should be colder. I can't digest this."

Cheseia took the mug and put it in a food locker.

"And what do you mean, 'here'?" Kivita asked. "We're already near Umiracan?"

Sar ran a hand through his black curls. "We should be

closing with the planet now. Shekelor knows me, though. We'll strike some deal until we leave the system. Anybody following can't track us because of radiation from the nebulae in the Expanse."

"That old spacer's trick? Okay, where to, then?" She cocked her head, hands still on hips.

"Wherever we can escape." Sar left the galley.

Cheseia handed Seul the mug and sat back down. Kivita sighed, then sat beside the Ascali as Seul sipped her drink. Only *Frevyx*'s dull engine ambience broke the silence.

"Where's your child?" Seul asked Kivita.

The back of Kivita's neck prickled. "What? I'm no mother."

"I saw a placard on your ship. A small female human, with hair . . . like yours." Seul almost gagged on the word "hair."

Kivita sipped from a water flask. "That was my father and me near Tejuit Seven, when I was a little girl. What of it?"

Clearing her throat, Seul lowered her eyes.

Kivita and Cheseia shared a baffled look.

"I never knew my mother or father, like you humans or Ascali do. I have a daughter, though she was birthed in the pediatric vats. I saw her once, before they implanted her cryoports."

Kivita's defensiveness evaporated. "What was she called?"

"Aldaakians are not allowed to know their children, not even by name. Those connections are old-fashioned. To survive, my ancestors shed what they considered unnecessary. And survive we have." Seul gulped the rest of the mug's contents.

"Never knew my mother, either," Kivita mumbled.

"I am truly sorry," Cheseia said. "My mother still resides on Sygma, my lovely homeworld. She would not abandon the traditional religion, as my sister and I definitely did. She tragically broke the Blood Bond with us."

"Blood Bond?" Kivita asked.

"An oath of loyalty usually severed only in death. An Ascali certainly never betrays, harms, or lies to one he or she has a Blood Bond with. Another's life and well-being irrevocably become that Ascali's responsibility, even if she must harm herself."

Kivita eyed the other two women as a sense of loss thudded in her heart. "That's sad about your mother. What happened to your—"

"I need you all on the bridge," Sar called outside the galley door. "Shekelor's ships have hailed us."

Moments later, with Sar in the pilot's seat and the rest of them leaning against the bridge walls, Kivita stared out the viewport. Ecrol, a super–red-giant star, shone millions of miles in the distance. It flared crimson, silhouetting Umiracan's sphere against the glare. She marveled at the even greater spectacle around the planet: churning, spacious nebulae, colored purple-gray, bluish orange, red-green. The celestial-sized arms of gas known as the Terresin Expanse formed one of the Cetturo Arm's outer fringes. Many of its depths had yet to be explored.

The speaker on Sar's console crackled with interference from the nebulae.

"Heh. Damn sloppy code sequence there, salvager. Wanna give a plumb damn good reason why we shouldn't board ya now?" The speaker's Meh Sattan sounded guttural, arrogant.

Sar pushed the mic button. "Tell Shekelor Thal that Sar Redryll wants that Umiracan Kiss he promised."

"What the hell is an Umiracan Kiss?" Kivita asked in a whisper.

"Best damn drink this side of the Arm. As long as the server doesn't slobber on you." He winked at Kivita.

Four ships came within sight outside the viewport. One was an oblong Inheritor transport. Two others had cylindrical Tannocci hulls. The fourth and largest was a saucerlike barge with a forward loading bay. No doubt dozens of armed pirates waited behind its cargo doors.

Kivita gripped the back of Sar's seat. "Shit. They mean business."

Sar reclined in the seat and looked up at her. "Easy, sweetness. Shekelor will talk."

Cheseia fixed her jiir-leaf headband. "I certainly do not like this. You know the coordinates, Sar. Key them in before something unavoidably happens."

"I hope these individuals are not part of the offer you promised?" Seul asked in a flat tone.

Sar said nothing.

Kivita smirked at Cheseia. "See how he treats us? Too damn mysterious in his relationships."

"If we are boarded, you must seriously hide the gem." Cheseia gripped Kivita's arm; the Ascali's fingers pressed into her flesh.

Kivita winced. "Yeah, okay, okay. Can I keep my arm?"

"Quiet," Sar said. The pirate ships changed their positions until each faced the planet rather than *Frevyx*.

"Well, Sloppy Redryll, ya can fly that trawler behind us down to the surface. You'll be plumb damned if ya deviate course. Got a fat slug with your Kiss waiting down there."

"Quite charming, aren't they?" Seul asked.

"And I thought you had bad manners." Kivita nudged Sar's shoulder.

Sar didn't reply as he piloted *Frevyx* toward Umira-can.

Still gripping his seat, Kivita almost touched Sar's back with her fingers. The closer they neared the planet, the tighter her chest became. Through brown cloud cover she made out cratered, desolate terrain with bone-yellow soil.

Cheseia took Seul and strapped them both to the bench outside the bridge, but Kivita hunkered down beside Sar's legs. With luck, he still hid a pistol under the pilot console. Then she'd feel more comfortable about bargaining the gem away.

"What the hell are you doing?" he asked without looking down. *Frevyx*'s gravity readjusted as it neared the planet's exosphere. Kivita's stomach jumped from the flux.

The space under the console held nothing. Great.

"I don't know what you've got planned, but I intend to get *Terredyn Narbas* back. Even if it means selling this silly gem."

Sar shot her a look. "That datacore is worth a thousand times your ship, Kiv."

"I'm not stupid. If this is like any other Vim datacore, why not get someone to read it and copy the information to some chits?"

"Not that simple—" Turbulence cut Sar off. His legs bumped into Kivita. *Frevyx* shuddered, then leveled off as Sar maintained course.

Kivita's head tingled. "Maybe Seul Whatever-Her-Name-Is can help."

Sar grunted and blinked, a flush spreading over his cheeks. Kivita sighed.

"Listen to me. She could contact the Aldaakians, and after selling the gem, I could buy my ship back from them—"

"No." Sar's strained voice gave her pause. "You've no idea what you have. Trust me, Kiv."

Kivita said nothing else, but she'd do anything to reclaim her ship. Her whole life rested within its confines. Mementos, equipment, clothes. That placard of her with her father.

After clearing the turbulence, *Frevyx* settled on Umiracan's surface with little incident. Kivita entered the airlock chamber, where Cheseia examined Seul's flexi bindings. During their year in cryostasis, the bleach solvent had eaten up the Shock Troopers' blood and left traces of dust. Seul's polyarmor lay in a bundle near the wall.

Sar left the bridge and opened the inner door to the other airlock. The dead Aldaakian was gone.

"Where is he?" Seul asked in a level tone, though her eyes dug into Sar.

"I jettisoned him before we neared Umiracan," he replied. "I know your ways, about meeting Niaaq Aldaar and all that. He'll be frozen out there forever now."

Kivita's brow furrowed. "Huh?"

"Commander Niaaq Aldaar led my people into the Cetturo Arm from Khaasis," Seul said. "He drew away our enemies so others might escape. His ship is out there somewhere, with him and his loyal Shock Troopers in cryostasis. We prefer to dispose of our dead in the same manner. A cryopod deposited into the vacuum. Your method is . . . acceptable, Sar Redryll."

"Khaasis?" Kivita asked as a chill crept up her back. Before touching the Juxj Star, she'd never heard the name.

"It's the home system of my people," Seul said. "You know of it?"

"No. I guess . . . it just sounded familiar." Kivita looked away.

Sar gave Kivita a strange look and cleared his throat. "Gravity's normal out there, but the atmosphere's carbon dioxide and helium. I've got six envirosuits with full air canisters. May have to walk half a mile or so before we reach his fortress."

"Allow me to wear my polyarmor with a borrowed helmet," Seul said. "Your suits will irritate my skin."

"You'll be fine," Sar replied.

"There are rough fibers in the liners of human suits. I'd like my own armor. With it attached to my cryoports, I'll use less oxygen and conserve more heat." Seul smiled with the whitest teeth Kivita had ever seen. Aldaakian hygiene must be formidable.

"C'mon, let her wear it. It's not like she can do anything to us in it." Kivita smiled, too, as Seul glanced at her several times. Asking her more about Khaasis was a priority.

"Paint it or discolor it." Sar went toward the storage lockers. "Shekelor's men won't appreciate a Shock Trooper dropping in for a visit."

"Thank you," Seul said, though her eyes met Kivita's.

Several minutes later, Kivita waited with Sar at the secondary airlock. They both wore miner envirosuits, the name tags pried from the shoulders. Ever since their landing, he'd avoided her, making little eye contact. She started to ask why as Cheseia arrived in the her own envirosuit. Seul followed, wearing an Inheritor helmet with a yellowed faceplate. Her polyarmor had been dabbed with red marker paint, used by dry-dock mechanics to indicate repairs.

Sar rested a hand on the door release. "I used to deliver goods to Shekelor years ago, but he doesn't owe me anything. He'll expect barter or gifts. Let me deal with him, and stay together. These pirates might kill you just for what you have on."

He pushed the release, and they all stepped onto Umiracan's hard-packed, sulfur-colored surface. *Frevyx*'s airlock snapped shut behind them. Sar double-checked the security-code pad, shielded under an armor plate. Once again Kivita envied Sar's oblong trawler, more than twice the size of *Terredyn Narbas*.

Far ahead lay a stone-walled structure overlooking a great ravine. Ecrol shone above them like an angry red eye gazing into their minds. Stiff wind laden with dust buffeted them every few seconds. The craters she'd spotted from orbit dominated a valley beyond the ravine.

Sar led the way, with Kivita and Seul following. Cheseia guarded the rear with the beam rifle, and Sar wore two small blades and a kinetic pistol. Kivita wore a steel polymer shortsword from Sar's armory. Seul, of course, carried nothing.

Two of the pirate craft she'd seen in space headed for the fortress. Blowback from the ships' passage threw small rocks against their envirosuits. Ugly brown clouds broiled above them, and a pink sky lent the landscape a diseased look.

Fifteen figures appeared from a swerving door in the fortress wall. As her group drew nearer, Kivita spotted sentries and gun turrets along the battlements. On their right, the ravine stretched into a plain pitted with square depressions larger than an Inheritor battleship.

"What're those?" Kivita asked.

"Old Ascali slave pens, from feudal times," Sar said in a tight voice. "Keep silent. They'll be monitoring our radio traffic."

Kivita wanted to punch him, but she chewed her lip. Perhaps her suggestion about trading the Juxj Star had angered him. Events had happened so fast since leaving Vstrunn, and Kivita hadn't contemplated where Sar planned to take her. She was helpless without her ship.

The fortress walls stood seventy feet high, with cracked stones and crumbled towers. A ditch she hadn't noticed earlier had been dug several feet from the wall. Bones lined the rough-cut trench. Long blond hair still clung to an eyeless skull.

Sar glanced at her in detached warning before Kivita could voice her shock and revulsion.

The fifteen pirates wore a hodgepodge of envirosuits. One stood out in blue-and-white polyarmor. All greeted them with brandished swords, kinetic pistols, and spike batons.

"Where's your flaming cargo, Redryll?" a high female voice said over Kivita's helmet speaker.

Sar didn't move. "I make deals only with Shekelor himself, not you. He'll like what I've brought."

"Right, fucking like the Ascali. Plumb straight for this teensy redhead, too," a rough male voice stabbed through the speaker.

"Shekelor." Sar pointed at the swerving door.

The pirates stared at them from tinted faceplates, but

she imagined scowls and cursing lips behind them. Wind yowled as it gusted through the ravine. She wondered if slaves' ghosts cried out instead.

"It's your flaming ass, Redryll, not mine. Now, is it?" the female voice said. "Hand over your weapons."

"I don't think so. Shekelor." Sar touched his pistol handle. Cheseia casually brought the beam rifle around. Even Seul didn't blink her startling white-within-azure stare. Kivita had been in tight spots, but their collective backbone impressed her.

"Quit wasting time and air," a gravelly voice said over the speaker. "Let 'em in. Redryll, you get the usual . . . escort." The figure in blue-and-white polyarmor gestured for them to follow.

Sar beckoned Kivita and the other two on, and together they passed through the swerving door. The pirates trailed after them, and the door clacked shut, followed by a harsh echo.

Inside, a rock floor contrasted with a pocked red ceiling. Two gun turrets tracked their every move. Murals of naked Ascali dancers covered the stone walls. The one in polyarmor motioned them up a stone ramp leading to the next fortress level.

Kivita stayed close to Sar as they entered a covered courtyard. Old starship engines, mining tanks, and gas skimmers filled it. A few pirates watched from dark corners. A pretty woman giggled as two pirates tugged at her clothes. Angry voices reverberated from the level above.

"You can remove ya helmets now, if you wanna conserve air." Their guide tugged off his own with a small pop. A gray beard, mustache, and mohawk dominated his dark features. "You may not remember me, Redryll.

Orstaav, Shekelor's old partner? Now I run security for him and all that."

Sar pulled off his helmet. "I remember. Still growing that blacklight cactus I sold you?"

Orstaav laughed. "That thing still makes the tastiest damn juice. C'mon. Shekelor hopes ya brought nice stuff for him."

Kivita caught the warning look in Orstaav's gaze.

The four followed Orstaav up another ramp onto a third level. Dung, urine, sweat, and vomit odors attacked Kivita's nostrils. Seul grimaced, but Cheseia wheezed and covered her mouth. Kivita guessed the stench choked the Ascali's keen olfactory senses.

Stone cubicles separated scores of families on the third level. The noise of mixed voices grew in volume. Humans, a few Ascali, and even a score or so Aldaakians convalesced in the poorest conditions Kivita had seen. Not even the farmer hovels on Haldon Prime matched this.

People dressed in ragged wool or stapled-together burlap cloaks munched rancid gruel. Flimsy cloth curtains served as doors to each cubicle. Arguments, sexual moans, infant wails, and coughing filled Kivita's ears. The wet crunch of someone getting bludgeoned, the hard slap of thighs thrusting against a rump, the splash of piss on stone . . . She wanted to put her helmet back on and mute it all.

"Gotta take these slaves away soon," Orstaav said. "Damn babies' crying driving me and the rest crazy."

Seul stumbled over a man vomiting outside a cubicle. His ribs showed through sickly skin. Kivita caught Seul's arm, steadying her. They both shared a determined, disgusted look. While Cheseia's eyes narrowed and her shoulders stiffened, Sar acted as if nothing bothered him. How many times had he been here and seen this travesty?

A narrow hall led from the third level to another ramp. Pirates sat on the stone incline, gambling with Naxan dice, functional in any gravity. Many studied Kivita and Cheseia with calculating, lustful eyes. Measuring them for profit, pleasure, or both.

Kivita's knuckles burned; she'd been gripping her sword handle without realizing it.

"Hurry up. This way." Orstaav climbed a metal latter into a loft where orange and green light flickered. Eight hefty pirates guarded the bottom of the ladder.

Sar looked straight at Kivita. "Say nothing unless he speaks to you. All of you." Something different from before swam in his brown-and-green-flecked eyes. Worry, maybe even dread.

Kivita had no choice but to follow.

After trailing Sar up the ladder, she paused and stared. The loft measured a hundred feet square. Old windows had been fitted with viewports cannibalized from starships. Strobe lamps flashed green and orange, while the scents of alcohol and perfume choked the air.

Gold-thread tapestries hung from torch sconces like misplaced towels. Chipped mosaics filled with armed men and women decorated tables. Counters overflowed with steaming dishes. Coral chandeliers from Susuron dangled from the ceiling, each holding a nude dancer.

The pirates themselves wore polyarmor with a double-headed green-and-red snake painted on their cuirasses. Humans from Bellerion, Dirr, Bons Sutar, and Tejuit rubbed shoulders. Ascali with designs shaved into their fur stood tall and brawny. Renegade Aldaakians in polymail looked like albino ghosts under the flashing lights.

Orstaav shoved a path through the crowd, and the pirates grew still. Greedy stares followed Kivita and Cheseia. Weapons clicked with Seul's passage. A few whispered Sar's name.

"Right through there." Orstaav pointed at a battlement entrance in the stone wall. A curtain embroidered with a two-headed green-and-red snake draped the doorway.

Sar walked past the curtain without obvious reservations. Kivita followed, helmet clutched under her left arm, right hand above her sword hilt. Seul and Cheseia came in behind her.

Before them rose a stepped dais in a room larger than she'd expected. A gem-encrusted throne rested on the dais. Crimson, pink, and green pillows lined the floor. Huge feudal tapestries and Sutaran glass sculptures rivaled the decor in the Rector's Compound. Two coral chandeliers holding white lamps lit the room. Six human and four Ascali females lay at the foot of the throne, dressed in transparent red-and-green shifts.

"Sar Redryll. What lovely companions you have. I already possess some of the finest beauties from across the Cetturo Arm, as you can see," a cultured voice said with Sutaran tongue inflections. A figure rose from the shadowed throne.

Kivita bit the inside of her cheek to keep from gasping.

Shekelor Thal stood about her height, but wide shoulders and corded limbs made him look as intimidating as a Kith. Dark green polyarmor covered his body. Black braids hung from his head. He had one brown and one purple eye.

Normal characteristics ended there. His left arm ended in three Sarrhdtuu coils, and his flesh bore the olive tint of one who'd undergone Sarrhdtuu Transmutation.

"They're nice. You've done well over the years." Sar smiled.

As Shekelor walked down the dais, the females scattered from his path. His eyes focused on Kivita. "I might make an exception for this one, Redryll. Yet, if I know you, these three are not here for you to bargain. That means they shall have to part our company while we conduct business."

Kivita tried to look aloof and tough while Sar remained silent. What was he waiting for?

"Come, now. You are my guests and shall not be harmed. Eat, drink, copulate—I care not! If you wish, there is a second covered courtyard where other activities are to be found. Orstaav will show you." Shekelor dismissed them with a look.

Sar spoke without turning. "You all heard. Wait for me out there."

Kivita didn't speak as she, Seul, and Cheseia entered the pirate hall again. Without seeking Orstaav, she barged through a doorway on her right. Just like Shekelor had said, a second courtyard waited. Rock shacks, stalls, and three dismantled starships filled it. The people wore better clothing, and several children peeped from dark windows. Kivita realized these were the pirates' families and personal slaves.

Cheseia stopped in the hall doorway. "Sar will not take long, I truly hope, and—"

"What the hell has Sar gotten us into?" Kivita asked. "What kind of deal is he working up there with that green-rigged brute?"

"I will not accept any offer from a Sarrhdtuu ally like that one," Seul said.

For once, uncertainty tainted Cheseia's voice. "I definitely do not know."

"So, how often do you and Sar spend a romantic getaway out here? What a charming little shithole." Kivita's face grew hot and she lowered her voice. "Have you no shame, dealing with these scum?"

"Do you stupidly think we would save you, just to mercilessly leave you to these people?" Cheseia's whisper cut into Kivita, along with her hurt glare.

"Arguing will get us all killed." Seul flicked her gaze to either side as pirates filed past them into the hall.

After studying Seul for a moment, Kivita undid the flexi around the Aldaakian's wrists. "Here, you're free."

Seul nodded once. "I'd prefer your company for now. I don't like this planet or its people."

Cheseia slung the beam rifle over her shoulders and tied the helmet to her envirosuit's belt. "Sar would certainly not have brought us here without good reason. Remember—he knows coordinates to a genuinely safe location."

"Yeah, like this one?" Kivita stared at the ceiling and sighed. "Damn it all to the void. I need a drink."

She left Cheseia in the courtyard and returned to the drinking hall. Seul followed, a strange look on her sharp features.

11

"It looks different here since my last visit." Sar glanced at Shekelor's throne; the man must think himself a king. "More pirates, more ships. More girls. Too bad we didn't have all this in the old days."

Shekelor's purple eye looked Sar up and down, but his brown one remained fixed on Sar's face. "One likes to stay busy. My followers are culled from the transients orbiting Tejuit. Former mercenaries or Tannocci lords fallen on hard times. And you would not believe what a starving family will trade in exchange for a crate of moldy foodstuffs."

Words came to Sar's lips, but thoughts of Kivita stopped them. She'd better not be pawning off the Juxj Star in the drinking hall.

"So, what did you bring me, Redryll?" Shekelor caressed the face of a tawny-furred Ascali. "You look like a man on the run."

Sar held his helmet in one hand and ran the other through his hair. He never could hide things from his old friend. "The Inheritors have something planned. It might be bad for everyone in the Arm—even you."

He tried not thinking of what'd flashed through his

mind after bumping into Kivita earlier. Sights of unknown planets, details on cryogenic colony ships he'd heard about only in spacer legends. What had happened to her since their days together at Gontalo? The strange mixture of loathing and expectation in Kivita's eyes now ... Her lithe body in that outfit he'd selected for her ... No, he needed her for his rebellion.

"I doubt it." Shekelor smirked. "Judging from the company you keep, I would say things aren't bad for you, either. Even that Aldaakian is rather easy on the eyes."

Sar returned the smirk, though he didn't feel it. Kivita was far more special than the lover he'd abandoned. Telling her about his Thede allegiance would've been folly, considering her wish to sell the Juxj Star. "The Inheritors are—"

"I do not prey on them anymore," Shekelor said. "Raiding Aldaakian and Tannocci shipping has been more lucrative for me of late. You still seek revenge on those silly prophets? I would have thought your double-sided game had ended by now. The Fall of Freen is in the past. Leave it there with the dead, Redryll."

Caitrynn's charred body invaded Sar's thoughts, but he continued. "Help me against the Inheritors like you used to. My allies will pay."

"I care not. The prophets will not dominate the Cetturo Arm forever."

Stiffening, Sar met Shekelor's eyes. The man had never interrupted him twice in the same conversation before. "And you'll be satisfied raiding trade routes forever? Or have you forgotten your own dead family?"

Shekelor's coils snapped at Sar's neck. "Revenge is something I understand, Redryll. But it does not feed or protect me. The Thedes lack the payment I require for such a risk."

Sar smiled to hide his concern. He'd never told Shekelor who he worked for. "So, the Sarrhdtuu feed and protect you? Never thought you'd enter the slave trade. Who buys all those people?"

"The Sarrhdtuu pay me in ways your rebels cannot," Shekelor said. "The prophets killed your sister. They killed my son. Years ago, they burned half my body away during that failed raid at Tahe. But I am a pirate now, not a freedom fighter. I sell slaves, so I do not become one."

"Then be a pirate. Cover my tracks from this system," Sar said.

"The Expanse's radiation hides my presence here, Redryll. You must really expect to be followed. Of course, that means my operation here might be exposed. I shall require something special for this inconvenience." Shekelor paced before Sar.

"I've got Susuron water on *Frevyx*, Naxan fruit trees—"

"Who is the human with you?" Shekelor asked.

A chill formed in Sar's gut. "The friend of an ally. I brought her from Inheritor Space."

Shekelor's eyebrows rose. "She resembles Kivita Vondir. I have seen her placard in spaceports. It seems she is as skilled a salvager as you. Rather attractive, she is."

"No." Sar kept his gaze firm.

Shekelor laughed. "Do not reject my offer before you hear it."

Sar had intended to lose any pursuers in the Terresin Expanse while escaping to key Thede coordinates. Shekelor's fleet could at least provide a diversion, but the warlord wasn't the same man Sar remembered; those slave pens and captive beauties revealed a new ruthlessness.

"She's not for sale."

A faraway look stole over Shekelor's mismatched eyes. "Once I believed that about certain liberties I considered unassailable: free will, safety, love. In the end, they are cheaper than dust, upon realizing you will trade them to destroy another."

The chill in Sar's gut stabbed his spine. He'd never be like that. His revenge could be achieved without sacrificing his morality.

"I see you are mulling it over. We shall discuss it over drinks, since I owe you an Umiracan Kiss." Shekelor pointed at the doorway.

Sar exited the room first. Kivita, sitting at the wooden counter with all the other pirates, stared right at him. Damn, why did those hazel eyes have to be so unforgiving? He'd been cold to her on purpose and ignored her again. The more others realized her value, the deadlier her situation would become.

And the greater his pain if something happened to her.

Kivita tried not to inhale the mollusk vapors drifting from the end of the counter. Three pirates bent over a decanter, sniffing the spicy aromas. Within seconds they staggered into each other, giggling like children. She started to move, then glanced around.

Orstaav ogled Kivita from across the counter with a sneer.

Best stay in this seat, then. With no empty stools beside her, at least the bastard couldn't get too close.

As Sar and Shekelor sat at an adjacent table, the pirates

raised their mugs and cheered. Sar still avoided looking at her. Cheseia sat beside him, and they shared a few whispers. The Ascali clutched Sar's leg beneath the table.

Kivita's cheeks burned.

Orstaav held up a mug and pointed at her, slowly licked his lips. If the man's antics didn't make her nauseous, Kivita would flirt with him just to annoy Sar. Yeah, like he'd notice.

Seul nudged a drunken pirate aside and sat beside Kivita. For all her military demeanor, the Aldaakian seemed disgusted by the behavior around them. Every now and then, she tried to wipe spilled ale from her armor as pirates jostled past them.

"I don't like this." Kivita kept staring at Sar, but he paid no attention.

"Neither do I," Seul said. "You have dealt with Sar before?"

Frustration smoldered in Kivita's chest. "You could say that."

"There's something you should know, Kivita. Commander Vuul might be searching."

"For you? You his girl or something?" Kivita avoided looking across the counter at Orstaav.

Scowling, Seul leaned close to Kivita. "I'm not his daughter."

Kivita's brow furrowed. Then she barked a short laugh. "No, I meant, are you his woman? His lover. You know, his—"

Seul's eyes widened and her hands balled into fists. "You crusty vacuum turd. No, I'm . . ." She banged her elbow against Kivita and grinned. "What a morbid sense of humor you humans have."

No, the joke was on Kivita. Sar had seemed desperate

to escape the Inheritors, but now he wanted to party with Shekelor Thal? And he still hadn't bargained with her or Seul as promised, either. She wondered if Orstaav had a ship, and if she could get him drunk enough to steal its access code. . . .

Ugh. Now she was the one getting desperate.

"If Vuul has tracked our coordinates, then it's you he seeks, not me." Seul gripped her arm. "We are both prisoners here. Help me and I will help you."

Despite the hall's clammy warmth, Kivita shivered. "Your commander. If he's really searching, would he be willing to make a deal?"

"Yes, Vuul would . . ."

Seul's words faded as Kivita's mind swam with images: *yellow-suited Rectifiers patrolled the large cryopod chamber she'd envisioned before. Autohandlers on metal tracks maintained occupied cryopods with moisture canisters.*

"Kivita?" Seul's voice brought Kivita back to the drinking hall.

"Huh? Yeah, sorry." Now the strange dreams disturbed her waking thoughts, as well, ever since she'd touched the Juxj Star.

Cheers and laughter deafened Kivita as she collected herself. She slumped forward to avoid the sloshing mugs behind her.

Shekelor beckoned a topless dancer to his table. "My friends, Sar Redryll has traveled many light years for a specialty only we can offer. The Umiracan Kiss!"

The half-naked dancer poured ale, wine, and blacklight cactus juice into her mouth. Holding the liquid in her cheeks, she smudged a bone-yellow stone, taken from Umiracan's surface, over her closed lips.

Sar leaned over the table, and the dancer placed her

lips on his. The pirates roared with approval as the dancer spat her mouth's contents into Sar's. A tiny spark lit between their lips.

"Orstaav, bring in more Susuron drinks!" Shekelor called, his eyes sweeping over Kivita.

The dancer sat in Sar's lap and jiggled her breasts. Whistles and laughter filled the hall, and Kivita glared at Sar as her cheeks grew hotter. Musicians played grind boxes; the electrified vibrations drowned out all other sound. Pirates danced, pushed, and puked all around them.

"To hell with this." Kivita pushed her way from the hall and entered the courtyard. A knot rose from her stomach and enveloped her heart. She pretended to adjust her envirosuit while contemplating her situation: no ship, trapped on a pirate planet, holding the greatest salvage of her career. And spurned again by the man she used to love.

A hand grabbed her arm.

"Shekelor says to take ya to your room," Orstaav said. The alcohol on his breath wrinkled Kivita's nose.

"Think I'll pass, smoothie." Kivita tried to back away.

Orstaav's drunkenness vanished, and he held up a kinetic pistol. "Ya didn't gulp enough in the hall to be flirting, Red. Move your pretty ass up to that turret over there."

Kivita's mind raced. "Redryll will break off his deals with your boss for this. I'm his, uh, lounge girl. Take your hands—"

"Shut it, and smile real sexy." Orstaav yanked her shortsword and tossed it into a corner. His pistol barrel dug into Kivita's back. They climbed a stone staircase leading up to the turret's loft.

"I can get you inside Redryll's ship. Think he came all the way to Ecrol for that stupid drink?"

"The Sarrhdtuu's gonna pay us whatever we want for ya, Red." Orstaav swatted Kivita's rump. "Whatever we want. Now get up them steps."

The Sarrhdtuu wanted her and not the Juxj Star?

Kivita turned over more lies in her head. "Hey, I thought you ran security for Shekelor? You command all the guards. Maybe Shekelor doesn't need all that reward, huh? If we steal Redryll's ship, maybe you could make your own bargain?"

Orstaav stopped and frowned. "Redryll keeps that damn ship locked."

"I could decode his airlock pad from here, if I had access to a radio transmitter," Kivita said. In truth, she wanted to send out a distress signal. To whom, she had no idea. Rector Thev would still want the gem, or Seul's commander might. Anybody to distract these assholes while she escaped.

"Walk on up these steps. Got my pistol aimed, ya try anything," Orstaav said.

Kivita hurried up the stairs with Orstaav behind. No one else occupied the turret. At the top, after mounting dozens of steps in a spiral, she halted before five metal doors. Though her heart pumped a steady beat, she didn't feel taxed by the climb. Her captor gulped for air and glared at her.

"Don't get any flaming ideas. My shot will follow your pretty ass even if my legs won't."

"Why do the Sarrhdtuu want me? C'mon, doesn't Shekelor trust you enough to tell you anything?"

Orstaav yanked Kivita up against him. The pistol barrel slid toward her crotch. "Shut your yap. All I know is it's a hell of a lot more than we get for the typical trash we sell 'em. Ya being plumb straight about that lock?"

"Yeah, you bet. I'm getting tired of Sar, anyway." Not a total lie, but her chest constricted.

"Go on through the fourth door, then," Orstaav said.

Kivita entered a narrow walkway sheltered with rectangular viewports. Through them, Umiracan's surface stretched down into the cratered valley. The pink sky darkened as night approached. Below, an uncovered courtyard contained a vessel beneath their feet. From the ship's armored hull and the number of guards, Kivita assumed it was Shekelor's.

They left the walkway for a second turret loft, where three pirates in polymail stood guard with swords. Two large terminals with multiple consoles filled one corner, and a wide viewport showed the slim, conical antenna of a deep-space radio transmitter outside. A gray-green coil was wrapped near the base.

Sarrhdtuu tech.

"Orstaav, what you doing here with that?" one pirate asked, undressing Kivita with his eyes.

"Never ya boys mind this," Orstaav said. "Now wait outside."

The three men left the room and shut the door.

Kivita jerked as Orstaav slashed down the back of her envirosuit with a blade. The suit flapped around her thighs as she backed against the wall.

"Take that crap off. I wanna see what makes Kivita Vondir so damn special." Orstaav blocked the door, pistol raised.

She slipped from the envirosuit, and Orstaav whistled.

"Lounge girl, huh? Plumb gonna enjoy this. Then we'll talk about Redryll's ship. Off with it—all ya clothes. Now!"

Kivita pursed her lips and grinned. "Maybe you should do it." Playing up to him made her skin crawl. Orstaav hurried over, unsnapping his polyarmor.

The flat of Kivita's right palm slammed into his chin; then her left hook crunched his cheek. Orstaav stumbled back, but she punched again. His nose snapped in a red spray, and he bellowed. As Kivita drew back for another strike, his armored foot slammed into her left shin. She crumpled onto the floor.

"Bitch! Ya don't plumb fuck with me like that!" Orstaav spat on her. The door opened. All three pirates raced inside, swords raised.

"He's going to steal Shekelor's ship! Quick—stop him!" Her heart sank as the three snorted and laughed. "I'm serious, he's going to—"

Kivita rolled aside as Orstaav fired. The pistol made a whizzing noise. The round blew a hole in the stone wall. Masonry shards stung her backside as she jumped up at him. His fist glanced off her right shoulder, but Kivita rolled with the blow and tried to get behind him.

A pirate rammed a knee into Kivita's right leg; a sword pommel struck her shoulder and knocked her back down. She gritted her teeth and tried to rise, refusing to register the pain throbbing through her body.

Orstaav wiped blood from his face. "Fucking get her up! We'll all four plumb ram her until she can't flaming walk!"

One of the pirates choked. The crack of a snapping neck echoed in the room, and the man collapsed. Behind the dead pirate stood Seul, who snatched his sword.

12

Surging with energy, Kivita rolled to her feet. A sword jabbed at her, but Seul parried the weapon and slapped aside its wielder.

Orstaav backhanded Kivita to the floor, then fired at Seul. The shot clipped Seul's shoulder armor. Shrapnel cut across the Aldaakian's left cheek.

Shouts from the doorway alerted Kivita a split second before two new pirates entered and aimed their pistols. Adrenaline obliterated her pain as she plowed into one pirate, clawing at his throat. Orstaav tried to fire at Seul, but the Aldaakian elbowed his chest, then whipped around and gutted one of the original pirates. The screech of metal jabbing through polyarmor mixed with the intake of sharp breath.

"Bitch!" Orstaav punched Seul's jaw; she wobbled but slashed his chin. Both landed powerful strikes on each other's armored bodies.

The pirate Kivita had grappled with rammed his fist into her right side. Kivita jammed a thumb into his eye and slapped his pistol down as he fired. The round blew off the man's foot. She cut his scream short by crunching the apple of his throat.

Orstaav yanked Kivita by the hair and brought his pistol up to her chest. She kicked his legs, then punched his face until her knuckles bled. Right before he fired, Seul slammed a pirate into Kivita, knocking her from Orstaav's grasp. The kinetic round ripped into the pirate's stomach instead. Orstaav thrust the dead man aside and yelled a curse.

Kivita kicked Orstaav's knee, knocking him off balance, while Seul grabbed his neck. A pop and a gurgle, and a lifeless Orstaav slid from Seul's grasp.

The last two pirates struck at Seul with blades; her polyarmor absorbed the first blows. One man pierced her right vambrace, drawing blood. Seul shoved her sword though his throat.

The final pirate raced for the door, but Kivita seized and fired Orstaav's pistol. The kinetic round went straight through the man's back and out his chest. He tumbled into a gory heap.

Blood pounded in Kivita's ears. Every muscle ached; every bruise and scrape flared. She wanted to vomit as her gaze swept over the twisted bodies. Yeah, she'd been in spaceport brawls and a few firefights. She'd even killed in defense, but never enjoyed it. Those times she'd been able to leave the scene and get on with her life. Trapped on Umiracan, she knew only more blood awaited her and Seul.

Standing in the center of the room, Seul appeared as calm as a pool of frozen water. Blood wept from the cut on her cheek and over her bruised jaw.

Kivita rose, rubbing her shoulder. Blood leaked from her right nostril, stinging her busted lips. She checked the pistol's magazine: three rounds left.

Seul shut the door, barred it with one of the pirate's swords, and waited. "I hear no one coming."

"Damn. We're both luckier than a blind spacer in a zero-G toilet." Kivita winced as adrenaline faded and more aches stung her body. Spots appeared in her sight, and the room blurred.

A firm grip encircled her waist. Kivita shook her head, and her vision cleared. Seul stood beside her, providing support. Respect glinted in the Aldaakian's white-within-azure stare.

"I saw you leave the pirate's hall. Orstaav followed you. I didn't like the look on his face. I suppose Sar and the Ascali are still being entertained by that abomination."

A cool sensation rippled through Kivita. Did Sar have anything to do with selling her to the Sarrhdtuu? He'd always talked about secret allies. It would explain his recent behavior, as well as him rescuing her on Vstrunn.

"You think they betrayed us," Seul said.

"I . . . I don't know. We've got our own problems." Kivita pointed at the antenna outside the viewport. "Can you send a signal to your people? I want my ship back. Your commander can have this damn gem for it— I don't care. I've had enough of this craziness."

Seul's eyes widened, and then she nodded. "You activated that signal. My superiors would be honored to speak with you."

"Yeah, yeah, that's great. Can you do it?"

"They'll only come if they're already looking for Sar's ship," Seul replied.

"A chance we'll have to take." Kivita secured the pouch with the Juxj Star to her slim belt.

Seul keyed a frequency into a terminal. A series of beeps followed the last few keystrokes. Through the viewport, the antenna rotated a few degrees. The terminal readout displayed a short broadcast in a repeating pattern.

"How long?" Kivita asked.

"If Commander Vuul is searching, then perhaps two Aldaakuun days." Seul glanced at Kivita. "Twenty Inheritor hours. But only if he traced the trajectory we traveled to this system."

"Guess what. We don't have that long." Kivita sighed, then extended her hand. "Listen. I owe you. Those guys would've . . . well, you know."

"I've fought these pirates before. They steal from my people and take slaves. That makes you more than a worthy ally." Seul gripped Kivita's hand.

"Now what?" Kivita asked.

Seul stared. "What do you mean? This was your plan."

"Yeah, that's what bothers me. What did you put in that message?"

"I requested Commander Vuul's assistance with retrieving the Juxj Star from Umiracan." Seul pointed at Orstaav's body. "You should put on his armor. There's no blood on it. You could fool these scum."

Kivita grimaced. "Shit. He'd better not be naked under there. Help me put it on."

After removing the armor—thankfully, a jumpsuit covered Orstaav's still-warm corpse—Kivita stood still while Seul fastened its buckles. She waited for more pirates to burst into the room any moment. Even Seul stole glances at the door. They had little chance of making it. Three kinetic rounds and two swords against dozens of pirates?

"We can do this, Kivita." Seul snapped a buckle closed. "Focus on the now, not what might happen."

"Yeah." Their eyes met. Strength swelled in Kivita's chest. Knowing someone else would stand with her and even die with her eroded much of her fear.

Minutes later, Kivita stood in Orstaav's blue-and-white polyarmor; it stank worse than a farmer's mud socks. She snapped on her helmet and darkened the faceplate manually.

"Well?" Kivita asked.

"Shave your silly hair, and you could be an Aldaakian."

Kivita snorted. "Will Vuul pick us up?"

Seul frowned.

"Didn't think so." Anxiety shortened Kivita's breaths for a moment. If Sar had betrayed her, she'd have to leave him and Cheseia on Umiracan. Leave him for good and bury the desires she'd harbored.

Kivita holstered the kinetic pistol in the polyarmor's belt. "Well, I'll just take the Juxj Star to Vuul. Ready to steal Shekelor's ship?"

Together they descended a flight of spiral steps to the other side of the battlement. The dull, distant boom of music from the drinking hall came through the stone walls. At the bottom of the steps, before a small door, Kivita swallowed. Her fingers flexed above the holstered pistol.

Seul nodded, and Kivita opened the door.

A vaulted chamber with a skylight awaited them. A ragged red carpet covered the floor, and pictures adorned the walls. No pirates around, just four women in flimsy clothes on a stained bed. Kivita strode on in. If she crept, it would raise suspicion. Even so, while making for another door across the room, she hesitated.

"We don't have time," Seul whispered.

"I know, but look at these," she whispered back.

Kivita pointed at a collection of feudal-style paint-ings hanging on the wall. Dust caked the brushed-oil canvases, the etched metal frames. One portrait stood out: black hair, strong jaw, heavy brows. It was Shekelor Thal, younger, dressed in the doublet of a Sutaran no-bleman. So the throne room hadn't been a total play on the warlord's ego.

A second portrait of a young man resembled Shek-elor enough to be his son. The skylight's pinkish glow cast shadows over the teenager's face.

He'd had a child? A family? Kivita shivered, wonder-ing what had caused Shekelor to devolve into the mon-ster he'd become.

The four women regarded Kivita with frightened grins so false, she almost laughed. Wait—it had to be the armor. Orstaav must have sampled every slave girl on Umiracan with rough relish. She'd lose no norm sleep over his passing.

"Come." Seul took her by the arm and cleared her throat. "Let's continue, Orstaav."

Kivita took a deep breath and opened the next door. The tingling returned to her head while the pain of be-trayal reawakened in her heart.

The grind box's music grated on Sar's nerves as he scanned the counter. Kivita had disappeared into the crowd. A dozen half-naked dancers added further con-fusion.

Years ago, Umiracan had been a safe haven for reb-els and less despicable pirates. Now he feared losing Kiv-ita here if he but turned his head. Shekelor and Orstaav watched her too much, and not just in a sexual manner. He should have taken Kivita somewhere else. No matter what he did, those he cared about were always placed in danger.

Suppressing a curse, he reached for the cup of Freen ale before him, but Cheseia grabbed his hand. He shot her a look, but her tense gaze made him pause.

"I see your Ascali beauty acts like the wine tasters of old Naxan courts," Shekelor said. "They possessed such excellent noses."

As the music subsided, the dancers cavorted from the hall with a band of drunken pirates. Eight men and women remained. All of them possessed the same olive skin as Shekelor.

Cheseia squeezed his hand, and for the first time Sar realized she'd neither eaten nor drunk anything.

Sar faced Shekelor. "So you use poison these days?" His lips still tingled from the combined alcohol, electric shock, and slight orgasmic reaction from the Umiracan Kiss.

"Only when needed." Shekelor leaned back in his chair. "You patriotic fool. Did you really expect me to welcome you with open arms? A Thede posing as a salvager, transporting a Savant wanted by the Arm's great powers?"

The eight pirates aimed guns at Sar and Cheseia.

Heat stifled Sar, but he kept his hands on the table. "You son of a bitch."

"I keep a brain-pulse analyzer above the curtain in my throne room, so I would have known, regardless. But I was already expecting your fetching companion."

"I wish you had truly listened to me," Cheseia whispered.

Sar smirked without humor at Shekelor. "So, who gets Kiv? That bald Rector, or the Sarrhdtuu surgeons who green-rigged your callous ass?"

One of Shekelor's coils shot out and wrapped around Sar's neck. The tentaclelike appendage squeezed off his air, its biomechanical ridges suctioning onto his flesh. Cheseia reached for her beam rifle, but two pirates shot her chair from under her. Wooden splinters flew through the air as the chair was atomized by the shots. Cheseia fell into a crouch, corded muscles ready.

"Kivita goes to the one who will soon rule the Cetturo Arm, Redryll. You might as well get used to this around your neck." Shekelor yanked back the coil, and Sar's head slammed into the table.

Before Sar could rise, rough hands tugged his arms behind his back. Two pirates hauled Sar to his feet, flinging aside his chair and the table. Cheseia finally stood as three closed in with their pistols.

"You Sutaran filth," Sar said. One pirate kneed him in the gut.

"Toss them into a holding cell. No food or drink for them tonight. I shall join Orstaav in *Fanged Pauper*'s courtyard." Shekelor headed for the hall doorway.

"You might as well have killed Byelor yourself," Sar muttered.

Shekelor paused but didn't turn around. "My son took my heart with him upon dying, Redryll. Your own was left on Freen with Caitrynn. We both wander the space lanes as heartless wraiths, hoping everything we do might bring them back to us. Thus we cannot be expected to act as men. We act as something worse."

Chest heaving with angry breaths, Sar told himself Shekelor was wrong. Told himself Kivita would've been captured anyway. Such mental reassurances failed to quiet the screaming rage in his heart.

The pirates led them into the courtyard, where two

turret entrances awaited them. Shekelor entered the right one, and the pirates led Sar and Cheseia into the left. A thick mildew stench rankled the air. Cheseia gagged, while Sar's stomach sank.

The stench of Sarrhdtuu starships.

Inside the turret entrance, a cluster of lockers stood upright against dark-lit walls. Gray-green carapace covered the lockers. Beside them, a table had a pump attached to transparent tubes running with yellow-green liquid. Sar tensed as several shapes moved in the shadows; then he wished they had remained there.

Six more green-rigged pirates, each possessing coils for hands, inserted a tube from the pump into their chests. Right into the skin or armor, like a finger through mud. As the liquid raced through the tubes into them, the pirates grunted and spasmed, eyes rolling back in their heads. Green moisture leaked from their tear ducts.

As a burn victim, Shekelor had repaired himself with Transmutation, but why did these pirates undergo it? Fear thudded anew in Sar's heart for Kivita. The things such madmen might do to her . . .

A dim stairwell led into a corridor lined with metal doors. The pirates opened one and shoved Sar in; then Cheseia's lithe form bumped into him as the door shut. A single, flickering lamp illuminated the five-by-five-foot cell.

Cheseia squirmed against his body and coughed into his shoulder. "I cannot bear that fantastically awful smell. What do you roughly think Shekelor will do with us?"

"Hard to say. He might sell us as slaves. He might kill us."

Full, eager lips brushed his. "I wish I could magically stop all this. Protect you from what is coming." Concern and fear warred in her gaze, mixed with something he couldn't identify.

"Not now," he whispered.

Cheseia looked into his eyes. "Your troubles weigh deeply on my own heart. You have been cold since we landed, especially to Kivita. Why did you not—?"

"I wasn't positive she was a Savant. It doesn't make sense. Why would Dunaar hire her, then hire me, but now the Sarrhdtuu want her?" Sar paused. Dunaar must have known about Kivita's Savant talent. The bloated pig also knew Kivita might sell the Juxj Star to the highest bidder. So Dunaar had hired him to . . . what? Secure the Juxj Star?

"She angers me with all the pain she has callously brought upon you." Cheseia hugged him tighter.

"Stop. Kiv's been hurt by me."

Cheseia released him and looked away.

"Will you listen? Everybody wants Kiv now. It has something to do with that signal Seul mentioned."

"You should have gone directly straight to Navon— not here," Cheseia said.

Since she was still a Thede recruit, Cheseia lacked the coordinates to the Thede rendezvous point; it was a security issue. Perhaps he should've heeded her advice after all.

Sar leaned so close his lips brushed her ear. "I've seen things in my mind every time Kiv's touched me since leaving Vstrunn. Stars, images of a cryogenic ship, coordinates to places I've never been. Never heard of anybody able to do that, not even Thede Savants."

Her furred hands dug into his envirosuit. "Then the Rector certainly will buy her from Shekelor."

"I think—"

A chattering wail echoed from a speaker in the corridor outside.

"An alarm," Cheseia said.

"We're under attack!" a muffled voice yelled outside.

13

Kivita and Seul paused before a doorway leading outside the fortress. With most pirates in the drinking hall, they'd passed only a few on guard duty. Every second spent in Orstaav's armor set Kivita's nerves further on edge.

"Are you sure this is the correct path?" Seul put her helmet on.

"I saw his ship from above. Something that big must be in the next courtyard." Kivita double-checked her own helmet and opened the pressurized door.

The pirates outside the turret exit stepped aside for Kivita. Seul trailed behind her, face impassive, though the cut on her arm still bled. Wind scattered dust over them as Umiracan's chill leeched through Kivita's polysuit. Sure enough, through the doorway, Shekelor's ship waited.

Two more pirates inside the courtyard barred their path.

"Ya gotta wait, Orstaav," one heavyset pirate said. "Shekelor said he'd be along in a few minutes."

"Thought you was supposed to be toting that plumb cute redhead with you?" He fingered his holstered pistol. "And who the hell is this bleeding Aldaakian?"

Kivita had no way of imitating Orstaav's voice, and she doubted a simple shrug would answer their curiosity.

An alarm blared. The pirates' faces hardened as one reached for his pistol.

Seul gasped and staggered toward the two pirates. While both focused on the Aldaakian, Kivita drew the kinetic pistol. The heavyset man turned as she squeezed the trigger. The shot ripped through his polycuirass, and his eyes glazed over. The report echoed throughout the courtyard.

Kivita aimed at the second pirate. "You have a choice. Give me the code to this ship's keypad and you won't end up like your buddy here."

The man held up his hands. "I plumb fucking don't know it! Shekelor, uh . . . nobody knows that code but him."

Seul stared at the man. "I don't think he's lying."

A voice called from the stairs behind them. The pirate punched Seul's wounded arm and fled up the steps. Seul stumbled into Kivita, cradling her arm.

"Damn. You all right?" Kivita ushered Seul toward the ship.

"Only if we break that code," Seul said through gritted teeth. Fresh blood flowed from the crack in her vambrace.

The ship before them measured more than four hundred feet in length. A K-gun placement on each side and cracked hull armor testified to many rough encounters. Kivita and Seul ducked under the forward landing pylon as pirates shouted into the courtyard. A square keypad, covered with a hinged armor plate, waited beside the entrance ramp.

"No shooting near the ship—rush 'em!" a voice called. Four pirates ran across the courtyard under bright floodlights.

Crouching, Kivita fired from the ship's underside. A pirate clutched her stomach and fell. Two pirates raced back to the stairway, while one charged forward.

"The keypad!" Seul yelled, then met the pirate with her sword.

Kivita flipped up the armor plate, but gray-green chitinous material covered the keypad. Shit—more Sarrhdtuu tech. She wondered what connections Shekelor possessed and what they cost him.

While more voices shouted from the stairway and Seul battled the pirate, Kivita tried several hack codes. The chitinous material writhed with each keystroke, but none of the codes worked. She grimaced and tried her best hack. Still nothing.

Seul sidestepped the pirate's spike baton and swiped her sword through the man's faceplate. Wheezing, the pirate crawled back to the stairs, but collapsed before reaching them.

Heart racing, Kivita tapped random numbers until a tingling interrupted her thoughts. An eight-digit sequence came to mind. Kivita punched it in as six pirates spread throughout the courtyard.

The ship's hatch opened.

"C'mon!" Kivita grabbed Seul's good arm and ran up the ramp. Three pirates raced after them.

A spike baton pierced the polyarmor over Seul's left thigh. She grunted and shoved her sword into the man's faceplate. He staggered off the ramp, the blade stuck in his skull. Kivita fired her last shot, shattering another pirate's helmet.

After shoving Seul inside, Kivita slammed the hatch-lock lever. The entrance slid shut as weapons struck the other side. Lamps activated along the bulkheads, and life-support systems came on. A mildew stench greeted Kivita when she removed her helmet.

The interior was fitted with weapon racks and troop alcoves. Each rectangular viewport had a beam rifle welded into it. At the end of a hundred-foot-long corridor, *Fanged Pauper* was painted over the cockpit entrance.

"Can you pilot this vessel?" Seul leaned on a rack, her faceplate fogging up. Blood flowed from the puncture in her thigh.

"Yeah, no problem." Kivita helped Seul limp to the cockpit. "Let me get us out of here; then we'll fix you up."

"My armor's inner liner should—" Seul winced as her polyarmor hummed. Blood ceased running from the two cracks in her suit. "Should seal long enough for us to escape."

"No wonder you wanted to wear your own suit." Kivita strapped Seul into a nav-station seat, then eased herself into the pilot's gyro harness. As she buckled the straps, the alarm's wail grew in volume outside the ship.

"Bet you an energy dump they found Pretty Boy's body in the transmitter loft." Kivita pulled the thruster ignition, activated the gravitational stabilizer, and gripped the manuals. With practiced ease, she lifted *Fanged Pauper* from the courtyard.

All around her, darkness covered Umiracan. Ecrol's glare had given way to one of the most beautiful night skies Kivita had ever seen. The Expanse's purple-gray, red-green nebulae stretched across the entire vista, with stars twinkling here and there in a kaleidoscope of possibilities.

Though tension left Kivita's chest, she tightened her grip on the manuals. With a starship at her call, nothing could hold her down.

The console beeped with a new scanner readout. Kivita's heart jumped with excitement. It detected another ship in the Ecrol system—with an Aldaakian beacon signal.

"Seul, I think your friends have answered."

After removing her helmet, Seul grimaced. "I hope they hurry. This vessel's stench will poison us."

While *Fanged Pauper* gained altitude, flashes of light winked below. The scanner beeped again.

"Kivita, there are other ships lifting off the surface. We have been discovered."

"Yeah, you think? Hang on. We'll see what else that green-rigged bastard's got wired into this thing." Kivita yanked the manuals and barreled the craft to stern. It obeyed her command with smooth precision. Smiling, she thumbed the thrusters again, and *Fanged Pauper* catapulted into Umiracan's upper atmosphere.

"Good-bye . . ." Kivita swallowed a lump, unable to speak Sar's name. What if he and Cheseia had also been taken prisoner and not betrayed her to Shekelor? Well, there was nothing she could do for them. Besides, she still had the Juxj Star. Everybody wanted it, right? Hell, nobody wanted Sar . . .

"We had no choice but to leave them behind," Seul said.

Kivita just nodded. She swore she was better off without him.

* * *

The thrum and boom of ships taking off outside shook Sar's cell. Years ago, Shekelor had possessed only six craft. Judging from the sounds, he must have three times as many now, enough to rival an Inheritor battle fleet.

"Sar, this is probably the time to tell me the truth." Cheseia touched his cheek. "Have you ever truly loved—?"

The cell door slid open. A coil shot out and punched Sar to the floor.

"Who, really, is Kivita Vondir?" Shekelor asked. "No one else knows the code sequence to my ship's keypad!"

"You tell me," Sar said. "The Sarrhdtuu not offer you enough, then?"

Two pirates hauled him and Cheseia into the corridor, where several others waited, weapons bared. Tense voices echoed down from the covered courtyard as the wailing alarm finally stopped.

"Who do you think is stealing my ship? Who do you think killed Orstaav and sent a signal into space?" Shekelor aimed a pistol at Sar's head. "It seems we both wanted to use that lovely weapon. She will not get far."

"I'd already be dead if you didn't plan on selling me, too. Guess you'll need two ships to carry all that loot from the Rector and the Sarrhdtuu?" Sar studied Shekelor's wide-eyed glare. Something else had happened.

"Kivita will net me what I want. You are simply a bonus—for now." Shekelor waved the pirates on.

The group left the battlement turret, walked through the courtyard, and entered the drinking hall. The pirate behind Cheseia carried her beam rifle. More pirates rushed about, collecting weapons and armor. Shekelor wouldn't place the entire fortress on alert just to capture one ship. Sar had to try something to escape. Old tales of Ascali songs and the Sarrhdtuu dislike of music gave him an idea.

Sar glanced at Cheseia and blinked twice.

Cheseia shrieked a high-pitched note only an Ascali could manage. The green-rigged pirates paused and covered their ears, but Shekelor aimed his pistol at her. Ears ringing, Sar rammed his elbow into the warlord's left side.

In one motion, Cheseia slammed her knee into Shekelor's other side, then turned and kicked the pirate behind her. She snatched her beam rifle back and fired. Two more pirates toppled, torsos sliced from their legs. Sar grabbed Shekelor's pistol and aimed it at him. The other pirates halted, weapons ready.

"You're going to walk us to *Frevyx*." Sar snapped his helmet on. Cheseia did the same, holding the rifle one-handed. "You even spit, you're dead."

Shekelor smiled. "I cannot breathe out there, Redryll. I need a suit, too."

"Move." Sar minded Shekelor's coils as he and Cheseia followed the warlord down the ramp. The pirates backed away with reluctance, their eyes filled with murder.

Shekelor stared at Cheseia. "Interesting way of destabilizing my followers. Very interesting. But they shall pick you off as soon as you exit the fortress."

"I doubt if their aim is as good as mine. Move." Sar half squeezed the trigger, the gun aimed at Shekelor's head.

They made their way down the ramp slowly, the pirates following them. In the slave pens below, people fell silent as they watched two people lead their chief captor at gunpoint. The temptation to pull the trigger ate away at Sar. Shekelor's betrayal had voided all the things they'd once fought for together.

They passed through the slave pens and walked down the next ramp in tense silence. In the adjacent barracks, dozens of men and women suited up in polyarmor. All stopped their preparations at the sight of their captive commander.

Shekelor stopped. "Go ahead, shoot me. Kivita Vondir will still end up as someone's asset. Not yours." The pirates behind them came closer, and dozens on the ramp below crept toward Sar.

"Nice bravado," Sar said. "Let's see if—"

The swerving door leading outside blew apart. Chunks of stone and mortar bowled over several pirates and crushed others. Shouts echoed in the chamber as green beams swept through the opening. More pirates, bodies sizzling or limbs dismembered, screamed.

"The air! Close that door!" Shekelor dove into the crowd below the ramp.

Sar fired point-blank at a rushing pirate. The man's head exploded in a red-gray geyser. Cheseia leveled her rifle and singed two more. More pirates rushed for envirosuits and face masks as Aldaakian Shock Troopers charged through the hole in the wall.

"We are not pirates!" Cheseia cried.

A squad of Shock Troopers lined up and incinerated a dozen of Shekelor's followers. Green beams swept the air, lopping off heads, hands, and torsos. Umiracan's noxious atmosphere flooded the fortress, choking any unprotected pirates.

Shekelor and his surviving followers fled up the ramp while Sar and Cheseia leapt from it into the breach. A pressurized portcullis shut at the top of the ramp as all air became contaminated. Several pirates asphyxiated with jerking motions.

Two suited pirates turned their way, but Cheseia decapitated both with a single blast of her rifle. As both of them rushed from the hole, Sar slammed into a Shock Trooper while exiting the fortress. The soldier stumbled as Cheseia ran by and lashed out with a powerful leg. The Aldaakian collapsed, clutching his head.

"Run!" Sar shouted into his helmet mic.

They fled across Umiracan's dusty surface while more Shock Troopers disembarked from a distant shuttle. A second shuttle descended from the sky, its retro thrusters raising dust. Floodlights activated along the fortress's parapets; then gun turrets cut down several Troopers, leaving broken bodies in yellow soil turned red.

Sar ran for his ship, fear powering his stride. If Shekelor was right about his stolen vessel, then Kivita was already in space by now. He might still detect her beacon signal if they hurried, but Kivita would make a light jump as soon as possible, especially if she still had the Juxj Star.

Frevyx remained in place, but six pirates and four Aldaakians lay dead around it, their bodies smoking. Five pirates still guarded the airlock, guns raised. They turned just as Cheseia squeezed off a shot. The green beam sliced off their rifle barrels as the pirates ducked.

"That was certainly all of it!" She brandished the rifle like a club.

As three pirates charged with drawn blades, Sar fired his last shot. The round shattered one pirate's shoulder. In the Umiracan night, the whooshing swords and armored figures reminded Sar of the Fall of Freen: Inheritors attacking at nightfall, slaughtering innocents. Old hatred erupted in him.

He dodged a strike, a thrust, then hammered a pirate's faceplate with the pistol. The plate broke, but the pirate smashed her elbow into Sar's side, then cut Sar's kneecap. His envirosuit beeped a contamination warning. A second pirate lunged at him, but Sar drew his blade and ruptured the man's suit. Blood poured out as the pirate flailed, his air gone.

Cheseia busted the empty rifle over one of the remaining pirates' helmets. The pirate fell to his knees, as another grazed her arm with his blade. Now both of their envirosuits had been punctured.

The pirate with the smashed faceplate came again. Sar kicked her back and sank his sword into another pirate's chest. It stuck there, and the man toppled into yellow dust.

"Key in the pad sequence!" Sar ducked another swipe from his assailant. Nothing would stop him. Not blades, bullets, or the alien atmosphere seeping into his suit. Kivita would still light the fires of rebellion, even if none burned in her heart for him.

Lacking a faceplate, the pirate held her breath; the olive tint of Sarrhdtuu Transmutation colored her flesh. Umiracan's chill frosted over her lips and nostrils, but she attacked Sar like a maddened snake. He avoided an overextended thrust, then punched her jaw. She drew back, mouth not even opening.

Cheseia kicked aside her opponent and raised the protective plate over the airlock keypad. The kneeling pirate rose and dived with his blade, but Cheseia dodged and slammed the pirate into the hull, cracking his helmet. She brought an elbow down across his neck, and he went limp.

Sar grunted as the female pirate punched his side, then kicked his left thigh. He stumbled and broke her nose with a right hook. She staggered back, sucking in Umiracan's poisonous atmosphere at last. Sar picked up a dead pirate's spike baton.

"Cheseia!" he yelled.

The last pirate cracked his rifle butt across her back. She fell on her hands and knees, her faceplate frosting over from carbon dioxide contamination.

With a furious yell, Sar struck the pirate's back with the baton, its spiked head puncturing polyarmor. The pirate tried to turn, but Sar swung again. The tapered edge entered the man's neck. Blood spurted as the pirate fell to his knees.

Seething with hate and pain, Sar bludgeoned the pirate again and again. He wanted to bring down the foul yellow Inheritor banner. He yearned to rip Shekelor to shreds. He needed to crush . . .

Hands numb, Sar stopped swinging the baton. The pirate's pulpy remains made him turn and force bile down his throat. The baton dropped from his grasp, and cold shame doused his conscious.

"Sar," Cheseia's weak voice cracked over his helmet speakers. Had she seen him beat the pirate to death?

Sar tapped the code into the keypad and closed the armored cover. Hefting Cheseia up, he entered the airlock. Every breath wrung his lungs; every exhalation fogged his faceplate. Hearing a noise, he turned around.

The female pirate tugged the helmet off a prone companion. Her olive face convulsed and her eyes rolled back before getting the helmet on. She collapsed into the yellow soil.

The airlock slid shut. Sar's breaths hurt his chest.

Frevyx's onboard systems activated with life support, heating, and gravity operating by the time he stumbled into the bridge. Cheseia hunkered down on the bench and tossed off her helmet.

"Sar," She coughed violently and slid off the bench. "Take off."

"Hold on. Got to . . ." His words came with painful effort as his lungs took in *Frevyx*'s oxygen. That green-rigged pirate had survived too long before succumbing to the toxic air. How many such followers did Shekelor possess?

Outside the viewport, a squad of Shock Troopers approached *Frevyx*. Eschewing the seat restraints, Sar started the engines and fired the thrusters. The ship lifted as he pulled the manuals back, even as concentrated green beams passed before *Frevyx*'s bridge viewport. Sar gritted his teeth, fired the retro thrusters, and flew over the fortress.

The scanner readout showed at least three Aldaakian ships orbiting the planet. Perhaps a cruiser, a few shuttles. An Inheritor beacon signal streaked from Umiracan's orbit.

"Damn it, Kiv. What the hell were you thinking?" Sar had no doubt she and Seul had taken Shekelor's personal ship. For a moment he feared the Juxj Star might have shown her something none of the rest of them could see. A place he couldn't track her to.

Brown clouds enveloped *Frevyx* for several wracking seconds. Cheseia moaned louder from the airlock chamber, and turbulence jarred him from his seat. Sar gunned the ship faster until it exploded from orbit.

Cheseia gasped as she crawled to his side.

"How bad?" Sar asked, trying to eye her body and the ships ahead.

"Concentrate on flying," she breathed. "My wind was simply knocked out of me."

In the nebula-covered void ahead, a lone ship sped toward the Aldaakian one. *Terredyn Narbas* was clamped beneath the Aldaakian cruiser.

"Kiv, you're mad," he whispered.

"Commander Vuul has brought *Aldaar* here much sooner than I expected," Seul said. "He must have followed us right after I was taken from Vstrunn."

The Aldaakian cruiser stretched over a thousand feet in length, glimmering with a polished black finish. Beam weapon emplacements protruded from below the bridge, the underside, and from each geometric, angled wing.

"How many of you are on that thing?" Kivita asked.

"Perhaps six hundred crew and Troopers, with most in cryostasis," Seul replied. "Just a typical strike force."

Kivita, once so sure of her actions, now battled a dozen doubts and anxieties. The Aldaakians might pay nothing for the Juxj Star and still keep her ship. They might even leave her in *Fanged Pauper*, with a ruined reputation and a horde of pissed-off pirates chasing her. Salvagers always took risks, but staying on Umiracan would have landed her on a Sarrhdtuu ship. She had no idea why they wanted her. It had to be the gem.

She opened her mouth to ask Seul about hailing the Aldaakian ship, but raw information filled her thoughts.

Kith awaited her orders as Kivita entered information into a Vim datacore by sheer thought. Information in its purest, most immortal form: the collective memory of a species, stored in nature's hardiest materials. Only the Children of Meh Sat could read the secrets within the datacores. Secrets scattered in Vim Cradles.

"Kivita!" Seul screamed.

Fanged Pauper veered to port, then back to starboard

as Kivita regained her senses and control of the ship. Her hands trembled over the manuals; sweat trickled down her cheeks. *Aldaar* loomed above her like some gigantic beast of prey.

Kivita considered what she'd just envisioned. "Children of Meh Sat" was an ancient term for humanity in the Cetturo Arm. So ancient even the Inheritors couldn't tell what it meant.

"You'll find something special out there someday. Just gotta keep looking for it."

She touched the place in her polyarmor where the Juxj Star resided. Damn it, why lie to herself any longer? All those stellar vistas, all those coordinates . . . all the wonders she could discover, using this gem. She'd found something far greater than just another relic to barter.

Glancing back at Umiracan, Kivita's heart throbbed. Found something, yes. But what had she left behind?

Kivita cut *Fanged Pauper*'s engines as she brought it alongside *Terredyn Narbas*. The parallel airlocks magnetized. With numb fingers she unbuckled herself from the gyro harness and left the cockpit.

"Kivita, what are you doing? Commander Vuul has not received the Juxj Star yet. He will not agree to you entering your ship until you've made a trade and spoken with our Archivers about the Vim signal." Seul tugged off her buckles and stood, suspicion in her eyes.

"There's other things on board my ship I have to arrange. Then I'll speak to the commander, whatever his name is."

Seul barred her path to the airlock. "You lie."

They stared at each other. How could Seul understand? She expected weird things from Kivita, a miracle to save her people or something. Kivita had to save herself first.

"Yeah. I'm sorry." Throat tight, Kivita raised the pistol. "But I can't give up the Juxj Star. Not yet."

Neither spoke for a moment. Seul's eyes darted about, as if searching for a weapon.

"I saved your life. I helped you steal this ship. All so that you can lead us to the Vim!" Seul winced and clutched her thigh wound.

"Seems like we used each other, huh?" Kivita tried to smile.

Seul glared, then looked away.

"I hope you see your daughter someday," Kivita said. "I mean that."

"Go. I will tell them . . ." Seul faced Kivita. "I'll tell them I was your prisoner, and you left me here. Even though I know you already fired your last shot." She moved from the airlock.

The cockpit speaker crackled. "Kiv, what the hell are you doing? Kiv?" Sar's voice made her cheeks burn.

"I hope your heart finds what it needs." Seul glanced at the speaker.

"Thank you, Seul Jaah." Kivita jumped into *Terredyn Narbas* as its airlock slid open. As she turned, Seul watched her with forlorn eyes. They reminded Kivita of melting ice shards.

The airlock shut, and Kivita ran to the bridge, wondering how she'd disable the Aldaakian clamps. Wondering if she'd ever see her new friend again.

14

Terredyn Narbas's gravity still lay under the Aldaakian cruiser's influence, but Kivita managed to strap herself into the gyro harness. There had been no sign of Shock Troopers on board—they'd have stopped her at the airlock, anyway. She opened the bridge viewport and gripped the manuals.

Kivita closed her eyes, and her breath shook through trembling lips. A cold, hard reality stole over her: she was leaving Sar behind. Leaving Seul and any possible bargain with the Aldaakians, too. The Juxj Star might show her more things—things she'd only dreamt about as a little girl staring up at the stars.

The console speaker awoke with static. "Kiv, wait. Your beacon can still be traced. Follow me and—"

She cut off the speaker and muted the mic. Too late, Sar Redryll. Too late.

The scanner readouts showed nine of Shekelor's ships closing with the Aldaakians—and thus her own craft. Kivita flicked on her radio transmitter and tapped in a code sequence. Once she'd cracked a pirate-ship computer in the Raderon system by hacking its clamp release.

The console beeped a negative. Yeah, so she lacked familiarity with Aldaakian code syntax. Kivita tried again. Nothing.

Shekelor's ships came closer. Kivita pounded new numbers into the keypad. C'mon, work, dammit!

The scanner picked up a shuttle exiting *Aldaar*, while *Frevyx* evaded two of Shekelor's vessels. Kivita rubbed her brow. The shuttle would have a boarding party. This time, Sar and Cheseia wouldn't be around to help repel it.

"C'mon, Kivita, think." She tapped in two more codes, but the clamps remained fixed on *Terredyn Narbas*'s hull.

On the scanner, *Frevyx* outmaneuvered a pirate vessel attempting to magnetize airlocks, while the Aldaakian shuttle boarded *Fanged Pauper*. She hoped Seul would be okay.

Her fingers neared the keys again as the tingling returned to her temples. The sensation of ice sliding through her skull made Kivita gasp and thrash in the gyro harness. What the hell was happening to her?

A long code sequence entered her mind; binary, but with complex syntaxes she'd never heard of. Kivita's eyes fluttered and she tried to concentrate. Where had it come from? The code slid through her thoughts as she stared at the keypad.

"Get out . . . Get . . ." The code corkscrewed into her mind as she stared at the console. Get away from *Aldaar*; get away from the pirates . . .

Her proximity alarm honked as *Aldaar*'s clamps released her ship.

Sucking in a deep breath, Kivita opened her eyes. The bulkheads creaked as a mild gravity flux rippled through *Terredyn Narbas*; then the craft was free.

Kivita glanced from the viewport to the keypad. Her fingers had not tapped in a single number.

"What . . . ?" She couldn't breathe. The icy pain in her head spread, and she gritted her teeth. Breaths finally came, fast and ragged.

How did I do that? The code went from her mind through the keypad, to Aldaar's computer. . . . It wasn't possible. Her heartbeat thrummed in her ears.

Maybe Seul had told her comrades to let Kivita go, or they wanted to ditch *Terredyn Narbas*'s extra mass to combat the pirates. There had to be a reason.

Kivita punched the thruster control, pushed the manuals, and sped away. Dunaar had lied to her, Sar may have betrayed her, and Shekelor wanted to sell her to the Sarrhdtuu. Why? She'd done nothing but find this gem, right?

She needed to get away and think. Needed to study the Juxj Star.

On the scanner, *Frevyx* slowed as another pirate ship drew alongside to magnetize with its other airlock. Two more ships flanked *Frevyx* and used their gravitational fluxers to destabilize it. Sar would be boarded for sure. It would serve him right. But he'd saved her on Vstrunn and let her keep the Juxj Star instead of taking it.

"Like your Umiracan Kiss now, Sar?" Kivita's finger lingered over the light-jump button. What could she do to save him? *Terredyn Narbas* had no weapons.

She punched the thrusters again and grunted as *Terredyn Narbas* turned about. G-forces tossed her in the gyro harness, and the gravity generator sputtered until she switched it off to zero-G. Though all her instincts begged her to leave, Kivita banked to port and angled *Terredyn Narbas*'s braking thrusters to starboard. As she sped alongside the second pirate ship docking with *Frevyx*, Kivita fired the thrusters.

The brief burst of heat and energy shook her ship, and debris slapped against the starboard hull. Two damage indicators blinked on her terminal, bathing the bridge in red light. The scanner displayed the pirate ship swerving away from *Frevyx*, chunks of its hull floating away.

Kivita swerved to starboard, fired her port-side braking thrusters, and wheeled *Terredyn Narbas* around to make a pass on the other pirate ship. G-forces slammed into her chest and stomach. Her eyes rolled back in her head and her vision narrowed into near darkness. She gasped for air as a structural-integrity alarm blinked.

"Kiss this," she mumbled, and urged *Terredyn Narbas* onward. Her thumb barely pressed the break-thruster button for the starboard side. Another proximity alarm hinted at success. Red warning lights on the console zigzagged across her tumbling vision. Dings and thuds echoed through her ship as debris struck it.

The gyro harness bit through her envirosuit, while G-forces yanked her around the bridge, but Kivita tugged the manuals. One pirate ship used its fluxer again. *Terredyn Narbas* shook, and Kivita's stomach crawled into her throat. Everything became a blur of red and yellow lights, black void.

Kivita's scalp flared; her mouth went dry. The fluxer—have to stop that stupid fluxer before it disrupts my flight path too much, before the pirates board *Frevyx*, before they hurt Sar. . . .

Her jaw popped with a racked cry as paths blazed into her thoughts. An icy feeling sheared through her body. Numbers emptied from Kivita's mind as her consciousness reached out toward the pirate ship.

Terredyn Narbas stopped shaking and its flight stabilized. Per her scanner, the pirate ship's fluxer had ceased operating.

Twice she'd forced something to happen on another ship just by thinking about it. Twice! Her wide-eyed stare drank in the celestial vista outside the viewport. Two times meant this couldn't be a coincidence. The stars and nebula all seemed to brighten in agreement.

Shivering, she flew *Terredyn Narbas* away from her handiwork. On the scanner, the two pirate ships appeared as flaring shapes on either side of *Frevyx*.

"You owe me one, smoothie," Kivita whispered.

The scanner beeped. Four pirate ships, one of them the large saucer with the forward cargo hold, closed in on her position. She'd done what she could for Sar and Cheseia. Anyway, if Sar was still half the pilot he used to be, he'd escape.

Terredyn Narbas's engine whined, and she frowned. All warning lights and alarms came on, assaulting Kivita's eyes and ears. The ship sputtered and slowed down.

No, not now. Please, girl, not now. Her mind churning with icy rawness, Kivita forced herself to focus on the console's readout display.

The ship was losing power; the phased energy dumps would need a manual reset. Just enough remained for a light jump. Great.

Her fingers darted over the keypad as a hundred different coordinate sets raced through her mind. Before finding the Juxj Star, she'd never known so many. At random, Kivita punched one in and hit the activate button; then cold agony whipped across her temples. Why couldn't all this damn information leave her mind?

"That's it, girl. Take us out of here. C'mon." The engine sputtered again. Kivita loosed a wordless shout, wanting the energy dump to reset, wanting to get the hell away. Wanting it to reset without her having to touch the lever.

With a dull roar, the engine awoke. The viewport shut as *Terredyn Narbas* light-jumped away from Umiracan.

After reactivating the ship's gravity, Kivita unbuckled herself from the gyro harness. The next instant she lay on the floor, palms and knees smarting from the impact. It took all her will not to vomit.

"Sar, you asshole." The words took more effort than she'd thought, but she needed to say them. The wringing nausea in her gut faded and Kivita stood. She pulled herself along the ship's corridors to the cryo chamber. All her bruises and cuts hammered at her nerves.

She needed light medical attention, food. But sleep first. As her cryopod hissed open; the Juxj Star spilled from her pouch and plunked into the cryopod. The gem's glassy red surface reflected her own face back at her.

"What the hell are you?"

15

Inside *Aldaar*'s hangar, Seul stood still while a medic unlocked her polyarmor. She grunted as the armor's rodlike inserts retracted from her cryoports. Cryonic exhaust wafted from her body.

"Cut wound on the right tricep. Puncture wound on the left quadricep," the medic said, wrapping cold packs on her injuries. "Small laceration on the right cheek. A few bruises. Are you able to walk, Captain?"

Seul gave him a cool glance. Of course she could walk. A few cuts wouldn't stop her. But she'd let Kivita escape. Maybe even lost the best chance her people would ever have of finding the Vim. Of finding her daughter.

"These wounds should hold until you reach the Medical Ward," the medic said. "We have more wounded coming in."

Shock Troopers hurried from another returned shuttle, carrying dead or wounded companions. Every Trooper in two different squads had been killed or maimed, and two other squads all bore wounds and cracked armor. Many had smashed faceplates, their faces blue from suffocation. Shekelor Thal's pirates had fought harder than usual. In past confrontations, these scum had fled in droves. And this time they'd made a stand before fleeing? Seul didn't like it.

"What is the battle's status?" she asked a nearby operations officer.

He gave her a brisk nod. "The pirate ships have fled, but nothing of worth was taken from the fortress, Captain."

"What of the slaves the pirates kept?" Seul's mind flashed to the ragged human children down there.

"Forward reports have indicated all noncombatants were left planetside, Captain." The officer hesitated. "Commander Vuul expects a briefing."

Seul nodded and headed to the bridge. More incoming Troopers passed her, speaking of pirates augmented with Sarrhdtuu coils or carapace armor. No wonder the pirates had fought so well.

"What did those animals do to you, Captain Jaah?" a voice behind her asked.

"Nothing I won't survive from." Seul turned. "Kael?"

Kael nodded in salute. "I am very glad to see you back, Captain. We feared you had been lost over Vstrunn."

"Help me to the bridge." Seul leaned on his shoulder and placed his hand around her waist.

Looking around, Kael gulped. "Captain, I . . ."

"That's an order." Seul wrapped her left arm around his waist, and they continued. A few crew members frowned at them in passing. She didn't care. Seeing how Kivita missed her own lover made Seul openly appreciate Kael.

"What happened after I was taken?" Seul asked.

"An Inheritor battleship carrying the Rector himself

fired on *Aldaar*. Commander Vuul ordered a with-
drawal, based on the second human trawler's trajectory.
The one you were on." A glance from him told Seul he
had missed her. Good. "The Archivers have been woken
from cryostasis. They are speaking with Commander
Vuul now."

Seul squeezed his hand as they neared the bridge.
Smiling, he squeezed back and walked away.

His words sobered her, but Kael's smile made Seul's
cryoports gape open. She needed it, after letting Kivita
go. The human woman had lied and threatened her with
an empty gun, but Seul found no bitterness in her heart.
Kivita's comment about Seul's daughter had sounded
sincere. No Aldaakian would have said that.

Seul's musings faded as she entered *Aldaar*'s bridge.
Three Archivers waited, their solid white uniforms
topped with black collars. Each held a computer chit
booklet.

Vuul stared at her with cold eyes.

"Commander Vuul." Seul inclined her head and
touched both chest cryoports.

"Captain Jaah," Vuul said. "Due to your message, *Aldaar* was able to track your location. The Terresin Expanse would have garbled our scanners for days. Yet I
see no Vim datacore in your possession, as mentioned in
your radio message."

Seul's cryoports tightened. "Commander, the datacore
was never in my possession. I've been a prisoner until I
was liberated by my comrades. The Juxj Star is on one of
the human ships that departed."

Vuul strolled over to her, hands behind his back.
"Which ship? Nine squads searched the planetside fortress. We suffered heavy losses."

"Kivita Vondir's ship," Seul said. "She asked me to send the message."

The Archivers mumbled among themselves while Vuul's staff shared uneasy looks.

Seul fought down frustration. "She wanted to bargain the gem for her ship, or perhaps—"

"Do you suppose she could send another signal to the Vim?" Qaan, the lead Archiver, asked.

"Track that vessel's course and make the jump," Vuul said. "Send a message to all Commanders in Aldaakian Space: mobilize for a possible Inheritor invasion."

The orders sent a noticeable ripple of tension through the operations staff. Seul almost stepped forward, but caught herself. Alerting the other Aldaakian fleets would accomplish nothing. It would take years to assemble them, and for what? Kivita would be out of their grasp by then.

"The human craft's trajectory leads to the Tejuit system," an operations officer said.

"Commander Vuul, Kivita still might bargain for the Juxj Star. It stands to reason that the pirate ships forced her to flee." Seul remained at attention, her wounds throbbing through the cold packs.

"You could renegotiate a deal with this salvager?" Vuul asked.

"A Shock Trooper is not trained in the correct disciplines to make this human understand her importance," Qaan said. "Kivita Vondir must be questioned by us."

Seul kept her face expressionless. "Shekelor Thal had a Sarrhdtuu-enhanced keypad on his ship, Commander Vuul. Kivita knew the keypad's sequence."

Qaan sniffed. "Impossible! Sarrhdtuu codes are too complex."

Silence fell over the bridge as Vuul held up a hand. *Aldaar* shuddered as it made a light jump and left Umiracan behind.

Seul took a breath and spoke, ignoring protocol. "Commander, Shekelor planned to sell her to someone, perhaps the Sarrhdtuu. Others want her."

Vuul sat in his command chair and glowered. "The signal you sent contained traces of a Sarrhdtuu message. Kivita's ship is equipped with a Sarrhdtuu beacon, and she knows Sarrhdtuu codes? She cannot be trusted."

"She activated the Vim signal sent from Vstrunn," Seul said. Years of training and authoritarian conditioning kept her tone respectful, but . . . hadn't Kivita spoke her mind?

"Commander Vuul, the pilot of the impounded trawler also cracked *Aldaar*'s clamp code," a staff officer said.

Vuul's expression darkened.

Seul's cryoports sank into her flesh. "That is how she escaped?"

"And you withheld this information, Commander Vuul?" Qaan murmured.

"What can a human mercenary do to save our tattered civilization?" Vuul's flat tone cut through the air. "Listen to yourselves. The Inheritors are gathering to destroy us this time. Our way of life, our children, our species! We should trust our weaponry and training, not the slim possibility this human woman and that gem represent."

"Statisticians proclaim an eighty-eight percent probability that Kivita Vondir is a Savant," Qaan said. "Yet reports state that brain-pulse analyzers detected no Savants or datacores in the fortress."

Vuul stood. "The leader of the Inheritors himself appeared after the Vim signal was sent. This is all a ploy to lure us into disaster."

Qaan cleared his throat. "Our enemies want Kivita, and that is enough. We must interrogate her about the Vim signal, Commander."

"I think she is more than a Savant. Everything so far has happened because of her." Seul glanced from Qaan to Vuul. To her surprise, the Archivers nodded in assent.

"That is why we are following her ship, Captain Jaah," Vuul said. "But not to feed into the hysteria that is building aboard this ship. Since you may be able to sway Kivita, I am assigning you the task of acquiring her. Use all means to find her, but I want the Juxj Star most of all."

"This human may not come peacefully, Commander Vuul," Qaan said. "Or relinquish the gem."

"Then execute her. Is that understood, Captain Jaah?"

She inclined her head, though her cryoports clamped so hard, they hurt. "Yes, Commander Vuul."

Vuul's fear that Kivita might be a Sarrhdtuu tool or an Inheritor plant nagged Seul as she left the bridge.

She'd not hurt or kill Kivita.

Disobeying orders, though, would earn her own death sentence. Kivita wouldn't give up the Juxj Star, else she would have done so at Umiracan. Seul had never seen such hope on the faces of the operations staff. How could she destroy it?

Inside the Medical Ward, several Troopers squirmed on bloody cots. One still had a human sword protruding from his left side. Another's hand had been sliced off, and one was missing her eye. Less fortunate ones passed

Seul on covered stretchers. They'd join Niaaq Aldaar and his loyal host, floating forever in the void.

An attendant removed Seul's cold packs and lathered her wounds in amino jelly. One medic examined her cryoports with prongs and scrapers. Afterward, Seul stripped and stepped into a vat filled with chemical slush. Her lungs labored to work in the subfrozen liquid.

Three flat displays highlighted Seul's diagnostics. One showed the infant name list. Seul's heart jumped.

"Signs of corrupted pseudoadrine seepage. We'll have to clean your teeth and palate," the medic said, as she studied the displays. "No unusual menstrual activity since your last examination. Your ovaries might produce a few more eggs for the Pediatric Ward. Those humans don't use enough radiation shielding on their ships. How they manage to breed so much is beyond me."

Seul felt like she could float from the vat. Once her people reunited with the Vim, maybe a security clearance would allow her to birth and raise her own child. Her excitement spawned a grin as Kael entered the room.

The medic frowned at him. "Shouldn't you be in cryostasis?"

"Officer Kael can help me to my cryopod when you are finished," Seul said.

Kael knelt beside the vat's edge as the medic walked away. "Vuul must have been easy on you."

Seul's grin faded. "I've been assigned to find Kivita Vondir, once we exit this jump. I'll need *Aldaar*'s best pilot. I won't accept a negative, Officer Kael."

"Is she that dangerous?" Kael touched the scratch on her cheek. "I heard Vuul thinks she is a threat."

"No, but I think she is linked to the Vim somehow."
Seul glanced at the infant list once more.

"Why are you looking at that again?" Kael asked in
an amused tone.

The chemical slush made her shiver. "One of those
names could be her. I don't like the way you said that."

Kael withdrew his hand from her scarred cheek. "Forgive me, Captain Jaah. But the Pediatric Ward knows best."

Swishing through the slush, she gripped his hands. "If
your sperm had fertilized my egg, how would you feel
about it?"

"I . . . Captain Jaah, please." Kael's cryoports gave an
audible squeeze.

She gripped his hands harder. "Would it shame you,
then?"

Embarrassment left his eyes. "I would be honored,
Captain Jaah."

Seul sank to her neck and beamed. "I'll need your
help once we reach Tejuit. Will you keep a secret?"

"Yes, but—"

Seul pulled him closer to her and lowered her voice.
"We're not going to kill Kivita Vondir. We're going to
save her."

Zhhl's hologram stared back at Dunaar. "*Terredyn Narbas* and *Frevyx* escaped. The Aldaakians have left. Our
ally is reclaiming his ship and planetary fortress."

Dunaar mopped sweat off his head with a yellow
towel. "At least five years have passed on Haldon Prime
since we departed. I cannot be away much longer. You
are certain our quarry will be coming here?"

Outside the viewport, the pink, blue, and green gas

giant of Tejuit Seven dominated the scene. The system was the largest trading hub in the Cetturo Arm. Inheritors, Tannocci, Naxans, and even Aldaakians sent merchant fleets there to conduct business. Like his predecessors, Dunaar participated only to maintain a presence in the system and to spy on rivals.

"The beacon on *Terredyn Narbas* will reveal Kivita Vondir's position," Zhhl said. "The Aldaakians will realize Sarrhdtuu involvement. Confrontation is unavoidable now."

Dunaar smiled. In addition to *Arcuri's Glory*, he had six cruisers and two other battleships waiting in the system. More would be coming. "How difficult will it be for Kivita to remove the beacon? Surely she knows about it by now."

"Sarrhdtuu technology inlays itself into the hull. Kivita Vondir will either have to dismantle her ship or reverse the implantation code, which only a Sarrhdtuu can accomplish." Zhhl's voice slurred.

"Very well." Dunaar risked the Thedes getting the redheaded salvager and the gem, since Tejuit was clogged with starship traffic. The reward still outweighed such dangers. "When can I expect the arrival of your own ships?"

"Soon, Prophet of Meh Sat." The connection ended.

Dunaar leaned against a quartz wall mural and swathed his face in the towel. Though Haldon Prime was in the hands of subordinate prophets, Dunaar had never been this far from the Compound. But no one else could be trusted with these tasks.

The fabricated news brief from Vstrunn had already been dispatched in a wideband signal. By now, most in orbit around Tejuit would have seen it. What else would these fools think if Dunaar didn't give it to them?

He tapped the intercom panel in his quarters. "Captain Stiego, keep *Arcuri's Glory* at the farthest fringes of the system. When the Sarrhdtuu signal from *Terredyn Narbas* is detected, you may alert me. Until then, all aboard will remain in cryostasis on the usual shifts."

"As you wish, Rector," Stiego replied, and Dunaar exited the chamber. Near the end of the corridor, two Proselytes opened a doorway. Inside, Bredine sat on the floor, eating gruel with her hands. Her cryopod waited nearby. Dunaar motioned to the Proselytes, who yanked Bredine to her feet.

He gouged a finger into her right breast. "Tell me again what this shows you about Queen Terredyn Narbas." Dunaar touched Bredine's head with the Scepter. "Before I enter cryostasis."

With a gasp, Bredine went limp, and the Proselytes held her up by her armpits. Her eyes moved beneath closed lids.

"Colony ship. Sixteen thousand in stasis." Bredine's voice lost the broken, chaotic phrasings she usually spoke in. Whenever she decoded a datacore, it seemed a different woman spoke.

"Yes?" Dunaar asked.

"The Rectifier. He stands in his yellow suit, watching. It is his responsibility to maintain the Handlers so all are cared for." Bredine's eyes fluttered.

Dunaar tried to imagine what she must be seeing: a huge starship filled with cryopods, with one man protecting all. Even in ancient, prefeudal times, a Rectifier ensured the Vim's children achieved their destiny. A Rector, as the position came to be known, knew what was best for all.

"And where does the ship come from?" Dunaar asked in a whisper.

Bredine pursed her lips. "Meh Sat. Yellow, warm light."

Dunaar caressed her forehead. "Do you still see Terredyn Narbas coming to the Cetturo Arm from that system?"

"Yes. She leaves a world of inferno, her ship afire. It crashes on a world of deep blue oceans."

His hand traveled down her neck and nestled between her breasts. "What did she flee from?"

"She fled the enemies that are still waiting for us. Beyond the blackest void."

Thank the Vim. Some new information this time. Dunaar leaned into Bredine, his bulk making the Proselytes brace themselves. Sweat from his face trickled onto hers.

"You mean the Aldaakians? This information will prove them as enemies of the Vim once and for all." He sucked the flesh of Bredine's neck between his teeth.

"Not Aldaakians. They are . . . they . . ." Bredine's voice faltered. "The pain . . ."

"More," he breathed into her ear, and rubbed her crotch. "Who are they?"

"The pain!" she screamed.

Dunaar shoved the end of the Scepter into her mouth and clutched her throat. "How can this dead queen still haunt us? Tell me, bitch! Tell me!" He pulled the Scepter from her mouth and pressed it under her chin.

Trembling, Bredine's eyes fluttered again. "Hmm? Rector, Rector. Don't turn void black. Yes?"

The return of her normal voice made Dunaar step back and slap her. Blood flew from her busted lip. He slammed the Scepter into her right side. Wheezing, she vomited up gruel. Dunaar rapped her across the knees with the Scepter as sweat poured down his back, over the bridge of his nose.

Her green stare remained fixed on him.

"You will reveal the rest later. Place her in cryo," Dunaar said.

Stomping back to his chamber, Dunaar's anger gave way to a new idea: Kivita could read the Scepter for him instead, before he turned her over to Zhhl.

The Scepter felt warm in his grasp. The means mattered little.

16

Still in her two-piece underwear, Kivita gaped at Tejuit Seven's massive curvature outside the bridge viewport. She'd visited the Tejuit system only once, as an eight-year-old with her father. Those memories seemed to stare back at her from the gas giant's blue, green, and pink storms.

She studied the console's readout scan, just like she'd done so many years ago. One-hundred and three thousand miles in diameter. A seventy-eight-hour day, coupled with an 8,053-day year. The numbers, the scale, the galactic majesty—they still amazed her, like they did then.

"I've been looking, Father, but I don't know if I've found it yet," she whispered.

Kivita studied the console readout again. It was Charter Year 11,414, and . . . wait a second.

Tejuit was fourteen light years from Haldon and six from Ecrol. For *Terredyn Narbas*, six light years meant a two-year journey. Her pod's life monitor claimed she'd been in cryostasis for only eight months.

Those strange coordinates she'd entered had cut her trip by two-thirds.

A fresh tingle at her scalp sent a wave of nausea over Kivita. Who or what was giving her this information? The code to open Shekelor's starship, the code to unlock *Aldaar*'s clamp, and now coordinates that defied time and space. Kivita covered her mouth and gripped her stomach. What was happening to her? Could anybody help, or—?

Oh, shit.

She'd forgotten about the Sarrhdtuu beacon aboard her ship! Trembling in the cold air, Kivita hunched over the computer console.

She did a wideband scan. The usual merchant and refugee traffic occupied the system, and a gathering of Tannocci vessels orbited the other side of the planet. Kivita set the proximity alarm to full, which would warn her of any approaching craft. Holding her breath, she performed a quick check of *Terredyn Narbas*'s systems.

"Worked you over good, didn't I, girl?"

Those wild maneuvers over Umiracan had scorched *Terredyn Narbas*'s starboard sensor couplings. A portside braking thruster lacked full power, and surface abrasions now pitted the iron-polymer hull. The pirates' fluxers had destabilized the aft gravity generator. *Terredyn Narbas* still functioned, but she might be stranded in the void the next time she needed to escape.

She glanced at the pouch on the console, wondering if the gem was worth all this trouble.

Kivita pulled the Juxj Star from the pouch and lay in her hammock. At her touch, the gem glowed from within. She tried peering through it, as if mere sight could reveal its secrets.

"Just what the hell are ... ?"

Her eyes shut as the vision of the cryopod ship came

back. *Albino figures in gray suits watched over the cryo-pods. Traces of hair covered their heads, and their eyes had a light blue tint.*

They resembled Aldaakians.

A dull, frigid ache entered her brain.

The scene changed. The growth tubes filled with hir-sute creatures she'd seen before now sat empty. Their contents had splashed onto the floor, the tubes smashed. Some of the creatures stumbled around, their bodies cov-ered in wet fur. Thick manes flowed, damp and stringy over their shoulders.

"Ascali," she mumbled. The ache grew into a consis-tent throb in her temples.

Coordinates clicked through her mind, as if she keyed them into a jump console. They seemed impossible, even foolish: directions to the ship she'd just seen, eighty light years outside the Cetturo Arm.

An icy, burning sensation whipped across her tem-ples, and Kivita dropped the gem. The pain subsided. Was it playing with her? Chest heaving, she scratched her head.

The gem stopped glowing.

"What are you really meant for?" she asked the Juxj Star. In its crimson surface her face looked pinched and shadowed.

She rose from the hammock and entered her galley. Unlike Sar's well-stocked one, hers consisted of a small, square oven, hot-wave disk, and grimy dry-disher. A crate filled with preserved foodstuffs stood nearby, along with three Susuron water drums. Kivita took two protein slabs and dried sugar reeds from the crate and warmed them on the hot-wave disk.

Soon, she gulped down the salty slabs and sticky-sweet reeds, then drank water mixed with Bellerion turtle-egg spice. Just something to settle her stomach and fuel her body. All the while, she stared at the Juxj Star. Sure, it hurt like hell to use it, but the things it revealed . . . almost like she were there in person.

It glowed again.

"All right. Show me more, then." She picked it up. A burning cold gripped her skull.

Her mind beheld another cryopod transport and its coordinates, thirty-three light years beyond the Terresin Expanse. Rows of pods with black-armored figures filled the interior. The image changed to a sticklike vessel with one end shielded by a giant panel of shimmering material. Somehow she knew the ship measured eight miles in length, and possessed a power output greater than all the Inheritor fleets combined.

Its coordinates, nearly five hundred light years from the Cetturo Arm, drove an icy dagger into her mind. Kivita cried out and dropped the gem. The Juxj Star rolled along the galley floor into her living quarters. Kivita cursed and ran after it.

The images and coordinates ruled her thoughts. *Blueprints for the Aldaakian shuttle she'd seen. Alternate phased fusion-dump settings, allowing faster light-jump speeds. Schematics for an energy-saving cryostasis router that cut power consumption by thirty percent.* Every new piece of knowledge further seared her brain.

"Stop!" she yelled, though whether to her racing thoughts or the rolling gem, she wasn't sure.

She finally snatched the Juxj Star before it rolled into the hammock's corner. As her fingers traced over the gem, a new image coalesced in her mind. *An oblong ship, with a polished hull and yellow-lit viewports. A*

name formed through the dreamlike relay of informa-
tion: Narbas.

Hissing between clenched teeth, she tried to hold the
image in her mind while controlling the pain. Second by
aching second passed. Her jaw numbed from the agony.
Finally she loosed a chest-wrenching sob and let the image go.

After tossing the gem into the hammock, Kivita
paced the floor. Though her toes, hands, and nose grew
chill from *Terredyn Narbas*'s low heating, she still didn't
grab a bodyglove. She wanted the vacuum cold to seep
into her, wake her up from this crazy shit.

She scratched her hair again, bit her lip. Shifted her
underwear on her hips. "There's no way this is real."

Kivita hurried back to the bridge. Tejuit Seven's gargantuan presence, along with the undeniable time lapse
listed on the life monitor, confirmed what she'd refused
to accept.

Somehow, the Juxj Star had informed her of coordinates
to reach this system from Ecrol, in the seldom-traveled Terresin Expanse, in one-third the time. Coordinates entered
during a stressful moment.

She'd entered a wormhole rift, decreasing the distance. An interstellar shortcut. Kivita had heard of such
cosmic anomalies, but to think of one from thin air
made her shudder. Inheritor dogma claimed that knowledge remained a blessing of the Vim, and was not to be
tampered with by the unworthy. The fact that she of all
people had gleaned this strange data exposed such beliefs as lies.

The information revealed to her had been gathered
by someone, though whether it remained current was
unknown. Even if she could travel the five hundred light

years to that massive ship, it might not be there then, if it was even there now. Though Kivita had never believed in the Vim as gods, no other race came to mind that could have assembled this data.

"Let's try something, then." She picked up the Juxj Star with both hands. "Okay, show me where the closest, richest salvage is." Kivita closed her eyes and waited.

A schematic for a deep-crust mining machine came to mind.

"Oh, c'mon. Give me something I can use." She thought of an uncharted paradise world yet to be discovered in the Cetturo Arm. Maybe even a planet she could claim as her own.

Data on adapting Ascali jiir trees to various terrestrial environments drifted through her thoughts, with a renewed headache for her trouble.

"Shit. Okay, maybe . . . yeah." Kivita concentrated on the secrets of Sarrhdtuu beam weaponry, something everyone in the Cetturo Arm would want. The concepts of critical thought from some unpronounceable philosopher entered her thoughts instead.

She gave up trying to force information from the Juxj Star. Before setting it back down, though, Kivita thought of her mother. The way Rhyer had spoken of her: strong-willed, brave, with great love for her baby daughter.

Rhyer had never told Kivita her mother's name. Whenever she'd asked, he'd grown silent or changed the subject.

The same image appeared in her mind of an oblong ship, similar to current Inheritor designs. Crushed port thrusters; dented hull. Flickering viewports. So opposite of what she'd seen before. In the dark void behind it, a huge, gray-green crescent shape closed in. A Sarrhdtuu vessel.

A new wave of agony spread across her temples, but Kivita grunted and continued.

The image shifted, with humans being interrogated on board the Sarrhdtuu ship. Green jelly bodies and slimy coils lashed out at the captives.

These new images combined with her dreams, the ones she'd seen since touching the Vim datacore near Xeh's Crown. Now the faraway nebulae she'd dreamt of lay three hundred light years away. A Cradle. The word still remained mysterious.

Kivita secured the gem back in the pouch and took a quick bath in the mist ionizer. Her device saved more water than Sar's. Thinking of him made her heart thud in her chest. Even though he'd been so cold on Umiracan, she missed him. Had he been a pirate, or had he planned on using her?

Her salvaging career in Inheritor Space was over. The Sarrhdtuu wanted her, and their reach was long. The Aldaakians probably wanted her, too. Looking all around her living quarters, a lump rose in Kivita's throat.

Who was she now? Where would she go? What could she do?

She dressed in a maroon bodyglove, black leather chaps, and the same polyboots. A gold-meld cuirass hugged her breasts and stomach. Kivita strapped on a shortsword, a slim Tahe knife, and a purple half cape. She needed to look tough but clean if she planned to deal with Tejuit's merchants.

Last, she attached the pouch with the gem to her belt, and looped the strap three times to ensure it wouldn't come away.

Later, as she flew into Tejuit Seven's gravity well, Kivita frowned at the starships orbiting the equator. Refugees who refused to obey the Inheritor Charter, or ones who'd fled after the Inheritors conquered their worlds. Some claimed ancestry back to the feudal kingdoms centuries ago. Those aristocrats had become known as the Tannocci, with their own small armies and fleets. United, for the time being, against Inheritor aggression. Maybe they would help her.

Cylindrical Tannocci ships orbited in tandem with oblong Inheritor craft. The curved, graceful vessels of Naxan merchants had magnetized their airlocks to create hive ships of fifty vessels and more. Bulbous, saucer-shaped craft from Bons Sutar stayed close together, housing renegades, merchants, or refugees.

Had Sar been right? Did the Juxj Star contain information so priceless it would be worth more than a thousand of these ships? Kivita's mouth went dry, and she urged the manuals forward.

Tejuit Seven's swirling hydrogen and methane storms caught the sun's rays and bathed the bridge in indigo, lime, and rose shades. Kivita flew past four small asteroids and a tiny cratered moon caught in the planet's orbit. Good; she still could maneuver despite the damage she couldn't fix yet.

"Here we go, girl." Kivita nudged *Terredyn Narbas* alongside a Naxan hive ship with a gleaming silver hull. Some spacers claimed the Naxans blasted their starship hulls with sand from their homeworld to achieve that characteristic polish.

An automated greeting crackled over the console speaker, but Kivita thumbed a button to accept Naxan trade regulations so she could board. Three seconds later, a code sequenced with her beacon, clearing her to dock with the shining vessel.

The Naxan hive ship played host to dozens of human craft and even a few Aldaakian shuttles. After orbiting it three times, Kivita finally found an unoccupied airlock on the ship's underside. *Terredyn Narbas* shuddered a moment while she magnetized its port-side airlock with the Naxan one.

"Yeah, here we go," she repeated in a whisper.

17

The muffled beat of Susuron drums reached Kivita's ears while she passed the airlock checkpoint. A Naxan trade rep in a dark green jumpsuit with silver piping and tassels clicked his tongue in greeting. Like all human cultures in the Arm, the Naxans spoke their own deviation of Meh Sattan.

"May your transactions go smoothly," he said, then clicked once and handed her a chit stack. Like on Haldon Prime, once a chit was activated by glue pen, it bound her in agreement with a merchant. Hack attempts met with permanent expulsion from Naxan consortiums, sometimes even a beating from their mercenaries. Not that she'd ever tried that.

Trying to look casual, Kivita glanced into corners, down aisles. Had anyone followed her here?

Kivita walked by an antiquated pathogen detector, where an Ascali male played the conch drums. A nearby stall sold Naxan clapper sticks, in case travelers could communicate only in yes or no answers. Years of detritus and carbon filth caked the metal-grate floor. Multicolored ceiling lamps lit her way into the first cargo chamber.

Twenty wall platforms contained an airlock, with each magnetized to a customer vessel. Decent heating, gravity, and life-support systems kept everything comfortable, but the air scrubbers needed changing a decade ago.

Aisles crammed with stalls lined the circular bay, while mercenaries hired by the Naxans patrolled the area—Ascali, human, and Aldaakian freelancers, armed with swords or batons. Firearms were prohibited, as much to protect hull integrity as customer safety.

Kivita hurried along, disregarding the proffered wares. One Inheritor carpenter sold wooden Vim idols, with each piece resembling a tall humanoid with solemn features. A Naxan florist sold cultured roots, fruit shrubs, and vegetable pots, though some already wilted from the carbon-heavy air.

"Give thanks unto the Vim for their blessings of technology! Without their wisdom, we would not be able to survive in space!" An Inheritor prophet walked the aisles, waving a yellow banner. "Who taught you the secret of artificial gravity? Who revealed to you the faster-than-light capabilities all starships now enjoy?"

A Solar Advocate, dressed in a shimmering silver tunic, preached in an adjacent aisle. "From the stars we were born, and to the stars we shall return. Heed the wisdom of the Solars! We all contribute to the structure of the universe. We are all centers of gravity and energy."

Sighing, Kivita strolled into another aisle. When she'd visited Tejuit as a child, all the products and the worlds they came from had fascinated her. Now they were all shallow bits of cracked nostalgia. Most people possessed the same tired, lonesome look of spacers who had left behind homeworld, family, and friends.

She paused to finger the glittering merchandise of a Naxan jeweler, though the necklaces and bracelets didn't interest her. All those years spent in cold stasis, all those trips to debris fields and disparate worlds . . . all of it the empty glories of a fool blinded by wanderlust. But she'd seen so much. Kivita touched the Juxj Star in its pouch.

She wanted to see more.

A Tannocci woman attired in a studded black skin-suit traded in cloaks, shawls, smocks, and even rare ply underthings. The fabrics glimmered as Kivita thumbed them, silky smooth and durable.

"You would look even more gorgeous in my wares." The Tannocci woman's Meh Sattan had thick glottal stops after each *e* sound. Red rouge stretched from her eyes in a thin line to her chin.

Kivita chose her words with care. "You have great stuff here, but I'm looking for any Tannocci Sages that might be aboard."

From the corner of her eye, she could see an Inheritor merchant studying her.

"Then find him with this. My relatives sewed this fine red cap, maybe just for you," the woman said, then lowered her voice. "Two cargo bays over."

Kivita scrawled two packets of Haldon bread on a computer chit and handed it to her. "Will this cover it?"

The woman took the chit and grinned. "Stay gorgeous!" She blinked three times slowly—an old Tannocci warning sign.

Kivita donned the pillbox-shaped cap, which matched her bodyglove and cape well. Leaving the aisle, she jostled through the crowd. A few hands brushed her bottom. A pimple-faced teenager bumped into her, but Kivita slapped his hand away from the pouch.

She winked. "Wasn't born last sleep cycle, you know." As the teenager fled, a figure darted behind a stall in her peripheral vision. Flesh prickling, she walked faster.

Even this far from Inheritor space, the prophets had agents searching for any sign of heretics. Sages, outlawed by the prophets, might know something about the gem.

Deeper into the hive ship, merchants from across the Cetturo Arm called out offers of Naxan sauce garnishes, Tannocci sword training, refined Freen copper, and dozens of other goods. She fought salvager instincts to inspect the best deals. In the next cargo bay, thick aromas from food stalls made Kivita's mouth water: fried Susuron algae, Haldon bread, and Bellerion reed cakes. An Aldaakian booth doled out protein slush and Touu gelatin, while an Ascali one traded jiir juice, alcohol, and bark powder.

A slight tingling irritated her scalp. Kivita's body flushed with heat, and she licked her lips. Was more alien data about to enter her thoughts? She couldn't blame it on a cryomalady anymore. Something had changed within her.

After several minutes of pushing through hungry crowds, Kivita reached the bay mentioned by the Tannocci woman. Extra mercenaries patrolled its dim-lit aisles, and refugees huddled near the bulkheads, begging passersby. Contrasting the fare offered in the previous bays, prostitutes, drug purveyors, and Sages sold their services.

"Look like you come outta a lonely, cold cryopod, honey," said a male prostitute in chaps and skinsuit. "I'll get you warm and wet real fast."

Kivita continued without answering. Other prostitutes tried to woo or beckon her along the way. Now, though, Kivita wanted only one man, and he'd rejected her. Just seeing Sar had made her feel alive again, in ways she'd thought herself long dead. Damn him.

Aldaakian armorers and tool smiths watched her pass with flat stares. One sold cryomasks for those addicted to the chilled air. Other dealers sold varieties of vapor-producing mollusks and decanters to inhale the fumes. Several spacers stumbled or lay near such stalls, no doubt having bartered away a full cargo hold for a few minutes of bliss.

At the end of the aisle, a Tannocci man in a black cloak and jumpsuit studied her with bored blue eyes.

"I'm looking for a Tannocci Sage," Kivita said in a low voice. Behind her, a mollusk-vapor addict moaned and urinated on a stall.

"So you think all Tannocci men in a Naxan hive ship might be a Sage?" he asked in a soft voice.

"No, and I don't think all Tannocci men are assholes. Are you the guy or not?"

He rubbed his chin. "Did a woman who sold you that red cap send you?"

"Yeah."

He smiled. "Then enter. I don't get as many customers like the others in this bay. The Naxans always place low-traffic merchants with these types. I am Jandeel."

Kivita stepped into a collapsible stand built from metal and canvas. The thin walls allowed little privacy. Jandeel sat at a table fashioned from a scrapped terminal, and crossed his arms.

"Now, what would a comely Inheritor like you want with a Sage?"

Hmm, how to answer . . . A Sage memorized everything he or she saw from texts, songs, poems, to starship blueprints. Though honored as scholars on Tannocci worlds, the Inheritors arrested them as heretics.

"Quickly, now, I haven't got an entire waking cycle. You dress like an urbanite, but your drawl betrays lowly origins. Farmer? Perhaps even a salvager?" Jandeel grinned.

"Yeah, yeah, you have me there. Bet you don't get many salvagers with questions about the Vim." She leaned on the table, staring at him.

Jandeel's grin faded. "The prophets have a conversion stall three cargo bays over. I'm sure they can answer your questions."

"Do I look religious? Okay, you're suspicious because I'm from Inheritor Space. But I need a Sage, not a prophet. You guys are always gathering stuff from old paper books, chits, and whatever datacores you can get your hands on."

"Yes, but few really listen." Jandeel's gaze turned hard as steel.

Kivita leaned closer and whispered. "I can write an entire crate of Haldon foodstuffs on this chit. Fortified with protein and antioxidants. I even have sugar-powdered reeds."

"You salvagers always boast. Fill out the chit now, so I'll know you are serious." Jandeel's left hand crept beneath his cloak while he scanned the aisle outside.

She did as he asked and handed it over. "C'mon, Sage. The Vim?"

Jandeel put the chit into his belt pouch. "The Inheritors claim the Vim placed humans in the Cetturo Arm to punish them for some ancient misdeed. They hope if they assemble the wreckage and debris left behind by the Vim, they can leave the Arm and rejoin them in the galactic Core."

Kivita snorted. "I'm from Haldon Prime, remember? I know all that."

Jandeel leaned so close, she smelled Naxan sauce on his breath. "What the Inheritors don't teach in their trite state programs is that the Vim were not gods. They did exist, but no one really knows why they left the Arm. The Inheritors also do not mention why humans, Ascali, and Aldaakians all breathe the same atmosphere, or why all three races have the same physiology. The same red blood, the same gravitational sensitivities."

Despite her dim surroundings, Kivita squatted beside Jandeel's chair with interest. Old fears of zealots spying one's every move made her whisper in his ear. "Go on."

Jandeel seemed to sense her trepidation, and whispered back. "Even the Kith have two arms, two legs, a head. Why? Only the Sarrhdtuu are different. Many Sages have postulated that the Sarrhdtuu are not only the Vim's ancient enemies, but may have wiped them out. The Vim may not even exist anymore. Are we in the Cetturo Arm their children or their former slaves?"

Kivita's thoughts switched to images she'd received from the Juxj Star: cryopod-filled ships, or the Ascali leaving those tubes. Kith building crystal structures, and Aldaakians with light hair on their heads. Ships hundreds of light years away, hinting at a past waiting to be discovered at the edges of her consciousness.

And the word "Cradle" repeating over and over in her mind.

"Vim datacores?" she asked, shaking away such thoughts.

Jandeel waited until five laughing prostitutes traveled down the aisle. "The Inheritors hoard them, never revealing what they find. Other humans hide them if found, like Tannocci nobles or Naxan merchants. The Aldaakians want them, but what they use them for, who knows? Only certain gifted humans can decode them, using brain waves. Have you heard of Savants?"

"No. Go on." Kivita's head tingled.

Two male Ascali mercenaries walked by. One glanced into their stall.

Jandeel fidgeted beneath his cloak. "Savants can recall a datacore's contents by touching it. Someone else must copy the information while the Savant recites it. Like a Sage."

"So that means a Savant doesn't remember all of it afterward?" she asked.

"Yes."

Kivita bit her lip. Nothing she'd received from the Juxj Star had faded from memory. "Anything else?"

"The Inheritors either kill or imprison Savants, according to rumor. Out here in Tannocci Space, some claim Savants are sheltered by the nobles. I bet you've never heard of the most famed one, since you come from an Inheritor world. Most have forgotten her name, even in my trade. A human queen from Susuron, who lived during feudal times."

A lump rose in Kivita's throat. "What was her name?"

"Terredyn Narbas, from a lineage shrouded in legend. The Inheritors executed her, the story goes. She wanted to spread knowledge contained in the datacores."

Kivita's hands shook as the tingling in her head strengthened. "Are you ..." She scanned the aisle behind them, her heart beating faster. "Are you a Thede? Will you help me?"

Sweat beads broke out on Jandeel's brow. "Help you with what? The Thedes are rebels, even in this system. Why, if an Inheritor merchant so much as heard you, you'd be reported—"

"Can you help me?" She gripped his hand. Images of the colony ships from her visions came to mind again. From Jandeel's bewildered gaze, it seemed he'd just seen the same thing in his own thoughts.

His eyes widened. "Are you a—"

A gloved hand covered Jandeel's mouth as a dagger sank into his left side.

Kivita leapt up as two hands grabbed her from behind. A cold blade touched her throat.

"You are far more pleasing to the eye now than when you wore Orstaav's polyarmor," Shekelor Thal said, withdrawing the dagger from Jandeel's side. The Sage gasped and slid from the stool. Four burly pirates in polyarmor entered the stall. One of them held a small device with a blinking screen. When the pirate turned it off, the tingling in Kivita's head stopped.

The bastards had tracked her. How?

"The Naxans will have your head if I so much as scream. Everyone knows who you are." Kivita tried not to look at Jandeel as he squirmed on the floor.

Shekelor smiled. "You flatter me, but my name is known, not my face. Cooperate, or I shall remove your fingers. Blood won't show in that pretty bodyglove you're wearing."

How had Shekelor found her here, much less escaped the confrontation over Umiracan? His purple eye ticked, as if lacking full control of his green-rigged augmentations. Shekelor's other eye stared at her with a sinister gleam.

"Yeah, you're such a charmer. Guess Sar got a good profit for me, and you're here to collect? Bind this man's wound, and I'll come as quietly as a summer snail. I know you need me alive." Kivita's nonchalant tone differed with the furious pounding of her heart.

Shekelor frowned. "Redryll is the reason I had to come to this system in the first place. If I ever find him, I shall haul that fool behind *Fanged Pauper* on a cable until he freezes in his suit. Now keep silent." He gestured to one of his men, who ripped off Jandeel's cloak and bound the dagger wound with brusque motions.

A strange hope surged through Kivita. Perhaps Sar had acted the way he did for a reason. Or the supposed deal with the pirates had gone awry. Maybe it'd all been an act. Whatever the case, it meant he wasn't Shekelor's ally, and still lived.

"I've spent two chits. The Naxans won't release my ship until I've paid." Kivita fought back a gasp as one of the pirates holding her squeezed her fingers until the joints popped.

"He told ya to plumb shut ya mouth," the pirate said.

Stalling for time, Kivita forced a smirk on her face. "And leave *Terredyn Narbas*? It's better than any ship in your little fleet, Shekelor. Why not share what I'll get for selling the Juxj Star? Hell, I'm not greedy." She hoped the Naxan mercenaries would pass the stall again.

Shekelor's three coils stretched out to her. One gripped her throat, one fondled her breasts, and one slapped her thigh, burning the skin underneath her chaps. "I am capable of treating you in many ways, Kivita Vondir. Remember that. Your ship is meaningless. What I shall get for you is beyond your meager ambitions. Now smile as if you are going to spread your legs for all of us."

She didn't struggle as they led her into the aisle. One of the pirates slapped her bottom every few moments, giving the impression they'd just purchased sex from her. Kivita finally laughed with fake merriment after the other pirate squeezed her hand again.

Shekelor led them from the dim-lit cargo bay into the adjacent one. Tannocci and Naxans sold tool kits for starship engines, modified energy dumps, and cryo equipment. A few dealt in nav computers and galley appliances. She tried to make eye contact with a few merchants; maybe they'd see her distress. But none paid her any mind.

The pirate stopped slapping her rump and rubbed it, and the other licked her cheek, his breath worse than a sewer. Kivita maintained her smile so much, her face hurt. C'mon, think of a way to escape these assholes, or cause a disturbance the mercs will notice.

Refugees filled the next bay, where three dapper Naxans in green jumpsuits with golden tassels ordered people into groups. The Naxans studied each refugee, examining mouths or ears with a handheld lamp. Since these people might starve, some sold themselves as indentured servants. Many would work in Sutaran strip mines or harvest desert vegetables on Nax. Most contracts lasted ten years, though many never returned from their postings.

"Plumb stupid bitch," the pirate who liked rubbing her said. "Our slaves could have netted some good fucking things until you ruined it all." He pinched her rump so hard, it brought tears to her eyes.

"Say, she's nice. How much?" a skinny Naxan asked Shekelor, pointing at Kivita.

Shekelor stopped with reluctance. "I purchased her for my crew. She isn't negotiable."

Kivita had to restrain herself not to shout or at least do something. But what?

One of the pirates laughed in her ear as the group continued. "Ya worth plumb more than all these skanks, Red."

Fury swelled in her chest. First chance she got, she'd cut off this scum's—

"Beautiful hair. Face to die for. How much?"

Kivita's heart stopped at the familiar voice.

Shekelor turned, a deep frown on his bisected features. "I said, she is not negotiable—" His frown became a scowl.

Someone pushed through the crowd behind them. Naxan mercenaries along the bulkheads glanced up and headed in Kivita's direction, as refugees made way.

Sar and Cheseia approached the pirate band.

Kivita had never thought he looked so handsome in his gray bodyglove and polycuirass. His brown-and-green-flecked eyes measured her with their old care, desire, and charm.

Nostrils flaring, Kivita tried to slow her excited breaths.

"Everything's negotiable around Tejuit Seven, Shekelor. Even your life." Sar's hand rested on his sword hilt. Cheseia gripped a baton.

Kivita could almost taste the tension as both pirates holding her squeezed her arms. The pain didn't register as she met Sar's eyes. Her leg muscles tensed, ready to spring.

18

"Release her," Sar said. "Naxans don't like pirates."

Kivita's heart beat with expectation, though none of the Naxan merchants or refugees gave her situation notice. More than anything, she wanted to draw her sword and lash out at her captors.

Sar shot her a warning look.

"There is nothing you can do here, Redryll." Shekelor recovered his smile and studied Cheseia for a moment. "And I am wise to your lovely Ascali's voice. The mercs will toss you from an airlock if you draw blood here."

Sar laughed, but his stare could have cracked diamonds. "Who said anything about blood?" He cleared his throat. "Fraud!"

The Naxan merchants stopped inspecting the refugees and stared at Sar. Kivita sighed with relief as the two men holding her eased their grips. Even Shekelor appeared surprised, until his face morphed into a disdainful mask.

"You don't have a—"

"Chit for her? Here it is." Sar held up a computer chit covered in glue pen notes.

Kivita's muscles tensed, and she held her breath.

Shekelor stalked toward Sar as three Naxan reps approached. Two Ascali and three human mercenaries trailed the Naxans, hands on their weapons.

"What is this about a purchase fraud? Such an insinuation is not made lightly aboard our ships," a Naxan said.

"I bought this prostitute's services before these guys took her. Got the proof right here." Sar handed the chit to the Naxan.

Coils writhing, Shekelor's lips peeled back from his teeth.

The Naxan studied the chit, glanced at Shekelor, then clicked twice with his mouth. "You?" he asked Kivita while pointing at her. "What is your name, and did this man purchase your services as he has stated?"

Kivita kept her voice level. "I'm Kivita Vondir. Yes, we made an agreement before these brutes came along."

The Naxan stepped closer and clicked four times. "To verify this, what . . . services did you offer?"

Kivita's cheeks warmed and she licked her lips. "Some damn good sex—that's what."

The Naxan studied the chit again and looked at Shekelor. "This man has a contract with this woman. Since this chit hasn't been turned in and collected, you may not interfere with that contract. Release her."

The two pirates didn't obey until Shekelor finally nodded to them; then they let go of Kivita with a shove. No way were they just going to fling her away without something in return.

Wheeling around, Kivita shoved her knuckles into one pirate's nose, crushing it with a pop. As the other reached for a weapon, Kivita slammed her knee into his groin.

Two Ascali mercenaries restrained her in grips even more formidable than Shekelor's men had, while on-lookers cleared the cargo bay. Sar drew near Kivita with a scalding stare.

The Naxan merchant raised his hands. "Violence is not tolerated in a hive-ship consortium! Remove her license for one Tejuit week. Escort her to her ship, if she has one."

Sar held up a hand. "I still have a contract with her. Prefer she fulfilled it on my ship."

The Naxan shrugged and clicked twice. "Make the best of what you've gained. Take her away."

A chill traveled up Kivita's spine after she scanned the cargo bay. Shekelor and his men had already left the area.

As the two Ascali led her back through the cargo bays she'd passed through, Sar and Cheseia walked on either side of them. His jaw tightened, but Sar didn't look at her, and no one spoke. When the group passed Jandeel's stall, the Sage wasn't lying on the floor.

"He's fine," Sar said as they wormed through a crowd of bulky Sutarans carrying trade crates.

Kivita blinked. "Jandeel? You mean—?" She hesitated, but Sar didn't answer.

Right before Shekelor's arrival, Kivita had suspected Jandeel of being a Thede, or at least a Thede sympathizer. Sar's so-called allies might be Thedes after all, not pirates. In the time they'd spent over Gontalo, he'd been critical of the Inheritors—nothing more. But suspicion darkened her relief into frustration.

She was tired of him saving her, tired of wanting him.

"So, how long will you require my services, kind sir?" she asked as they passed through the bay filled with food stalls.

"I just saved your ass, Kiv. You're welcome." Sar still avoided her eyes.

She started to retort, but one of the Ascali escorts nudged her. "Be speaking to each other once you are boarding your ship. Until then, stay being quiet."

Though the mercenary's professional but unyielding tone silenced her, Kivita glared at Sar until the sound of the drums filled her ears again. The same Naxan greeter waited near the airlock magnetized with *Terredyn Narbas*.

"Do not be entering any Naxan hive ship in this system until a Tejuit week has been passing," the other Ascali said. Both of them looked over Cheseia, murmured respectful words to her, then left.

Ignoring Sar, Kivita approached the Naxan. "Have any chits been turned in for my ship?"

"Why, yes," the Naxan replied, then made several clicking noises while operating his console. "A Tannocci garment manufacturer and a Tannocci Sage?"

"Yeah," she replied, shooting Sar a look. Someone had aided Jandeel; the wounded Sage couldn't have turned in his chit already. Who else on this damn ship was helping Sar? Once again he had her . . . but not for long.

After the Naxan keyed in the sequence for her to re-enter *Terredyn Narbas*, Kivita stomped to the bridge. Sar and Cheseia followed.

"Yeah, just come on in, make yourselves at home." She enabled the autoloader, which deposited the required goods from her cargo bay. After several minutes with no one speaking, the transaction was completed. Kivita finally regarded Sar with her coolest stare.

"I see you followed me here, just like that pirate asshole. Well, come and get it, smoothie. My services are all ready for you."

Cheseia scowled. "He has just truly saved you. You should be definitely thankful."

Kivita wanted to rub her arms and hands where the pirates had gripped her, but refused to show discomfort in front of Sar. "Oh, I'm thankful. You just made me embarrass myself in front of all those people. Plus, Shekelor's still around."

"Want to join him instead?" Sar asked. "Help yourself, sweetness. Jandeel will live; we passed him after we'd spotted you with the pirates. But what were you doing talking to a Sage, Kiv? Not your usual stop in a spaceport." He tossed the unused chit onto Kivita's hammock. A hint of worry rose in his eyes, and he looked away.

Kivita crammed her new hat and the purple cape into her locker. "Maybe I wanted to find out something."

Sar neared her, hands clenching and unclenching. "Did you ask him how the hell you managed such a shortcut from Umiracan?"

"Would you rather the journey take the full two years?" She looked away and tried to suppress a shiver. Did they know what else she could do?

Did she?

Cheseia studied Kivita with narrowed eyes. "Explain to us why you certainly stole Shekelor's ship with Seul and fled Umiracan. Why you did not answer Sar on the radio when he surely hailed you over the planet." The command in her voice dared Kivita to lie.

"Maybe the Rector was right. You got a deal with the Aldaakians, Kiv? They let you go pretty easy. Shock Troopers showed up all nice and quick, too. That almost got us killed." Sar glowered at her.

Kivita poked a finger against Sar's polycuirass. "Then

maybe you should explain all that bullshit about a deal with Shekelor. You were practically kissing his ass. For all I knew, you planned to sell me into slavery after Orstaav led me from that hall! Hell, I wanted my ship back, okay? Not my fault the Aldaakians arrived so soon."

"You knew the Aldaakians would surely be coming?" Cheseia flinched as if bitten by a wood snake.

Sar frowned. "How, with all that radiation in the Expanse? No way they'd have detected us so soon."

"The transmitter room in the fortress had Sarrhdtuu tech," Kivita said. "Seul sent out a signal, okay? I told her that her commander could have the Juxj Star for my ship. I changed my mind, though, once I neared their cruiser on *Fanged Pauper*. Seul let me escape, believe it or not."

Sar shook his head. "Lot of good it did. Seems the Aldaakians were on our trail, anyway. Dammit, I told you to trust me. I wanted Shekelor to confuse any who might be following us while we escaped the system."

"He violently tossed us into a cell after you left the hall." Cheseia smoothed her mane with frustrated strokes. "Shekelor mentioned he would certainly sell you to someone."

"The bastard was expecting us, Kiv," Sar said. "Knew your name, everything."

Kivita's guts churned. "C'mon, sell me to the Sarrhdtuu? Why?" Did her visions have anything to do with it? If what Jandeel said about Savants were true, and that story of the executed Susuron queen . . .

"Has to be the Sarrhdtuu," Sar replied. "Someone put one of their beacons on your ship, and Shekelor didn't have all those Sarrhdtuu enhancements the last time I knew him."

The vision of Sarrhdtuu torturing humans taken from a wrecked ship came to mind. Her hand bumped into Sar's, and she blinked the thought away.

Sar jerked his hand back, lips tight. Cheseia gave him a confused look.

Kivita's cheeks burned again. "Well, excuse me. Guess you don't want my services, huh? Got your Ascali beauty for that. Well, you've got your answers. Get the hell off my ship. I'm sick of your games."

"Dammit, this isn't a game!" Sar grabbed her by the shoulders. "I see things when I touch you, Kiv! Stars, planets, images I don't understand. Seeing them even now." He jerked her close. "What did Jandeel tell you? That you're a Savant?"

She'd never seen him explode with such emotion. The cold, fearful look in his eyes appeared again, and now she realized its origin: he'd feared for, and had been afraid of, her since entering the Umiracan system.

"Let go of me." Kivita trembled at his touch.

"Shekelor had a brain-pulse analyzer in his throne room. He knew what you were the whole time on Umiracan. How long have you known? Son of a bitch, Kiv. How long?" Sar's last question came out in a whisper.

"Ever since touching that datacore from Xeh's Crown, I've had headaches. Weird dreams. After touching the Juxj Star, now I see them all the time."

"Don't you understand?" Sar asked. "The Rector must've known, too. Inheritors scan all adults on a regular basis. He knew about you. You can't go back. You can't just sell that gem now."

Kivita recalled the tingling she'd felt on the hive ship, up until the pirate had turned off the small device. Jandeel's words about Inheritors executing Savants made the tremor in her stomach grow until it shook her whole body. She'd been set up for something. Something beyond her ken.

"Now you're seeing some of the things I've dreamt about since Xeh's Crown." She stared off into space as an image of Kith guarding Vstrunn entered her mind.

"Kith on Vstrunn," Sar murmured, then slowly released her. "I know a few Savants. None can put thoughts into another's mind like that."

"Jandeel's a Thede, isn't he?" Kivita stepped back from Sar. "So are both of you, right? What's happening to me? Why'd this gem choose me?"

"Wish I knew," Sar replied.

Cheseia plopped on the floor and jerked her mane from its headband. "You will never be truly free of enemies again, Kivita. Sar, we should definitely leave Tejuit and take her to the Thedes."

"She's right, Kiv. Until the Arm is free of the Inheritors, you'll never be safe. The Thedes are the only ones you can turn to now."

Kivita blew out a breath, rattling her lips. "Wait right there. Since leaving Vstrunn, you two have dragged me across the light years. Wow, now you've saved me twice. But this is me you're talking about, not just this damn gem anymore. If we go anywhere, I'll be the one deciding."

"With that Sarrhdtuu beacon on this ship? They'll track you all over the Arm. Longer we stay here, sooner they'll find you." Sar's face fell, as if all the years he'd spent in cryostasis now weighed down on him. Cheseia, though vibrant with typical Ascali vitality, possessed haggard eyes. Maybe they really intended her no harm and wanted her safe.

Sar paced Kivita's quarters. "Shekelor will be watch-

ing out for us. Need to lose him somehow. Need to scrap
or hack your beacon, too. Don't know how myself, but
we're a meteor running from a supernova until it's deactivated. They will catch you."

"I'm not ditching *Terredyn Narbas*," Kivita said.

"We need to leave this hive ship." Sar looked straight
at Kivita. "You help the Thedes, it'll bolster resistance in
the Arm. There might be some information in the Juxj
Star to bring this war into the open. This won't be a salvager run, Kiv, with a big payment at the end. The Inheritors will want you dead afterward. Will you help us?"

Kivita studied the old placard of her with her father.
What would he think of his daughter being a Savant?
Now she was the salvage everyone desired, the most
wanted individual in the Cetturo Arm. That meant she
needed friends, allies. Her gaze bored into Sar.

"What if I won't help the Thedes? Will you refuse to
help me then? I need to know, both of you: does your
friendship depend on what I can do for you? If it does,
then just go. The airlock's right there." Kivita crossed
her arms.

Cheseia rose, her beautiful features pinched in anger.
"You unfortunately accuse us too much! Why would we
truly save you if all we wanted—"

Sar touched Cheseia's shoulder. "Kiv's right to ask.
You know what I hope you'll do, sweetness. But if you
don't want to help the Thedes, hell, I'll still help you any
way I can."

"Will you? You once told me that no one with an
agenda could be trusted." Kivita pursed her lips.

"Trust me like you did in the old days," Sar said.

Cheseia pushed Sar's hand away and faced the airlock, her jaw set.

"First we lose Shekelor Thal . . . then I'll decide." In truth, Kivita preferred the Thedes over the Inheritors, but she wouldn't be used. You don't waste air on a fair-weather crew.

"Good enough. Cheseia, care to find some refugees who want to earn a crate of foodstuffs?" He didn't take his gaze off Kivita. The way his eyes roved over her, the glimmer in them . . . it was the same way he'd looked at her when she'd wore those flashy clothes on *Frevyx*.

"What for?" A flush came over Kivita.

Sar smirked. "Diversion."

"I will definitely meet you back at *Frevyx*'s airlock in a few minutes," Cheseia said in a low voice, then exited *Terredyn Narbas*'s airlock into the hive ship.

As soon as the airlock slid shut, Kivita wanted to ask Sar so many questions, but none of them reached her lips. Chest tight, her eyes roved everywhere and paused on her hammock. His computer chit still lay there—a promise at future passion she doubted either of them would keep.

Kivita bit her lip and rubbed her hands. The knuckles on her right hand still shone red from breaking the pirate's nose. As she walked to the bridge, Sar took her hands and rubbed them himself. His fingers kneaded the soreness from her joints and digits. The flush on her skin blazed into a furnace at his touch.

"Sar, don't—"

"Salvagers need good hands. Gripping the manuals, using excavation tools." He studied her hands, not looking up.

Kivita took shallow breaths. Saliva filled her mouth. His fingers caressed her skin the same way he'd done over Gontalo. As much as she adored his attention, Kivita wanted to shoulder her own pain.

"I'm not the same lonely salvager you teamed with at Xeh's Crown," she said. "I can survive whatever this universe throws at me. But I'm sick of wanting you back, sick of needing you. Sometimes I hate you for it. Don't you understand?"

Her lips quivered as he continued massaging her hands. Sar said nothing.

"You're not being fair to Cheseia. I see her love for you in her eyes. Doesn't that make you feel guilty?" Her question came out as a whine.

Sar pulled her close, still looking down. Heat flooded her body.

"You can't save me every time, Sar. Sometimes I don't want you to. Are you listening to me?" She reached up and tilted his chin until his gaze finally met hers. "I don't want you to."

"What about right now?" he asked.

Kivita kissed him on the lips.

Her fingers ran through his black curls; her thighs rubbed against his. Cupping his face in both hands, she tasted the pseudoadrine residue in his mouth as their tongues writhed. Her nipples tingled while her legs rubbed against each other in eager anticipation. A hungry moan traveled up her throat.

Sar didn't touch or embrace her.

Moaning deeper, she sucked his lower lip, squeezed his rump, and swished her tongue farther into his luscious mouth. Kivita loved and hated him in the same moment. Wanted him to feel her pain, her passion. She would make him want her; just a few more kisses, a little more touching. All the hurt from being left alone, all the tenderness she'd saved just for him, gushed from Kivita.

He pulled back, lips moist from her kisses.

Her skin cooled in an instant, and she turned away. "Guess you cashed in that chit."

Sar grasped her by the shoulders and made her face him. "Don't you understand? Every time we touch, I see those things. It hurts my own brain, trying to break down these images and sensations. How you manage it, I don't know. Guess the universe is telling you what I've always known."

Kivita trembled in his grasp. Their bodies were so close, yet light years away. "Yeah. What's that?"

"That you're one special woman."

Shivering, she pushed away. "Don't. Nothing will change once this is over. I know you."

"Kiv . . ."

"I loved you once. It already isn't easy to want you so much, but then to be told I can't even touch you now? Goddamn pirates didn't seem to mind." She bit off the last words to keep from sobbing.

Sar pressed her against his chest. "That's bullshit! I try to tell you how much I . . . But you just keep being so damn fickle." He shoved her away and stormed toward the airlock.

Kivita ran after him and barred the airlock doors with her arm. "The hell I am! Just tell me one thing. Did you feel anything while sleeping in the cryopod with me from Vstrunn?"

He tugged her aside; she'd forgotten how strong he was.

"Anything at all?" she asked, voice thick with emotion.

He reached for the airlock lever.

"Goddammit, did you?" she cried.

Kivita tried to bar him again, but Sar wrapped an

arm around her waist and kissed her. While his fingers brushed through her hair, Kivita squeezed herself to him. She languished against his chest after their lips finally parted. A long moment passed with him rubbing her back, her inhaling his scent.

The emotions inside wanted to spill out and drown him, cleanse them both of ill feelings and lost time. Kivita tightened her hold. The universe had taken so much from her—her parents, her career. Sar could still be hers, if she just—

He gently pushed her back and wiped tears from her cheeks. Before Kivita could say anything, he hit the airlock lever and left *Terredyn Narbas*.

"I know you did," she whispered.

19

Kivita hit the speaker button on the bridge console. "Yeah, Sar?" Her voice came out sure and strong, contrasting the uncertainties in her heart.

"Shekelor will be watching for you to leave the system. I've got a way to lose him; then we'll discuss plans." Sar's voice sounded flat, unemotional. She wished she didn't love him.

"You mentioned a diversion?"

"Kivita, I truly hired three humans," Cheseia's smooth voice came over the speakers. "They have happily agreed to help us before we demagnetize airlocks."

"Going to ditch a few food crates in the refugee fleet traffic," Sar said. "With commotion on both the hive ship and in the orbital lanes, we'll make for the exit lanes. Our beacon signals should get mixed with all the other ships there, and we'll escape during the confusion."

Kivita snorted. "Sounds like an insane plan. We'll never be allowed back in this system again."

"It's either this or abandon your ship, sweetness," Sar replied. She imagined him smirking. Damn, he was such an asshole!

"Fine, whatever. Ready when you are." Kivita strapped

herself into the gyro harness and turned off *Terredyn Narbas*'s gravity. Several red and orange lights blinked on the console, reminding her of the damage the ship had suffered over Umiracan. Her chest tightened.

"Kiv...keep up. You're more important than you know," Sar said.

Important to him or his ragtag rebellion?

Kivita took a deep breath and demagnetized *Terredyn Narbas* from the hive ship. Nudging the manuals, she edged away from the Naxan collection of vessels and waited.

Outside her viewport, dozens of Inheritor, Tannocci, and Naxan ships passed in an orbital traffic lane around Tejuit Seven. She counted three ships across, five ships deep. Although it was originally done for protection against pirates, she'd heard that some ships magnetized with others and never departed the system again. Families and renegades dwelling in fluctuating gravities, exiled to a blue, green, and pink horizon of uncertainty.

She closed her eyes and inhaled again. To what horizon was she flying now?

Sar's voice crackled over the speaker. "You might hear some Naxan radio chatter, but try to keep the channel open."

Kivita rolled her eyes. "Great. Let me know when something happens."

Three hundred feet away, an Inheritor transport docked to the Naxan hive ship demagnetized and drifted away. Then a Tannocci cruiser did the same. Both ships drew near the orbital fleet traffic. Unease crawled up Kivita's spine.

"What the hell? Sar, got two ships here, ready to collide with the—"

Sar's voice blared from the speaker. "Those people I hired released these ships for us. Wasn't cheap, either. Try to follow my lead."

Before she snapped back a reply, *Frevyx* skimmed past her port-side viewport, aft thrusters flaring. Naxan traffic controllers spoke over her speaker on an open channel.

"Attention! Two unmanned vessels have departed Naxan Consortium Fifteen Delta and are on a collision course with traffic over Sector TJ-Seven-One-Eight. Repeat, two vessels . . ."

Kivita flew after *Frevyx* as the two unpiloted craft entered the traffic lane. Incoming ships veered in every direction to avoid collision, and numerous thrusters fired throughout the traffic, resembling small starbursts. She squinted and dove under a cargo barge angling to starboard. *Terredyn Narbas* shuddered; more red lights activated on her console.

"Sar! You crazy ass!" she called into her mic.

Pulling the manuals back, Kivita fired all port-side thrusters. *Terredyn Narbas* evaded two incoming craft as they avoided the rogue Inheritor transport, while the rogue Tannocci cruiser slowed under the planet's gravity well. Two refugee vessels stalled and cut their engines. More craft swerved around the growing obstacle.

Ahead, *Frevyx* dove around three refugee ships, then ascended between two Inheritor barges. Backwash from its thrusters dusted the ships' hulls. Kivita shrugged and, without even glancing at her proximity readings, copied Sar's maneuvers with ease. Smirking, she increased engine power and corkscrewed around eight refugee craft.

Naxan traffic controllers practically screamed through the speakers.

"Yeah, let's see you top that." Her smirk fell as three craft flew in tandem with her, and three with *Frevyx*.

Off to port, *Fanged Pauper* mirrored her movements. *Frevyx*'s thrusters flared, and Kivita activated hers, as well. Shekelor's ships kept pace as a new grouping of orbital traffic came up ahead. She deactivated life support and heating aboard *Terredyn Narbas*, save for the bridge. With slightly more engine power, Kivita gunned her trawler straight into the traffic.

"Kiv, pull up," Sar's voice broke in between Naxan warnings.

She winced while her port-side braking thruster, damaged over Umiracan, sputtered. *Terredyn Narbas* wobbled as traffic sped past.

"Pull up!" Sar shouted.

"Dump the cargo!" she shouted back into the mic.

Refugee and Inheritor ships flew out of the traffic ahead, though longer Tannocci ships tried to maintain course. Kivita swerved starboard, port, then starboard again. She braked the port thrusters and pulled the manuals back as three crates tumbled from *Frevyx*'s loading bay.

One port-side braking thruster lost all power. *Terredyn Narbas* jerked toward a Tannocci cruiser.

"Kiv!" Sar called, but she pulled the manuals and wove right between *Fanged Pauper* and the two other pirate ships. One pirate vessel swerved toward the other. A bright flash almost blinded Kivita as the ships smashed into each other.

Terredyn Narbas's proximity alarm rang as debris banged against its starboard hull. Kivita flinched as a chunk struck and cracked her starboard viewport. Without slowing, she closed the damaged viewport's blast cover. Some oxygen sucked out into space, making her breaths labored.

Fanged Pauper swerved at her port-side hull, but Kivita dived just as more ships sped past in the orbital lane. *Fanged Pauper* now flew on her starboard side. Five other craft had slowed to examine Sar's dropped crates.

One of the damaged pirate vessels limped into Tejuit Seven's orbit, its thrusters crushed. The other pirate craft floated in place, its port-side hull ripped open. Small forms floated in the void.

A pirate craft tailing *Frevyx* slowed until it flew parallel with her port-side hull, with *Fanged Pauper* on the other. Both ships drew closer, sandwiching *Terredyn Narbas*. All three formed a triumvirate of doom while orbital traffic veered as a whole into Tejuit Seven's upper atmosphere.

Sweat rolled down Kivita's face. The harness dug into her skin, stretched taut from rising G-forces. There really was nowhere she could go without being followed.

"He's not buying it, Sar," Kivita said.

Fanged Pauper came even closer, its port-side airlock linking up with her single, starboard-side one. The pirate ship on her port side drew in, keeping her from pulling away. Below, traffic resumed, preventing her from diving.

Warning lights bathed the bridge in red shades as her ship jolted. Her stomach fluttered; *Fanged Pauper* had activated its gravity fluxer.

"He's going to board me, Sar!" Kivita started to pull up, but the vessel on her port side fired its starboard thrusters. An integrity alarm rang in her ears.

"Kiv, try to pull forward—" Sar's voice cut off as a

green beam darted past her viewport. It struck one of the pirate craft flanking *Frevyx*, cutting straight into the hull behind the bridge. Debris and bodies flew out as the ship careened away.

The speaker buzzed. "Kivita, this is Seul Jaah. Hang on; we have those pirates in our sights."

Heart leaping into her throat, Kivita gripped the manuals and increased speed. "Seul?"

The clank and suction of *Fanged Pauper*'s airlock joining with hers echoed through her ship. Kivita increased the onboard gravity to high-G. The gyro harness bit through her bodyglove as she sank toward the floor.

Air levels dropped as someone forced her airlock open.

Terredyn Narbas shuddered again. The ship on her port side came even closer.

Through the viewport, *Frevyx* blasted toward the exit lanes. A green beam hit the last pirate craft trailing Sar's ship; the vessel spun into a Sutaran saucer in a shower of debris.

Heavy, booted steps reverberated from Kivita's airlock chamber.

"They're inside my ship!" she yelled into the mic.

Kivita drew her kinetic pistol, but under high-G, the gun seemed to weigh fifty pounds. Her right biceps bulged, but the weapon clanged to the floor.

"The Sarrhdtuu will give me my own world for you, Kivita Vondir," Shekelor's cultured voice came from her quarters. "Make it easier on yourself. The Sarrhdtuu shan't care if I deliver you without your arms and legs."

"Kiv, hold on!" Sar yelled over the speaker. Ahead, *Frevyx* slowed and ascended.

"Almost there, Kivita," Seul said.

Through the forward viewport, two orbiting asteroids drew near.

Kivita squirmed in her gyro harness as *Terredyn Narbas* continued along the gas giant's curvature. In her struggles, the Juxj Star rolled from her pouch, pulled out by the high-G.

Three coils grasped the bridge doorway just as Kivita caught the gem in her right hand.

Shekelor's coils lashed around her right arm, and his smile shone through his envirosuit's faceplate. His mismatched eyes glared death.

"Get off my ship, you son of a—" Kivita screamed as Shekelor yanked her arm out of socket.

"Bitch? My mother means nothing. My son means everything." Shekelor's coils pulled again.

Chest heaving, Kivita tasted bile in her throat, and the high-G seemed to mash her organs to the floor. Blazing, tearing pain traveled up her arm. The viewport became a raging blur of lights.

Through it all, she still held the Juxj Star.

Kivita recalled things the gem had revealed, then met Shekelor's stare. All became focused, attuned. Forceful. Kivita showed him the vastness of space outside the Cetturo Arm. The flurry of coordinates; the awesome alien vistas. Crammed it into his mind, drowning his thoughts with the invasive knowledge the Juxj Star had given.

The coils relaxed their grip as Shekelor gaped at her. Grunting, he tried to retract his coils.

With high-G hampering her every move, Kivita maintained her stare. Cold pain pressed in on her temples and her forehead numbed, but she focused the raw data into him. Even without touching Shekelor, she sensed it rattle his brain.

Agony rippled through her skull. Oh, shit; couldn't hold the data flow, couldn't control it! She groaned and spasmed. The pirates would still capture her. If only she could demagnetize from *Fanged Pauper*.

Kivita thought about shoving the manuals down.

Terredyn Narbas climbed at a sharp angle.

"Stop! Get out—" Shekelor fell back through the bridge doorway. His coils wrenched from her arm, and Kivita cried out. Concussive popping noises sounded from the airlock. As both asteroids grew larger in her viewport, Kivita slammed the gravity controls and wanted the ship to dive.

Terredyn Narbas dived of its own volition.

Alarms invaded her ears. Pure static blared from the console speaker. *Terredyn Narbas* hummed in her mind, while the tingling numbed her skull.

On her port side, the other pirate vessel smacked into both asteroids. A brutal dismantling of hull, engine, and flung bodies accompanied a brief dust ball.

Even in her gyro harness, Kivita smacked into the bridge wall as gravity returned to normal. Her left leg flared with pain. Groans and curses came from her quarters, *Fanged Pauper* ground into her starboard hull with earsplitting noises. She unbuckled herself with the quick-release button, grabbed her pistol, and stumbled into her quarters.

"Kivita, report your status," Seul's worried voice came over the speaker.

Shekelor started to stand as Kivita cracked her left polyboot into his right side. Two pirates rose from the floor, pointing guns, but Kivita fired point-blank into one's faceplate. Blood and melted polymer dusted her bulkheads. She aimed at the other pirate, but *Terredyn Narbas* tilted. The pirate ducked and shoved his gun into her stomach, then aimed it at her head.

"Disarm her!" Shekelor stood up.

The pirate rammed his armored knee into Kivita's gut. A terrible ache spread through her abdomen.

The pirate she'd shot rose, half his olive-tinted face shot away. "Plumb stupid bitch, ya should—"

Fanged Pauper finally demagnetized from *Terredyn Narbas*'s airlock with a pop and a whoosh. Decompression yanked them all off the deck, but Kivita gripped the end of her hammock. Sharp agony traveled from her fingers up to her dislocated shoulder. Air sucked from the cabin, and the vacuum pulled the mangled pirate with irresistible force through the airlock. His scream ended as the void claimed him.

Shekelor, coils wound around the airlock lever, sneered. "The Sarrhdtuu have ways of reviving the coldest-hearted bitch, Kivita. Go ahead, let go. You cannot escape."

As the second pirate neared the airlock, his form blocked the vacuum suction for an instant.

Kivita leapt toward Shekelor and fired. The shot blasted through two of his coils, breaking his grip on the lever. Landing beside him, she kicked him away and clutched the lever.

In the next second, the pirate clattered through the airlock. With the opening unblocked, the suction ripped Shekelor into space. Kivita's body lifted off the floor toward the airlock. Air was ripped from her lungs. Awful cold numbed her skin. A few more feet, and she'd be lost out there forever . . .

She pressed the lever.

The doors slid shut just as her boots clanked against them. She fell onto the floor, knocking what breath remained from her body. Blood bubbled from her lips. She coughed, bringing up more.

Kivita gasped with suffocating fright, since most of the cabin's air had emptied into space. She forced herself up, right arm numb. From a nearby locker she snatched a breath mask and breathed deep. The vacuum quiet seemed to last forever, until a faint buzzing tickled her ears. The sound grew louder until her ears popped back to normal in the repressurized cabin.

Sar's yell echoed from the speaker on the bridge. "Kiv? Kiv! Dammit, I'm coming aboard!"

She staggered onto the bridge and leaned against the console. With numb fingers she turned all of *Terredyn Narbas*'s life-support systems back on and activated the mic.

"I'm ..." She gasped, then sucked in more air from the mask. "I'm okay. Shekelor's taking the ... long way to Umiracan." Wheezing, Kivita strapped the mask on before she fainted from lack of air.

"Your old trawler is listing starboard, toward the gas giant. Can you trail me, at least from its gravity well?"

Kivita's breathing regulated, but as adrenaline wore off, her stomach throbbed. She coughed; blood splattered the inside of her mask. She ripped it off as life support resumed normal levels.

"With my eyes closed," she whispered.

Slumped over the manuals, Kivita forced herself into the seat. The Juxj Star rolled against her right boot. The fact that the gem hadn't been sucked into space gave her a chill.

Through the viewport, *Frevyx* reappeared above her and blasted away from Tejuit Seven. Kivita flew after them as Cheseia's voice came over the speaker.

"We must definitely leave the system, Kivita. The Naxans have sent their mercenary transports to investigate, and Inheritor ships are unfortunately everywhere."

Kivita glanced out the viewport and almost let go of the manuals. The two asteroids and crushed pirate ship had lumped together into scrap and dust particles. *Fanged Pauper* limped to the other side of Tejuit Seven, leaving several floating forms in its wake.

"I need . . ." Kivita bit back a groan, barely staying in the harness. Her right arm, left leg, forehead, and stomach all came alive with renewed agony.

Seul's voice popped from the console speaker. "Kivita? I've been ordered back to *Aldaar*, so please follow my coordinates. My people can help you. I want to help you."

Three Inheritor battle cruisers appeared over the gas giant's horizon.

The speaker crackled. "All human craft seek shelter in sector TJ-Five-Three-Zero. Inheritor ships have been deployed for your safety against Aldaakian aggression." The arrogant voice brought a cacophony of protest over the radio channels.

Two more Inheritor warships appeared.

Terredyn Narbas shuddered and new warning lights lit up the console. Two starboard thrusters were gone. The port-side hull had lost its outer layer of iron-polymer coating.

"Give me some coordinates, Sar," Kivita said on a direct channel to *Frevyx*.

"Too late for that. Inheritor military is in the system now. Every one of their ships will have locked on to your beacon. If Shekelor hadn't given such a chase, we might've made it. Didn't expect such craziness, even from him. Must want you bad."

"Yeah, a gal likes to be popular." Kivita clutched her aching stomach. The movement sent fresh waves of pain up her right arm. "Listen, I'm pretty banged up, but I can still make a light jump. Send your coordinates."

"Kivita, it is simply too late. They will certainly trail your beacon," Cheseia said in an aggravated tone.

A knot formed in her stomach along with the pain. She slammed the console button. "I'm not leaving *Terredyn Narbas*!"

"Then let me pilot her. You and Cheseia take *Frevyx* to the coordinates." Sar paused. "Coming alongside now. Two merc ships are nearing the pirate wreckage. They'll be after us next."

"No, I won't—"

The speaker replied with static.

"Sar?" A wet cough ended her protest. Crimson droplets spattered her terminal.

She knew he spoke truth, but abandoning *Terredyn Narbas* again cut her heart with a dull knife. She glanced down at the Juxj Star. Gritting her teeth against the pain, she put it back into her pouch.

Within moments, after her airlock magnetized with his, Sar rushed in, wearing two pistols and a tooled leather satchel. Upon seeing her, his face fell.

"Your arm . . ."

"I'll make it," she said, but he touched her forehead, smoothed her hair, felt her neck. This time, she caught a slight reaction every time he contacted her. After forcing raw data into Shekelor's mind, Kivita realized Sar's struggle.

"Hold still." Sar reached for her right shoulder.

"Hell, no—" She bit her bodyglove sleeve to keep from screaming while he pushed the dislocated arm back into place. Hot dampness flooded her crotch. Tears misted her eyes, but she restrained a wail. He had to see she was strong, no matter what. Breathing faster, she glanced up at his face without wincing.

"Cheseia's ready; I've already keyed in the coordinates. Any trackers will follow me in *Terredyn Narbas*. And there will be trackers, Kiv." Sar looked her in the eye. "Damn it, take care of yourself. I swear this ship will be fine—don't worry. But you listen to Cheseia; she'll help. Promise me." The fear in his voice sunk like a stone into her heart.

"But when will we link up?"

He looked away.

She grabbed his collar with her good hand. "Don't you dare! Don't sacrifice yourself for—"

"I'll find you." The tremor in his voice stopped her heart. Sar hefted her into his arms and carried her to the airlock. Cheseia helped her through *Frevyx*'s airlock, but Kivita stopped.

"Sar, take good care of her, will you?" She fought back fresh tears and kept her voice firm.

"Hope she's not as fickle as her owner." He smiled sadly and squeezed her hand.

Kivita wanted to pull him along with her, but Sar released her hand and backed into *Terredyn Narbas*. The vacuum outside nipped at her skin as Tejuit Seven's multicolored atmosphere reflected in his eyes. She wet her lips.

"Sar, I—"

Both airlocks slid shut.

20

Dunaar paced before the bridge viewport while Stiego and his officers watched with tense faces lit by red and blue console screens. Outside, the traffic lanes orbiting Tejuit Seven had slowed to a crawl. Dozens of ships had already left the system after Captain Stiego's wideband announcement. Dunaar smiled. Let the gnats escape. Soon there would be nowhere to run to.

"Rector, *Terredyn Narbas*'s beacon is still broadcasting in this system." A hologram emitted from Stiego's monocle, showing Kivita's ship a short distance from the gas giant. "Surely, if we act now—"

"It takes cool resolve to achieve our goals, Captain. Kivita Vondir must depart without our involvement. Then we will follow her to the Thedes." Dunaar ran his sweaty palm over the Scepter of Office. "What is the status of our blockade?"

Stiego's monocle hologram flickered and displayed a diagram of the system. "Two cruisers have taken position near the jump lanes, preventing further egress from Tejuit. One cruiser is in pursuit of the Aldaakian ship we spotted earlier. Our other two cruisers are maintaining order in the traffic lanes."

"And the Naxans?"

"Three hive ships have agreed to await inspection by our boarding parties, but six have split up and have made for the jump lanes," Stiego replied. "There is nowhere they can go, though. The system is ours, Rector."

Dunaar swept his gaze over the pathetic panorama. Yes, the system was theirs, but the sight of so many rebels, heretics, and petty nobles sent a pang into his heart. None of these people had to live like this. Residing on outdated starships, orbiting a beautiful but worthless gas giant. How many children on those ships could be fed by Haldon grain and tutored by wise prophets? How many could he save by taking them to the young yellow stars in the Core?

By the Vim, he would see it done. As long as he had the strength to do what was necessary.

"Captain, order those cruisers policing the traffic lanes to target a few random Aldaakian craft and destroy them."

Within seconds, the order passed to the Inheritor battle cruisers. From his vantage point, Dunaar glimpsed small flashes and hurtling debris. Stiego's monocle hologram projected data sent back from their cruisers: four Aldaakian merchant ships and two frigates destroyed.

One did not lead by mere words. Sometimes people had to be shown what they should fear, and whom they should beseech for salvation.

"That is sufficient. I shall—"

A terminal beeped, interrupting him.

"Rector, I have just received a report from our fleet at Bons Sutar," Stiego said, his monocle hologram deactivating. The bridge officers perked up with expectant eyes.

"Finally, some news from that treacherous Tannocci strongpoint." Launching campaigns across the light years tested even his patience.

"The system has been taken, though casualties have been heavy." Stiego's right eye twitched.

"Of course those Sutaran brutes would fight well. Give me the numbers," Dunaar said.

"Out of the thirty-five thousand troops sent, sixteen thousand were killed or wounded. An additional two thousand are still unaccounted for."

The bridge staff blanched. Stiego's shoulders sagged slightly.

Dunaar clasped the Scepter in both hands and took a deep breath. "We shall not forget those brave men. When we reach the Core, we will reunite with them there, bathed in the Vim's light. The Sutarans have joined our cause. It is up to us to bring as many as we can when the time for departure arrives. The Sutaran losses, Captain?"

A mirthless smile stole over Stiego's face. "More than two hundred thousand insurgents have been eliminated, Rector. Internment camps have been set up as you requested. Their quotas, at the time of this message, were full."

The pang in Dunaar's heart lessened as he stared out the viewport again. One of the tiny points of light out there was *Terredyn Narbas*. Sweat dripped down his chest, rolled down his cheeks. Any moment now, Kivita would lead him to his destiny.

"Where're we going?" Sitting on the bench outside *Frevyx*'s bridge, Kivita coughed again. Blood speckles stained her hand.

"To hopefully see Navon and the Thedes." While she sealed the viewports and activated the light jump, Cheseia fidgeted. Did she know what she was doing?

Frevyx shuddered and departed the Tejuit system.

"You didn't want him to do this, did you?" A knot of emotion strangled Kivita, knowing millions of miles now separated her from Sar.

Cheseia stepped into the crew quarters and stripped down to her breechcloth. Lamps along the ceiling and floors winked out in the galley and bridge while *Frevyx's* air chilled as the heating system relented its output.

Kivita shambled to the cryo-chamber doorway and blocked Cheseia. "Did you?"

Cheseia's russet eyes burned into Kivita. "Your bridge mic was still on after I truly left *Terredyn Narbas*. When I boarded *Frevyx* to unload payment for the three humans, I unfortunately heard some of your . . . conversation."

"Yeah, so? Maybe I wanted something you've taken from me." Kivita tried to straighten, but the pain in her stomach made her double over. She hacked up blood again.

"You are so truly foolish and ungrateful." Cheseia lifted Kivita as if she were a child, then leaned her against the medical cabinet. "You will speedily receive proper treatment once we reach our destination. I hope these thogens will definitely stop your internal bleeding."

Kivita swallowed the thogen powder after Cheseia spooned it into her mouth. Neither said anything. Cheseia's bosom rose with sharp breaths.

"How long have you loved him?" Kivita asked.

They gazed at each other for a tense moment.

"Certainly not as long as you," Cheseia finally replied,

face drawn with anxiety. "He surely knows my feelings. Which makes it tragically hurt all the more when I saw how he looked at you."

"I don't need him. I don't want him." Kivita forced down a sob. No way in hell she'd cry in front of Cheseia.

"He truly wants you." Cheseia's furred fists clenched. "Sar would definitely never have gone to Vstrunn, never gone to Umiracan, certainly never stayed at Tejuit, but for you!"

Before Kivita could reply, Cheseia lifted her carefully in both arms and carried her into the cryo chamber. Running lights winked out in the corridor behind them.

"I didn't ask for him to," Kivita muttered.

"Sar told me you and I truly deserve better than him. If not for him, I certainly would . . ."

"Jettison me out the damn airlock? C'mon, just say it." Kivita glared.

Cheseia stiffened and said nothing as they entered the chamber. The same cryopod she'd slept in with Sar awaited Kivita, hatch already open. As Cheseia set Kivita inside, the movement sent painful shockwaves up her right arm and left leg. Kivita gasped and tensed, which made her stomach throb anew.

"Bet you like seeing me like this," Kivita rasped.

Cheseia gave her a flat stare. Her furred hands trembled over the cryopod's console.

Kivita started to say more, but Cheseia shook and closed her eyes. Before, she'd refused to believe anyone loved Sar as much as she did. Refused to admit the pain she'd seen in Cheseia's eyes. Now, with Cheseia nearing an emotional breakdown, the truth shamed Kivita.

"I'm sorry," Kivita whispered. The thogens slurred her words, blurred her vision.

"So am I. Soon you will truly understand." Cheseia swallowed and shut the hatch. While *Frevyx*'s lights winked out altogether, Kivita glimpsed the Ascali wiping her eyes inside her cryopod. So she hadn't wanted to cry in front of Kivita, either.

As she closed her eyes, cold, black sleep stole over Kivita's consciousness.

In her mind, an ancient ship crash-landed on Susuron. Ocean waves rose and receded. Grains of sand as numerous as the stars sank beneath her naked feet.

Forgoing the gyro harness, Sar hurried into *Terredyn Narbas*'s pilot seat. On the console scanner, *Frevyx* made a light jump and vanished. He knew it would take Kivita and Cheseia one Haldon day to reach *Luccan's Wish*, the Thede ship waiting just outside the Tejuit system.

"I had to lie, Kiv," he whispered, gripping the manuals. Sar had no idea when he'd really see her again, if ever. She wouldn't have understood. Maybe he didn't, either.

Behind *Terredyn Narbas*, the Naxan merc ships had completed their examination of the pirate and asteroid debris. A Naxan voice came over the console speaker, but Sar muted it.

Terredyn Narbas protested his commands, creaks and groans reverberating throughout the ship. Judging from the damage he'd seen while on *Frevyx*, Kivita's old trawler shouldn't even be together, let alone fly.

While prepping the ship for a light jump, Sar reviewed his options. In no way could he follow *Frevyx*, at least not from Tejuit. The nearest systems—Wraith Star, Ecrol, Senul Tur, and Soleno—offered no refuge. Someone would follow, and he'd no idea how to disengage the Sarrhdtuu beacon.

Orbital traffic scattered as a large Inheritor battleship and five battle cruisers formed an erstwhile blockade. Sar's brow furrowed. Wherever he went, these bastards followed.

Many Aldaakian craft, including the cruiser and its shuttles, had fled. What was Seul's agenda, and why had she blasted those pirate ships? He believed Kivita when she'd claimed no deal had been made with the Aldaakians, but something was up.

"Can't do anything sitting here," he muttered. With luck, everyone in the system had detected his beacon signal. The quicker he left and their enemies tracked him, the better chance Kivita and Cheseia had of making it.

Terredyn Narbas was too damaged to pull off any fancy maneuvers, much less evade an airlock link. Sar ran several coordinates through his mind, rejecting each set in turn, until one set made him pause. The coordinates would lead just outside the Tejuit system, perhaps an hour in light jump. Sar had never remembered these coordinates before.

Not until Kivita had kissed him earlier.

Sar sealed the other viewports, keyed the coordinates, then hit the jump button. The ship shook, and red warning lights lit up the darkened bridge. The engine screeched. He held a breath and didn't move. A full minute passed before the trawler shuddered into the jump.

"Need some new equipment, sweetness," he mumbled.

Images of derelicts floating in unknown systems flashed in his mind. What had Kiv done to him? He'd managed to resist its flow during those wonderful moments before leaving the hive ship. Moments lost to him now.

Terredyn Narbas's engine groaned, and the entire ship trembled. Bulkheads popped with pressure changes.

Sar ran to Kivita's lockers and pulled out a breath mask and cold lamp just as the gravity changed to low-G. He floated off the floor. Grabbing the locker door to anchor himself, he put the mask on. A proximity alarm rang from the bridge. Sar braced himself for impact or disintegration.

Nothing happened.

Sar pulled himself along the bulkheads, using regularly spaced handles for such situations. With excruciating slowness, he reentered the bridge. Each breath came out long and deep, just like he'd been trained. Red and yellow warning lights bathed him in shades of terror.

The console displayed a large asteroid field, hanging listless in the infinite space between systems. Sar unsealed the bridge viewports and stared.

Terredyn Narbas flew amid the interstellar rocks, with the closest three thousand miles away. He sighed, thankful the coordinates had been accurate. By all rights, he should have slammed into an asteroid.

Sar almost laughed at his luck until a glimmer caught his eye.

A small life capsule floated two hundred feet away from *Terredyn Narbas*. Its cylindrical golden-meld hull reflected distant starlight back at him. Unlike standard life capsules, this one emitted no beacon distress signal. He'd heard of only feudal ones with such a hull.

"Must've been royalty," he murmured.

The console gave an awful beep.

"Shit." Sar ran a diagnostics check: the engine had

ceased working, two-thirds of *Terredyn Narbas*'s thrusters were inactive, and he had life support for only eight Haldon days.

With deliberate keystrokes he routed all the ship's power to the cryo chamber and Kivita's single cryopod. The console and terminal both darkened, the viewports sealed. Sar flicked on the handheld lamp and pulled himself along the handholds from the bridge.

Terredyn Narbas floated dark, silent, and cold in the asteroid field.

Sar's breathing escalated. He might never be found out here. Millennia might pass, the engine power would deplete, and he'd die in cryostasis. Frozen forever like Niaaq Aldaar, the Aldaakian legend. The Inheritors would crush the Thedes, and Kivita would never know his fate. She'd spiral through space, running until her enemies found her. He wouldn't be around to save her.

Hyperventilating, Sar snatched after the next handhold. Quick, before he froze to death, before Kivita went too far and got herself in too deep and—

"Stop, damn you," he whispered to himself upon reaching her quarters.

Sar took slow, deep breaths, casting the fears from his mind, willing himself to stop shaking. He'd known the risks. Known them when he'd squeezed Kivita's hand. The lamp's bluish-white beam lit up her quarters, illuminating clues from her life.

It passed over glue-pen and Ascali claw graffiti, over placards of beefy males and buxom females. The beam came to rest on a placard of Kivita and her father. The child's wide smile and hazel eyes hinted at the beauty Kivita would mature into. The man, though, looked nothing like her.

He smiled as the beam revealed the chit he'd bought her freedom with at Tejuit. It had wedged itself into a crack beside the placard; a damned miracle the chit hadn't been sucked into space.

Utter darkness ruled the ship now. As a child he'd been frightened of the dark, whether the black void of space or the depthless fissures in Freen mines. Caitrynn had convinced him there was nothing to fear in the darkness.

As he dragged himself into the cryo chamber, Sar's eyes narrowed. When the Inheritors had conquered mineral-rich Freen, Caitrynn had been among those who resisted. She and her two children, almost teenagers, both died in the fighting. Her husband, stricken with black-mouth disease from mine work, had been executed by Inheritor soldiers afterward.

He hesitated and shut off the cold lamp. *In the dark, the faces of Caitrynn's son and daughter stared up at him from a bloodied mine tunnel. Bullet holes smoked in their chests. Yellow paint covered their foreheads, placed there by Inheritor troops to mark a defeated heretic.*

"Damn you." His whisper summoned the headless body of Caitrynn's husband, cast onto a pile of corpses. Men, women, children.

Sar's face pinched and his chest sank in.

Caitrynn still clutching a sword and pistol, her body sprawled over a burned-out Inheritor tank. The back part of her skull shattered open. Eyes closed, with a yellow-painted dagger shoved into her mouth.

Raging, uncontrollable emotions surged through his being.

He screamed at the darkness, the ship's chilled, decaying air hurting his throat and lungs. He stumbled into the nearest bulkhead. Goddamn them! Gritting his teeth, Sar mashed the lamp's button. Its light banished the darkness, erased the images from his sight but not his heart.

Kivita might be able to end it all. Why else would everyone want her? A Savant like her could spread knowledge like no other. Send data to pinpoint and destroy Inheritor armies, coordinate assaults, direct battle fleets.

The lamp's beam flickered. Sar loosed a ragged breath and shook his head. Shekelor had been right after all.

Like he'd told Cheseia once, she and Kivita deserved someone else. Someone free of darkness, whose heart didn't have the chill of a vacuum.

Sar eased himself into Kivita's cryopod, shut off the cold lamp, and removed the mask. The cryopod's hatch snapped shut. Cold air filled his nose and mouth.

Caitrynn used to tell him stories—an older sister helping her brother cope with the hellish conditions in Freen's subterranean mining society. Stories of a paradise world just outside the Cetturo Arm, where people never died, never slaved in deep mines.

It was called Frevyx.

Before closing his eyes, Sar hoped the Juxj Star would reveal it to Kivita someday.

21

Seul's cryoports clamped shut and her spine went rigid. On the shuttle's console display, the remains of several Aldaakian ships floated in Tejuit's traffic lane. The two frigates had been the only Aldaakian military presence in the system—and Tejuit was a strategic cosmic crossroads, usually well defended by Aldaakian warships.

With other fleets still recovering from the Sarrhdtuu attacks into Aldaakian Space, the path to her people's worlds now lay open to the Inheritors.

"Captain Jaah, the Inheritor blockade of Tejuit has made this war official," Vuul said over the console speaker. "Aldaakian forces in the vicinity are on full alert. The Inheritors may strike at Aldaakuun, or even Aldaak Emtar, through the Aldaakian Corridor in the Terresin Expanse. However, I think they have other plans."

"Yes, Commander Vuul?" Seul gripped Kael's shoulders while standing behind his seat.

"Follow *Terredyn Narbas*. By your own report, the trawler was heavily damaged. It could not have jumped far."

"It is done—"

"Captain Jaah? Your orders are now to destroy Kivita's ship on sight. No chances can be taken."

The other Troopers aboard shared confused glances. Seul's fingers dug into Kael's chair.

"It is done, Commander Vuul." Seul took a deep breath, and her cryoports tightened. "Officer Kael, I want the Sarrhdtuu beacon trajectory from *Terredyn Narbas*."

Kael studied his console, thumbing a few keys. "Inheritor scanners will detect us, Captain Jaah. We've orbited the system for hours."

"That's a chance we'll have to take." Seul had never fought the Inheritors, since the peace treaty had been stable since the Nebulon conflict years ago. Why would those humans do this? The Inheritor battleship seemed to be waiting for something, which bothered her even more.

Seul exited the cockpit and paced between the launch tubes. Their shuttle's energy dump could power them six light years, so she had to find Kivita—fast. Seul wondered whether she'd have let the human escape if she'd suspected Kivita's importance on Umiracan.

Something about that placard on Kivita's ship still made Seul's chest tighten. A father with his daughter. Both had looked happy.

By the void, she wouldn't kill Kivita. The human was the best chance of contacting the Vim—but Vuul wasn't telling her something.

"Trace found, Captain Jaah," the female navigator said.

Seul hurried back into the cockpit. "Where does it lead?"

Kael frowned. "Captain, the trawler departed to unknown coordinates."

It was too easy, too clear-cut. Kivita knew about the

Sarrhdtuu beacon on *Terredyn Narbas*, knew she'd be followed.

"Captain Jaah, with your permission?" Kael asked, worry in his eyes.

She had no choice. Vuul's orders were for Seul to destroy Kivita, not follow her instincts.

"Make the jump." Seul returned to her launch tube. It closed over her, acting as troop carrier and cryopod. Inserts entered her cryoports as her polyarmor unlocked. The pilots keyed in the coordinates, shut the viewport, and retired to their own cryopods. The vessel shuddered, making the light jump.

Seul tried to imagine what she'd say to Kivita. The redheaded woman was running from everyone. What did she really know? Seul wouldn't use force to find out. Guns and blades had spoken too long for her people.

A proximity alarm roused Seul from cryostasis, and the tubes retracted from her cryoports. She flexed her muscles and let her polyarmor lock in place, then opened the launch tube hatch. Gravity activated on board.

The life monitor showed that she'd been asleep for less than an hour.

Seul hurried from her cryopod, limbs trembling from lack of proper warm-up. Joining her, Kael opened the cockpit's forward viewport. The shuttle had entered a wide asteroid field.

"How did this happen?" Seul asked, while the other Shock Troopers roused from cryostasis.

Kael strapped into his seat. "Look, Captain Jaah."

Outside the viewport, a hammerlike oblong shape floated five hundred feet distant.

"It's *Terredyn Narbas*," the navigator said. "Scanners

show low engine power, though the beacon is still transmitting."

Seul activated the console mic. "Kivita? This is Seul Jaah. We're here to help you." She avoided looking at her comrades. Vuul wasn't around, and neither was his murderous agenda.

No answer.

"Kivita?" she asked again.

Terredyn Narbas sat silent. What if Kivita had been injured when the pirates boarded her ship? Seul's cryoports squeezed.

"Captain Jaah?" Kael asked.

Seul grabbed her helmet. "She won't answer. Prepare to board."

As they neared Kivita's ship, Seul left the cockpit and selected one squad. "I have point. Point Two, follow me once Auxiliary One has cut through the airlock doors. Flanks Three and Four follow. This is a rescue mission. I want all rifles and blades left behind. Batons only."

The Troopers all frowned, though none commented. Seul took position beside the airlock and donned her helmet.

After magnetizing *Terredyn Narbas*, Seul stood back while the sliding doors opened. Auxiliary One readied his beam rifle, then hesitated.

"Captain Jaah, the lock has already been cut."

The clamps on the airlock's four sides had been sliced by a beam weapon. Seul signaled her squad, and Flanks Three and Four flung open the doors with a pry bar.

The interior lay shrouded in absolute darkness, but after a few steps, faint running lights activated along the bulkheads. The same quarters she'd studied over Vstrunn greeted her again.

"If those lights came on, everything else should have, too," Seul said. "Stay alert, everyone."

Hefting her baton in zero-G, Seul waited as her poly-boots magnetized to the floor. "Point Two, Flank Three, and Flank Four, follow me. The rest of you, stay here."

Seul continued into the bridge. No one sat in the seat or gyro harness, so Kivita must be in her cryopod, if she still lived.

After a few minutes, Seul passed the living quarters, galley, and launch-capsule entrance to an even smaller cryo chamber. Stillness ruled the empty trawler. As the cryo chamber's lamps ignited at her presence, Seul gaped.

Cut marks lined the far wall. Sliced bolts and cooled slag floated over the floor. Energy couplings dangled from the wall and floor in the zero-G, having been disconnected from a large device.

No cryopod waited within the chamber.

Kael's voice came over Seul's helmet speaker. "Captain Jaah, scanners have detected a departing beacon signature leading back to the Tejuit system."

"All Troopers, return to the shuttle," Seul strained to say. "There is no sign of Kivita Vondir, and her cryopod is missing."

After boarding, Seul had a Trooper close and seal *Terredyn Narbas*'s airlock. For some reason, she wanted it protected, as if Kivita still lay inside. Asleep in a frozen tomb, like Niaaq Aldaar himself.

Cryoports snapping, she entered the cockpit. "Take us back to Tejuit, Officer Kael. Commander Vuul must be alerted. We will not enter cryostasis this time."

Seul turned without waiting for an answer. With the cryopod gone, she dismissed theories of Kivita sending

Terredyn Narbas here unmanned, to fool pursuers. Someone had taken her while Kivita slept in cryostasis.

More than ever, Seul feared for her race, the Vim, and her red-haired friend.

"Stop," Kivita whispered through chapped lips.

The Kith crushed the Sarrhdtuu warrior with its hulking arms. Three more Sarrhdtuu, gilding over the floor on their gray-green coils, sliced the Kith apart with sicklelike blades. Kivita's point of view switched to her seeing everything from the tower's crystal floor. Blood formed a pool around her as the last Kith defenders collapsed under Sarrhdtuu beamers. Each dead Kith dissolved into fine metallic dust.

One Sarrhdtuu propped her up against the wall. Kivita's sight dimmed as the Sarrhdtuu holding her produced a red gem—the Juxj Star.

Something burned her gums. Her eyes fluttered.

The cryopod hatch opened. Kivita coughed and wiped pseudoadrine from her lips. Feeling returned to her chilled limbs as she tried to rise from the cryopod, but her stomach flared with pain.

"Wait until I truly come back for you," Cheseia called, exiting her own cryopod. "I must certainly check our location." The Ascali slipped on leather boots and left the cryo chamber.

Like she wanted to move. Besides, Kivita hadn't wanted to wake just yet, since she'd hoped to glimpse the crash-landing on Susuron again. Whoever had collected data into the Juxj Star had been present for so many different events. It wasn't possible, since the viewer from the Sarrhdtuu attack must have perished.

Cheseia came back dressed in chaps, polygreaves,

and a jiir headband. "I will help you get adequately dressed. Your condition surely demands attention."

Minutes later, Kivita gritted her teeth as Cheseia finished tugging an envirosuit on her. "Now place your left hand around my waist and simply lean into me."

"I'm not a cripple," Kivita said.

"You will be, unless you attentively listen." Together they neared the starboard airlock, Kivita wincing with each step. Her left leg burned, and soreness stabbed her right arm.

"Where are we?"

Cheseia pulled the airlock lever while *Frevyx* powered down around them. "I have certainly never been here."

They stepped into a short, circular tube magnetized with *Frevyx*'s airlock. The transparent sides revealed a star-studded void with a yellow sun millions of miles away. Several gas giants orbited it.

"Tejuit?" Kivita asked.

Cheseia said nothing while they passed through the tube and into an airlock bay filled with supply crates. Two terminals blinked with small screens, while three circular hatches waited under dim lamps.

The center hatch opened, and Jandeel entered the bay, smiling. "Welcome to *Luccan's Wish*."

"The Thedes?" Kivita whispered, tasting blood in her mouth. She slumped against Cheseia, her scalp tingling.

"Summon the medics!" Jandeel called.

A sharp throb pierced Kivita's gut.

22

Kivita tried to straighten, but stumbled into Cheseia. "No, I need . . ."

Pain stole her words, seared her thoughts. To stifle a cry, she pressed her face against Cheseia's shoulder. The Ascali's fur smelled of exotic bark vapors, used for perfume on certain worlds. She tried to think of such places . . . anything to ignore the pain.

"Stop moving," Cheseia said in a gentle tone. "The medics are certainly coming. You should not be foolishly walking."

"Going to meet them." Kivita grunted and took another step. "On my feet."

Cheseia shared a look with Jandeel, and they helped Kivita along. Jandeel limped, favoring his right side.

They entered a large chamber filled with lockers, cushioned seats, and bright lamps. The smell of sweat and stuffy air filled the space. Six men and women in polyarmor waited, kinetic pistols in hand.

Jandeel held up a hand to the guards. "The human tested positive on a brain-pulse scan. We can question her later."

A door on the other side of the chamber opened, and

two humans and two Ascali rushed through. They brought medical satchels, a collapsible stretcher, and cold packs.

Shivering, Kivita tried to stand on her own again. She'd never been in a stretcher, never required surgery. All her ills and aches had been healed during long cryosleeps while wrapped in blue tape. She didn't need all this . . .

Cheseia helped Kivita onto the stretcher after the medics opened it up. "Her bruised stomach still prevents her from truly walking. She has certainly not coughed up any more blood since we arrived."

"Anything else you've told them about me?" Kivita winced and held her abdomen.

Cheseia didn't answer as two guards escorted the Ascali from the room. Jandeel nodded once to Kivita, then followed Cheseia. The medics lifted Kivita's stretcher and carried her; each corridor they passed through had a slightly different scent. She guessed the pressurized atmosphere needed more regulation. Patch welds and mismatched bulkheads hinted at constant repairs.

In the infirmary, two autohelpers swerved and clicked in one corner, caring for a dozen different patients on cots. Both consisted of nothing more than metallic cylinders on wheels, with ratcheted arms ending in pincers. In another corner an Aldaakian medic talked with an Aldaakian mother, who held an albino infant.

Over a scarred terminal an image flickered, showing a man holding a blue hibiscus flower and describing it. Kivita wondered if it was a hologram, something only Inheritor prophets were allowed to use. How did these rebels get one?

The Aldaakian medic approached, while the others

lifted her from the stretcher and placed her onto a cot. The cot's coarse fabric creaked beneath her. Cheseia entered the room and stood beside the cot while the Aldaakian examined Kivita's eyes, ears, and mouth.

"She is not unfortunately contaminated." Cheseia smoothed her mane back, eyes darting everywhere.

The Aldaakian medic sniffed. "She may require surgery."

Kivita squirmed on the cot. "It's not that bad, really. I don't want—"

"To die." The Aldaakian placed a mask over her mouth and nose. The air inside it stank of thick musk and seemed to fill her mouth with sand. She tried to speak, but her eyes wouldn't stay open. Hands tugged off her envirosuit.

The familiar tingle traveled across her temples and forehead. What would she see? Sar, escaping the Tejuit system? Stupid Juxj Star. Why couldn't the damn thing show her the future instead of the past?

The pain in her stomach subsided.

When she reopened her eyes, Kivita lay on a softer cot in a different room. White, indigo, and yellow hibiscus flowers surrounded her in red-brown pots. The air reminded her of a crisp Haldon breeze, and soft light came down from large ceiling lamps. Light gray walls surrounded her, along with eighteen other cots. Only four cots contained a patient.

The circular door hissed open and Cheseia entered, still wearing her breechcloth and headdress. A thin white tunic contrasted her dark mane.

"Your fever has finally relented. The medics worried you would tragically enter a coma." Her soft voice caressed Kivita's ears.

"Coma?" Kivita asked, her tongue thick with pasty medication. "How long have I been lying here?"

Cheseia knelt beside the cot and studied Kivita's hair. "I truly envy your mane color. Of all the lovely hues humans have, I have always liked yours the best."

Kivita snorted. "C'mon, how long?"

"Six Haldon days. The surgeon repaired your awfully ruptured stomach and properly set your right shoulder. Your other bruises have truly healed."

"Yeah?" Pushing down with her arms, Kivita lifted herself into a half-sitting position. Her right arm, left leg, and stomach gave no ache, though all were numb. Confidence swelled in her chest.

Kivita sat up completely and touched Cheseia's mane. "Seems you saved my life, then." The Ascali's long tresses resembled the finest threaded ply rather than hair, and the fur on her cheeks felt like plush cushions. No wonder Sar had taken up with her. Kivita wished she were this beautiful.

Cheseia smoothed Kivita's hair. "It is what Sar truly would have wished."

The tension between them was so damn petty in light of recent events. War loomed between the Inheritors and Aldaakians, pirates wanted to sell her to the Sarrhdtuu, and Sar could be anywhere. Kivita decided to swallow her pride for once.

"I didn't want him to take my ship. I . . ." Kivita's throat tightened. "I'm not angry with you for loving him. For keeping him happy, since . . ." Emotions spilled up from within her as she realized years might have passed wherever Sar had escaped to. He might be older, with gray in his lovely curls. He might be dead.

"He will certainly find us. I think you amazingly

opened his heart, Kivita. If not for you, I truly doubt Sar would have humored me." Cheseia smiled.

Kivita's laughter eased the tension in her throat and chest. "Yeah? I had to push myself on him at times. He's not like a Naxan seducer, who won't leave you alone. A gal has to approach him on his own terms."

"Which you definitely did not, of course." Cheseia grinned.

Kivita laughed louder. Two other patients looked in her direction. "No, you're right there. Just barged into his feelings when I wanted him."

They shared a long, thankful look.

"The medics say you are certainly well enough to leave this infirmary. I know you tire of what Sar and I endlessly tell you about yourself and the gem. Now you will hopefully see."

Kivita balked. "Wait—where is it?" She lifted the thermal blanket, as if the Juxj Star might be in the cot with her.

"Navon has it, though he supposedly has not studied it yet. He awaits you, once you have satisfyingly eaten." Cheseia helped Kivita up from the cot.

Kivita opened a small locker and changed from the white shift into her polyboots, chaps, gold-meld breastplate, and maroon bodyglove. All had been cleaned and repaired. A new red pillbox hat had been set aside for her. She donned it all in a hurry, eager to meet the infamous Thedes. So far their kindness had refuted more of the Inheritors' lies.

Leaving the infirmary for a long corridor, Kivita stared at the intricate Ascali claw graffiti along the walls. Rhyer had told her the Ascali of Sygma carved poems and songs into trees or mud, which dried into stone.

Away from their homeworld, the graffiti was applied with paint or glue, like the examples before her.

"Those are lyrics from the 'Chant to Revelas,' right?" Kivita pointed at the graffiti. "My father once went to Sygma. Told me they sung him the most gorgeous songs."

Cheseia studied Kivita with wide eyes. "You truly know this? That would certainly explain the graffiti I saw on your ship."

Kivita smirked. "Yeah, I'm not just another Inheritor farmer. I'm cultured. Well, a little."

Another circular hatch opened, and Cheseia led her into a galley where people sat at tables cobbled from spare motor parts. A rectangular viewport, twenty feet long and ten feet high, remained sealed. Hibiscuses, orchids, and flowered cacti lent the place a peaceful ambience.

Kivita received curious stares from the others, a collection of mixed races and origins. Naxans drank reed ale with Ascali, while Tannocci and ex-Inheritors ate with a few renegade Aldaakians. A burly Sutaran woman laughed with a swarthy Freen man. A few children cried or played beside their parents. One Ascali male sung low, soothing notes accompanied by a man playing a nine-pipe reed whistle. Placards of old feudal nobles hung from the bulkheads, crusted with age.

Cheseia nudged Kivita to the serving counter. "Woodsnake milk, please."

Leaning on the counter, Kivita cleared her throat. "A protein slab, jiir tea, and some sugared reeds. How much?"

The server, a middle-aged woman with curved tattoos along her temples, handed the food over. "Stars shine and wink, miss. Costs nothing, since you are on our rations list.

You're the one who's brought Vim knowledge? The one Sar Redryll sent us? Blessings of water and sun on you, miss."

Kivita's cheeks warmed. "Um, yeah. Blessings of water and sun to you, too."

She accepted the food and walked with Cheseia to a table beside the viewport. As they sat down, a few in the galley pointed at Kivita and whispered.

"What was that all about?" She sipped the jiir tea; its sweet warmth, tinged with a wholesome aftertaste, warmed her heart, as well. Accustomed to bawdy spaceports, Kivita hadn't expected such respectful friendliness.

"*Luccan's Wish* is visited only by other Thedes and allies who can be sincerely trusted." Cheseia drank her milk, then licked the brownish-white foam from her lips. "This is truly also my first time here. Sar secretly spoke of it often."

Kivita munched a sugar reed. "How many live here? How far from Haldon are we?"

"This cruiser houses more than four hundred right now, but can accommodate double that number," Jandeel replied as he neared their table. "Our best scientists, Sages, and tactical leaders plot all Thede activity from *Luccan's Wish*. We departed from an uncharted location near Tejuit. The Inheritors would have paid a hefty price for those coordinates."

"Departed? For where?" Kivita almost stood up, but Jandeel raised a hand.

"Navon will reveal that when you meet with him. Kivita . . . this ship never leaves the Tejuit system, so that Thede agents know where to send reports. That's how important this signal is." He grimaced and limped beside them.

Kivita grunted, chewing the salty protein slab. "So, how's that wound?"

Jandeel gave a slight bow. "If you hadn't convinced those brutes to make that shabby tourniquet, I may still be in the infirmary. Sar spotted me and signaled allies on the hive ship to help. I repay a good deed in kind, Kivita. I've convinced the others that you aren't a spy. Please don't make a liar out of me." He grinned.

A dark-skinned Dirr boy approached their table with childlike curiosity. Kivita offered him one of her sugared reeds, which he took and ran back to the serving counter. She smiled and studied the other children. Healthy, happy, well cared for. The life her father would've wanted for her. The life she'd once dreamt of with Sar.

Jandeel nodded in the children's direction. "They are our future. Raised here in peace and educated by our resident Sages."

"Guess that's you, huh? You always do a brain scan when someone visits?"

"One cannot be too sure in these times. When you have finished your meal, come to Level Six. Navon has been waiting to see you." He left them alone, walking slowly.

"Wow, all these kids . . . Sar always tried to convince me to quit the salvaging business before radiation made me sterile like him." Kivita finished her last drink of tea.

"I do not think Sar is actually sterile," Cheseia whispered.

Kivita jerked back and stared. "What?"

"I am not truly certain, but I think he unfortunately misled you. He always ate little green pills before we excitedly shared one another. Sar has also told me to
· surely seek someone else."

"Yeah. That's Sar, all right." Kivita bit her lip. Focusing on Sar right now would only spiral her into depression. "Guess I'd better go see this Navon guy."

Cheseia gathered their cups and took them back to the server, while Kivita entered a nearby lift. It led to Level Six. *Luccan's Wish* had ten decks. Where'd these people find such a large ship?

The lift door opened to an observation deck lined with vegetable, fruit, and flowering plants, where two older Naxan women argued in playful tones over how much water the plants needed.

"This way." Jandeel stepped from behind a giant indigo hibiscus.

"Some woman with a red cap sent me." Kivita smirked and touched her new hat.

Jandeel chuckled and led her from the observation deck into a dim-lit, cubicle-filled room. In each cubicle, a Sage instructed several students. Two holographic displays in the room's center showed various educational images: humanoid anatomy, planetary rotation, or Bellerion-reed growth cycles. Students of all ages discussed Naxan philosophy of the individual, Ascali respect for nature, or the pitfalls of ancient autocratic human kingdoms—subjects forbidden in Inheritor universities.

Not that Kivita had attended an Inheritor university—hell, any university—but she'd slept with enough students in spaceports to know. For the first time, that bothered her. Had she been nothing but spacer trash all these years?

"Don't feel disconcerted. Many others have yet to see our brand of education," Jandeel said.

"No, I'm okay." She pushed back red-blond bangs and continued on.

One Sage sketched engine schematics on a slate board for five adult students, pointing out the flaws in current light-jump technology and offering suggestions. Kivita recalled the vision she'd had about tweaking phased fusion-energy dumps.

"Hey, if you smash the protons together faster in the energy dump, I bet you could shave jump speeds by a third," Kivita said.

The Sage and students stared at her as if she'd turned orange.

Jandeel took her arm and passed the cubicle by. "Later, Kivita." They exited the room via another circular doorway. "Though I like your attitude. This is what the Thedes do: share knowledge. You'll have a chance to share everything soon."

They passed through a room cramped with rusty terminals and maps printed on oversized placards. Three men and two women, their faces stern, examined the maps and discussed military strategies. Kivita glimpsed plans for aiding the insurgencies on Haldon Prime and Tahe, and for arming Sutara against Inheritor aggression.

One placard mentioned *Frevyx* and showed routes for weapon smuggling in Inheritor Space. One route passed by Gontalo. So, Sar had been a gunrunner all this time? The time they'd spent on Gontalo, had it all been a cover while he supplied Thedes with armaments? She turned away from the placard, eager to change her train of thought.

"Where did this ship come from?" Kivita asked. "Doesn't look Inheritor or even Tannocci."

"Luccan Thede, the founder of our organization, discovered it abandoned near the Tahe system. With much effort, he and many allies refitted it. Luccan used knowledge from Vim datacores and engineered a null beacon that rejects scanner signals."

A reinforced door opened to another corridor. "So where's Luccan now?" Kivita asked.

"The Inheritors assassinated him," Jandeel replied.

"Just because he fixed an old starship?" Kivita's eyebrows rose.

"Luccan was a Tahe mercenary under Inheritor employ," Jandeel said. "After seeing how the prophets wasted so much wealth—and lives—in their wars with the Aldaakians, he decided to educate people about the costs of such ruinous decisions. As he discovered more, Luccan revealed the breeding programs of the Rectors, their lecherous Oath of Propagation, and just how impoverished Inheritor citizens were in comparison to their leaders. This caused riots and unrest on several Inheritor worlds. The prophets hunted him down, executed his family. They even razed his home city to the ground, when they finally conquered his homeworld."

Kivita had salvaged for those bastards many times, and all she'd had to show for it was a beat-up trawler and the thought that she was free.

"How did he die?" she asked, staring at the placard with Sar's old route on it. A heaviness pressed down on her heart.

"One of the Rector's own Proselytes finally killed him in a raid near Tejuit," Jandeel said. "But Luccan's work continued. He'd dubbed himself a 'Thede,' an old feudal word for 'teacher.' All his followers gladly accept this moniker."

"So what do Thedes teach?"

Jandeel patted Kivita's shoulder. "Navon can answer

your questions far better than I. Only because of your own gift, and because Sar sent you, do we trust you in his presence."

"You have my word," Kivita said, meeting his eyes. "I just want some answers."

"I hope you have some for all of us." Jandeel limped away.

A second reinforced door opened, and the scent of jiir juice and silver lotus stung Kivita's nose. Two plush couches, three grass mats, and two telescopes filled the room. A shelf packed with old paper books, computer chits, pieces of stone, thin crystals, and metal shards reached the ceiling.

A human male rose from one of the grass mats and smiled. He stood over six feet tall and had sea-green eyes. His gray hair hung in thick Bellerion coils, and he wore a green bodyglove.

"You are welcome here, Kivita Vondir. I am Navon." His deep-timbre voice and Bellerion accent gave his diphthongs a warbling sound. He gestured at one of the couches. "Please rest. I am glad to see you walking." He sat back down on the grass mat.

Kivita wanted to be polite, but impatience took hold. "Where's the Juxj Star?"

He pointed at the viewport sill. The gem rested there, almost obscured by a telescope stand. Kivita finally nodded and sat on a couch.

"You are correct to be forthright," Navon said. "I have never seen a gem so large used for a Vim datacore. As you can see on my bookshelf, I have collected several others. I am glad you trusted Sar and did not sell it to those who do not share."

Crossing her arms, Kivita leaned forward on the

couch. "Listen I . . . I don't understand any of this. I keep having these dreams, and when I touch the Juxj Star, I suddenly see and know things I shouldn't. I can even make others see them."

Navon nodded. "And you do not like it, do you? Neither did I at first. Being a Savant is not something you can cast aside. From what Cheseia has told me, there is a possibility the Sarrhdtuu know this. Shekelor Thal does, and he will not keep it secret."

Kivita stood and paced the floor. "Well, now what? Jandeel told me strange things. Things that match some images I've seen in my thoughts since touching the Juxj Star."

"I know. I felt the signal the first time you touched the gem on Vstrunn."

"What? How?"

"We have long known about the Juxj Star, but never suspected the tower that housed it was some sort of antenna. Your signal, sent out from your brain through that tower, reached me aboard this ship almost two Haldon years past. In that time, no one has deciphered what the signal means, only where it leads."

"But I've never felt these things before. Why me?" She placed her hands on her hips.

"Savant talents are hereditary, Kivita. The Inheritors, Aldaakians, and Sarrhdtuu can detect the difference in electrical pulses from the human brain. This makes itself known only in early adulthood, however. What I wish to know is how you broadcasted that signal. How you make others see what you see, by thought or touch. I can only decode a datacore. Your abilities astound me." Navon's brows furrowed.

She sat cross-legged before him on the same grass

mat. "Do humans, Ascali, and Aldaakians all come from the same race? Did the Vim make us and the Kith? I've seen cryo ships, growth tubes, coordinates to massive ships five hundred light years from the Cetturo Arm. Even the Sarrhdtuu attacking the old colony ships."

Navon leaned forward, eyes wide. "I have not touched the Juxj Star myself, for I wanted to speak with you first. Thede scholars have theorized that those three races are related, yes. I do not know which race came first. I do think the Vim had a hand in it, and there can be no doubt the Kith defended the Vim against the Sarrhdtuu. They have been enemies for millennia."

"Really? I haven't seen any clues why the Sarrhdtuu attacked those colony ships. It seems they drove some of the humans into the Cetturo Arm, though." Kivita described to him all her visions concerning the ship crash-landing on Susuron.

"The Narbas lineage . . . I have long suspected this."

"Go on." Kivita licked her trembling lips.

"Terredyn Narbas, the ancient queen of Susuron, was the first Savant capable of doing what you can do. Cheseia says your vessel was named after her?" Something gleamed in his eyes.

"Yeah, my father named it. I think it's so strange he would have chosen that name, and here I am, a Savant, too." She smiled but wrung her hands.

Navon sat back. "Yes. Two Savants who can send information across the cosmos by mere thought. Whatever happened to your father, Kivita?"

She frowned. "He died in a salvaging accident when I was seventeen. Saving passengers from a ship whose reactor had . . . Well, even though Inheritor law forbade it, I got Father's ship. They let that slip because I started salvaging for them right then. Father taught me how to fly when I was four, so I knew everything about starships already. I never knew my mother."

Navon rose and walked over to the bookshelf. He took down a piece of rock, pitted like the Vim datacores she'd seen near Xeh's Crown.

"You must decode some of the information from this datacore, Kivita. It will save much time and explanation on my part."

Kivita started to speak, but Navon placed the stone into her hands. The room faded.

A smoldering starship on a Susuron beach filled her mind.

23

Blue-green waves lapped the beach as Kivita stumbled past smoldering debris. Ruptured bulkheads, cracked cryopods, and mangled bodies littered the sparkling sands. The ship lay on its starboard side, with half the port-side hull torn away. Deep scorch marks had penetrated the craft in two perfect vertical cuts.

"Beamers," Kivita whispered. The tingles burrowed into her temples.

Hundreds of survivors gathered near the shore: people in maroon jumpsuits, soldiers in feudal polymail. Children wailed. Smoke billowed from the wreckage.

One soldier in polymail and a purple cape turned and bowed to Kivita. He had Rhyer's face, Rhyer's eyes. Even his gentle smile, but younger. No wrinkles, no gray in his long brown hair.

As her breath caught, the other people turned and bowed, and upon seeing Kivita, their grief lessened. Frowns became smiles; weeping became determination.

Icy pain sliced into her skull.

The beach shifted into a vaulted courtroom, like the ones her father had spun tales about: coral chandeliers, ply drapes, knitted grass carpets, and a pillow-strewn dais. Kiv-

ita leaned forward on her throne, which was worked in gold, rubies, and glitter wood. Sentries in gold-meld cuirasses stood at attention while two men wheeled a small cryopod into the courtroom. A woman in nursing fatigues followed, carrying an infant swaddled in golden cloth.

Whomever Kivita witnessed this scene through stood from the throne and descended the dais. Her delicate, bejeweled hand caressed the infant, who began to cry. The babe's hazel eyes and blond wisps made Kivita swallow.

The nurse placed the infant into the cryopod. A strong throb emitted from Kivita's brain. She knelt beside the cryopod, her vision blurring as if the viewer wept. Rhyer stood nearby with a worried face. Outside the courtroom window, a golden-hulled life capsule waited beside a small Tannocci-style vessel.

Trying to fight the pain in her head, Kivita gasped so hard her throat hurt.

"Navon? What is this?" she cried out.

Inheritor ships hovered in the sky, and yellow banners fluttered in the air. Thousands of peasants waited in a city square below a sandstone podium. Her sight trembled, as if the viewer experienced great anguish.

Kivita wished she could feel the emotions of those who'd recorded this data.

Wished she could reach into the past and ask about the infant.

Soldiers in old-fashioned steel armor led Kivita onto the podium, where a man with an axe stood beside a stained wooden block. Kivita tried to move faster, but the viewer walked to the block with agonizing slowness. A crisp breeze ruffled Kivita's hair. Its earthy scent was unmistakable.

"Haldon Prime," she said.

Kivita knelt before the wooden block. The executioner raised his axe. An overpowering contraction loosed from the viewer's brain as the axe came down.

A mind-numbing ache throbbed in her skull.

Tears running down her face, Kivita tried to drop the stone datacore, but her mind reeled.

An unmanned freighter with thousands of tons of cargo was 238 light years away. Blueprints for larger autohandlers with weapons zipped through her mind. An abandoned Sarrhdtuu colony was just three thousand light years away, using a Vim engine capable of reaching fifty times the speed of light.

The pitted datacore left Kivita's hand. She slumped over, trembling with sobs while she clawed at the grass mat. Gentle hands lifted her and placed her onto one of the couches.

"Three hours have passed," Navon said. "I did not pull the datacore away until I was sure you had seen what you needed to see."

Kivita sat up straight and glared at him. "Damn you. Why'd you let me see that?"

Navon sat back down on the grass mat, his eyes grave. "I suspected, the first time I visited you in the infirmary, that you might be a descendent of Terredyn Narbas. When Cheseia told me the details—your ship's name, your Savant talents, ignorance of your mother—I became certain. You are the very image of the ancient Susuron queen who lived a thousand years ago."

She tried to laugh, but it came out as a moan. "I'm not that old. Neither was my father."

"Rhyer Vondir was not your father."

She rubbed her temples and shivered. "Liar. You don't know anything about—"

"You know it is true."

Kivita rose and stalked to the circular door. "This is insane!"

"Your father was Queen Terredyn's Seneschal," Navon said in a calm voice. "A skilled soldier and commander, from what I have uncovered about that era. I have no doubt he loved you very much, Kivita. Rhyer knew about the ancient law regarding Savants, however. I cannot fathom why he raised you on the very planet your mother was executed on, in the midst of your enemies."

Fists clenched at her sides, she paused near the door. Rhyer was her father. Had to be. She loved and missed him too much for it to be otherwise.

"Your mother ordered you set afloat in space before the Inheritors captured her. I suppose Rhyer hid you in a secret location, in stasis, then returned under his new identity as an Inheritor salvager—centuries later. He must have spent decades at a time in cryostasis."

"Then why did the Rector hire me?" So hard to think, so much pain still in her head ...

Navon's voice flattened. "The Inheritors destroy historical archives, so I doubt if any of their current leaders recall your mother. Rhyer must have learned something, to name his trawler after his queen and begin raising you himself."

Kivita squeezed her eyes shut to stop the tears. "Then who wants me? The Sarrhdtuu? They tried to kill ... tried to kill her." She found it hard to call Terredyn her mother.

"The Sarrhdtuu are the Inheritor's benefactors, Kivita. For some reason, they have supported the Inheritor's rise to power, their wars against the Aldaakians, and their persecution of the Thedes." Navon stood and sighed. "This is not how I wanted our first meeting to transpire. But you must realize your importance. Sar Redryll may have given his life so you could be safe, just as your ancient mother did."

"I didn't ask him to." Kivita stormed back to Navon's side. "I didn't! How do I know this isn't some trick? Using me like some sort of symbol for your cause."

His eyebrows rose. "Cheseia described the wormhole you found, leading from Umiracan to Tejuit. Was that a trick? The Juxj Star gave you the information. As a Savant, you used it."

"Listen. I'm Kivita Vondir. Father didn't find me in some stupid life capsule. There's no way I slept in space that long." Her voice sounded weak in her own ears.

Navon looked at the datacores on his bookshelf. "Beyond the Cetturo Arm is where your mother really came from. Where we all originated, I am willing to believe. I know you saw the coordinates for the Sarrhdtuu colony, the supply freighter. Will you be like the Inheritor prophets, who deny their people the truth while hoarding the best technology for themselves? Will you act like the Aldaakians, who keep searching for a Vim miracle to save their way of life?"

Her breathing quickened. "No, I'm—"

"Or will you regress back to the mercenary salvager, who sold the past to the tyrants of the present, so there will be no future for anyone?" Navon faced her, brows lowered.

Kivita stumbled back, flabbergasted. Anger rose in her mind, but guilt flooded her heart. Sar himself seemed to be reprimanding her instead of Navon. Now he might be dead or floating in the void forever. . . . Like she might have done as an infant.

Navon clasped her hands in a tender grip. "The most powerful forces in the Cetturo Arm know your name, your face. Wherever you go, you will be followed. Your powers are traceable through space, beyond any reckoning. I am not asking you to act as a symbol for anyone or anything."

"Yeah? Then what do you want? Cheseia didn't bring me here and Sar didn't do what he did just so I could find out who . . . who I might really be." Kivita still didn't want to accept it. The fact that the kind, weathered man who'd taught her to fly, who'd instilled a wonder for the stars, might not be her father crushed her heart.

"I will not live forever," Navon said. "The other Savants on board this ship learn all they can from me, but that is not enough. The Vim mirrored their datacores on a biological brain, constructed from nature's hardiest materials. The perfect data receptacle. A brain can store, process, and retrieve information. It can pass this information on to each successive generation. There are talented Savants among us, but none that can match what you have already done."

"I can't even handle what the Juxj Star has shown me. How do you expect me to take on all that you know?" Kivita quelled her sobs and stood straight. She'd thought being a salvager had toughened her, thought Sar breaking her heart had tempered her. The idea of Sar dying for her made her chest tighten, but the scene of her mother's decapitation churned her stomach and dampened her vision with tears. Kivita resisted the urge to rub her neck.

Navon placed his hands behind his back. "I asked Jandeel to lead you through the teaching cubicles. Did you like what you saw?"

"Who wouldn't? If even a fraction of the worlds in the Cetturo Arm shared this stuff you've told me, we'd all be in better shape. But the Inheritors claim you're terrorists, saboteurs, killers. Dissenters who want to deny us the glory of the Vim and all that."

Navon shook his head. "We Thedes are not terrorists. Yes, Sar—whom I admire greatly—advocates armed rebellion, but what we really do is share knowledge. Knowledge enlightens us, sets us free. So many in Inheritor Space still live in superstition and fear. The prophets, despite their foolishness, know that if knowledge spreads, they will lose power. The Sarrhdtuu also know this. However, I think the prophets have the right idea—the Vim might still be out there somewhere. Finding them and sharing what they know will bring peace to the Arm."

"Maybe they don't want us to find them—you ever consider that? Maybe the Cetturo Arm is a prison. Maybe the Vim fought a war with us and drove us here. Or this is some . . . some Cradle."

He chuckled, a deep, infectious sound. "Good, you are thinking about the possibilities. You are correct to refer to the Cetturo Arm as a Cradle. We can discuss that later. Now that you know what the Thedes are really striving for, will you—"

"No," Kivita said. "I should leave here right now. You say I'll be followed wherever I go. Well, I don't want this station and its people to suffer. I've seen enough pain inflicted in the search for me and the Juxj Star." She thought of the little boy in the galley, the other children.

"You know it will not stop even if you flee," Navon said in a low voice.

"Will it mean I'll have to live here the rest of my life? If we share what we know, I mean."

Navon paused. "No. You are your own person. One who I think has both strength and morals. I would not have asked you if I thought you would betray us or waste knowledge."

"C'mon, how does one waste knowledge?" Kivita asked, still unsure of her decision.

"By not using it."

They stared at one another for a long moment. Kivita finally bit her lip.

"Are there more ... scenes of my mother in these other datacores? In your mind?" Her mouth went dry speaking the word. *Mother.*

"Only one as far as I know. Should you choose to go through with this, then you will see it. I also want to focus on the Juxj Star. Your talents are strong, but you must learn to control the pain of data transfer from a datacore to your brain. Whereas a Savant forgets much of the information after taking their hand off a datacore, you haven't. I have no doubt the pain is worse for you as a result."

A few minutes later, they sat cross-legged on the middle grass mat. She'd removed her hat and chaps. The Juxj Star rested on the mat between them.

"When touching a Vim datacore, your mind should be clear, your breathing calm," Navon said. "The first data transfers are usually minor ones. Let these flow into your mind; do not resist them. When large chunks of data surface in your thoughts, try to focus on each individual one and absorb it in its entirety. This will be difficult at first. Once you have mastered this, a datacore can reveal most of its secrets over a few hours of study."

"And the pain?"

"That will fade if you control the flow of data. Focus, attune, and absorb. You must learn how to do all three. Let this be your first lesson."

Kivita nodded. Together they reached out to the Juxj Star until their fingertips barely touched the smooth, round surface. The red gem glowed from inside. Navon's eyes widened in surprise.

She closed her eyes as details on an air recycler entered her thoughts. *Improved air scrubbers, a more conservative moisture intake valve, catch pockets for pathogens, and insertion tubes for liquid medication, which could be vaporized into an air supply through the recycler.*

As she followed Navon's advice, the data didn't bombard her consciousness this time.

A system for improved hydraulics on starship lifts came to mind, then coordinates for a tiny world with rich farming soil just eighteen light years outside the Cetturo Arm. An analysis of interstellar asteroids, showing how each could be mined for exotic new bulkheads, stronger hulls.

Her temples ached. "I see what you mean. Now I can—"

A bulk of data hit Kivita's mind. She concentrated, fingers balling into fists. Sweat ran down her cheeks.

"Focus," Navon said.

Her skin crawled with chill bumps. Electric, tingling sensations ran over her scalp. Jaw-popping pain shot into her skull.

"Attune and absorb," Navon whispered.

An old memory of her father surfaced in her mind, telling her to be patient with the manuals as she piloted Terredyn Narbas *over Haldon Six. Showing her how to judge short distances with the eye, almost feel the starship in the void, without depending on the navigational computer. His kind, crooked smile urged her on.*

The memory merged with her having piloted *Terredyn Narbas* over Tejuit by thought alone.

"Rhyer showed you how to link your brain with your ship's navigational system?" Navon asked. "Uncanny."

The pain in her temples crept into her forehead. Kivita concentrated harder, slowing the data flow in her mind. *Different starship designs to hold more cargo and use less energy, farming techniques to revitalize soil with natural bacteria and fertilizer, rather than coarse chemicals or slash-and-burn tactics. Medication to relieve Bellerion bog diseases or Haldon winter flu.*

The Juxj Star offered many such beneficial technologies, but why nothing on weaponry or warfare? It made the dogma of the Vim imprisoning humanity in the Arm for past sins ludicrous. Now she understood why the Inheritors considered the Vim superior beings, even gods; there seemed to be no limit to their scientific marvels. There had to be a reason, beyond mere posterity, why the Vim would have left the datacores behind.

What did the Vim gain by doing all this when they were gone?

Instincts told her the far-flung coordinates she'd gleaned, the origins of colony ships, even the Aldaakian homeworld of Khaasis, all resided in other Vim Cradles. The Sarrhdtuu had either destroyed or conquered some of them. What their designs might be for her and the Cetturo Arm chilled Kivita's skin.

Navon grunted and shuddered, but Kivita increased her focus. Icy daggers cut into her brain, so cold they burned. Her mouth opened, loosing a silent cry.

Genetic coding for different human classifications entered her thoughts. Bulked soldiers, reed-thin pilots, fine-boned individuals adapted for low-G. Ones who could adapt to cold and gravity fluctuations: Aldaakians. Bulky individuals with increased metabolic rates and environmental tolerances: Ascali. Kith genes, and their use of hydrogen as food, then Sarrhdtuu code indices to integrate with their ships.

Navon shivered, and she grabbed his hand before he fell backward. Her other hand still remained on the Juxj Star.

Her breath caught at a memory of Sar meeting Navon on Bellerion. He looked a little younger: his eyes brighter, his smile easier. Kivita didn't want to intrude on Navon's life, but information flowed into her like water through a sieve.

One image stood out from the Juxj Star, though, and Kivita absorbed it over all others.

The viewer holding a hazel-eyed baby girl before a seashore fortress—Susuron Palace.

A frigid hammer blow smashed into her mind. Everything went dark and numb.

Kivita rolled over on her side, gasping. Sweat drenched her clothes, hair, and face, while chills ran along her body. Her tongue sought moisture in a bone-dry mouth. A humming in her ears matched the cold throb in her temples.

The Juxj Star remained on the mat, its divulgence still tickling her mind.

Navon lifted her to her feet, still shaking himself.

"You kept absorbing the data from the Juxj Star. I could not endure any more, yet you went on . . ." A few new wrinkles lined his face.

"I saw her. I saw her holding me. But how? If she was the Savant, then who recorded the data and how?" Kivita asked.

"Somehow the Savants of old were able to record their experiences, their thoughts, their knowledge in the datacores. How, I do not know." Navon sat on a couch and massaged his temples. "It also seems Terredyn could send her thoughts to datacores far away, which recorded them. Like that stone one, or the Juxj Star. Like you did within that crystal tower on Vstrunn."

"How'd I see your thoughts, then? Those memories of Sar."

"As I said, the human brain is the biological version of a datacore, Kivita. What else did you see? The images confused me once I glimpsed the different kinds of humans."

Kivita described the Ascali, Kith, Aldaakian, and Sarrhdtuu data. Navon listened with intense focus, not even blinking.

"I think there's more, too." She wiped her forehead. "Don't think I'll be trying to get it for a while, though. I feel as if I've just finished a high-G training session."

Navon rose. "We must eat and rest for a few hours. I would like you to use the Juxj Star again, as well as take on my personal data." He smiled at her frown. "It is not intruding. I think of it as sharing. I have nothing to hide."

Kivita's cheeks burned as she realized he might have looked into her past. "Well? What's the verdict on me, then?"

"I have been honing my mind for years, Kivita

Vondir. You took on more data in your first true session of absorption than Savants handle their entire lives. Legends said Queen Terredyn struck fear into the Inheritors with her amazing abilities to absorb and redistribute knowledge. You are her daughter in every way."

Kivita said nothing. As the truth sank in, everything she'd ever thought about herself changed. No wonder her father hadn't taken her along on his salvaging runs. What had he really been up to? And what about her own wanderlust? Maybe she'd been salvaging all along to discover these secrets, without realizing it.

Navon gently squeezed her shoulder. "The man whom you knew as your father reared a baby princess. I see a ripe queen before me now. Maybe you will become a mature empress—not of worlds and servants, but of wisdom."

She faced him. "Where is this ship going? Jandeel said you'd tell me."

"As soon as you boarded *Luccan's Wish* and we knew you were the one who sent that signal, we agreed it was time to investigate the signals' coordinates. Our enemies may already have."

"How far is it?" Kivita asked in a whisper.

"Six and a half light years. A little over two for *Luccan's Wish*. All aboard enter cryostasis in four month shifts, so you will have plenty of opportunities to hone your Savant skills."

She turned from Navon and fought the tremor in her heart. The more she learned about herself, the further Kivita traveled from Sar and the life she'd wanted.

24

Harsh light stung Sar's eyes, and then pseudoadrine splashed into his mouth, invigorating him to a fully awakened state. He raised his hands and coughed. No polyvambraces covered his arms. Sar glanced down. No polycuirass, no polygreaves. Just his gray bodyglove and boots. Both kinetic pistols had been taken.

The light flared in his vision again, and he moved his head.

"So this is what the great Sar Redryll has become? Frozen on a derelict trawler that wasn't even his own ship, floating in an uncharted asteroid field? How pathetic."

Recognizing the voice, he moved his head again. The light lessened in intensity. His eyes opened.

Sar stood in Kivita's cryopod, which had been placed upright against a wall covered in quartz mosaics. Bright lamps shone from the ceiling, encased in Susuron coral enclosures. The light glittered off the sandstone floor as if he gazed at a night sky filled with stars. Gold-thread drapes hung on either side of a quartz throne in a round chamber.

Several figures moved before him as his vision focused.

"Shit," Sar muttered. In the depths of his heart, he'd known it would come to this.

Dunaar Thev walked toward him, dressed in a scintillating outer robe, clasping a stone staff. "Not to mention irreverent. Guard, show him what such a foul tongue earns him."

A soldier in a red jumpsuit slammed a baton into Sar's stomach. Sar heaved and doubled over. The soldier struck him again over the head. Though blood blinded Sar's left eye, he raised his hand in feeble defense as the baton rose again.

"That is sufficient," Dunaar said. "Shall we continue? Ah yes, that's better. Tell me, Sar, how many Thede agents do you think my loyal soldiers have killed in the past year in Inheritor space?"

Sar gripped the cryopod's sides and staggered onto the sandstone floor. Two soldiers with batons moved forward, but Dunaar waved them off. Behind the Rector, Shekelor Thal smirked at Sar. The pirate warlord wore different green carapace armor, and three new coils writhed from his left wrist.

"Not as many as will rise up and take their place." Gut throbbing, Sar forced down vomit and wiped blood from his eye. "Been expecting this a long time, Dunaar."

Dunaar laughed with good humor. "Yes, you should have. All traitors know what their eventual end will be. Like those on Sutara, recently liberated by my soldiers. Two hundred thousand dead. Such a waste."

Loss tore at Sar's heart, and his jaw clenched. He'd trained some of the Thedes on Sutara, smuggled weapons to them, given medicine to their children.

"You were a renowned pilot and salvager, famed throughout the Cetturo Arm. Who knows what path a man of your talents could have taken, even mastered? I could have placed you in command of this very ship." Dunaar sighed.

"What the hell do you want? I was busy." Sar glared at him.

Dunaar frowned and motioned a soldier forward.

The soldier came at Sar with the baton again. Sar waited until the last moment, then ducked and grabbed the soldier's collar. Using the man's momentum, Sar flung him to the floor and grabbed the baton.

Two more soldiers charged him, but Sar whipped the baton across the first man's jaw. Blood and teeth flew, and the soldier collapsed. The second struck Sar's left shoulder and elbowed Sar's right side. Sar rammed his palm into the man's left temple and knocked him to the floor, baton snapping the man's neck. Swinging around, Sar lunged at Dunaar.

Two coils slammed into Sar's side while another one yanked the baton from his hand. Sar collapsed to the floor, coughing. Shekelor stood over him.

More soldiers rushed forward, but Dunaar held up a hand.

"I appreciate this, Sar. Really, I do. I have long wanted you to kneel before the headsman's block since I discovered your true allegiances. Thanks to your former associate here, of course. But as much as I enjoy watching you suffer, we are wasting time."

Dunaar motioned to Shekelor, who dragged Sar to the center of the room, into a round mosaic. It depicted an Inheritor prophet touching a mysterious hand coming from a cloud. Blood dribbled from Sar's left temple and busted lip onto the prophet's quartz face.

"Where is Kivita Vondir? You were on her ship. You

were even in her cryopod, Sar. So where could she be? On your ship, *Frevyx*? Or hidden away somewhere in the Tejuit system? I doubt she is in the asteroid field where Shekelor recovered you." Dunaar sat on the quartz throne.

Nothing would leave his lips. These bastards could peel off his skin and he still wouldn't tell them.

Shekelor nudged Sar with his boot. "It is rather rude of you not to answer the Rector, Redryll."

Sar locked stares with Dunaar and spat on the mosaic beneath him. Shekelor wrapped a coil around Sar's throat, but Dunaar grunted.

"No, he will talk. It is still too early. I doubt you could wrangle her location from him with a simple beating." Dunaar pressed a button on his throne's armrest and a four-foot cylinder extended from the ceiling. A light flickered on the tip and shone down on the floor before Sar.

The hologram of a Sarrhdtuu with two eyes and a dozen coils appeared.

"This is not Kivita Vondir, Prophet of Meh Sat," the Sarrhdtuu said in a squishy, mucus-choked voice.

Dunaar wiped sweat from his brow. "Sar and his Thede allies have tried to trick us, Zhhl. I assure you it won't work."

Sar rubbed his throat after Shekelor removed his coil from around it. "You'll never find them. Search the cosmos; raze a thousand worlds if you like. You still won't find them."

"You Thedes think you are so clever, with a null beacon on that old ship," Dunaar said. "You cannot hide from the righteous."

Sar's heart jumped. Only Thedes knew about the special beacon on *Luccan's Wish*.

"Zhhl, we are now en route to find Kivita and the Thedes," Dunaar said. "*Frevyx*'s transmitting beacon was more than sufficient to give us the trajectory. Though I was surprised when your friends decided to investigate the signal sent from Vstrunn, Sar."

"This is acceptable. Kivita Vondir must be recovered. Sarrhdtuu ships have been deployed, Prophet of Meh Sat." Zhhl's hologram flickered over Sar like a god from a dark abyss, then disappeared.

Sar glowered. "You're lying about my ship's beacon, just trying to get me to tell—"

"I think it is time you met someone." Dunaar nodded at one of the soldiers, and the man left the chamber.

"The Sarrhdtuu are just using you," Sar said. "Just like they used you for that mission to Xeh's Crown."

"I think this will reveal who is using whom," Dunaar said as the soldier returned. Two Proselytes in copper-meld cuirasses and black masks flanked an Ascali female. She wore a translucent gown and full-face veil. Her dark mane, brown fur, and russet eyes made Sar frown.

"Zhara, your veil, please?" Dunaar rose from the throne.

The Ascali removed the veil, revealing a beautiful face with sharp cheekbones and full lips. The same face Sar had tried to replace Kivita with.

"Cheseia?" His skin numbed. A sharp pain stabbed his heart. "Cheseia!"

A Proselyte jabbed a nerve above Sar's collarbone with a finger. Sar cried out and fell to his knees.

"Not quite. My lovely double agent is aboard *Luccan's Wish* even now. Amazing what one will do, when one's twin sister is involved. When my spies discovered two female Ascali had departed Sygma with a merchant suspected of being a Thede sympathizer, I acted. Cheseia has taken long enough, but as you can see, patience brings fruition." Dunaar smiled.

"I am truly, deeply sorry," Zhara whispered, her delicate voice an octave higher than Cheseia's. Sorrow radiated from her gaze.

Dunaar whacked the back of Zhara's legs with his staff. She grunted and her lithe body struck the floor.

"You see, Sar? This one is strong like her sister. I hope you enjoyed Cheseia. Rutting in space like two beasts." Dunaar leered, sweat dribbling down his chin.

All his moments with Cheseia fell into doubt. Their relationship, her jealousy of Kivita, her incessant requests to meet with Navon and the Thede leadership. Always reminding Sar he possessed coordinates to their location.

Remembering how he'd handed Kivita over to her in those last moments over Tejuit.

Primal hate broiled in his heart. Sar punched the Proselyte in the face, but the man struck Sar three times in the chest. He teetered forward and grabbed the Proselyte's leg. As the man swung down, Sar rolled and kicked the Proselyte over, then rose and balled his fists.

Coils encircled his throat again.

Shekelor shoved him up against the wall. "Naxans and Aldaakians shall not save you from me this time." His breath stank of the mildew Sar had once smelled aboard a Sarrhdtuu ship.

"You're mad," Sar breathed. "This is the future you wanted for Byelor? You'll be next."

"Play the patriotic fool to the end if you wish. I know how to survive." He rammed an elbow into Sar's back. "That is for one of my ships shot down over Tejuit."

"You're their slave! Their tool!" Sar pulled at the coils with all his strength. Sleek like wet leather yet hard as steel, they didn't budge.

"This is for losing Umiracan." Shekelor backhanded Sar. Blood flew from Sar's busted lips.

Dunaar walked over, staff in both hands. "That is sufficient, Shekelor Thal."

"Zhhl told me I would be allowed to have him. Redryll owes me restitution, shall we say?" Shekelor's coils wrapped around Sar's arms.

Dunaar regarded the pirate warlord as one would a slug. "Leave us. When I am finished with him, you shall have what remains."

"And her?" Shekelor nodded at Zhara. "We had an agreement."

"Yes, as well as the Ascali," Dunaar said. "Her usefulness is at an end."

The coils dumped Sar onto the floor. "I shall hold you to that agreement . . . Rector." Shekelor kicked Sar's thigh and left the chamber.

"Such polite, fancy talk between you two. Doesn't change the fact you're both assholes." Sar smirked.

Eyes narrowed to dangerous slits, Dunaar approached Sar. "Bring them."

The two Proselytes hauled Sar to his feet and escorted him behind the Rector. Two others followed with Zhara. The group entered a wide corridor spaced with open doorways and hatches. Colored glass mosaics decorated the walls, and every ten feet a soldier stood at attention. Sar walked on his own, though the Proselytes held his arms above the elbow. A plush red carpet silenced his boot steps. He smelled the scent of clean-scrubbed air mixed with lotus oil fragrance. Gold-chased sconces and painted Susuron shells hung near every door.

"Grown fat in more ways than one, Dunaar," Sar said. "Too bad the Sarrhdtuu will take it all from you."

Dunaar snapped his fingers, and a Proselyte shoved a pacifier gag into Sar's mouth. The rubber nipple filled his mouth and touched the rim of his throat. Sar steeled himself against the urge to retch.

They led him past a hall where cryopods contained hundreds of Inheritor soldiers. Another chamber housed a dozen gorgeous serving girls in cryostasis. Sar had heard of *Arcuri's Glory*, the flagship of the Rector, but never realized so much was wasted for one man. Each gold-trimmed piece of decor reminded him of the Freen workers who'd died producing it.

The group entered a narrow corridor branching off from the main hall. Soldiers in full polysuits guarded a barred and locked doorway. Dunaar drew the bar aside and keyed in the lock sequence. The door opened from the inside.

Three chairs fitted with flexi restraints and rusted iron clamps waited in a room lit by a single lamp. Six small cells held four men and two women. All wore evergreen bodygloves and had malnourished visages.

"Kivita sends," one woman with large green eyes said. She gazed at Sar as if she knew him.

The Proselytes strapped Sar into the middle chair and removed the gag, while Dunaar sat on a stool opposite Sar. Zhara waited near the door, the two soldiers holding her. One of the imprisoned men whimpered.

"You think I am a cruel man, Sar. I did not harm Zhara to make Cheseia obey my commands. On the contrary, she willingly revealed your Thede allegiance upon hearing Zhara had joined my serving staff." Dunaar examined his fingernails.

"Get this over with. You know everything you want to know." Sar braced himself. Proselytes were known torture specialists, zealous and nonempathic.

"Yet you want to take away from everyone else. Do you feel no shame?" Perspiration coursed down Dunaar's nose. "What gives you the right to make decisions for millions of others? Who asked you to rescue them from the light and offer them darkness?"

"Kivita sends . . . Rector, Rector? Hmm." The green-eyed woman rocked back and forth in her cell, moaning. One Proselyte kicked the bars of her cell, and she quieted.

"You are the darkness," Sar said.

Dunaar glared. "Time is running out, do you not see? We shall all starve and freeze on cold worlds unless we heed the Vim's holy call. Everything I do is for everyone's salvation. Even yours. And how do you reward this generosity?"

A Proselyte pinched Zhara's neck. She shrieked and her body spasmed, but the soldiers forced her to remain standing.

"By trying to destroy everything I, and generations of Rectors, have striven to build."

The Proselyte jerked Zhara's head back by the hair and pressed a thumb into her temples. The Ascali grunted, gasped, then squalled in agony.

Sar wanted to kill them all. Cut up every last one of the bastards. Fists clenched, legs tensed, Sar remained silent. Everything would be in vain if he crumbled. All his life, all his struggles, had brought him to this moment. He would not fail Kivita.

"See? You do not care for others. One word from you, one piece of information, and this lovely creature would be free of pain." Dunaar rose from the chair and swung the staff with both hands into Zhara's gut. She wheezed and went limp in the guard's arms, but her eyes dared Sar to speak.

Dunaar pointed at Sar, and the other Proselyte jabbed a thumb behind Sar's right ear. Clenching his jaw, Sar squirmed in the chair. Nerve endings burned along his back.

"You resist because you think that I will kill you afterward. Or Shekelor, since he will take possession of you once I am satisfied." Dunaar stroked Zhara's cheek and sniffed her mane. "There is nothing noble about being a fool, Sar. Think about the innocents who have perished in Thede terrorist acts. The brave troops who gave their lives defending the faithful from your ilk."

A Proselyte pinched a nerve on Sar's left wrist. Fiery pain raced up his arm and blazed in his chest.

"I see mutation in your eyes, Sar," Dunaar said. "Had the Inheritors policed your homeworld earlier, you would have been born whole. You could have been something greater than a mere rebel. Caitrynn could have lived a long time—"

"You made me what I am!" Sar shouted. "By invading Freen, you son of a bitch! Killing my sister, killing—"

Grabbing Sar by the hair, Dunaar faced him nose to nose. "How many more would die if I allowed every world to decide its fate? How many children would starve, how many would fall in senseless wars? Millions! How long will you remain blind? The Vim are our only hope. Eventually we will destroy ourselves in this small, galactic spiral arm. We human beings were meant for something greater. We were meant to rise above this prison!"

"You built this prison, but people will rise and cut you down," Sar said through gritted teeth.

"Not after I have annihilated your friends. Consider all the minds you have poisoned, all the lives lost due to your sinful practices! What have the Thedes accomplished but the spread of suffering and hate? Look at my flabby face, my sweaty brow. A Thede bomb irradiated my glands as a boy. All my life I have hated your kind. You are scum, less than human. If not for the Vim and their prophets, you would still be living in mud huts or hiding in caves!"

Sar spat in Dunaar's face.

Both Proselytes throttled Sar. Fists pummeled his face, struck his chest. Blood and drool flew from his mashed lips. Dunaar shouted into his ears; the Rector's spittle and sweat splattered Sar's neck. All the while, Sar focused on the woman he loved, the one who'd wanted him to finish something, to stop running.

"Shekelor told me all about Caitrynn." Dunaar smacked Sar in the head with the stone staff. "He told me quite a bit about Kivita." He rapped the staff against Sar's knees. "Do you see a pattern here, Sar? Your hatred, your sin, has destroyed all that you love. By the Vim, I shall not allow you to destroy any more lives. All those thousands that perished on Sutara, and for what? Do you hear?"

Trembling in agony, Sar shook his head in the negative.

Dunaar laid the staff across Sar's neck and rammed his head into the back of the chair eight times. "Do you hear? Do you?" he screamed in Sar's face. Sweat coursed from Dunaar's hands and down Sar's numb, swollen face.

Old, raw emotions cracked open Sar's heart. Dunaar was right, just like Shekelor. Sar had planned to use Kivita, had endangered her. Even now Cheseia might be delivering Kivita into Inheritor or Sarrhdtuu hands.

She might be dead, or undergoing far worse horrors than his own, all because he couldn't control his selfish hatred. Sar squeezed his eyes shut. Tears still stung his bloodied eyelids.

"There, my son," Dunaar whispered, caressing Sar's curly head. "You are brave enough to face the truth of your foul endeavors." He stood before Sar and sighed. "He is ready. Open Bredine's cell."

One Proselyte opened the green-eyed woman's cell and nudged her forward.

Dunaar sat back on the stool, sweat pooling under his jowls. "Decode his brain. Find out what he knows about Kivita Vondir."

Bredine paused, then grabbed Sar's head in both hands. Sar waited for something to hit him, cause pain, or at least make his skin crawl. Nothing but a low throb traveled through his cranium. Bredine moaned and took deep breaths.

Numb with pain, Sar tried to resist, but Bredine cupped his head with surprising tenderness. Layers of memory peeled away as a distant whooshing entered his ears. The room faded as he lost himself in more pleasant recollections.

In reverse, Sar remembered his last moments with Kivita before leaving Tejuit. She'd almost told him she loved him; he was sure of it. *Their hungry kisses after the argument on* Terredyn Narbas, *rescuing her on Vstrunn, watching her chest rise and fall as she breathed through the mask. Exploring the ice cap on Gontalo together, then throwing snowballs at each other. Making love to Kivita in his hammock aboard* Frevyx *with the gravity turned off, her hands gripping his buttocks, her mouth melded with his. The first emotional stirrings toward her as they escaped the derelict near Xeh's Crown.*

The room faded back into view, along with his aching body. Dunaar watched him like a starving madman.

Bredine shook as she drew back. "So gushing hot. Hmm." She bumped against his right wrist.

A Proselyte shoved a finger in Sar's ear and pinched a nerve on his neck. Sar screamed, his limbs jerking in the restraints.

"Leave him be," Dunaar said in a casual voice. "Though you aren't a Vim datacore, Sar, Savants can still access your memories. My predecessors learned long ago how to train these mongrels to wrest information from others."

"What good will it do you?" Sar managed through stinging lips. He wasn't sure if the Proselyte's nerve attack or Bredine invading his mind made him shudder.

"He's in love. Love, love, love. Gushing hot in void cold, yes. Gushing hot with Kivita. Love with a Savant, Rector. Food? Food, food, food." Bredine pointed at herself and the five inmates.

Dunaar looked bored. "Don't look so shocked; Cheseia told me of your affair with Kivita. You took the mission to Vstrunn rather quickly, as I had hoped. Yet it was not meant to be. Kivita will enter my Savant breeding program as a host for my children. Imagine how much she will enjoy that." He chuckled.

Sar scowled at Dunaar. "Why the Sarrhdtuu?"

"Zhhl wants her, and once she births a few of my children, she will have served her purpose. Be content that Kivita fulfilled a role in guiding us to the sainted Vim. You should feel blessed being on the periphery of such a historical figure."

Emotion rose in Sar's chest again. Kivita might have fulfilled so much more. Seeing all those memories . . . all those precious, irreplaceable moments. He still loved Kivita, still had to hope she might make it. A reserve of strength he'd never realized existed blossomed into his limbs.

"Golden capsule? Hmm. Kivita slept in void cold. From baby to woman in golden capsule." Bredine backed away as a Proselyte motioned her back to her cell.

"Never worry, my son, for—"

Sar wrenched his head away from Dunaar's hand. "Go to hell."

Dunaar snapped his finger at the Proselytes. "Place him in cryostasis after he cannot scream anymore. Then you may tell that pirate he may claim him." He smoothed his robe and left the room. Zhara shot Sar a remorseful glance before the two soldiers elbowed her after Dunaar.

Gritting his teeth again, Sar prepared himself. As he flexed his fingers, the restraint over his right wrist loosened where a sharp bolt brushed his knuckles. He glanced at Bredine. She watched him with anxiousness, standing before her open cell.

The first Proselyte aimed a finger at Sar's ear again. As the gloved digit neared him, Sar wrenched his right hand free and shoved the bolt into the Proselyte's neck. Hot blood sprayed Sar's hand. The man jerked back and fell.

The other Proselyte backhanded Sar and pinched his left shoulder. Every nerve on his left side ignited in white-hot pain. Sar screamed and tried to punch, but his strike went awry.

As the wounded Proselyte writhed on the floor, the other Savants whimpered in their cells. Sar gasped and reached for the ankle clamps, but the second Proselyte kicked Sar's hand away and reached for the door alarm.

Bredine slammed her foot into the Proselyte's side, then punched his jaw. Sar tried to work the other clamps loose while the Proselyte rapped Bredine's left temple. She wobbled and slumped against the wall as Sar ripped away his ankle clamps. The Proselyte rounded on him.

Sar worked his left arm free just as the Proselyte punched. Ducking, Sar jabbed the man's stomach. Bredine strangled the Proselyte from behind as Sar rammed the flat of his palm into the man's nose. A crunch, a grunt, and the Proselyte struck the floor.

Without flinching, Bredine bent over and snapped both Proselytes' necks. One of the male Savants wept, and another urinated in his cell.

"Hmm. Too far gone. Gone, gone. Leave them here?" Bredine pointed at her fellow inmates.

His entire body aching, Sar caught his breath. "Guess so." A shiver rippled along his shoulder as the nerves finally settled.

Bredine looped his left arm around her slim shoulders. "Food, food, food," she muttered, gazing up at Sar with hope.

"Just help me get this guy's uniform on before they come back," Sar said.

25

Seul took shallow breaths as Vuul stared her down on *Aldaar*'s bridge. Fresh out of her polyarmor, she felt nude in the presence of the operations staff and two squads of armed Troopers. Qaan and the other Archivers brooded nearby, sharing worried glances. Why were they all wasting time? They needed to act.

Kivita needed her.

"Why did you not fire upon *Terredyn Narbas* before it made a light jump from the Tejuit system?" Vuul's tone stole the air from the bridge. "A crippled, unarmed vessel. Why, Captain Jaah?"

"Inheritor ships had already entered the system." Seul's cryoports tightened. "I thought it best—"

"You were under orders, Captain Jaah. When under orders, you do not think. You act."

"Someone captured her before my squad arrived, Commander Vuul. The main Inheritor battleship has just exited this system, while their other ships remain. That can't be a coincidence. Kivita is important to them. She must be aboard that battleship." Seul wished Kael could be at her side, but she didn't want him to face Vuul's wrath, too.

The operations staff looked at one another with pinched expressions. One of them cleared his throat and spoke.

"Commander Vuul, Captain Jaah may have a point. The basis for the Vim signal we detected from Vstrunn contained a powerful brain-pulse signature. It came from a Savant of a magnitude never recorded. This signal contains the coordinates taken by the Inheritor battleship."

Vuul's brows knitted together. "So you theorize that the Inheritors plan to use Kivita Vondir for more such signals?"

The three Archivers talked among themselves.

"Well?" Vuul glared at the Archivers.

"The Inheritors are known only to execute Savants, though intelligence reports state that they may keep some in captivity," Qaan replied.

Seul almost stepped forward, then remembered herself. "But the Inheritors hired Kivita—"

"There can be no doubt they are mounting an assault on our worlds. Any warning message sent will not reach Aldaakian Space in time." Vuul's words left a tense silence on the bridge.

Seul waited out of respect and protocol, but she burned inside. Didn't he understand what was at stake? Without Kivita or the Vim, there would soon be no Aldaakian worlds to defend. Bravery and discipline were no longer enough. Her people needed help this time.

"Your orders, Commander Vuul?" one of the staff asked.

"*Aldaar* will pursue the Inheritor battleship. Kivita Vondir must be eliminated." Vuul paced the bridge, hands behind his back.

A weight plummeted in Seul's gut but she gazed at Vuul, unflinching. "Commander Vuul, Kivita is the very thing all Aldaakians have been hoping for. We must save her."

"We cannot engage in combat with such a larger ship," one of the Archivers mumbled. "It measures over four thousand feet and bristles with kinetic gun batteries. One broadside from it would cripple us."

"We should retreat to Aldaakian Space and regroup with our fleets, Commander Vuul," a staff officer said. "To follow that battleship would be suicide. Kivita Vondir's fate is out of our hands."

Qaan straightened. "No. She cannot be allowed—"

"You all have your orders." Vuul sat in his command chair.

Seul's cryoports clicked shut, and she stepped before Vuul's chair. "We have fought for our survival for centuries, and adapted our race to starships and cryopods, just to keep running? Niaaq Aldaar never retreated. He fought the Sarrhdtuu against all—"

"That is enough, Captain," Vuul said.

"It is never enough! We've allowed the Sarrhdtuu to corner us here in the Cetturo Arm. This is our one chance."

Vuul rose from the chair, white-within-azure eyes receding into a contorted face. "Are you implying I am unfit for the command of this vessel?"

Seul met his stare. "I'm saying we follow those coordinates and help Kivita, Commander Vuul. How can we stand by and argue while the Inheritors—and perhaps the Sarrhdtuu—rush to those same coordinates? What if they lead to a Vim ship or a colony? What if the Vim appear, after so long an absence, and their old allies are not there to stand with them?"

"I am not a coward!" Vuul roared.

"Then what is it you fear?" Seul asked.

Troopers and operations staff gaped at her.

"They must know . . . Commander Vuul," Qaan said.

Vuul turned his back on Seul. "Tell them," he whispered.

Qaan clasped his chit booklet in both hands. "Before the Fall of Khaasis, the Sarrhdtuu had difficulty in defeating our fleets. Our Troopers prevailed; our vessels held firm. We took the battle to them, thus safeguarding our worlds. It was our undoing."

Everyone on the bridge listened, as still as cryo ice sculptures. Seul's anger subsided, and her cryoports relaxed. The Fall of Khaasis had always been blamed on Sarrhdtuu aggression; this information wasn't part of the Archivers' curriculum.

"In our zeal we left the Vim undefended. We left Khaasis undefended." Qaan raised the booklet over his head, and his normally rough voice cracked. "Undefended not from starships, but from within. They turned our ships against us, controlling our vessels by thought alone. We underestimated the Sarrhdtuu. They used human Savants to undermine and weaken us."

"Kivita activated the Vim signal. She isn't being used by anyone," Seul said.

Qaan continued as if she'd not spoken. "The Sarrhdtuu crushed any who made a stand. Niaaq Aldaar and his Troopers held off many ships while the survivors escaped in colony-ship caravans . . ."

Vuul turned back around, an ageless guilt in his eyes.

"A Sarrhdtuu fleet attacked our ancestors. Something caused many of their ships to crash into one another. An image was transmitted to some of the surviving craft." He nodded to Qaan, who opened his chit booklet.

The display screen inside the booklet showed a bloodied human male wrapped in gray-green coils. He knelt on what appeared to be the deck of a Sarrhdtuu ship. The agony on his face made Seul's cryoports clamp shut.

In the human's hands was the Juxj Star.

Seul blinked. Kivita had shown impressive piloting skills over Umiracan and Tejuit—too impressive for a salvage trawler to handle, much less while damaged. No. Kivita had to be the one.

"I have kept watch over Vstrunn for decades," Vuul said. "Now you know why I have attacked any humans who made it off the planet's surface. Those the Kith did not kill, we eliminated. The Juxj Star was safe."

"We have guarded the very thing that might have destroyed us and the Vim. It might yet destroy us." Qaan's shoulders sagged.

"Perhaps we are destroying ourselves." Seul's fingers brushed her cryoports.

The tension on the bridge gave way to shamed, crestfallen visages. Even before Seul's birth, Archivers surmised that the Aldaakians had failed the Vim, failed to fight the Sarrhdtuu with every last ounce of Aldaakian blood. So many worlds had fallen, so many fleets reduced to space dust.

It would end. No more running. Seul swore it. The silent oath filled her with strength.

Vuul said nothing and stared at a flat display. Reaching out toward him, Seul hesitated. What was she doing? Kivita wouldn't have hesitated. A well of inner strength burst forth and she touched his shoulder.

"Let us investigate Kivita's signal. She isn't the enemy. Let us reclaim the honor of our ancestors, but not for ourselves. For those who come after."

"Have all crew wakened one hour before we exit the jump," Vuul finally said in a low voice. "Send a message to our people that *Aldaar* is taking action, and then follow that battleship's last beacon trajectory."

The operations staff lost their stunned looks and obeyed Vuul's orders. Within moments *Aldaar* shuddered as it made a light jump.

"To your cryopods, everyone." Vuul glanced at Seul. "Save for you, Captain Jaah."

While everyone else filed out, she maintained her erect stature.

The bridge door hissed shut, and running lights dimmed as *Aldaar* prepped to shut down life support. The entire crew would enter cryostasis this time.

"I know you're not a coward," she whispered, eyes forward.

"And I know the hope you hold out for this human woman," Vuul whispered back. "Once, I too possessed similar hopes."

They looked at each other. *Aldaar*'s running lights illuminated Vuul's face in forlorn, blue-gray shades.

"Only once?" Seul asked.

Vuul looked away and placed his hands behind his back.

"Captain Jaah, you will have overall command of Shock Trooper squads, should the need arise to engage the enemy. Find Kivita Vondir and the Juxj Star. The order for her execution . . . is rescinded."

Seul nodded and gesticulated between her chest cryoports, a new strength blazing into her heart. "It is done, Commander Vuul."

For the first time, Vuul smiled at her.

26

"You can't escape!"

Kivita laughed and tickled Basheev, the dark-skinned Dirr boy, on the observation deck. After he squirmed into a corner beside a six-foot tall indigo hibiscus, she pretended to lose interest, then turned and tickled his armpits. Laughing, Basheev fled behind the two Naxan women, who mused over potting soils.

"Look here: there is to be no playing around these plants!" called Maihh, the head Naxan horticulturalist. Her gray hair was tied back in a bun, which shook when she moved. A green-and-yellow dress draped her thin frame.

"C'mon, let's go," Kivita said, but Basheev laughed and shook his head.

Maihh clicked twice and crossed her arms. "You are standing too close to that golden rhododendron, young man. It is a rare species."

Hands on hips, Kivita leaned toward the flower. With their mauve petals and brilliant yellow buds, the rhododendrons reminded her of her childhood. Rhyer had always brought back flowers from his travels, though often in small containers. This bush came to her shoulder, and had an eight-foot diameter. Kivita reached out to it, trying to imagine its native world.

Maihh lightly slapped Kivita's hand away. "They only remain as beautiful as you are, my dear, because they remain untouched." She clicked once and grinned at Kivita.

"I'm still amazed at the work you do." Kivita steered Basheev away from the rhododendron. "I've never seen such flowers."

"Nax is all desert, so my people had to master plants before we could master ourselves. Life is easier to cherish when it is so frail. So similar to us Thedes. Have you enjoyed your stay with us so far?" Maihh clicked twice.

Gazing around the observation deck, Kivita nodded. "It's like another world aboard this ship." From the corner of her eye, she spied Basheev trying to sneak away.

"Gotcha!" Kivita grabbed Basheev and tickled his belly. In his struggles, the boy's hand brushed a hibiscus blossom.

Maihh clicked three times, while the other Naxan woman shouted and waved her hands in the air. Laughing, Kivita and Basheev rushed through the circular door. They almost knocked over Jandeel in the adjoining corridor.

"You'll be banned from that room yet," Jandeel chided with a smile. "May we go to the library now?"

Kivita tousled Basheev's head before he ran off. "Yeah, yeah. I just ate after waking from cryosleep. Kinda hoped for a little relaxation before we started again."

Jandeel frowned. "I realize we're asking much of you. The Sages on board, including me, want more information to study from that Juxj Star. Believe me. I wish I could do this myself. But we don't know what awaits us at the end of this jump. We must be prepared."

"Yeah, you're right." Kivita paused and considered how far she'd progressed. Eight Haldon months had passed, with four months of it spent in cryostasis. Navon, Jandeel, and the others had taught her much about the Thede ambition: sharing knowledge with all, so everyone could be equal and content. Though not certain about such a lofty philosophy, Kivita relished the sense of community aboard *Luccan's Wish*.

Each time she saw the Thede children, like Basheev, Kivita thought of Sar. His lie about being sterile, or what he would think of her, the daughter of a long-dead queen. A princess without a crown, without a throne. Without her swarthy, curly-haired king.

"Are you well?" Jandeel asked, concern in his eyes.

"Still taking it all in, you know?" She gestured at the ship around them.

Jandeel smiled. "Let's grab a drink before you give the other Savants more tasks."

As they walked through pressurized corridors and chambers, people smiled at Kivita. Everyone knew her Savant talents, which now exceeded even Navon's. But how much longer could she handle all this attention? Gifts had been placed in her chambers: flowers, a Tannocci marriage contract requesting her hand, and even a lock of Ascali hair, a potent symbol of respect.

Why did they think she deserved all this?

She returned the smiles, but despite the new friendships and attention, Kivita missed the hammock on *Terredyn Narbas*, and Sar's mysterious smirk. She hoped he was . . . well, she just hoped.

In the galley two other Sages stopped Jandeel and

whispered to him. Kivita smiled at them and blew a kiss to Basheev. He shied away, then blew it back. The air smelled cleaner since her knowledge about the improved air scrubber had been put to use. As she neared the serving counter, the Dirr serving woman, Rhii, grinned.

"Stars shine and twinkle, miss! No wonder Basheev ran in here with that smile. I see you still have that Dirr braid I plaited for you." Rhii handed her a cup of woodsnake milk; Kivita now loved the thick drink.

"I might add one on the other side, too." Kivita touched the small, plaited tress dangling from her right temple.

Rhii grinned wider. "Stars blinking, miss! Beware of the third braid. Only married Dirr women plait three into their hair."

Cheseia stepped up to the bar beside Kivita. "I hear your studies have truly come along?" Since volunteering for the maintenance staff, Cheseia's cryostasis shift remained a month away. The beautiful Ascali hadn't aged in a noticeable way—save for her eyes. Those exhausted russet orbs always seemed occupied.

"Yeah, you wouldn't believe the things I've seen. Hey, you look tired. You okay?"

"I am definitely fine." Cheseia touched Kivita's braid. "You are so radiantly vibrant here. I must honestly admit, when I first saw you . . ."

Kivita smiled wanly. "Yeah, I know. I was a scruffy salvager tramp."

Cheseia squeezed Kivita's hand. "Now I know you thankfully are not. You are truly honorable." The Ascali released her grip and accepted a cup of jiir juice from Rhii.

"I . . . thanks. Hey, you going to the gym later? I liked that last workout we had." Kivita gulped her milk to alleviate the sudden dryness in her mouth.

"Yes, but now I must surely go to Level Two and continue my duties." After touching Kivita's braid again, she left.

Kivita sipped her milk, eyeing the Ascali's departing form as pride swelled in her chest. To think they'd once been enemies.

"Winking stars, but I still remember when Sar saved my boy and me from that Inheritor blockade," Rhii said. "Darkest stars, it was near Susuron, maybe thirteen Haldon years ago. Basheev was no taller than your knees, miss."

"Really?" Taking another drink, Kivita's pride deflated. All this time she'd hated Sar, cursed him, and he'd been saving people. Making a difference while she'd slept in cryo or caroused in dingy spaceports.

Jandeel joined her at the bar and accepted a mug of reed ale. "Everyone is growing more excited as we draw closer to those coordinates. People will grow more nervous, too. Everyone wants to know what's coming."

"Guess that's where I come in." Kivita finished her drink. "C'mon, let's go visit my favorite gem."

After exiting the galley and taking an elevator to Level Six, Kivita and Jandeel entered the ship's library. Sages, students, and Savants looked up from their studies. She was dressed in a blue skinsuit and chaps, and more than a few admiring stares came her way. Her cheeks warmed.

"Yeah, okay, so you know I'm in here." She smiled. Everyone chuckled and grinned back.

Jandeel sat at a desk with four other Sages, and three

male Savants sat on a bench opposite them. The students all waited, holding computer chits and glue pens. Kivita still felt uncomfortable while these people paid attention to her words, even the inflection of her voice, every time she described her visions.

Entering from another door, Navon smiled at Kivita. "I see Jandeel finally discovered you?"

Kivita sat on a grass mat in the center of the room. "Sorry I'm late. What's the lesson this time?"

A Naxan Sage dressed in evergreen robes cleared his throat. "Come, now, my dear. You promised to reveal the genus of the Haldon red-grain seed from the Juxj Star." He emitted three clicks.

Jandeel frowned and rubbed his chin. "What of those details about energy dumps?"

A Tahe Sage, her slender form swathed in white cloth, spoke. "We require new engines to test such theories, Jandeel. The resources are not present aboard this ship."

"I suggest we let Kivita focus on her former transmissions," Navon said. "Perhaps a hint at what this Vim signal is and the coordinates we are headed toward will be gleaned."

Kivita waited while Jandeel placed the Juxj Star on the mat beside her. Though she'd uncovered minor data from it since her first meeting with Navon, no further probing of its deeper knowledge had been attempted.

Everyone sat still, watching her. Waiting. Her heartbeat raced. She swallowed. No matter how many times she did this, Kivita knew she'd never get used to it.

Laying her palm over the gem's surface, Kivita closed her eyes, and a slight tingling traveled across her temples. Weeks of training allowed her to resist the cold throb in her skull. With acute focus, she skipped past the datacore's outer information layers.

Her skin numbed. Sounds around her faded.

The image of figures in white exoskeletons returned, one Kivita hadn't seen since touching the datacores near Xeh's Crown. The shapes moved with mechanical precision, lifting huge steel girders and beams. Other forms walked around the base of the figure, carrying tools and satchels. Upturned earth and mortared foundations waited nearby. Tall, angular buildings and ordered forests riddled the landscape around the worksite.

Kivita let out a slow breath. Focus, attune, absorb, like Navon had taught her. The frigid ache in her temples dissipated.

The image morphed into one where the buildings had been gutted and burned. Several large colony ships lifted off barren soil now devoid of foliage. The ships exited the atmosphere and hung in space, where spiral arms filled with blue, yellow, and orange stars blinked. The colony ships departed the dying world.

"Meh Sat," Kivita whispered. The human homeworld.

As the ships left, a glimpse of gray-green, crescent-shaped craft appeared. Violet beams of light darted from the vessels to the planet below.

"The Sarrhdtuu destroyed it," she said with a strained voice.

A similar image of Khaasis, with Aldaakian fleets scattering in desperation, appeared in Kivita's thoughts. Again, Sarrhdtuu ships arrived and demolished the planet from orbit. Jewel-blue atmospheres darkened from soot and ash blown from the surface.

Kivita shuddered and licked her lips. "They ... they destroyed Cradles."

The vision transformed. Kivita gasped as a Sarrhdtuu held her against a wall, waving the Juxj Star in her face. Purple-slotted eyes widened as moist, steely coils tapped Kivita's head. She got the impression the Sarrhdtuu wanted her to do something with the Juxj Star. Something the viewer hadn't wanted to do.

The images blurred in her mind. Focus, attune, absorb. She couldn't lose her control, her concentration. Not now, please not now.

Kivita's mind peeled away another data layer. A huge chamber filled with transparent tubes and pipes, each flowing with green or yellow fluids, contained rows of vats containing green jelly. Humanoid figures floated inside each vat. Booms with stalklike appendages lifted several figures from the muck.

Yes, another of the images from Xeh's Crown! But . . . the body reminded her of Shekelor Thal's green-rigged augmentations. Sarrhdtuu Transmutation, she now realized.

The viewer struggled until opaque green liquid engulfed the vision.

Coughing, Kivita doubled over. Her grip tightened on the Juxj Star.

The gem sent another scene into her mind, where Rhyer Vondir waited in front of Kivita, wearing his purple cape and polymail. The charred remains of a Sarrhdtuu hull lay on the stone floor. Kivita concentrated on the gray-green metal covered in knobby protrusions.

By thought alone, the viewer—Kivita's mother—caused one of the protrusions to open.

Teeth chattering, head throbbing, she almost brought up the milk she'd drunk earlier. Hands prevented her from slumping to the floor.

"The datacore has stopped glowing," the Naxan Sage's voice entered Kivita's ears.

"She is taxed. Please stand back so she can have air." Navon's voice.

Kivita coughed again and sat up. "I'm okay," she mumbled, then took a deep breath. Her trembling ceased. The throbbing in her head lessened to a dull mental fatigue. The faces around her gawked and stared.

"Did it work? Was the data recorded?" As she loosed a shaking breath, the icy tingles left her temples.

Jandeel gaped at her, clutching his head. "You planted it into our minds. Without touching us, without speaking."

The Tahe Sage slumped over the desk and whimpered. One of the other Savants had fainted. Several students wobbled, clutching chits filled with written information.

Navon steadied himself against the wall. "You transmitted it to all of us, Kivita. Even I . . . have difficulty with what you have just shown us."

"The Sarrhdtuu have been our ancient enemies long before we ever came to the Cetturo Arm," Kivita breathed. "The Aldaakians are right."

"We have nothing they need," Jandeel said. "By all accounts, they don't seek out datacores."

"The Sarrhdtuu ships, the green-rigged people—I think they're connected somehow. I don't know how, but . . . my mother manipulated that piece of Sarrhdtuu hull." Kivita stood. Unlike the others, her strength had already returned.

"The same as you managed with other electronic devices, like you have described to us." Navon gripped her hand. "Kivita, that is why they want you. That is why they destroyed those worlds. They fear what you can do. Fear it so much, they massacred civilizations to contain it."

The Naxan Sage clicked five times. "That is speculation. From that vision, they green-rigged the very Savant who sent that memory to the Juxj Star. The Sarrhdtuu also wanted something performed with this datacore. If they fear Savants so much, why commit those things?"

Kivita shivered as Shekelor's final words over Tejuit entered her mind: *"You cannot escape."*

"Aldaakians lack the Savant ability," Jandeel said. "Why destroy their worlds, too, Navon? I always assumed the two fought over resources."

Everyone waited for Navon to answer, but Kivita bit her lip and shook her head.

"Remember—the Sarrhdtuu chased my mother's ship into the Cetturo Arm. By all rights, they should have incinerated it. Maybe that's how she escaped? By doing something to their ship . . . with her mind?"

"More speculation." The Naxan Sage clicked once.

"So much death," the Tahe Sage murmured. "It serves no purpose. This is genocide, complete eradication. Why?"

Something teased at Kivita's mind, a notion born of intuition. It bothered her that such thoughts might not be her own, but data recollected from the Juxj Star.

"Maybe the Vim developed Savants as a weapon?" Kivita said.

Everyone shot her a contemptuous look.

"We spread knowledge, not death!" one Savant cried.

"That's ludicrous, Kivita," Jandeel said. "How would this be used as a weapon?"

"Yeah, but we already know someone—the Vim?— created humans, Aldaakians, and Ascali from one stock, then put us in these spiral arms called Cradles. But why? Why would the Sarrhdtuu chase Savants across the cosmos, just to kill them? Why capture and torture them? It has to be something more than just broadcasting data."

No one answered Kivita's questions.

"We must study these revelations," Navon said, his deep, warbling voice a comfort among such concepts. "Study and discern them, before *Luccan's Wish* completes this jump."

One by one, people left the library. The Tahe Sage still quivered, and one Savant had to be aided out by two others. Though Kivita also found the images disturbing, she failed to see what really troubled everyone. The Thedes were rebels. Weren't they used to death? Even Jandeel avoided her eyes as he left with the Naxan Sage.

She scratched her head. "I didn't mean to . . ."

Navon sighed. "They all refuse to entertain your theory, Kivita. Those who join the Thedes usually do so in rejection of war, forced coercion, and slavery. For you to insinuate—"

"What would the reason be?" Kivita crossed her arms.

"The Sarrhdtuu confuse me," Navon replied. "They destroy, then enslave. The Vim either abandoned us or were unable to cope with Sarrhdtuu aggression. So many of their wrecked craft are found in the Cetturo Arm, and no one really knows why. It is a mystery the Juxj Star may never reveal, but there are uncounted datacores still awaiting discovery. Perhaps one will cast light on our ignorance."

The mention of enslavement evoked the slave pens on Umiracan. Since Shekelor did not deal with the Tannocci, Naxans, Aldaakians, or Inheritors . . .

"Oh no," Kivita whispered. A chill crept over her body.

"What is the matter?" Navon clasped her hands.

"Shekelor is green-rigged, right? He also had scores of slaves when I was on Umiracan. We know he's a Sarrhdtuu flunky. Think he sells slaves to them?"

The color drained from Navon's face. "If that is so, that might explain other things."

"Navon?" Kivita walked over to him.

"Though it is unknown to most, the Inheritors press entire villages and townships into service from my homeworld," Navon said. "That is one reason I became a Thede. Villages that are desolate, their people vanished. Yet no Thede agent has ever uncovered any clues as to where these people were sent or their fate."

Kivita nodded. "Yeah, and you mentioned the Sarrhdtuu are the Inheritor's benefactors."

Navon gripped her hands tight. "We must pore over our available datacores, Kivita. We must try to find all knowledge relating to Sarrhdtuu Transmutation and its links to the slave trade. I fear what you have shown me today is but the first murmurs of an ancient nightmare."

"You cannot escape." Shekelor's warning sunk into her mind and burrowed into her heart.

27

Sar opened the Savants' cells one by one. Each huddled in a corner and regarded him as some reptilian predator from Bellerion. None left their cells.

All of them resembled Dunaar, but thinner and younger. They even shared his baldness and sweaty skin. Sar had to turn away from their pitiful stares.

"Food. Redryll?" Bredine pointed at the entrance.

Wincing at all his bruises, Sar stubbed the clothed Proselyte with his boot. "Put it on. It'll be easier to escape."

Bredine rubbed her arms. "I won't wear void black uniform. Hmm. Beatings, beatings."

With no idea who waited outside the chamber or how many aboard had already entered cryostasis, Sar considered his position. Either he could wait here and risk someone coming back or he could slip out and hope to hide somewhere aboard. Neither option appealed to him. He'd never been so brutally beaten in his life. It took all his strength just to stand.

"Fine. You lead," he said.

Bredine unlatched the door and peered outside. Sar stifled a grunt as his nerves woke fully to the damage he'd received. At least he'd not given away anything about his friends or Kivita.

"Redryll?" Bredine whispered, motioning him to follow.

No one stood guard outside, and the lamps in the corridor had diffused. His eyes darted to every corner. Disguised or not, his skin prickled. His breaths sounded too loud; each footfall was a cacophony.

"I lead. Hmm? Redryll. But you act the part." Looping her arm in his, Bredine walked slightly forward of him. He leaned on her more than he liked to admit.

As Sar followed Bredine through *Arcuri's Glory*, lamps flickered on at their approach, then faded after they walked past. Inheritor transports placed the crew in cryo, while a scant security detail maintained the ship. With luck, he'd avoid them. After the beating, he was too weak for resistance.

"Food, food. Hmm?" Bredine's green eyes measured Sar with hope.

He put a gloved hand on her shoulder. She cringed for a second, then nestled up to him.

"I promised you would eat, but keep still. We don't know who might be about."

Sar's breath came out in small clouds, which worried him. With *Arcuri's Glory* maintaining an air supply and the interior temperature not dropping as much as it should, it meant others remained awake, too. More than just a few crew.

Right around the corner, two soldiers snapped to attention.

Sar's heart almost leapt from his chest, but Bredine urged him on.

Two more soldiers stood guard at the end of the corridor. Sar did his best to shamble past them, but the next corridor contained an entire squad of the bastards. Dressed in red jumpsuits and gold-chased polyarmor, they were Dunaar's elite troops. All gave him and Bredine a wide berth and nodded in respect. Playing the arrogant Proselyte, Sar didn't acknowledge them.

Was Dunaar in his own cryopod? Even though Sar wore the Proselyte's outfit and mask, he needed to know. He pointed at a squad commander.

"Has the Rector entered cryostasis?" His voice sounded like flesh scraping over gravel.

The commander saluted. "Indeed, sir. His holiness's staff, servants, and retinue have also entered cryo." He frowned at Bredine. "Do you require assistance, sir?"

"The Rector wanted this one to eat before going into cryo." Sar hoped the man would reveal the location of the kitchen galley, but the commander nodded again and continued his patrol.

Pain stabbed into his knees and shoulders. Bruises along his body pounded his nerves. Dammit, the shock was wearing off.

"Redryll?" Bredine leaned him into her right shoulder.

Without knowing the ship's total jump time, he needed a cryopod. One where, upon waking, he'd not be captured again. Dunaar would discover his absence shortly after exiting the jump. A more immediate concern was his health. A good cryosleep where he could be pumped full of medicine would help, but he needed a doctor.

"Hmm? This way."

For a prisoner, Bredine knew her way around *Arcuri's Glory*. He tried to keep his footsteps silent on the sandstone and quartz flooring while they crept into another corridor. A humming, machinelike sound rose above the ship's gentle thrum: a hot-wave disk. The scent of cooked protein slabs wafted up his nose.

Bredine's stomach growled. He tensed.

"Hey, nobody's supposed to be on this deck," a voice called from a side galley. "Unless you're the Rector himself, get your ass back into cryo."

Sar stood straight and gripped Bredine's hand. Walking into the galley, he tried to adopt a Proselyte's stiff, arrogant gait.

"You hear me? Dammit." A crewman in a brown jumpsuit came out, holding a steaming protein slab. "Oh. I wasn't told one of you fellows would be still awake. Hey, prisoners aren't allowed on this deck. Rector's orders."

"Where are your comrades?" Sar asked in a gruff tone.

The crewman frowned. "I won't be waking my reliever on this deck until another Haldon week has passed. Hey, what are you—"

Sar punched the crewman's jaw, then jabbed his knee into the man's stomach. The man crumpled to the floor and reached for a large wrench on his belt, but Bredine kicked the wrench away and twisted the man's legs together.

"Tell me what I want, and I'll dump you in a cryopod trussed up, not as a corpse." Sar caught his breath, his bruises smarting.

The crewman went limp. "What the hell you need?"

"How many are awake in this section?" Sar propped himself against the wall. Damn, he hurt all over.

"One per deck, plus one in operations and one in the

engine room. So five others." The man winced as Bredine tightened her grip.

"Soldiers, hmm?" she asked. "Hmm. Still eight squads? Already eaten this shift?"

"Yes. How did you—" He gasped as Bredine wrung his left arm behind his back.

Sar tried to think of what else he needed to know. "Is *Fanged Pauper* docked with this ship?"

"Yes, the Vim curse your eyes. Who the hell are you?"

Bredine undid the crewman's belt, along with its attached tools. She hesitated, then removed the tools and snapped the belt with a smile. Sar hadn't expected her to still have all her teeth.

Turning the crewman over, Sar pulled the man's arms to the center of his back. Bending over made him grunt from his multitude of agonies. Bredine looped the belt around the crewman's wrists, though Sar shook his head when she drew it too tight. She relented, then rewound and fastened it into a thick knot.

"Where's your cryopod?" As Sar tried lifting the man up, his battered body and stomach and tingling nerves made him stagger. With strength belying her appearance, Bredine helped Sar bring the bound crewman to his feet.

"Two doors down. You'll be executed for this, whoever you are. The Vim won't have mercy on you!" The crewman spat at Bredine. "Filthy witch!"

Sar forced the man along until they entered the specified door. Nineteen cryopods held various crewmen; one was empty. Sar shoved the man in and closed the hatch. Though the crewman struggled and cursed, the hatch muted his voice. Sar waited until cryosleep took the man, then returned to the galley, limping at every step.

Bredine sat on the floor, eating the crewman's protein slab. A placard of Inheritor Charter tenements hung over the counter.

"You're not filth or a witch." Kneeling, he smoothed the dark bangs from her eyes. She watched him with wide eyes, chewing the slab.

"Food?" She pointed at an open food locker.

"Need a medical cabinet." He lifted the ply mask. "I'm Sar Redryll."

"Bredine Ov." She pulled sugar reeds and Susuron mussels from the locker, then gobbled them by the mouthful.

Though raw pain shot through his legs and stomach, Sar rose and pulled out a water flask. "Hold still."

He wet the ply mask and washed her face. Bredine didn't move, but he had to work around her continuous eating. A long scar ran down her left cheek; another went up from her right brow into her scalp. Around thirty years old, she looked attractive despite her abuse. Those green eyes . . . like those of an elderly woman. He wondered how long Dunaar had kept her in cryo.

Contrary to Dunaar's claims, Sar had aided many such victims of Inheritor hegemony. Bredine's dark hair and determination reminded him of Caitrynn, reminded him of what little his vengeance had gained him. He feared to abandon it. Shekelor had, and it had made the pirate even less honorable. Without retribution driving him, Sar wasn't sure what he might become himself.

"Grab a flask and let's go. Got to find a cryopod somewhere." Sar stood and rubbed his pounding face. For a moment, Kivita entered his mind. He wondered if Cheseia had harmed her.

"Kivita sending to you?" Bredine asked between bites.

Stomach throbbing, Sar bent over and shut his eyes. No tears came, but emotions shook his body, ripped his heart. His sacrifice had been in vain; Cheseia would lead Dunaar to the Thedes, and all of his friends and the woman he loved would die. Now Caitrynn and Kivita both would haunt his frozen dreams across the cosmos. Sar's knees buckled and he flopped onto the floor.

Something soft and damp caressed his face. Sar opened his eyes.

Bredine wiped his face with the wet mask, her green eyes solemn and noble. The damp cloth mopped away dried blood from his lips and nostrils.

"Gushing hot love for her. She'll forgive." Bredine popped another reed into her mouth. "Don't let heart get void black, okay? Sar Redryll. Redryll, Redryll. Hmm. Food?"

Wincing, Sar sat up. "No, thanks." He lifted her up with him. "Need some medicine."

"Brown face needs attention." She tugged his hand and exited the side galley. Now she walked more upright, exuding confidence and purpose. They passed four doors and entered a slim corridor. A keypad prevented entrance to a medical ward.

"Six, eight. Stupid binary. Ah, lock. Redryll? Hmm." She munched another reed and pressed the keypad's buttons. The door opened.

After passing rows of unoccupied cots, Sar rifled through a few wall cabinets, where he discovered thogens, cold packs, blue medical tape, and pink mollusk extract. With the aid of cryostasis, he might be fully healed before reaching their destination.

Had to be, if he planned to help Kivita.

Stripping to his underwear, Sar grimaced at the chill

air. All of his bruises flared up in aching protest. Bredine sat on a stool and ogled him.

Sar applied cold packs to his bruises, drank the extract, downed four thogen capsules, and wrapped blue tape around his neck where Shekelor's coils had left friction marks.

"Kivita is lucky," Bredine murmured as she finished the last of her food. "Very lucky with Redryll. Hmm."

Sar slipped back into his bodyglove and put the Proselyte outfit back on. Bredine helped, looping the copper-meld cuirass around his torso. Kneeling, she checked his boots and patted his black chaps with military crispness.

"How do you know this ship? This uniform?"

Bredine motioned for him to follow her into a storage chamber. Again, she knew the keypad sequence and opened several lockers, where she selected a soldier's red jumpsuit. She stripped from her bodyglove and donned it. Scars and more curved tattoos ran along her naked body, but she paid him no heed. The jumpsuit hugged her bony frame, which still retained toned musculature.

"Hurry. The thogens are making me drowsy." He leaned on a bulkhead while she finished suiting up.

"Hmm. Warmer now. Ah." She held up a hand. "My father. He might know. Redryll, Redryll?"

They passed into a carpeted, draped corridor. Several cryo chambers branched off from it, where dozens more soldiers lay in stasis. The temperature had dropped; their breath crackled as it turned into vacuum frost.

Bredine stopped at a large doorway framed in gold. Counting aloud, she tapped her fingers on Sar's cuirass. "Two, five, sixty. Hmm. It never changes." She pointed at the doorway.

"What's in there?"

She jabbed the keypad, and the door slid open. As they entered, yellow ceiling lamps activated. The round room had a sandstone and quartz floor, couches, and various consoles.

Ignoring the rich trappings, Bredine led Sar to another large door. She entered a sequence into the keypad and it opened.

Who was she, possessing such an intimate knowledge of *Arcuri's Glory*?

An adjacent circular chamber, larger than the previous one, gave Sar pause. Dozens of upright cryopods lined the walls. Vacuum frost on the transparent hatches blurred the faces within.

Bredine stopped before one and activated its waking sequence.

"Don't! We need to hide, not wake them up—"

He stopped at the look on her face. Bredine's mouth turned down and her eyes narrowed. Despite her seeming near madness before, she appeared dangerously sane now.

The hatch opened, and a wrinkled old man shivered inside. A tube extended and squirted pseudoadrine into his mouth. The old man coughed, his lungs rattling like a broken Naxan clacker.

"Leave me be, Thev. I wish to meet the Vim soon." His speech had archaic Meh Sattan trappings, as if he'd been asleep for a long time.

Bredine waved aside cryo exhaust. "Father. Hmm. I looked into their stones for you. Pictures, pictures."

The old man stared at Bredine, then Sar. "You are not the Rector! How dare you awaken me like this . . . ?"

Sar stepped forward. "Who are you?"

"Imbecile. I am . . . Rector Broujel. I should be . . ."
He paused and looked closer at Bredine. "What is this?
Bredine? You . . . cannot still be here. Unless . . ." Broujel's eyes bulged, and he coughed in great, racking
heaves.

"Unless she's been frozen on and off for centuries?"
Sar leaned on the cryopod's hatch as the pain of his
bruises mixed with the extract's tingling in his gut.
"Heard you prophets froze each other. Guess you'll all
kiss the Vims' asses together?"

Broujel scowled. "Blasphemer! You will be decapitated. Bredine, why are you here? Why are the codes the
same? You should no longer . . . know them."

"I've seen much Vim data for you. Hungry, hungry.
Cold. Hurt, hurt. Hmm. Redryll gushing hot for Kivita.
Gushing hot in love with a Savant. Narbas, father. Narbas!" She shook the old man by the shoulders until Sar
pulled her back.

Broujel hacked up mucus and leaned over the cryopod's lip.

"We eradicated that witch and her . . . progeny. A
blight on the salvation of all in the Cetturo Arm. Then
you turned against me, Bredine." Broujel coughed, his
breath wheezing through clogged lungs. "My best captain, my best general. You decoded things for the Dirr
factions, though. You damned yourself. I had safe-
guarded you from the Savant purges long enough. Now
you come back to haunt me in this cryo dream."

Sar nudged Broujel back into the cryopod. "What
witch? Tell me, Rector. Your successor has allied with
the Sarrhdtuu. He hired a Savant to take the Juxj Star."

Broujel shook with rage. "Thev? He should be con-
demned and replaced! I warned him about Terredyn

Narbas. That red-haired, hazel-eyed witch left no legacy. The Juxj Star ... Terredyn refused to obey us. ... Release me! I must warn the people, the righteous."

Forgetting his pain in an instant, Sar thought of Kivita. The name of her ship, her Savant talent, the remarks Dunaar had made about her—was such a connection possible? If so, he'd allowed the greatest salvage to slip through his fingers. Through his heart.

"Let's go." Sar tugged Bredine's arm. The cryopods around them seemed to be watching him, listening. Centuries of repression contained in the blood of frozen tyrants.

She ignored him. "Inheritor sun will fall, Father. Hmm. Cold, hurt, hunger. It will fall now. Sar Redryll loves Kivita Narbas. Dream of a witch reborn." Tears dripped down her cheeks as she pulled down the cryopod hatch. "Father, be warm."

Cryonic exhaust spurted as the pod's stasis cycle reactivated. Bredine fingered the pod's console as several lifetimes of pain, glory, and determination passed in her moist eyes.

Sar gently pried her from the cryopod and led her from the chamber. "Do you know where the airlock bay is?"

"Fly to Kivita? Hmm. Lucky her. Warm, warm, and warm again you'll be together." Bredine smiled and pulled him behind her through the ship, as Sar tried to work his thoughts around what he'd just heard.

Though Inheritor records weren't available to the public, he'd heard of Broujel from the Thedes; the man had ruled Inheritor Space five hundred years ago. Bredine had referred to Kivita as a Narbas, and Broujel had described Kivita's hair and eyes. The golden life capsule waiting at the end of those strange coordinates toyed with his imagination and fears.

"Airlock bay," Bredine whispered, while they descended stairs to a lower deck where machinery hummed around them. Metal grating clanked under their feet as Bredine finally led him into the bay itself. Eight forty-foot-wide airlock doors and twenty shuttles awaited them.

Fanged Pauper was magnetized to a smaller airlock.

A hundred feet away, a crewman walked onto a gantry and typed at a computer console. Sar and Bredine ducked behind a shuttle's landing pylon. If they subdued the crewman, anyone searching for them postjump would know they'd been in the airlock bay.

Bredine slid around the shuttle's hull and accessed the hatch's keypad.

Not daring to breathe, Sar expected the crewman to hear the slight hiss of the hatch opening. Seconds passed, and Bredine entered the hatch. Sar, eyes still on the crewman, followed.

An anguished cry echoed across the airlock bay. The crewman and Sar both jumped.

Shekelor tramped into the bay, his coils wrapped around Zhara. The gorgeous Ascali struggled and gasped, but the coils strangled meaningful resistance from her. Sar's neck marks burned, and a simmering anger ignited inside him.

The crewman made to protest, but Shekelor waved him aside. "I shall be taking her aboard *Fanged Pauper*, as per my agreement." The pirate's deep voice reverberated throughout the airlock bay.

While Shekelor and Zhara entered *Fanged Pauper*, a hand jerked Sar's collar. He backed into the shuttle and the hatch slid shut, but he waited a full two minutes before accepting the crewman's ignorance of their presence.

Though Cheseia had betrayed him, Sar hated to see her sister fall into Shekelor's clutches. The pain Zhara must have endured, knowing her sister turned traitor in a doomed attempt to save her . . . Sar had seen it in her eyes. Cheseia's professed love for Sar must have been part of the plot, but her russet eyes had never seemed false in those intimate moments. Perhaps he would never know.

One way or another, Shekelor and Dunaar would pay.

Inside the shuttle, the scent of gun oil and sweat tainted the air. Sar crept past the cockpit and troop harnesses until he found a chamber with four cryopods. He set his to wake him once *Arcuri's Glory* finished its light jump.

Bredine got in hers and sighed. "Warm, warm. Hmm. Kivita can send."

"Once they discover we're missing, they'll search the ship. Hopefully we can launch from this airlock bay as soon as we exit the jump." Sar got into the cryopod and closed the hatch.

He knew their chances amounted to nothing, but he had to make the attempt. Maybe he could warn the Thedes. Maybe even save Kivita one last time.

Maybe he'd finally save himself.

28

Kivita's wrists and forearms burned as she twirled the jump rope faster. Her bare feet bounced again and again off the floor in time with the swishing rope. Sweat stung her eyebrows, temples, lips. Damp hair clung to her cheeks, and she grinned, twirling the rope even faster.

A few others in the gymnasium aboard *Luccan's Wish* watched her with admiration. The fifty-by-twenty-foot room contained dumbbells, barbells, and Sutaran weight balls. She'd used them all, honing her body to the best condition it'd ever been in.

Basheev tried to keep up with his own jump rope, but tripped up. "Winking red stars, you're too fast!"

Closing her eyes, Kivita laughed. Delicious fatigue sank into her body, burned through her muscles. In contrast to her salvager days, now she relished the need for exercise. With every jump off the floor, it seemed she drew closer to something greater within herself. She wanted to share it, savor it.

Kivita twirled the rope six times in rapid succession, jumped once, then stopped. Facing the ceiling, she filled her lungs with air.

"Stars shining, Kivita. Momma says you work out too much." Basheev pointed at her left wrist. "Still like it?"

She touched the black ink sword and star Rhii had tattooed on her left wrist. "Oh yeah. She does great work." Kivita smiled and hung the jump rope beside a weight rack.

Rhii had told her the sword represented purpose, while the flaring star meant compassion. Long after Terredyn's death, Dirr natives on Susuron still used her insignia. In Dirr culture, tattoos placed near important veins symbolized a heartfelt conviction. For Kivita, it represented total acceptance of her heritage.

As she stretched to cool down, the dampness inside her skinsuit became palpable. Dark splotches had spread along the garment. As well as sweating out impurities, Kivita had also shed the mercenary salvager. Returning to such a lifestyle, much less living on an Inheritor world, seemed impossible now.

Basheev looked up at her. "Rising moon, I want something to drink. Race you to Momma's galley?"

Kivita rustled his braided locks. "Easy there, smoothie. Guess Cheseia's not exercising this cycle, either."

As they departed the gymnasium, Basheev took Kivita's hand. Though her sweaty body chilled in the ship's corridors, Kivita's heart warmed. She imagined how it must have felt for Terredyn to hold her on the Susuron beach. Giving birth to her, maybe even singing Kivita a lullaby. She squeezed Basheev's hand.

With Savant talents being hereditary, Kivita pondered her real father's identity. Terredyn had never married, and given Rhyer's closeness to the queen, he might have been her real father after all.

Something sank in Kivita's heart, all the way down to her stomach. Any children of hers would be Savants, too. Hunted like she was now. Fantasies of a family with Sar melted like ice in Haldon summer.

Exiting the corridor, Kivita bumped into Jandeel.

"Well, if it isn't the Sage Squad, come to ask for another headache." Kivita grinned.

Jandeel's long black hair hung in a ponytail, with bronze Tannocci clasps through the tresses. The purple skinsuit he wore made Kivita blush. Several aboard *Luccan's Wish* had started wearing purple and maroon, the old Narbas livery colors. Now she received the first plate at meal times, the best cryopod, the softest sheets for norm sleep. She hated all this preferential treatment. Hell, did she look like a queen now, all sweaty and sticky?

"Bursting stars, Jandeel, you almost stomped over us!" Basheev said. "You can't have Kivita right now. I'm taking her to get a drink. Twinkling stars, all right?"

Jandeel smiled at the boy. "I wouldn't dare break your, ah, date." The smile faded as he faced Kivita. "You're needed in Navon's quarters."

Kivita frowned. "What is it?"

"Refresh yourself, clean up, then come. We must speak before this shift enters cryostasis." With a quick smile at Basheev, Jandeel hurried down the corridor.

Before Kivita had time to consider Jandeel's concern, Basheev tugged her into the galley. Several others sat at tables, eating last meals before entering their cryopods. As she neared the end of her second waking shift, Kivita dreaded going back into cryostasis. Sixteen months aboard *Luccan's Wish* made everything before seem like a distant dream.

"Blinking stars, Basheev, you worry Kivita until she's sweating!" Rhii called from the serving counter. "Sun and water, bring her over here before the miss dehydrates. The usual?"

"Yeah, give me the wood-snake milk again. You're going to make me put on weight." Kivita leaned over the counter.

"Queens don't get fat." Basheev plopped on a stool and beamed at her.

Heat returned to Kivita's cheeks when other patrons looked her way. Maihh waved from her table, where she and other botanists pored over a deep blue hibiscus.

Rhii slapped Basheev's hand with a wooden spatula. "Inky void, don't be embarrassing her, now. Give her your blessings and hurry along. The shift change is coming."

Rolling his eyes, Basheev kissed Kivita's cheek. "Blessings of sun and water on you. Blessings of warmth and light."

Kivita hugged him and kissed his forehead. "See you when we all wake up again." She stared at his back as he left the galley.

"Warm sunrise, my son thinks highly of you, miss," Rhii whispered. "Many of us do. Put sun in all our hearts if . . ." She hesitated and touched the tattoo on Kivita's left wrist. "Best blessings of sun and warmth on you, Kivita. Would be blessings for us all, with one on the throne."

"Yeah. Hey, I have to get cleaned up. If you see Cheseia, tell her I'm in my quarters. Kiss Basheev again for me, okay?" Kivita smooched Rhii's cheek and hurried from the galley.

The hope in the people's eyes added to the weight

building on her shoulders. She wasn't a savior, a panacea to fix all their problems. By traveling with them, Kivita placed everyone on *Luccan's Wish* in danger. Besides, what was she supposed to do for them?

After entering her quarters, Kivita stripped from the damp skinsuit. Though she shared the room with Cheseia, the Ascali had avoided Kivita for the past two weeks. Where before they'd shared galley meals and gym workouts, Cheseia always claimed to be busy now. Others on the ship had mentioned the Ascali's attitude change.

"Yeah. I miss Sar, too," Kivita murmured. She shut the door to the mist ionizer and bathed.

Afterward Kivita sat on her bed, a soft Tannocci affair with thermal blankets and a ply pillow. Her garments lay scattered about the floor and bed, while Cheseia's hung in her locker, neat and pressed. Yeah, so what? Kivita didn't have time to clean her room, anyway. As she stepped into her underwear, Kivita wondered what really bothered Cheseia. She snuggled into her maroon bodyglove, polyboots, and black leather chaps.

Kivita spotted two Bellerion carb sticks on Cheseia's bed. Though *Luccan's Wish* possessed an adequate larder, she knew the galley lacked such delicacies.

Cheseia could have gotten the bars only from *Frevyx*. Maybe that's where she was?

Moments later, Kivita hurried out. Traffic in the ship's corridors had thinned already, though few guards remained at key positions, to be relieved in two-week shifts. Passing through the deck's cryo chamber, Kivita glanced over the assigned pods. Cheseia's numbered among the empty ones.

She hurried to the nearest elevator and descended to Level Eight.

Airlock Eight was empty save for supply crates and blinking terminals. The lamps had already dimmed. Kivita walked toward *Frevyx*'s magnetized airlock.

"Cheseia? Hey, you in there?" She pounded on the trawler's airlock hatch.

No answer.

Biting her lip, Kivita focused on the armored keypad beside the airlock. Sar had never told her his personal code sequence, and neither had Cheseia. Concentrating, Kivita stretched out with her mind. Cold pain rose in her temples, but she forced it away, using her recent Savant training. Kivita tuned her thoughts to the lock, its circuits, its mechanism.

The pulses from her brain sent and received information from the keypad. Numbers entered her mind.

"Well, hell." She smiled. The keypad's sequence consisted of the coordinates of Kravis, Gontalo's sun. Surely Sar wasn't so sentimental. The idea tickled her heart all the same.

Kivita keyed in the code. *Frevyx*'s airlock opened.

Light, heat, and fresh air emanated from within. The trawler's life-support systems had been turned on.

"Cheseia?" Kivita called. Though she hadn't been on the ship since her arrival, Sar's personal scent still lingered in *Frevyx*'s air. Taking deep breaths, she strolled toward the bridge.

"How did you assuredly get in here?" Cheseia eyed Kivita from the bridge entrance. Grease stains soiled her tunic and breechcloth.

Kivita bristled at the Ascali's accusing tone. "Hey, where have you been? Whole ship's about to enter the next cryo shift. Besides, what are you doing in here? Got a hankering for carb sticks?"

Coming closer, Kivita made out Cheseia's bloodshot stare. The Ascali's mane had become disheveled, and her lithe, muscular figure was slimmer, as if she'd been skipping meals.

"What's bothering you? I've missed you in Rhii's galley." Kivita meant it. In their time together, she and Cheseia had swapped stories about Sar and the places they'd traveled. Laughed over drinks at Rhii's bar, played with Basheev in the gym.

Cheseia avoided Kivita's stare.

"Well?" Kivita asked.

Sighing, Cheseia leaned on a bulkhead. "It is unfortunately only a matter of time before Sar will be truly found, if he has not been already. *Terredyn Narbas*'s beacon will definitely draw enemies to him."

Kivita frowned and crossed her arms. "I try not to think about it. I feel so useless here, while he could be—"

"You certainly realize that once he is discovered, and you are not truly found aboard *Terredyn Narbas*, that the search will begin anew?" Cheseia sighed again.

"What are you really trying to say?"

"You delightfully think this is a vacation, Kivita. You certainly fawn over the Sages' attention. You recklessly play with Basheev like he's your son. You superbly tell salvager tales in the galley. Outside this ship, people are truly . . . suffering. My— I mean, Sar may be definitely suffering. You seem to have magically forgotten how hard it is to live in the cold void."

Kivita grabbed Cheseia's tunic. "Forgotten? I've dreamt of Sar, my father, and my mother for months. I've wondered all my life who I really am, then struggled to accept it. If I don't talk about things out there, it's because I've never had it so damn good. How many times have you wiped vacuum frost off your father's placard? How many times have you paid for a cheap spaceport fuck and regretted it? Wondering why you keep going when you've got no one, nothing but a ship and the next jump, the next cryosleep?"

Shivering, Cheseia backed down. Kivita blinked in surprise. The Ascali had always been fearless in her stature and bearing.

"I am . . . I am so truly sorry. You are certainly right. Let us quickly go into cryostasis." She took Kivita's arm in a desperate grip.

Something pulsed in Kivita's thoughts. The closer she came to the bridge, the stronger the pulses became: a repeating sequence.

"Come, Kivita." Cheseia's musical voice cracked. What was her problem? Kivita had never seen the statuesque Ascali so distraught.

A slight beeping sound came from the bridge.

Kivita shrugged off Cheseia's hold. "All right, already. You going to shut down *Frevyx*'s systems or what?"

The pulse rang through Kivita's mind, quiet but powerful. It seemed to pierce through the trawler's hull and leap into the void outside.

"What the hell is—"

Kivita stepped into the bridge and paused. A green light on the console flashed in time with her mental pulses: an emergency beacon. Being in a light jump, all scanners on the Thede ship would have been deactivated. The signal's broadcast had gone unnoticed by all aboard.

Anyone seeking *Luccan's Wish* would now be able to do so.

A click sounded behind her.

"Goddamn you." Kivita slowly turned. Stomach chills contrasted with the heat building in her cheeks.

Cheseia stood in the bridge entrance, aiming a kinetic pistol with both hands. Tears streamed down her furry cheeks.

"I truly did not want to fall tragically in love with Sar," Cheseia whispered. "I just definitely wanted Zhara safe. The Rector unfortunately took her as his servant. I had virtually no choice!"

Kivita backed farther into the bridge. Tightness enclosed her heart and throat, and the sour taste of tension flooded her mouth. The dark-maned Ascali in Dunaar's service with russet eyes . . . Cheseia speaking about her sister . . . the Ascali Blood Bond . . .

"A twin sister?" Kivita asked.

"I truly am sorry." Cheseia's gaze crumpled with sadness and regret.

"You shoot me, the others on board will hear. They'll kill you. You can't demagnetize from *Luccan's Wish* during a jump, either. You'd be space dust." Kivita's jaw twitched. Damn her to the void!

"I certainly know." Her moist eyes gleamed. "Tell Sar I truly did love him. Tell him . . ."

Cheseia aimed the pistol at her own head.

Kivita leapt without thinking, her right shoulder connecting with Cheseia's right elbow.

A shot echoed throughout *Frevyx*.

Cheseia's eyes rolled back and she collapsed. A hole smoked on the bulkhead behind them. Blood covered the floor.

"You bitch. You ... Goddamn you!" Whimpering, Kivita cradled Cheseia in her arms. She didn't want the Ascali to die. She wanted her to suffer for the forces sure to destroy Sar and the Thedes. Destroy all she loved and had come to love. Even Cheseia herself.

Kivita's tears mingled with the line of blood along Cheseia's right temple.

"I'll ... I'll tell him." The words came out in heaves. Kivita's fingers brushed over the Ascali's face, exquisite even in death.

A faint breath exited Cheseia's lips.

Swallowing a sob, Kivita examined the wound. A deep graze.

Body numb, Kivita ripped off Cheseia's tunic and bandaged the wound. The white garment reddened with blood.

Kivita crawled to the console, flicked off the emergency beacon, and keyed the radio to the frequency on *Luccan's Wish*.

"Jandeel? Navon? Somebody send a medic to *Frevyx* at Airlock Eight! Hurry!"

"I truly ... want to die," Cheseia whispered in a weak voice.

Kivita knelt and pulled Cheseia against her chest. "Yeah, and I truly didn't want to be your friend when I first met you. But, dammit, I am."

Cheseia's eyes widened. Her tears coursed over Kivita's arms and made splotches in the blood on the floor. "You truly ... ?" The Ascali fainted.

What would happen now? Cheseia had saved her life, had loved the same man she did, then betrayed Sar and her both. Kivita gritted her teeth and squeezed her eyes shut. Maybe she should have let Cheseia end her life.

Deep in her heart, though, Kivita found no hatred. Spotting the Ascali's blood on her new tattoo, a throb pierced her heart. How many would die so that others could live in peace, free of ignorance? All those video streams she'd seen while on *Luccan's Wish*, showing Inheritor cruelty . . . Cheseia was the latest victim. Those who'd forced her friend to betray the Thedes gave Kivita a purpose.

"I swear I won't stop until everyone is free." Ignoring her own tears, Kivita kissed Cheseia's forehead.

Four guards in polyarmor waited at the infirmary door while the Aldaakian medic finished with Cheseia. The sleeping Ascali had been given thogens, and a bandage now swathed her temples. Root-spice disinfectant permeated the air. Navon, Jandeel, and the other Sages stood nearby, while Kivita knelt beside Cheseia's cot, her jaw tight.

"She'll recover with just a scratch. I recommend rest in cryostasis—where we all should be." The medic left.

"You should have let her go through with it." Jandeel scowled at Cheseia's inert form. "There can be little doubt Sar Redryll has been taken. The Inheritors are following us even now."

Kivita squeezed Cheseia's hand and stood. "I know she's done wrong. I know she's not to be trusted. I'm angry, too. But I won't let you kill her. What's done is done. I say we focus on what we can change."

Jandeel sighed. "Kivita, I'm not advocating her execution. But she cannot leave custody."

"She is right: all our energies must be dedicated to what befalls us when we exit this jump," Navon said.

"No one, other than those in this room, can know our voyage has been compromised."

"They have a right to know." Jandeel crossed his arms. "You would lead us into a trap, blind?"

Navon's brow creased. "No, but I think—"

"What did you want to tell me earlier?" Kivita stood between them. Arguing would get them nowhere. She'd been nowhere most of her life. Now it was time to leave it.

Navon paced between the other cots, hands behind his back. "We have finally deciphered the name of the coordinates' destination. They lead to a red-giant star system called Bōs-Euex. Nothing is known to exist there."

"But nobody's ever explored this system, right? Those coordinates don't even exist in Inheritor charting. No beacon signals from Vim derelicts, nothing." Kivita shifted her feet, not wanting to leave Cheseia's side. With everyone after her since the salvage on Vstrunn, Kivita felt responsible for Cheseia's predicament. Someone had maneuvered them both like pieces on a Tannocci chessboard.

"I fear we are being led along on this course." Navon stopped pacing. "The Inheritors and Sarrhdtuu have gone to great lengths to use you and then hunt you, Kivita."

"What else can we do?" The Naxan Sage clicked twice.

"There's never been a Vim signal in any of the recorded histories," Jandeel said. "We must investigate it. This is what Luccan himself hoped for, Navon."

Kivita cleared her throat. "Maybe we haven't dug deep enough."

Navon looked at her, brows knitted. "Explain yourself."

"What if I pool information from all the datacores we have? I haven't studied every one yet—and never at the same time." Kivita raised her brows and cocked her head to one side.

"Can you handle that?" Jandeel asked.

"No, she cannot. No one ever has." Navon wrung his hands and neared Kivita. "You are gifted, but even you might burn out your brain with that sort of activity. There is no guarantee that all the knowledge stored in our datacores is still valid. Some of this data may have become obsolete centuries ago."

She clasped both his hands in hers; his thick ones dwarfed her slender ones. "We need answers more than ever. I can hold it—I know. Everything I've been taught by you all or shown by a datacore, I can repeat verbatim. If we're heading for a trap, then we might be dead already. C'mon. We have nothing to lose."

"We can't lose you," Jandeel said.

"You won't," Kivita said.

"We will gather in my quarters," Navon said. "Jandeel, retrieve the datacores from the library."

Cheseia murmured on her cot. Kivita walked over and knelt beside her, while the others filed toward the infirmary door.

"I should truly, certainly die," Cheseia moaned.

"Hush. Things have been set into motion now. Just rest and heal up."

"And then what? I certainly have no future now," Cheseia said.

"That might go for the rest of us. You see me quitting?" Kivita clasped her hand. "Most won't forgive you for this. Maybe I shouldn't, either. You won't be executed, but I can't promise anything besides that. What did Dunaar Thev tell you? What did he want?"

"The Rector only truly wanted the location of *Luccan's Wish*. I also assuredly told him that Sar had loved you once. I have been so surely jealous of you. After Tejuit, when I saw how Sar definitely wanted you, and now this . . . I hate myself." Tears welled in Cheseia's eyes.

"And Zhara?"

"She and I secretly stowed aboard a Thede sympathizer's starship and left Sygma." Cheseia winced and touched her right temple. "Months after we left, Inheritor agents unfortunately captured my sister. I was ordered to lovingly attach myself to Sar. Ascali Blood Bond forced me to certainly honor Zhara's life, being her sister. She truly wanted to see other worlds. . . ."

"So, why didn't your mother come along?" Kivita asked in a whisper.

Cheseia gave her a sad smile. "She surely still worshipped Revelas, god of the Ascali on Sygma. She definitely thought we were heretics to think Revelas was just a silly starship, and that we should certainly not travel the Cetturo Arm. She tragically disowned Zhara and me, the greatest insult in Ascali society. I unfortunately have not seen her since."

Kivita touched her hand. "You ever think about her?"

"Every day." Cheseia touched the braid in Kivita's hair. "Maybe you can skillfully braid me one later."

"Yeah. Maybe." Kivita rose and exited the infirmary. Navon waited in the corridor.

"She might not have revealed those things under interrogation," Navon said. "Her sorrow is palpable, I must admit. An Ascali regards a Blood Bond breakable only by death."

"I can't bring myself to despise her. She doesn't need any pity, either."

"Nobility really does come from within, not from a crown," he said.

Shaking her head, Kivita touched the wrist tattoo. Cheseia's blood still stained the skin around it. "I'm not a queen."

He linked arms with her and headed for the nearest elevator. "You may not have a choice any longer."

29

As Navon led Kivita into his quarters, his gentle yet firm grip on her arm eased some of her tension. Jandeel and the other Sages waited inside, their faces grim. The Juxj Star, along with all the datacores the Thedes possessed, lay on a grass mat.

"Remember your training," Navon said. "Do not force the knowledge from the datacores."

Taking a deep breath, Kivita moved toward the mat. Jandeel touched her shoulder. "If you falter . . ."

Kivita sat on the mat, the datacores ringing her like a barrier. Shielding her from what may be coming.

This might be it. She took another deep breath, trying to calm her rising pulse. What she'd always wanted lay ahead: discovering what was really out there. The more she learned from her new friends and the datacores, the more she wanted to know.

The more she learned, the more she realized just how much she didn't know.

Closing her eyes, Kivita concentrated on the stones, crystals, and the Juxj Star. One by one their specific ambiences touched her mind, each one different. The crystals were bright, scintillating pulses of data, while the rocks crunched against her mind. The Juxj Star tried to flood her thoughts like before. Electrical sensations traveled along her scalp, penetrating her cranium.

The usual cold pain started in her temples, but this time it varied in degrees of intensity as each datacore threatened to batter down her psyche. Sweat traveled down her back. It hurt to breathe. Kivita licked her lips and repeated Navon's instruction in her consciousness.

Focus. Attune. Absorb.

"Slowly," Navon whispered, his voice miles away.

Concentrating, she compiled all the data signatures from the items. Kivita shivered as numbers, letters, and images pushed at the walls of her consciousness. Where before the datacores had offered glimpses, now they displayed long, branching paths. Countless lifetimes passed in her mind, and Kivita clasped her persona by a thin thread of willpower. So much data flooding her like an ocean . . . Mouthing a silent cry, Kivita channeled it all into one stream. Imagery and numbers from separate datacores linked and combined.

All of it led to a yellow star ringed by Vim starships.

Viewpoints shifted in Kivita's mind, each becoming a snapshot of the scene. The ships resembled those she'd seen before, siphoning energy from the main sequence star. In one image the vessels appeared stable, well-maintained. Next, each one had deteriorated to drifting hulks filled with energy dumps, datacores, and blobs of green jelly.

The floor seemed to vanish beneath her, and she wobbled. Her temples throbbed.

"Kivita?" Navon's voice sounded farther away than the vistas in her thoughts.

Without answering, she concentrated anew. Focus, attune, absorb. Willing the headache away, Kivita kept the stream of data going.

The Vim derelicts now orbited various stars: red giants, aging orange suns, young blue ones, or antediluvian white dwarfs. In each case, the basic orbital distance remained the same between the ships and the sun.

Just like all the wreckage in the Cetturo Arm.

Swaying, she spread her arms to steady herself. Breaths came in heavy gasps.

"Wait—let her keep going," Jandeel whispered.

The imagery transformed into a scorched, body-ridden starship bridge. A cracked, hundred-foot-tall viewport showed a healthy yellow sun in the distance. Sarrhdtuu warriors in carapace armor waited, while the viewer stepped over a dying Kith. Coils tightened around the viewer's waist.

"No," Kivita mumbled as sharp pains lanced into her skull.

The Sarrhdtuu squeezed, and the viewer, thrashing in pain, accessed a terminal by thought alone. Readouts along the holo console indicated the ship had begun siphoning the star's hydrogen, disrupting its internal-fusion process.

Kivita coughed. Her fingertips burned.

The scene changed. Now the same bridge was covered in vacuum frost. The star outside had swelled into a massive red giant.

The data flow altered and displayed several Ascali gathered in a circle on an arboreal world covered in green foliage. As one, the Ascali raised their gorgeous voices in song. Within the circle, a captive Sarrhdtuu warrior lay stunned by the aural resonance. Memories of Rhyer's journeys to Sygma, and Shekelor's comment about Cheseia on Tejuit, nudged her curiosity.

Licking her lips, Kivita plunged her mind into the datacores' shared information stream. She could hold it.

Nothing new emerged, except more scenes of the Sarrhdtuu destroying Vim projects.

"Tell me, Mother," she murmured. Terredyn Narbas had sent her thoughts into the Juxj Star, trillions of miles from Susuron. The gem datacore from Vstrunn loomed larger in her mind than the other datacores combined. Kivita stiffened; the time for peeling away the red gem's deeper layers had passed. Inhaling a ragged breath, she inserted her mind into them.

Crystallized neurons within the Juxj Star fired in reply. The barrier around Kivita collapsed with reality itself.

Observing the coral-ringed Susuron Palace through Terredyn's view, Kivita stared out the courtroom window. Night ruled the sky where stars twinkled in a visual code beyond human ken. Kivita gripped the windowsill, her legs numbing.

A message from deep space drifted into her mother's mind. Coordinates for an event a thousand years into the future—the same coordinates Luccan's Wish *now headed toward. Safeguarding her daughter to ensure a Savant could return the message; plotting with Rhyer to awaken Kivita at the right moment. But no information on why he reared her on Haldon Prime in the presence of the Inheritors, or why he'd posed as a salvager.*

Something within the Susuron Palace augmented the signal. But what could enhance a Savant's powers? Not even datacores could do that.

Terredyn's thoughts focused on a handsome man in a red Inheritor uniform. Dark hair, green eyes. The feudal surname of Ov came to mind. One of their bloodline, Broujel, had even become a Rector, Kivita knew from Jandeel's tutelage.

Kivita's vision blurred, as if Terredyn wept. A placard of the same man hung in a golden frame beside the windowsill. Terredyn kissed her fingers and laid them on the image.

Was the handsome man her father? She sank deeper into the Juxj Star's red-tinted depths, deeper into the recorded memories of her mother. Was he?

The datacores revealed nothing.

"Tell me," she whispered, concentrating harder still.

The Juxj Star's red-tinted depths gave way to coldest darkness.

"Tell me!" she screamed.

Quivering, Kivita opened her eyes. Salty stickiness stung her cheeks from dried tears. The datacores, including the Juxj Star, floated around her like planets orbiting a star.

Navon, Jandeel, and the other Sages lay gasping on the floor. Each stared at her wide-eyed and gaping.

"She knew all along. . . . Your mother knew she would not live." Navon pushed himself into a kneeling position.

Kivita stood, and the datacores came to rest on the mat. The Juxj Star glowed once.

"Yeah. Seems I answered that signal she wanted, too. From Vstrunn." Hugging herself, Kivita staggered around the grass mat.

"This unites all the theories and beliefs of the Vim." Jandeel wiped his damp forehead. "The Inheritors joining the Vim and their healthy yellow suns in the galactic Core, the Aldaakian Archivers and their tales of reuniting with the Vim, the Ascali songs, the Arm's dying stars—it all makes sense now."

"No." Navon rose and steadied Kivita. "All this means is that the Vim could not cope with Sarrhdtuu aggression and abandoned the Cetturo Arm. This signal sent a millennium ago proves only that another Savant, at a second Vim antenna, sent it."

Kivita shook her head. Why would her mother have given in to such a predetermined fate? Losing her throne, her daughter, her life, all so Kivita, someday, might return that mysterious signal? Rhyer had believed in and obeyed his queen. The Inheritors had killed Terredyn—the only known Savant capable of returning the message.

Why?

"They're using me against the Vim." Kivita drew back from Navon. "That's why Dunaar hired me, that's why the Sarrhdtuu have tracked me—"

"The Sarrhdtuu wouldn't need you, or any of us, to find their enemies." Jandeel's brows rose.

She sighed. "Yeah, and I told you my other idea: I might be a weapon. Every one of these visions has shown the Sarrhdtuu forcing Savants to do their bidding, and killing those who don't. Now we have proof of the Ascali combating the Sarrhdtuu in their own way. The Vim prepared us for something. C'mon, Jandeel, think about it."

"A Naxan butter knife can also cut one's throat," Jandeel said. "That doesn't mean it was intended for violent use."

Luccan's Wish shuddered.

The intercom crackled to life. "Navon, we have just exited the light jump, eight months early!" the pilot cried.

Navon, Jandeel, and the others froze with terror in their eyes.

Heart thudding, Kivita raced to the intercom console and pressed the button. "How? What's happened?"

"Seems to have been a wormhole or something," the pilot replied. "We've entered a system with a gas giant orbiting a red-giant star. There's ... there's a Vim derelict orbiting the planet, too. One hell of a strong beacon signal coming from it."

"Any other ships?" Kivita asked in a tight voice.

"None so far," the pilot replied. "But that signal is hampering our scanners."

Kivita glanced at Navon. "In all my salvaging, I never came across a Vim derelict that close to a planet."

Navon grunted. "We lack enough transports to evacuate this ship if need be. I will not risk all these lives on what must be a trap. Would you be willing to communicate with this derelict—the way your mother must have tried?"

The Naxan Sage clicked twice. "That is supposition. We should leave this system before we are caught. Cheseia's betrayal has already decided that."

"We may not have much choice," Jandeel said. "I believe in what Kivita can do."

"Then so shall I." Navon smiled sadly and handed the Juxj Star to Kivita.

"See, it glows again," Kivita said, as the gem flared red in her grasp. "Maybe it recognizes me."

"A star in hand. I hope it will always burn bright," Navon whispered. "Keep it on your person. If we are to evacuate *Luccan's Wish*, these datacores must be spread out among the Thedes." He took the stone one and handed it to Jandeel. "Awaken everyone from cryostasis. We will gather in the observation deck on Level Four."

The observation deck's large viewport was open, revealing a turquoise-hued gas giant. Storm swirls surged just beneath the planet's opaque atmosphere, matching the stony frowns on Thede faces. Kivita stood with crossed arms; Cheseia sat behind her. Four armed guards waited near the morose Ascali.

Jandeel pointed at Cheseia. "Cheseia is a traitor! Even now our enemies might be in this system with us. This system isn't safe. I say we make a jump now to Tannocci Space. Stand behind our queen!"

"Let us stay and fight any who comes! It's what Sar Redryll would have done!" a Sutaran called out.

Kivita's cheeks burned. Cheseia hung her bandaged head.

Many shouted in support, though several remained silent. Men, women, and children, fresh from cryostasis, all studied Kivita. Navon and the other Savants frowned, while the Sages whispered among themselves. A few people in maroon or purple clothes, including Rhii and Basheev, stood near Jandeel.

"I'm not anyone's queen," Kivita said. "Look. I'm no better than any of you. Because of me, we're all in danger now. Cheseia's actions can't be undone, okay? She will be punished, but not with death. I think this ship should leave while a few of us take a look at this derelict with *Frevyx*. We can't just ignore what these coordinates have led us to."

More than a few nodded in assent with her words, but Navon held up a hand.

"We must evacuate *Luccan's Wish*. Never before have the Inheritors tracked this ship. They will expect to find it here. If we are gone, the search will continue. So will our misery."

"Where will we truly go?" an Ascali asked.

"I say we fight!" a man shouted.

"With what?" Maihh asked, then clicked once.

"Lead us, Queen Kivita!" someone cried.

Kivita stepped forward. All grew quiet and watched her with hopeful stares.

"Listen. I've learned so much from you all. I've learned the universe can be a better place if we don't give up. But I'm no Inheritor saint or Solar Advocate come to lead you to something better. It doesn't matter who my mother was or what I can do. We're all equals here. But it does matter what we do." She swallowed, knowing all those adoring stares were something she couldn't live up to.

"We don't have the ships to evacuate everyone," Jandeel said. "Some will have to remain aboard for such a decoy plan, Navon. Too many."

"That is a ghastly choice," the Tahe Sage said, pulling her white bindings tighter.

"Without null beacons, they'll track us, anyway!" a woman in the back yelled.

"It's me they want," Kivita said in a loud voice, and the crowd quieted again. "So I'll stay."

People bustled and shouted. Basheev gripped Kivita's hand, fear in his brown eyes. Navon tried to calm the crowd, but most ignored him. Cheseia touched Kivita's back with a trembling hand.

Closing her eyes, Kivita concentrated. This time it was harder to withhold data rather than share it with everyone in the room. Her skull numbed and her hearing dimmed. The image of her mother holding her on the Susuron beach reached everyone's mind within the observation deck. Voices died away; pushing and shoving ended. As she opened her eyes, everyone gaped at her.

"Remember what I just showed you. My mother made sacrifices so I could be here today. So have many others. Luccan Thede, Sar Redryll . . ." Kivita cleared her throat. "I can't be your queen unless I can show that same courage."

"We still don't have the ships," Jandeel said in a low voice. "But I will stand by you."

Cheseia rose beside Kivita. "I will certainly stay behind."

Though màny shot the Ascali dark stares, Kivita took her hand.

Navon sighed. "We have four ships: *Frevyx* and three shuttles. In cryopods, I think one hundred could fit on *Frevyx*, and fifty on each shuttle. Of course, each ship would take some of our Vim datacores, books, and other things. Nothing would be left on *Luccan's Wish* pertaining to knowledge."

"That's only two hundred and fifty of us!" the woman yelled again.

"I know," Navon said. "That is why I ask for one hundred fifty adult volunteers to stay behind."

Though a few dozen stepped forward, many backed away. Some argued.

Kivita charged into their midst before fists took the place of words. "Wait! Listen! What if we draw lots, or—"

Luccan's Wish shook and wobbled. The floor quaked

under their feet. Alarms rang throughout the station as the intercom buzzed. "Integrity breach! Integrity breach!"

Outside the viewport, chunks of hull floated toward the gas giant below. *Luccan's Wish* trembled again and the intercom went staticky.

"What's happening?" Rhii asked.

Kivita's stomach churned for a moment, the same as it did whenever she entered a gravity flux. She pulled Basheev to her.

For a few seconds, they all floated into the air; then everyone slammed into the floor. People cried out and groaned, while some clutched broken arms or smashed kneecaps. Kivita, still holding Basheev, rose and pulled Navon to his feet.

A grinding noise reverberated from the deck above them.

Everyone fell into a deathly silence. People stared at each other or out the viewport. Several children wailed.

"Easy, everyone," Navon said.

"Make for the transports!" someone yelled.

Navon started to speak again as dozens rushed toward the exits. Shouts, curses, and weeping filled the air in a wall of noise. The pressurized corridors opened, and people spilled through them. Navon shouted for order, yet few listened. The intercom announced something, but the frightened uproar drowned it out.

Jandeel and others in Narbas livery rushed to Kivita. "We'll escort you to *Frevyx*. Hurry, before it's taken!"

"I'll gather who I can on *Frevyx*, but I'm not leaving," Kivita said.

"Stars flaring, miss, there's no time for that!" Rhii said. "We must leave now!"

Navon tugged on Kivita's arm. "Please. You are too important. You are our cause now."

Kivita stared him down. "Would you leave this boy here?" She clutched Basheev close. "Yeah, well, not me."

Jandeel gave Kivita a sorrowful look. "We will have to fight our way through."

"Yeah? Is this what the Thedes are? Squabbling, scared cowards?" A few still left on the observation deck stopped and listened to Kivita. "Is this how we'll defeat the Inheritors—trampling over each other to escape? Not me. All of you follow me. If I can't squeeze you on *Frevyx*, then I'll stack you atop one another."

A dull explosion sounded from the other end of the deck. *Luccan's Wish* tilted toward the gas giant as the gravity lightened.

"Run to Airlock Eight!" Kivita shouted, then pulled Basheev along as she and the rest rushed through the corridor. The hiss of decompression echoed behind them right before the circular door closed.

30

"How in the name of Arcuri did Redryll escape? You damned fools!" Dunaar wiped his sweaty face with a towel while hurrying to the bridge. The void take these cretins! Two of his Proselytes dead, and one crewman forced into cryostasis by a man posing as a Proselyte.

Bredine Ov was also missing.

Skeletal bitch. The favor he'd shown her, the luxuries he'd allowed her to partake of in his private chambers ... And he'd kept her as his, despite her barren womb! What in the name of the holy Vim did Redryll want with her?

"Rector, we don't know how it happened. They could be anywhere on board," a squad commander said.

"I want them found, imbecile. What of the Thede ship?"

"Captain Stiego has disabled it and awaits your presence on the bridge," a Proselyte said.

By the time Dunaar reached the bridge, his yellow robe was damp with sweat. Through the viewport, a feudal-era cruiser orbited a turquoise gas giant at an odd angle.

Luccan's Wish, just like Cheseia had described it to him.

"Have you hailed them yet?" Dunaar tapped the Scepter on the floor. Hope formed in his breast, despite the complications plaguing their entry into the uncharted system. No matter what Sar or Bredine did, the Vim's punishment for those foul heretics would still be meted out.

"No, Rector," Stiego said. "We have enfiladed their engine module with a single kinetic barrage, per your orders. The signal emanating from the Vim derelict has hindered communication, but the beacon signal from *Frevyx* has stopped."

Dunaar smiled. Cheseia may have been discovered and killed, but he cared not. Like her sister Zhara, that Ascali whore had served her purpose well. "And Kivita Vondir?"

"A signal we believe may be her is emanating from the craft," Stiego replied.

"The Vim have granted us a boon. The infidels must not have even realized what struck them. Captain, set an intercept course for that cruiser, and prepare a battalion of soldiers for a boarding action—lightly equipped, so they can search faster. Arm each platoon with brain-pulse analyzers." Dunaar wiped his chin.

"Rector, their gravity and atmosphere will be compromised by now," Stiego said. "The search may take some time."

"What is time but a gift of the Vim? They cannot escape." Stroking the Scepter, Dunaar gazed out the viewport. Bredine had warned him about enemies from blackest void, but it mattered not. The Vim had chosen him.

"*Fanged Pauper* requests permission to leave *Arcuri's Glory*," the security officer said.

"Granted. The sooner Shekelor Thal is gone, the better." Dunaar tapped a ringed finger against his lips. "Send this order to the platoon commanders: Kivita Vondir is to be taken alive. All others are to be exterminated. Let no Thede survive."

Sar waited in the shuttle cockpit, its viewport still closed. He'd buckled himself in right after waking from cryostasis. Bredine sat in the opposite navigator seat, counting her fingers and mumbling. Muted sounds reverberated in the airlock bay outside: voices, footsteps, fusion engines starting up. He checked the lock status of the shuttle's hatch again.

He would have to escape this battleship, and soon.

Rubbing his jaw, lips, and temples, he was thankful for the cryosleep. All minor bruises and scrapes had healed, due to an extended rest coupled with medication. More than enough large bruises still made him grimace.

"The Rector will cleanse. Hmm? Cleanse, cleanse. Like Susuron, Tahe, Freen, Bellerion." Scowling, Bredine popped her knuckles. "Cleansing to create ugliness. Redryll?"

Her words chilled his spine. No doubt she'd seen many Inheritor atrocities and invasions. Hell, maybe she'd even commanded some, based on what Broujel said earlier.

"Want to tell me who you are?" Sar stared at her.

"Ov lineage. Hmm. I captained *Arcuri's Glory* for Father. Captained, flew, decoded datacores. Redryll, Redryll. They hid my bloodline. Hmm? Yes, hid it to use it. But Rhyer convinced me. Soon, Rhyer's ally. I was caught and placed in void black cell."

Sar studied her. Though beaten, scarred, and en-slaved, Bredine had harbored a great conviction. Why she'd chosen his presence as an opportunity to escape bothered him.

"Why'd you help me? You seem to know Kiv, too."

"Rhyer was brave, so brave. Kivita hadn't started sending then. Rhyer saved other Savants from void-black cold. Poisoned by radiation. Hmm? Poisoned to save more like Kivita."

Sar lurched from his seat. "Kiv's father? You knew him?"

Bredine's face smoothed over in fond remembrance. "Seneschal, swordsman, pilot, general. He raised the princess on Haldon Prime. Raised until she could send the queen's message. Hmm? Ov family distracted proph-ets and protected Rhyer. Oh, Redryll, Redryll. Gushing hot love for a princess, a queen."

"What message?" Sar leaned toward her.

"Vim signal, yes? Expecting a reply. Expecting some-one like Kivita to send. Hmm? But she sent it to everyone. Now all are here to hear the Vim. Thedes, Rector. Maybe Sarrhdtuu." Bredine shrank back in her seat.

As he gripped the manuals, fear gnawed at Sar's mind. Kivita had been preserved, perhaps even groomed, for a higher purpose. Even if he rescued her and they escaped, he doubted she'd ever take him back. Under Navon and Jandeel's tutelage, she would've learned more from the datacores, as well as other things. She would not be the same person as before.

In his racing thoughts, Caitrynn's visage melded with Kivita's. His sister had died long ago. The woman he loved could still be saved from the blinding Inheritor sun. Even if it burned him to ashes.

Sar activated the console scanner, but the hull of *Arcuri's Glory* limited the signal. It still showed the faint outlines of a gas giant, *Luccan's Wish*, and a huge Vim derelict. Sar tried to fine-tune the frequency as the shuttle and airlock bay shuddered. Bredine floated off her seat a few inches, then fell back into it.

"Redryll? Hmm. I'll strap in." Bredine buckled the restraints and tapped her fingers on the console. "Black void. Cold, cold. Ready?"

The scanner flickered and beeped, while readouts on the terminal lit up. Studying the information, Sar frowned. The scanner beeped again.

Luccan's Wish had been hit, with the Inheritor battleship closing in.

"Hmm. Sarrhdtuu? Maybe they are doing something." Bredine drummed her fingers louder on the console.

The chill spread from Sar's spine to his stomach. The Sarrhdtuu's plan still baffled him. "Dunaar, you bastard."

Bredine pointed at him. "Redryll? Do something!"

He ran a hand through his hair. "Shut up a minute. Can't act until—"

The readouts indicated that shuttles had left *Arcuri's Glory*, bound for *Luccan's Wish*.

"Hell with this." He activated the shuttle's main systems. The cockpit viewport opened and the engine came online.

Outside the viewport, Inheritor soldiers in polysuits boarded the other shuttles, lamps reflecting off their yellow-tinted faceplates. Sar's throat constricted. Hundreds of soldiers had been wakened from cryostasis. The Thedes would be lucky to have fifty armed defenders aboard *Luccan's Wish*.

Across the bay, Shekelor Thal entered *Fanged Pauper* and turned around before its airlock shut. Despite the distance, his eyes met Sar's. A smirk spread over Shekelor's face. Then he pointed and shouted.

"Shit," Sar muttered.

"Redryll? Hmm?" Bredine's eyes widened.

Sar clicked on full engine control and steered the manuals. Their shuttle turned on the landing pad toward the nearest airlock doors.

Shekelor shouted again. Soldiers rushed across the floor, weapons drawn. The bay's lamps flashed red.

"Redryll? You will do something?" Bredine stopped tapping her fingers and stared at the approaching soldiers. Shekelor exited *Fanged Pauper*, aiming a beam rifle.

"As much as I can." Sar clicked the airlock relay on his console and fired the thrusters. Something exploded behind the shuttle, but Sar pushed the manuals forward. The airlock bay doors slid open.

"Yes, something. Yes, yes." Bredine peeked from the viewport, then recoiled as kinetic shots pinged off the shuttle's armored hull. A fine green beam sliced across the shuttle's nose from Shekelor's rifle. The airlock doors started sliding shut.

Dunaar's voice came over the console speaker. "Redryll? You sacrilegious offal! I will have you shot down as soon as you exit my ship!"

Sar concentrated on the view outside the opening airlock.

"You are too late to be a martyr for your cause," Dunaar continued, mirth in his voice. "Kivita Vondir is already mine—"

Sar punched the mute button, then fired both starboard and port-side thrusters. The airlock doors black-ened, and warning alarms blasted Sar's ears. Bredine tapped his shoulder and yelled unintelligible sentences.

Kivita's hazel eyes and easy smile beckoned him over the threshold.

As the shuttle shot into space, Sar stabilized its flight path, just as the battleship's starboard K-gun battery fired. The shuttle's hull creaked as he dove. G-forces shoved him back into the seat and made his head throb. Bredine gasped, eyelids fluttering.

Sar pushed the manuals to their lower limit. The shut-tle's proximity alarm resounded in the cockpit, tremors rocked the shuttle, and the star field outside blurred.

The sabot rounds darted past the shuttle's viewport.

Sar righted the shuttle and flew toward *Luccan's Wish*. The familiar shape of *Frevyx*, docked to Airlock Eight, caught his eye. Why no one had used it to escape deepened his anxieties.

As he drew near, *Luccan's Wish* tilted toward the gas giant. Debris and bodies floated into the eternal cold.

Sar's body sagged, and he lost his breath. Damn Dunaar to the deepest depths, damn him to—

Bredine gripped his arm. "No void black for Kivita yet. She still sends."

Sar slammed the manuals forward.

While *Aldaar*'s hangar filled with Troopers for the boarding action, Seul cradled her helmet. On a nearby flat display, Vuul stared back at her.

"Despite interference from the Vim signal, we have concluded the damaged human ship has not been evac-uated," Vuul said. "No beacon trajectories have exited this system. The fact that the Inheritor battleship remains reveals the presence of Kivita Vondir. Find her. We will hold off that battleship as long as we can."

"It is done, Commander Vuul." The possibility of a Vim rendezvous made Seul feel lighter than cryo exhaust. Above all, she would find her red-haired friend.

"The human craft has been damaged and breached, so stay in tight formation," Seul called. "Each squad's officer will have a brain-pulse analyzer in his or her poly-armor. Understood?"

Dozens of Shock Troopers spoke in unison. "Yes, Captain Jaah." Their voices echoed in the hangar.

Seul stepped away from the boarding ramp. "Officer Kael, a word."

Kael paused while Shock Troopers loaded onto the shuttle. "Yes, Captain Jaah?"

Taking his hand in her polygauntlet, Seul's cryoports tightened. Though everyone aboard *Aldaar* had woken from cryostasis half an hour before exiting the light jump, she'd been too busy to see him until now. Her excitement gave way to yearning.

"Remember what we discussed in the Medical Ward. . . . I don't want you to remember me this way." She touched her polycuirass.

Kael frowned. "We'll make it through this, Captain Jaah. Why are you acting like this?"

Biting back emotions, Seul wanted to just tell him. Say the words, verbalize her feelings. Touch Kael and make him see. All the Shock Troopers in the airlock bay, all the flat displays where Vuul might be watching, buried the words in her heart.

"Promise . . . promise me you'll do what needs to be done. Don't wait for me if something goes wrong." Seul squeezed his hand.

"As you command, Captain Jaah," he whispered.

Warmth rose in her chest as her cryoports clamped. Seul pursed her lips, then kissed Kael's mouth so quickly, he blinked in surprise. Her polyboots bumped into his as she drew away.

"As you were, Officer Kael." Seul shut her faceplate, unable to look him in the eye. What a clumsy, fleeting kiss. She almost wished she slept in Niaaq Aldaar's cryo chamber.

After striding aboard, Seul locked herself into a launch tube. Her heart hadn't beat with such painful rapidness since her first combat mission. How foolish of her to strain her combat effectiveness—the mission mattered most, not her personal wishes. No matter how much she repeated it to herself, though, Seul's heart grew heavier.

Aldaar wouldn't last long in this fight, but the Vim may be coming to save them. The Inheritors would be brutal, after coming so far for whatever prize the system held. All depended on saving Kivita from them and the Sarrhdtuu.

Saving a daughter who remained ignorant of her mother.

The shuttle departed *Aldaar* and made for the crippled starship. Its bulk would shield them from the Inheritor battleship's guns for a short time, since they wanted Kivita, too.

The vessel resembled an ancient human-colony ship, with multiple decks and a bridge tapering into a cone from the bow. Two precise sabot hits had struck near the aft engines and an airlock. Chunks of hull, crates, and bodies floated toward the blue-green gas giant and its ice rings below. Seul turned away from the humanoid forms.

Vuul's voice came over the cockpit speaker. "Enter through those two punctures, Captain Jaah. I want two shuttles to infiltrate each. So far, our analyzers show that no datacores or Savants have exited the hull's breaches. Kivita and the Juxj Star are still inside."

"Commander Vuul, how long will we have until the planet's orbit reveals *Aldaar*'s position behind the ship to Inheritor fire?"

Static crackled over the connection as the shuttle's artificial gravity shuddered from the gas giant's propinquity. Seul waited for Vuul to answer, unused to any hesitation from him.

"Perhaps half an hour before the ship's orbit deteriorates into reentry. Inheritor shuttles are nearing the vessel now. Do not seek engagement with hostiles. Retrieve Vondir and coordinate a fighting retreat back to your transports. *Aldaar* will standby, but should things go wrong, light-jump back to Aldaakian Space with Vondir."

The Troopers aboard glanced at Seul and gripped their rifles tighter, the resolve in their stares swelling her chest with pride. Aldaakians had long inured themselves to sacrifice. Now it could mean something again.

"Officer Kael, drop us at the earliest opportunity next to the ship's hull."

Kael glanced back at her, a gleam in his eye. "Coming up now, Captain Jaah. Five, four, three . . ."

She didn't hear him count the last two numbers. Lips trembling, Seul closed her eyes and imagined a world with a yellow sun, shining over snow drifts and glaciers. Her daughter running in the cold wind with arms outstretched. Seul reclining in Kael's arms, dressed in swath robes . . .

The launch tube ejected Seul into the vacuum right alongside the human starship. Her polyboots magnetized and snapped to the hull. The action of her fellow Troopers making contact with the hull vibrated up her body. The shuttle hovered nearby, awaiting recovery.

"Squad A, form up behind me and keep your rifles ready. Remember to minimize breaths to conserve air. If any of you experience gravity sickness, alert the rest immediately." Seul walked down the hull toward a hole shot through an airlock. With each step suctioning to the metal surface, her leg muscles pumped harder just to propel her along.

The hull stretched hundreds of feet in either direction, its smoothness broken by other airlocks, orbital thrusters, and sensory arrays. Far below, the planet dominated the view with its opaque turquoise atmosphere. The yellow-white ring of dust and ice twinkled. In the distance, the gray sticklike Vim derelict stretched at least eight miles in length.

Were they in that derelict, waiting for the right moment? Seul had to look away from the craft. The mission. Must remain focused on the mission.

Near the breach, supply crates drifted out into space, along with metal shards, melted globules, cooled slag, and one human body. No wounds or envirosuit, but the eyes stared at her with horror. Vacuum frost already coated the corpse's mouth.

Seul pushed aside smaller debris and gripped a protruding girder. Lifting her feet off the hull, she pushed herself from the girder into the breach, where her boots stuck to the ruined airlock's metal floor. Walking forward, she swept the area with her rifle.

"Jaah here. I'm in. Airlock is clear. Squad A, enter one at a time and form a ranging party, single file." Seul examined corners for any survivors or lurking enemies.

"Captain Jaah . . . is Vuul. The signal from . . . derelict is interrupting our scanners even more. Beware of . . . and blackout. Give me regular updates on . . . prog-ress . . . possible." Vuul's transmission broke up.

"It is done, Commander Vuul." Seul clomped toward two circular doors, while Troopers filtered in through the breach. She tried one door, but it had clamped shut. Through a small window on each door, humans gaped at her with shocked faces, then fled.

"I have a visual on live occupants, apparently un-armed," Seul said. "Judging from their movements, the station still retains adequate gravity in certain areas."

"Understood. Proceed and . . . Inheritor soldiers in-side, but . . ." Vuul's reply broke up again.

Seul waited until all Troopers had entered, then acti-vated the brain-pulse analyzer affixed to her right poly-vambrace. As soon as she cut through the door, those on the other side would lose their air. They would die. Seul fidgeted with her rifle, then checked her readouts on the inside of her extended collar.

The analyzer revealed the presence of five Savants on board the doomed starship. One emitted a more powerful signal than the rest, from the ship's fourth deck. Any enemies would be headed in the same direc-tion.

"Captain Jaah?" a Trooper asked.

She cleared her throat. "Squad A, the station's com-partments are pressurized. If we continue, occupants may perish. Point One, start hailing short-wave radio frequencies to alert all nearby passengers we mean no harm. Point Two, slice this door open. When you finish, weld it back."

Several minutes later, Seul waited while Squads A and B entered the corridor. Point Two finished sealing the cut door back into place.

"Don't demagnetize your boots yet, and maintain ranging order. Do not fire unless provoked. Is that understood?" Seul met each Trooper's gaze. All assented.

"Good. Remember—we are here to retrieve Kivita Vondir. Alive." Seul approached the next circular door and held her breath. It hissed open.

The room was empty, but a viewport displayed an open area in the underside of the ship for cargo bays and an exhaust trench. On the opposite side, the viewport to an observation deck was also open.

Seul's heart sank.

Several unmoving forms floated on the deck. Human, Ascali, even an Aldaakian woman. Beside her floated a small Aldaakian boy, dressed in Tannocci-style leather clothing. Seul hadn't seen any Aldaakian children since viewing her infant daughter in the Pediatric Ward.

Here, on this starship, an Aldaakian mother had been rearing her child. Away from Aldaakian society, free of strictures and routine. Now they'd both joined Niaaq Aldaar on his frozen journey.

"Keep moving." Seul gripped her rifle tight.

31

After squirming through buckled girders and cracked insulation, Kivita entered the next corridor. Whoever had fired on *Luccan's Wish*, their weapon had sliced through the entire ship at a diagonal angle. She feared even more damage had been done, with many passengers dead. Navon, Jandeel, Cheseia, Basheev, Rhii, Maihh, and two dozen others followed her past charred bulkheads and melted flooring.

A deep fear lingered in her gut. Their attackers hadn't finished off *Luccan's Wish*—which meant more was to come.

"The impact must have sealed some of these compartments due to the heat." Navon pointed at the corridor's ceiling. A blackened line ran above them, with cooled slag hanging in fat droplets.

"We'll need envirosuits," Kivita said. "We're still half a deck away from the next lift, and who knows what shape it's in."

"There is a maintenance shaft beyond this corridor," Navon said. "It might be even more dangerous."

"What if the next corridor has been compromised?"

Maihh clicked once. "When we open that door, we'll all be sucked in!"

Jandeel helped Rhii over a sharp bulkhead crease. "It's our only chance now. Try the intercom again, Kivita. Maybe the communication systems have come back online."

As Kivita neared an intercom panel beside the doorway, *Luccan's Wish* tilted again. Everyone scooted toward the viewport, where the gas giant loomed closer than before. One man slammed into the viewport, and Kivita held her breath. All grew quiet, as if fearing their weight might shatter it.

"We're not going to make it!" Maihh wailed.

Kivita crawled back to the intercom panel and pressed several buttons. Nothing but static answered her.

All those faces filled with hope, all the Thedes who believed in her—all of them dead or doomed now. Her heart sank into her stomach. A constant throb grew inside her head.

Kivita mashed the buttons again. "Hey!" she called into the mic. "If anyone can hear me—"

"You are doing no good like this. There is nothing that can be done." Navon placed a hand over the mic.

Kivita glared at him. "Some are still alive, and you damn well know it."

"I believe so, too," Navon said, his face calm. "That is why we must focus on those around us. The maintenance shaft, Kivita. Please." He gestured at Basheev. "For their sakes."

Jandeel, Rhii, and the others watched her with determination mixed with fear. Cheseia's jaw tightened and her muscles flexed.

"Yeah. Let's do this." She crawled toward the door and straddled the viewport below her. The next corridor lay empty through the door's small square window, but she'd no clue what the conditions were like. With a hull breach, each room and corridor might contain their deaths.

She swallowed and pulled the lever. The circular door hissed aside.

No decompression, no escape of their thinning atmosphere. Relieved sighs, weak laughs, and prayers sounded behind her as Kivita walked into the next corridor.

The air wasn't as thin, but the temperature had dipped several degrees. As in previous corridors and rooms, an eerie silence greeted them. For a damaged ship, *Luccan's Wish* gave off no creaks or groans yet. Since sound didn't travel in a vacuum, the silence only worried Kivita more.

Some queen she'd turned out to be.

Her temples tingled. What about the ship's mainframe computer? Focusing her mind, she tried to stretch out her thoughts to the computer. Navon said something, but she gritted her teeth and concentrated harder.

Luccan's Wish tilted again.

"No," she grunted, directing all her mental will into the ship's computer systems. In her mind, locking mechanisms activated, three braking thrusters fired, and life support returned to a few cabins. After a few seconds, *Luccan's Wish* stabilized. Kivita closed her eyes and fought back sharp pangs in her cranium.

"Kivita?" Jandeel grasped her arm.

"Leave her be," Navon said in a hushed tone. "You are connected with the ship. You are pouring its data into my thoughts. What if I—"

"Can't hold this for long. Which way?" she asked in a strained voice.

"There, on your left." Navon followed her into the next corridor.

As Kivita drew aside the shaft's thin metal safety door, a pounding erupted from the door into the next chamber. Through the door's square window, a Naxan man screamed at them in silence while floating with terminal slowness.

"Stars darkening and setting, no." Rhii pulled Basheev to her. The others all turned away and shuffled past. The Naxan continued to pound on the door, his lips turning blue.

"May the Solars have mercy on him," Jandeel whispered.

Clutching her bandaged head, Cheseia sniffled.

Navon blocked the view with his body. "We cannot help him. Come, everyone. This shaft should take us down to Level Eight, where *Frevyx* is docked."

Kivita gripped Cheseia's arm, while everyone crept into the shaft on their hands and knees. During her time aboard *Luccan's Wish*, Kivita had felt part of a family. When Navon moved from the door's window, she avoided looking through it.

"You certainly must abandon me here," Cheseia said, sagging against the bulkhead.

The throb mounted in Kivita's brain. Holding the ship in place would fry her brain unless she caught a break soon, but there was something else touching her thoughts. Familiar, yet alien. "C'mon, let's go."

Cheseia hung her head. "No, I—"

Kivita grabbed Cheseia's ripped tunic. "Listen to me. You can either weep about the pain you've brought these people or you can help a few escape. You think this is easy for me? I brought enemies here as much as you."

Nodding, Cheseia entered, and her sniffling ended.

Kivita ducked and wriggled into the shaft's cold metal housing, which measured three by three feet square. Noxious air made her gasp for breath. The others in front slowed down, their numbers depleting the shaft's available oxygen. Small lamps at ten-foot intervals gave spare illumination.

"Hurry the best you can." Kivita nudged two people who'd stopped to catch their breath. "You see anything, Jandeel?"

"There are three branches here, but I say we go straight across." His voice traveled through the shaft in a metallic echo.

Navon entered the shaft and closed the sliding door. The lamps flickered. Several people moaned.

In Kivita's mind, the ship's computer indicated multiple power failures. She concentrated. The power cells didn't fire; the energy couplings had burned through. Heart racing, she made the braking thrusters fire again. Nevertheless, *Luccan's Wish* dropped slightly toward the gas giant below.

Kivita bit her lip. "Yeah, Jandeel, sounds good. C'mon, everyone. We can't stay here."

She coaxed the others as they crept along the shaft. The air chilled and thinned as the shaft resonated with their collective heaves. Dropping temperatures made Kivita's lungs hurt and chapped her lips and nostrils.

Maihh faltered to her knees and gasped.

"Here." Kivita clasped Maihh's hand and they continued together. Maihh clicked three times and murmured her thanks.

For several freezing minutes, the group traveled the shaft. Kivita's palms numbed from touching the frigid metal, until she rolled her long sleeves over her hands. Basheev gasped and winced, flexing his fingers. Rhii ripped patches from her skinsuit and fashioned makeshift gloves for him.

"I see another shaft door ahead," Jandeel called back, wheezing.

Tasting carbon in the air, Kivita breathed only through her nose. She glanced back at Navon, who plodded on with slow, measured breaths. Cheseia kept pace though her arms trembled.

A passage on their right creaked; then air hissed somewhere and stopped. Something scraped over metal above them.

Kivita reached out her thoughts to the ship's computer, but nothing useful returned. Though her head throbbed, she feared to release her hold on *Luccan's Wish*.

"Almost there," Jandeel said.

A dull thud, followed by an explosion above, shook the shaft. Its metal walls vibrated from the force, creating an earsplitting racket. Everyone cried out in pain. Kivita slammed palms to ears and closed her eyes in agony. The reverberation made her teeth chatter, her heart flutter. Cheseia bumped into her; then Maihh coughed and stumbled into Navon.

The throb became an incessant drumbeat in Kivita's mind. It pumped in her veins, constricted with each heartbeat. She blinked as a repeating sequence entered her thoughts. It wasn't from the ship's computer mainframe. A chalky taste violated her mouth.

The sequence formed into an inquisitive sensation.

Words came to Kivita's lips, as if someone else spoke them.

"I'm here," she whispered.

Warmer air blasted over them from the front. Light flashed into the shaft.

"Hurry it up!" Jandeel yelled. "The door's open!"

The shaft shifted a few inches to the right. People yelled and screamed. Maihh tried to turn back, but Kivita caught her and, with Navon's help, forced her forward. The hissing from the right passage grew louder.

"C'mon, go!" Kivita pushed those before her. The shaft shook again. Jerky light filled the shaft. Jandeel held the door open while Rhii, Basheev, and the rest climbed out, gasping. Maihh patted Kivita's shoulder and rushed out.

Kivita exited the shaft with Cheseia and Navon as a screeching noise echoed inside it. Jandeel slid the door shut and locked it. They all jumped back as it buckled from within, but held.

"Decompression," Navon said. "Let us find a lift."

Shivering, Kivita tried to learn from the computer the location of the closest lift. This time, though, more sensors had shorted out. *Luccan's Wish* was all but handicapped.

Focusing her will, Kivita barely managed to keep control over two braking thrusters and some life support.

"The computer is almost dead, so where now?" she asked, looking around.

They'd entered the other side of Level Four, across the thruster exhaust trench and cargo bay on the underside of *Luccan's Wish*. On their left, a small galley held five cringing Thedes. Tiles had fallen from the ceiling, and one lamp flickered like a crazy firefly. Air and gravity remained normal, but the temperature was still dropping.

Kivita ran to the lockers and flung them open. "Everyone get into an envirosuit!" She grabbed one and slipped into it.

Her fellow Thedes also suited up. Even the five in the galley came and put one on. Navon faced them while he fastened wrist clamps around his gloves.

"Have you seen anyone else? What has happened?"

A Sutaran man with a broken arm answered. "We all ran to the airlocks for the ships. The whole ship shook, and the lights went on and off. We heard screams and hissing air from ahead, so we turned back. The corridors started collapsing, and . . . So many are out there now. . . ." He looked down.

"Out where?" Basheev asked as Rhii handed him a helmet.

"In space," Kivita said. No use avoiding the issue. "Damn it. What about the lifts? Should be one the next corridor over." She tried to contain the strange sequence running through her mind, but it almost blotted out everything around her.

"Broken," the Sutaran man said. "It won't come back up from Level Ten."

Jandeel found an intercom panel and pressed the button. "Can anybody hear me?"

Static crackled on the speaker, and then a small girl's voice came across it. "We can't get out! We can't get out! Please come get us out!" The connection clicked and went dead.

Cheseia glanced at Kivita, russet eyes wishing for her own death. Part of Kivita wanted to reach out to her; the other wanted to strangle the Ascali traitor. Across light years and depthless revelations, she'd finally learned to control her feelings. Vengeance amounted to an empty pursuit, and Kivita had others than herself to worry about now.

A strained male voice broke over the intercom speakers. "We're on Level Six. I don't know what the hell happened. We still have air but no gravity. Where are you? Can you get to us?"

Navon touched Jandeel's shoulder. "Do not reveal our location, for we cannot help them. We still do not know who or where our enemy is."

Kivita burned with helplessness, and the Thedes' reaction to the attack still angered her. Damn fools, thinking they were untouchable. If they didn't reach *Frevyx* or the other ships soon, they'd die within hours for lack of air.

"Whoever fired on us didn't want to destroy *Luccan's Wish*," Kivita said. "Just disable it and cause confusion. We have to assume they've boarded, so I'm not sticking around. To hell with the lifts. I say we find a roll of flexi wire and rappel down the shaft to Level Eight."

Rhii shook her head. "Stars darkening in the night, miss. We have wounded and children. How can we do that?"

"Carry them," Kivita replied. "It's what I'm going to do. We can't just—"

Luccan's Wish slanted a few degrees toward the planet. An alarm rang from a cryo chamber on their right. Behind them, the maintenance shaft door buckled in farther. Concentrating on the computer, Kivita tried to make the braking thrusters fire. One did, but the other lost power.

"Put your helmets on!" Navon shouted. Everyone obeyed him.

Kivita rifled through the lockers until she found two flexi rolls, perhaps fifty feet each. She handed one to Cheseia. "I'll go down the shaft first. We'll have to open the lift doors to Level Eight manually."

Two explosions vibrated far above on their right. *Luccan's Wish* shook. The lamps flickered off, and some didn't come back on. Kivita felt her steps getting lighter as the ship's computer finally went offline. Her slight control of the last thruster and scant life support ended.

Kivita affixed one end of the flexi line to a girder just inside the lift shaft. "Make sure it'll hold us."

Cheseia tugged it and nodded. Darkness waited below.

Jandeel nudged Rhii and Basheev after Kivita. "Hurry. I'll make sure the flexi holds up here before following."

"May the stars shine for us, miss." Rhii pressed a portable lamp into Kivita's hand, while Basheev passed out more to the others from a nearby locker. The ship vibrated again, longer and with greater intensity. Pods creaked from their casings in the cryo chamber. Crockery and foodstuffs spilled from the galley.

The intercom speaker buzzed and popped. "... And we can't ... no! ... coming in ..."

The whizzing noise of a kinetic shot ended the connection.

"Let's get going," Kivita said in a flat voice.

Cheseia helped her down into the lift shaft. Its spherical sides bore sensor pits and gravitational accelerators, which moved the lift without cables. Kivita activated her lamp, clamped it to her helmet, and hoisted herself down. They needed to travel four decks down, from Four to Eight. Each lift stopped at fifteen-foot intervals.

Kivita swiveled her head left and right, the cold lamp lighting her descent in quick glimpses. A tug on the line signaled others were following after her.

"How much farther, Kivita?" Jandeel asked over the helmet speaker. "I've lost all gravity up here."

"Yeah, down here, too," Kivita replied. "I'm nearing Level Five now. With less gravity, there'll be less weight on the line. Cheseia, bring the other flexi roll and send everyone down. No one let go of it."

A hissing sound exploded in the chamber above. Kivita vibrated on the line for a second; the galley had finally decompressed.

Shouts and sobs came over her helmet speakers, but Kivita magnetized her polyboots and descended, hand over hand on the flexi line. The lift exit for Level Five passed her by, and the one for Level Six came within sight.

"Everybody still with me?" she asked. "Just hang on to the line and try to keep your feet on the shaft wall." Kivita's muscles burned with the effort of pulling the rest behind her. Lugging all those small loads through zero-G derelicts paid off now.

Luccan's Wish trembled for an instant. The flexi line shook.

Kivita glanced up. Cheseia had wrapped the flexi around her waist and now helped Kivita pull the others via the shaft's sensor pits.

"Just keeping going. We are truly right behind you," Cheseia said.

Along the shaft, several lamps shone their beams over the walls and across her fellow Thedes. Almost thirty of them. Kivita had no idea, out of four hundred, how many still lived aboard *Luccan's Wish*. The thought drove her on. Her shoulders and legs shook with exertion; sweat pooled in her envirosuit collar.

"Kivita, there's—" Jandeel's voice cut off.

"Just hold on, I'm nearing Level Seven," Kivita said, unable to keep the relief from her voice.

"Flaring red stars, someone's shining light on us from up there!" Basheev cried over their helmet speakers.

Maihh clicked several times. Some of the others mumbled and cursed, but no one stopped moving along the flexi line.

"Don't panic. It could be friends," Rhii said.

Impacts vibrated down the shaft into Kivita's legs. "Jandeel? Jandeel, can you hear me?"

No one answered. The lights kept shining from above.

"Kivita, keep going!" Navon shouted.

A hard shake traveled down the flexi line. Kivita glanced up as something flashed far above them; then the line went limp in her hands. Cheseia bumped into her. With her boot soles knocked from the shaft wall, Kivita plummeted down.

The gravity had reactivated.

"It's been cut!" Basheev screamed over the speaker.

Though the gravity remained weak, it still yanked Kivita down with terrifying speed. Below, her lamp illuminated the top of the lift on Level Ten.

Mind racing, Kivita shouted over her mic. "Shit— grab the sensor pits!"

Her fingers scrambled over the shaft wall. Some of her fingertips caught on the pits, and her feet skidded along the surface. Kivita's polyboots stuck to the wall again as Navon and the others scrabbled past her.

"Grab me!" She leaned out and took Navon's hand until he found a foothold near the next lift entrance.

Rhii got a handhold opposite them and clasped Navon's other hand. An Aldaakian latched onto Rhii's ankle. Above, Cheseia held Basheev with one arm, but the weight of the rest slid the flexi down her waist and past her ankles.

The other people fell past them. Without atmosphere in the shaft now, Kivita heard no impact. The flexi line sunk in noiseless gloom.

Voices came over her speaker: people in pain, afraid, cursing, calling for help. Kivita walked up the wall as two light beams shone from above.

"Hurry, Kivita! Those are not friends!" Navon called. Rhii and the other hangers-on climbed down using the sensor pits for handholds.

Kivita pulled Basheev from Cheseia's strained grasp. "Here, climb on my back." She took Cheseia's arm. "And, you, hang on to me."

"I am definitely coming," Cheseia said, renewed strength in her gaze.

Glancing down, Kivita's lamp revealed more than twenty Thedes lying in a crumpled heap atop the lift. Some had gained their footing, but most remained motionless. Maihh stood, hands reaching up to Kivita.

Level Eight's lift entrance waited three feet away.

"Kivita, definitely put me on that lip next to the lift door," Cheseia said. "I will certainly try to open it. With your boots, try to help as many down there as you truly can."

Kivita released Cheseia and Basheev on the lip and walked down the wall. Her heart thudded in desperation as she tried not to think about who watched them from above, shining lights on them. Who had cut the flexi line.

While Kivita neared those atop the stalled lift, Cheseia grunted and strained with the door; Navon helped her. Kivita reached for Maihh's hand as it came up to meet hers.

"The Solars bless you, dear," Maihh said.

"I've got you now. Just—"

The lift shook and slid away from Kivita with increasing speed. Maihh's fingers brushed hers, then disappeared into the darkness. The wall vibrated under her boots. After a few seconds, the lamps of those who'd fallen winked out.

Kivita's gloved hand remained extended. Ready to save a life, to give hope.

She wanted to scream, wanted to follow and help them, but her lamp didn't penetrate the black hole beneath her.

"Kivita, come back! The lift must have gone to the power level," Navon said. "We have forced the door open. We've got gravity—"

"They're still alive!" Kivita yelled.

"Please, Kivita," Navon said over the speaker. "Help these others. We are being followed now."

Far above, the light beams still scanned the shaft's walls. Shapes moved in the entrance to Level Four.

"You fucking bastards," she whispered, then walked up the wall toward the others, where faint light emanated from Level Eight's entrance. Inside her envirosuit, the pouch containing the Juxj Star weighed her down. She'd thought her knowledge had illuminated the darkness of her life, and would have brightened the ignorance blanketing the Cetturo Arm.

Now it seemed to envelope her as it swallowed those she cared about.

32

Sar maneuvered the shuttle closer to Airlock Seven. One deck below, *Frevyx* was docked to Airlock Eight. He gripped the manuals tighter while examining the damage to *Luccan's Wish*. The ship had tilted twice more toward the gas giant since he'd escaped Dunaar. Outside the shuttle's starboard viewport, the Aldaakian cruiser waited. It didn't fire on him, though three assault shuttles maintained a tight flight perimeter near the decks above.

"Bet they've sent Shock Troopers aboard." Sar flew parallel to Airlock Seven and initiated the shuttle's magnetizing array. With a shudder and a clank, both vessels linked airlocks; then Sar yanked off his restraints and rose from the cockpit. The scanner beeped twice. Sar studied it and cursed under his breath.

Fanged Pauper had docked on the starboard side of *Luccan's Wish*, while the Inheritor shuttles drew closer to Airlock Three.

He needed more time, not more enemies.

"The Rector will find Kivita. Hmm." Bredine followed him, face drawn in concentration. Since leaving *Arcuri's Glory*, she'd been quiet.

"Dunaar wouldn't still be in the system unless Kiv was trapped on board." Sar slipped into an envirosuit and snapped on a helmet with a dirty faceplate. "You're free, Bredine. You want this shuttle, it's yours. Once I have Kiv and my friends, I'm leaving on *Frevyx*." The words held more confidence than he felt. It would be madness inside the disabled ship.

After suiting up, Bredine stared at him with a strange clarity. "I want to see the queen. Hmm. Redryll? Kivita sends."

"Whatever. Just stay behind me." He snatched a spike baton from a small weapons locker; it held no swords or pistols. Once the shuttle airlock opened, momentary weightlessness gave way to normal gravity as they entered Airlock Seven. Red warning lights flashed inside, where supply crates, toolboxes, and gas canisters lay overturned. An intercom buzzed with static, which meant the bay hadn't decompressed yet.

It'd been more than fourteen years since he'd boarded *Luccan's Wish*. The only family he'd had since Caitrynn's death needed him more than ever.

"Kivita sends," Bredine said over his helmet speaker.

"What? Don't distract me unless it's important." He neared one of three circular doors leading from the airlock bay. Through the first-door window, light flickered in the adjacent corridor. Shards from a broken viewport floated inside. Sar approached the second door; utter darkness barred its window. His heart beat faster, and his breath fogged up his faceplate before it could defrost.

The third window revealed a Tannocci man in an envirosuit, leaning against a bulkhead. Several people sat behind him, their faces pallid from stale air.

"Jandeel?" he muttered, then rapped on the window. "Jandeel!"

Eyes meeting Sar's, Jandeel rushed to the door, a strained smile on his lips. The others rose and hugged each other. Jandeel tapped the window and mouthed words.

"Enemies aboard. Don't use main radio frequency. Kivita and Navon are trapped," Sar whispered as he interpreted Jandeel's silent words. He glanced around the airlock bay. "Bredine, how much air in here, you think?"

She turned the nozzles on five different air canisters. "Hmm. Not enough for you to argue with Kivita." Jets of gas blew from the nozzles.

"What the hell does that mean? Never mind." Sar pecked on the window and pointed at the canisters.

Nodding, Jandeel turned and gestured to his comrades. The other Thedes' faces shone with new purpose. Sar wondered how they had accepted Kivita and her abilities, and Cheseia's betrayal. Did they even know that she was a traitor? What a fool he'd been.

"Redryll? You can let them in." The more Bredine spoke, the more coherent her sentences became.

Sar motioned for Jandeel and the others to stand back. Holding his breath, Sar removed his helmet and inhaled. The canister air had a metallic taste, having not gone through a proper scrubber. Jandeel nodded and led the others toward the door. Sar pulled the release lever.

The pressurized door slid open with a hiss. Those inside the corridor poured into the airlock bay, weeping, laughing, gasping.

Jandeel removed his helmet and sighed. "I couldn't leave them in there, and we feared the bay had lost all air. It's so damn good to see you again Sar. Thank the Solars."

Sar clasped his hand. "Glad that knife wound healed. How was Kivita the last you saw her?"

"She's doing things beyond anything we ever dreamed." Jandeel beamed.

The other Thedes neared the airlock, then gaped at the Inheritor shuttle docked outside. They murmured among themselves and shot glances in Sar's direction. Bredine stared at them with the authority of a military commander.

"Where is your queen? Black void out there. Cold. Hmm."

Jandeel stiffened. "Everyone, Sar came here to rescue us. It should be his decision when we depart *Luccan's Wish*. We still might save others."

Sar raised a hand. "No. The Inheritors have fired on the ship. Shock Troopers have boarded, too."

"Add pirates to that list," Jandeel said. "Brutes in polyarmor separated me from Kivita, Cheseia, and the others as we descended a shaft to Level Eight. I managed to escape, and found these other survivors."

So, Cheseia was still alive. Why did that bother him?

Sar gazed into the corridor. "The shuttle will take all of you, but an Aldaakian cruiser and other ships are out there. Best chance is to make a jump as soon as you can."

"You're leaving?" Jandeel's brows rose.

"Hell, no. I'm getting Kiv and taking *Frevyx*."

"I'm coming with you." The intense loyalty in Jandeel's eyes made Sar grip his hand again.

The other Thedes opened the airlock and rushed onto the shuttle, but a few waited, guilt on their faces.

"Go while you still can," Sar called. "I'm not leaving without Kiv."

Seconds later, the shuttle, and Sar's nearest escape, departed.

"Kivita sends." Bredine's breath exited in cold clouds as the temperature dropped.

Jandeel looked at her with amusement.

"She's a Savant that Rector Thev held captive on his ship," Sar said. "I'll explain later. What about everyone else?"

Jandeel frowned. "I don't know. So many compartments have lost gravity, life support, or simply decompressed. We could have used that shuttle to link with Level Eight." He gestured behind him. "We saw bodies floating on the opposite deck across the cargo trench. I have no idea how many have survived."

"Why the hell weren't the security protocols I came up with put into action?" Sar kicked a supply crate. "Told you we couldn't hide forever, that we'd have to fight sometime."

Sighing, Jandeel raised his hands. "There was such panic when the attack came, and—"

Luccan's Wish shook. Sar steadied himself against a bulkhead, while Bredine reacted with precise reflexes, gripping Jandeel's arm and the airlock handle. An explosion vibrated through the decks above them. The bay's red warning lamps clacked off. Only the gas giant's turquoise glow lit the chamber.

"Did you try to reach Level Eight again? Should be another lift nearby," Sar whispered to Jandeel.

Helmet still on, Bredine tugged Jandeel with her toward Sar. She pushed damp hair from Jandeel's face, making the Tannocci Sage view her with exasperation.

"I wanted to try, but those I was leading feared the airlock bay may not have air, and none of them had an envirosuit." Jandeel's eyes narrowed. "I know you're right. We didn't even use the old evacuation plan, and . . . Cheseia betrayed us. We'll never defeat the Inheritors like this, Sar. If the organization is to survive, we need Kivita to—"

The ship tipped again, making all three of them slide toward the far wall. Sar snagged his hand on the corridor doorway and crawled inside. Jandeel grabbed hold of Bredine's waist, and together they followed. Though some of the canister air had seeped into the corridor, its foul carbon taste made Sar grimace.

"We can't stay in here," Sar said. "The planet's gravity is pulling *Luccan's Wish* down bit by bit. That son of a bitch Dunaar knew what systems to target."

"Dunaar Thev? The Rector himself is out there?" Jandeel balked.

Sar shrugged. "We need a lift to Level Eight."

"My group passed a second lift that still worked," Jandeel replied. "But some of those pirates guard it, Sar. I think they want *Frevyx*, but don't know or can't hack your keypad sequence. My group refused to fight them, so we moved on."

Sar forced down his rising anger. Shekelor and his men had moved fast—too fast, considering he'd left *Arcuri's Glory* before that backstabbing asshole. His former comrade had gained more things from the Sarrhdtuu than just coils.

"Then we force our way in. Without *Frevyx*, there's no use in searching for the others." Together, he and Jandeel pried open the lift entrance. The darkened tube echoed with screams and clanging metal from below.

Sar hefted his baton and crept just over the ledge. Jandeel donned his helmet, drew a curved Naxan dagger, and followed with Bredine in tow.

Through the lift entrance, more shouts drifted up, followed by whimpers and laughter.

"Plumb stupid fucks," a gruff voice said. "Gimme the girl, and ya can keep ya fingers." Laughter followed the man's comments.

After locking his helmet back on, Sar freed one hand for climbing. He stepped from the ledge into the shaft, then clawed into the sensor pits with his fingers. Below, the lift hovered near Level Nine.

Sar had climbed Freen's jagged landscape in his childhood, and clambered through some of the most heavily damaged derelicts in the Cetturo Arm. Descending one-handed while using his boots for leverage, however, taxed his muscles to their limit. Though flickering yellow light shone from Level Eight's entrance, Sar knew one slip would cost him his life. Jandeel and Bredine climbed down after him.

"Guess they wanted to leave on Redryll's ship," a thin male voice said below. "Stupid bastard will pay for that shit on Umiracan. My brother died, and we lost all those slaves."

A woman screamed. The pirates laughed; Sar guessed at least six occupied the airlock bay, maybe more. Only with surprise could he even hope to succeed.

He finally drew near the entrance. The lift door had been blown off and lay just inside the airlock bay, charred and dented. Three mangled bodies lay near the far bulkhead. They bore the sliced cheeks and cut throats of Sutaran execution rituals, no doubt influenced by Shekelor. Once, Sar had done the same to Inheritor soldiers. How close had he come to being one of those pirates?

A small Ascali girl lay in her own blood, her amber eyes staring right at Sar.

Bredine came down and spotted the bodies. Before he could stop her, she dropped into the airlock bay and leapt forward. Shouts echoed from within, traveling up and down the shaft. Ringing metal, and a painful grunt followed.

"Kill the Thede bitch!" a pirate shouted.

Grasping the corner, Sar yanked himself into the entrance. He stepped fully into the airlock bay as Bredine jammed her elbow through a pirate's faceplate and grabbed the man's sword. Another pirate lay at her feet, head and neck leaning at opposite angles. Five other pirates rushed at her with swords, while three more aimed pistols. All of them had olive-tinted flesh and Sarrhdtuu carapace armor. A dozen Thedes lay strewn on the bay floor, dead or dying. Seven others cringed in one corner.

Bredine crushed a pirate's cheek with her foot, then ducked and sliced off another's fingers. A kinetic shot slammed into her left arm, but she kept swinging. Sar charged forward and drove the spike baton into a pirate's lower back, then swung with both hands. The spikes crunched through the man's cuirass and snapped his collarbone.

As much green as red blood splattered from the pirates' wounds.

A pirate kicked Bredine across the floor and into a wall, and the sword clattered from her grasp. Sar slammed the baton into the man's stomach, then brought it down across his neck. Blood sprayed from the ruptured polyarmor, but the pirate rammed a knee into

Sar's right side. Grunting, Sar broke the pirate's neck with the baton. The man crashed onto the floor.

The other pirates took cover behind supply crates and fired again.

A shot grazed Sar's left leg, and he dove for the wall on his right. Jandeel jumped from the lift entrance and shoved a pirate woman into the crossfire. She went down with a smoking hole in her back, green-rigged flesh popping.

One pirate slashed through the back of Sar's enviro-suit. The blade drew a deep nick through his skin as Sar turned to defend himself. A kinetic shot struck the wall a few inches from his helmet. His faceplate cracked from shrapnel impacts.

The pirate raised his sword, but Bredine snapped his neck from behind. The man went limp and crumpled at Sar's feet, while Jandeel scrambled for the man's sword. Bredine ducked and rolled toward the pirates as they trained their guns on her.

Sar flung the baton. It knocked one pirate's gun from his hand, as Bredine tumbled up from her roll and struck with both palms. The pirate fell back, faceplate, nose, and mouth crushed.

The last pirate struck Bredine across the face with his pistol, then aimed it down as she fell.

Sar ran forward. "Here, you bastard!"

The pirate aimed at him and smiled.

"Sar!" Jandeel lunged for Sar as the pirate fired.

The shot blew away the left side of Sar's helmet in an explosion of faceplate particles. Sar fell on his back, tasting blood as a thousand prickling stings materialized on his face. He rolled over and opened his eyes. They stung.

With both hands, Jandeel crammed the sword into the pirate's chest. Polyarmor cracked, and crimson ran along the floor. A heavy mildew stench mixed with the scent of blood. The pirate batted Jandeel aside and punched Bredine's helmet. Scrambling to get up, Sar glimpsed the pirate's feet melding into the floor.

"Now I'll plumb—"

The pirate's head atomized in a cloud of blood and faceplate shards. Jandeel knelt nearby, holding one of the fallen pirates' pistols.

Her own faceplate cracked, Bredine unlocked her helmet and tossed it aside. Jandeel grasped her wounded left arm and steadied her against him. Seven Thede captives raced from a corner and attacked any pirate still living. Two they stabbed to death, but one morphed right through the floor. The mildew stink thickened. Patches of olive liquid lay on the floor where the pirate had been.

"By the Solars," Jandeel breathed. For the first time, Sar recognized fear in Bredine's eyes.

What the hell were these pirates now?

Sar clambered up and wiped his face. A Dirr woman applied a cold pack to his left cheek. "Stars wink and glow! They found us in here, and—" She sobbed. "We tried to fight them, but they were too strong."

Jandeel stared at the other Thedes as Bredine wiped sweat from his brow. "We should have stayed together. This shouldn't have happened." He kicked a dead pirate's body.

A Tannocci man, his temple bleeding, hung his head. "We have hidden too long. We thought that with the Narbas line reborn . . ."

Bredine seemed more concerned with Jandeel's state

than her own, though she was trembling from exhaustion and her wound. Sar wondered how dangerous the woman would be if nourished and healed.

Sar allowed the Dirr woman to pick faceplate shards from his forehead. "Stars fade, but you are right, Jandeel. Even though the stars turn black, you are right."

After gently stopping Bredine's ministrations, Jandeel bound her arm with medical tape supplied by the others. "Sar, we still have to find Kivita. I'll come with you."

Wincing, Bredine studied Jandeel. "You can't go. Kivita is sending. I feel her. Hmm. Redryll?"

Sar took a sword and pistol from the bloody floor. "Sending? You mean you can sense her? Then she's right, Jandeel. Get *Frevyx* ready. If I don't return with Kiv, then leave the system with these people."

"There are more survivors on Levels Three and Five," the Tannocci man said.

Jandeel gripped Sar's arm. "Kivita is more than just a Savant. She's integral to our cause now."

"Not doing this for me, Jandeel. Go to the other airlocks; get what survivors you can. Meet me back here." As he keyed in the sequence to *Frevyx*'s airlock, Sar realized Kivita had infected these people with loyalty to her—a far cry from the selfish salvager he'd rescued on Vstrunn.

"We'll meet back here, then." Jandeel ushered the other survivors—three other adults and two children—to *Frevyx*'s airlock.

Bredine strapped on a sword and clasped two kinetic pistols. "Hmm. Kivita's coordinates. Yes, they are sent."

Sar gave her an exasperated look. "What?"

"Redryll? Kivita sends, and I follow." Bredine looked at her ruined helmet and pointed at the lift tube.

"Kiv would've made her way to Airlock Eight." Sar turned to the Dirr woman. "Were there any more pirates? What did they talk about?"

"Six others went down in the lift," the woman relied. "Stars winking out, they talked only of . . ." She glanced at the bodies and whimpered.

Sar took Bredine's arm. "Track Kiv. And keep still." They headed for the lift tube.

"Sar?" Jandeel called after him.

Sar turned as an explosion rocked the shaft. Faint light flickered from another entrance.

"Luccan's dream will die on this ship if Kivita does." Jandeel stepped back into *Frevyx*, and its airlock hissed shut.

Sar wasn't sure of his own survival or Kivita's. The only certainty remained the one he'd felt since Kivita had kissed him at Tejuit. The certainty of regret, and of what he should've told Kivita all along.

33

A shot whizzed past from the chamber ahead and Seul ducked back into the corridor. Point One's faceplate shattered and he keeled over. Another Trooper collapsed, blood seeping from her cuirass. More shots zipped into the corridor, striking two more Troopers. Shrapnel dusted Seul's polyarmor.

"Point Two, Flanks Three through Six: lay down a suppressing fire! Point Three, follow me in after the first barrage!" Seul waited until her Troopers fired green beams into the next chamber. Screams and the hiss of sliced, burned bodies reached her helmet's aural sensors. By the void, was every Inheritor aboard this ship?

"Go!" She ducked and charged into the chamber where several Inheritor soldiers lay dead. More than a dozen others aimed kinetic pistols at her.

Seul fired, sweeping the rifle in a horizontal line. Four humans hit the floor, heads cut from their bodies. A shot grazed her right thigh armor, but Point Three charged in and mowed down three more Inheritors. The humans fired again, then fled into the next corridor. Flanks Four and Five crashed to the floor, both shot through the chest.

"Secure the area," Seul said as she stood. A wide observation deck, forty feet high, rose around them. Rectangular viewports offered a wonderful view of the gas giant, but with the ship's tilting, she and her Troopers had to keep their boots magnetized or else walk on the viewports themselves.

Flank Three dispatched wounded humans with her blade while others checked corners for hidden enemies. Potted plants and flowers filled the deck; some had been burned in the brief exchange. Their gaudy, colorful bulbs and petals seemed a waste. Who would rear plants for beauty but not food or medicine?

The real waste, of smoking bodies and still forms, lay around her. One dead Inheritor soldier clutched a carved wooden statuette. What was that likeness? It seemed familiar, like something from a cryo dream. Another soldier moaned a prayer to the Vim before Flank Three ended his life.

"Fools," she mumbled, then studied her own Troopers. Just like the Inheritors, they wanted reunification with the Vim.

What did she really believe? Was it worth all this death? Seul's jaw tightened, and she had to look away from the shattered bodies. She'd see these faces, friend and foe alike, in her dreams.

Were Kael and her daughter worth it?

They had to be. What else was there to die for? Victory could be had as long as she still drew breath. First she had to find Kivita.

Her helmet speaker crackled and popped. "Vuul here . . . and it isn't . . . Qaan says the Vim derelict is siphoning . . . Jaah, give . . . status report."

Seul sighed in relief; *Aldaar* still waited outside.

"We've reached Level Eight, and so far we've encountered nothing but dead Thedes and a platoon of Inheritor soldiers. Squad A has all been killed or wounded, and Squad B has two dead. Squads C and D have been completely annihilated."

Through spotty radio contact, she'd heard Squad C and D's last moments near the engine-module breach. Such losses meant several human platoons had infiltrated the ship. She feared the Inheritors might have taken Kivita already, considering their stubborn resistance.

"Captain Jaah, everyone's rifles are on one-quarter power," Point Three said.

"Cannibalize guns from the Inheritor dead," Seul said. Dents and graze marks, as well as frozen blood, scarred her polyarmor. Bruises protested along her left side from a close melee with Inheritors two corridors back. These human zealots demanded lives for each area relinquished.

Seul studied the brain-pulse readout on her collar's extended lip. "Scanner shows several Savants and the Juxj Star are on this deck. Form up, everyone."

As her Troopers reformed ranks, Seul's helmet speaker buzzed. ". . . commit evasive . . . Jaah, engaged with . . . aft batteries are gone . . . retrieve Vondir and . . ." Vuul's voice cut out.

Swallowing, Seul tapped her arm panel. "Commander Vuul?" If *Aldaar* was in distress, then what about the assault shuttles? She tapped the panel again with a trembling finger. "Officer Kael? Kael, do you read me?"

A low hum came over the speaker, building into a stream of musical notes, whispered words, and machine-like jingles. Some invisible force made the entire starship vibrate, and Seul wanted to cover her ears. As soon as it began, it stopped.

The brain analyzer went off the meter, as if twenty Savants waited in the adjacent chamber. It had to be Kivita.

"Go!" she shouted, leading her Troopers in a run. The next corridor entrance hissed open. Kinetic shots rained down on her squad.

Seul hunkered down and shot down two Inheritors in a smoky haze. Their bodies floated in place, their poly-boots still magnetically gripping the floor. A shot struck inches from her left leg. Shrapnel pinged against her armor. She flinched and scooted to the right.

Her rifle's ammo counter was empty.

"Kael . . ." Drawing her sword, Seul charged through the haze.

Dunaar leaned forward in his seat, gazing out the viewport as *Arcuri's Glory* closed with the Aldaakian cruiser. "Fire again, Captain Stiego. Their airlocks this time. I do not want any of their shuttles returning."

Alarm lights drowned the bridge in red hues as Stiego's holo monocle displayed the sights for the portside K-gun battery.

"Concussive sabots," Stiego said. The security officer nodded, and the console beeped. Three shots sped toward the Aldaakian craft, where four breaches along its hull marked the first salvo's results.

Dunaar smirked. "The fools must have thought to delay us."

A green beam flashed from the Aldaakian cruiser. *Arcuri's Glory* shook, and breach klaxons rang along the terminals.

"Damage?" Stiego's monocle flickered on and off. "Dammit, man, answer me!"

One of the staff hunched over his console. "Cryo Chamber Eight has been compromised on Deck Two, Captain. The breach has been contained and the surrounding chambers sealed off."

Through the viewport, he could see the sabot rounds crash into the Aldaakian cruiser. Armor plating, hull, and mangled debris spilled out into space. The vessel reeled to starboard, while three assault shuttles maintained a close screen around it.

Dunaar licked sweat from his lips. So the Aldaakians wanted to steal what the Vim had sent the faithful? Let the pallid infidels try. "What news from the Thede vessel?"

"Rector, the Vim derelict's signal has cut off all communication with our troops," Stiego replied.

"What?" Dunaar rose. Were the holy ones themselves aboard the derelict? Had he done something wrong? Sweat ran down his legs and pooled in his slippers. "Play the signal on the bridge speakers."

Stiego cleared his throat. "Rector, it might—"

"Play it!"

Stiego nodded to an officer, who switched the signal to the speakers. Voices whispering in an unknown, guttural language; high-pitched musical notes; and metallic pings blasted through them. The hair on Dunaar's neck prickled; his vision blurred. The barrage pierced his mind and demanded something of him. Dunaar covered his ears until it ended.

Everyone on the bridge stared out the viewport in stunned silence.

"What in the name of the sainted Vim was that?" Dunaar frowned as the Aldaakian cruiser repositioned itself. "Is that some sort of new Aldaakian weapon? That could not have been the Vim speaking to us!"

"Signal from unknown origin, Rector," the nav officer replied.

An awful chill gripped Dunaar. Was this a message from the enemies Bredine had warned him about?

Stiego moved beside him, face pinched with worry. "Rector, almost three platoons have been destroyed at last report. The Aldaakians on board the Thede ship cannot escape. Perhaps a short truce to negotiate for the Savant?"

"How do you expect us to redeem ourselves in the eyes of the Vim? We have the upper hand here, Captain. I shall have Kivita Vondir if I have to sacrifice every soldier aboard. Their martyrdom will not be in vain." Dunaar gripped the Scepter with slick fingers.

"Rector, a Sarrhdtuu ship has entered the system," the nav officer said. "Their leader wishes to speak with you."

"I shall converse with him here on the bridge." Pride surged through his body, puffing his chest and filling his lungs. With the Thede leadership doomed, and Aldaakian military might being swatted aside, Dunaar had only to give Kivita to Zhhl. Then the Inheritors would take over the Cetturo Arm once and for all.

All humanity would be redeemed and ready to meet the Vim.

"Have faith, my children. What you have seen in this system is a sure sign from the Vim themselves." He smiled, though sweat dripped over his parted lips. The bridge's holographic display activated.

Zhhl's image flickered into the air before Dunaar. It

had only two coils and two eyes this time. The hologram possessed a misshapen continuity, as if another frequency mixed with it.

"Prophet of Meh Sat. Our scanners indicate the Juxj Star is still aboard the Thede starship. Kivita Vondir would not have abandoned it. Your soldiers must act faster."

Dunaar smiled. "My followers shall acquire it. Regardless of whether the Shock Troopers are victorious, they will have great difficulty once their cruiser is destroyed. They cannot escape."

Zhhl's holographic coils lashed out at Dunaar. "Do not tarry, Prophet of Meh Sat."

Annoyance made Dunaar's ears burn. "The Aldaakians will not just hand Kivita and the datacore over. They have one measly cruiser. Patience, Zhhl."

"You must destroy the Aldaakian cruiser. No delays. We await your maneuvers, Prophet of Meh Sat." The hologram faded out.

Dunaar fingered the Scepter. The Sarrhdtuu had never shone such anxiety before.

"Captain Stiego, close with that Aldaakian cruiser and engage," Dunaar said. "Ensure that nothing remains."

34

Gravity fluxed up or down every few seconds in the corridor that Kivita entered with Navon. Cheseia and Rhii checked the next circular door, while Basheev and four others leaned against the bulkheads, faces ashen.

"What do you see?" Navon asked Cheseia.

"Everything seems truly fine." Cheseia pointed out the door window.

"Stars blinding, we're on Level Eight now. I think we should run straight for *Frevyx*, miss." Rhii clutched Basheev, who stared off into space. Kivita knew the child would never forget these horrors. None of them would.

Kivita steadied herself against a bulkhead while datacore imagery passed through her mind. Though she'd learned to bury such data until she needed it, it now flowed through her thoughts with ever-increasing intensity—ever since she'd heard the strange whispers and sounds. Kivita almost mouthed some of the coordinates, until Navon touched her hand.

"Who do you think cut the flexi line?" she asked.

"I do not know, but we must continue," Navon said. "Kivita, you are sending strange data to my mind. I cannot think clearly."

"Yeah, sorry. I don't know why I'm doing that. Just nervous, and . . . you know. Airlock Eight should be just a few chambers away. I know *Frevyx*'s airlock code." Kivita brushed past the others, but Navon barred her path.

"Then you should share it with the rest of us. There's no telling what might happen between here and there." Navon's firm voice contrasted with the genuine apology in his eyes.

Cheseia stood behind Kivita. "I also certainly know it."

Rhii scowled at Cheseia. The others turned away.

"No, he's right. Here." Focusing on the keypad sequence, Kivita broadcast it into the thoughts of everyone in the corridor. During her training on *Luccan's Wish*, she'd always transmitted data to willing minds. While escaping from Shekelor over Tejuit, it had been the opposite. But Kivita swore she'd never abuse it.

"Now you know why you are so important." Navon moved from her path.

"Yeah. C'mon, let's go." Kivita pulled the lever and passed through the circular doorway.

Gray-green coils wrapped around her throat and yanked her into the next room. Choking, Kivita tried to stand, but the appendages dragged her to her knees. Despite her helmet and air supply, Kivita couldn't breathe as she pried at the coils around her neck.

A brown eye and a purple eye gazed into hers. A green-tinted face smiled.

"Finally, after searching this wreck, you come to me," Shekelor said. Behind him, six pirates aimed pistols and beam rifles at Kivita's friends. "I don't require the rest of you, though." He nodded to his followers.

As they raised their weapons, Kivita forced raw data

into their thoughts. Shekelor flinched and drew back, while his pirates stumbled into one another.

Navon leapt from the corridor and rammed his knee into one pirate's chest. The man wheezed and fell back into his comrades. Kivita tugged at the coils, still unable to breathe. She met Shekelor's eyes and let the asshole see how the Sarrhdtuu had harangued humanity and all its relatives for millennia: the Narbas family, the Ascali, and the Aldaakians.

Shekelor staggered back, and his coils released her throat.

Gasping, Kivita slumped onto the bulkhead. Her throat refused to cooperate, but her lungs pumped with demand. She massaged her esophagus while the other Thedes charged the pirates. Cheseia snapped one man's neck, then shoved two others to the floor as they fired their pistols.

The shots cracked the viewport on the right. A whistling noise screeched in their ears.

Shekelor whipped Navon across the face with his coils, then skewered one Thede with his sword. Cheseia snatched a kinetic pistol and fired right into a pirate's chest. Navon punched Shekelor's jaw, but the warlord battered him to the floor.

"Run, Kivita!" Navon cried, before Shekelor hauled him into the adjacent chamber.

Kivita leaned into Cheseia as the Ascali ushered her into the next corridor. The pirates, who were not wearing envirosuits, turned and fled after Shekelor. The whistling noise behind them exploded into a defeaning boom. A klaxon integrity alarm rang in the corridor.

Gunfire and shouts echoed ahead.

"Kivita!" Basheev cried from the corridor behind

them. Rhii charged through with her son just as the corridor decompressed. The circular door sank in with a screech.

Kivita coughed as her breathing regulated. "I'm here! C'mon!" Together, she and Cheseia hurried into a cryo chamber. Two lamps faded in and out, losing power. Cryonic exhaust drifted into the air from a busted conduit.

Though Rhii and her son gathered behind Kivita and Cheseia, none of the others had made it. Kivita swallowed a hard lump in her throat. What good were these damn abilities if everyone kept dying around her?

"Navon?" Kivita called, her voice cracking from Shekelor's grip.

Her faceplate defrosted as a green beam sliced through the forward bulkhead. The opposite door burst open and four Inheritor soldiers ran through, aiming pistols at Kivita.

"The redhead is the Savant we're looking for! Cover me!"

The beam fired again, burning a hole through the soldier's chest.

Turning, the Inheritors fired back through the doorway. A body in black polyarmor fell, while a second one waded in among the soldiers with a sword. Blood and screams filled the entrance. Another shot fired. Then the human soldiers lay dead.

Two Aldaakian Shock Troopers entered the chamber, their magnetized boots clanking on the floor. One raised a beam rifle, but the one with the sword held up a hand and pointed at Kivita.

Through the Trooper's faceplate, Seul Jaah stared at Kivita, her white-within-azure eyes wide.

"Kivita! You must come with me. I have searched and lost so many. . . . My orders are to rescue you. Please hurry!" Seul's firm tone belied the relief playing across her face.

Luccan's Wish rocked back and forth. Gravity disappeared for an instant, then returned. The lamps dimmed; the integrity alarm died. Three more Shock Troopers entered the chamber, their polyarmor battered. With their magnetized boots, neither she nor the Aldaakians had lost their footing.

Kivita's heart raced. "Can you save the others? How bad is the damage? Who fired on us?"

Shekelor and his pirates popped from behind the cryopods on their left and fired. Two Troopers crumpled to the floor, shot through their faceplates. Seul's remaining comrades returned fire, reducing the walls to orange-yellow slag.

Smiling, Shekelor morphed through the wall itself. Kivita gaped and staggered back, but Shekelor reappeared from the other side of the wall and shot down another Trooper.

Seul ducked down and beckoned. "Kivita, don't delay!"

As Kivita gripped Cheseia's hand and ran, Inheritor soldiers charged into the chamber, and Shekelor's pirates surged forward. Another Trooper collapsed, shot three times in the chest. Polyarmor shards enfiladed Kivita as she reached for Rhii and Basheev. Cheseia shielded all three of them, the shrapnel ripping her envirosuit in several places.

"Kivita! I—" Seul's words ended as Shekelor slashed her cuirass with his sword. She clanked to the floor, limp.

"You filth!" Kivita yelled at Shekelor.

The surviving Aldaakians fell to numerous kinetic bullets. Holes smoked in black polyarmor; gauntleted hands trembled on rifle triggers and fell still.

Rhii lay on the floor with Basheev. Horror filled their eyes as Inheritor soldiers aimed pistols at them all.

"Is this what you seek? The blood of the innocent?" Navon, now held by two pirates, asked. Like Shekelor, they all morphed through the walls. The action made little sound and left olive stains in their wake.

Ice-cold fear sank into her gut as Kivita wondered how the pirates breathed, since so much air had been sucked out from the cracked viewport in the last corridor.

"No one is innocent—only those who claim to be," Shekelor said. "Take her. Bring the Ascali, too."

Kivita flinched as two pirates affixed her wrists together with flexi. Others did the same to Cheseia and Navon. The Inheritors waited, as if supporting Shekelor's deeds.

Shekelor spoke into a mic inset into the carapace armor covering his arm. "Bring *Fanged Pauper* to Airlock Eight. Inform Zhhl that I have her."

Concentrating, Kivita tried to shove raw data into her enemies' minds again, but Shekelor snatched up Rhii and Basheev with one hand.

"Continue, and I shall kill them right now. The boy I shall take my time with."

Kivita glowered at Shekelor. "Goddamn you. No wonder you're so cruel. You can't have a heart, moving through walls like that."

"This is just the beginning," Shekelor said. "The Sarrhdtuu keep their promises."

"Whatever they've promised you, you'll still suffer," Kivita said.

Shekelor shoved Rhii and her son into the hands of another pirate. "You know nothing of suffering. Nothing."

The pirates led them through corridors coated in slag, corpses, and body parts; dead Inheritors sliced in twain; crumpled Aldaakians with pierced armor lying in pools of frozen blood. Here and there, a Thede Kivita had trained with in the gym or studied alongside in the library lay dead. With fierce effort, she fought back tears.

"I know it needs to end." Taking a deep breath, she began sorting all the data in her mind for one final broadcast.

Sar paused while Bredine concentrated on what she claimed was Kivita's position. They stood in a corridor filled with Inheritor and Aldaakian dead. Slag pools still cooled at their feet, and the walls had been blasted to the bare framing underneath. He snatched another kinetic pistol, since none of the Shock Trooper rifles retained any power. It surprised him they'd left their dead, and made him even more concerned for Kivita.

"Hmm. Kivita is on this deck. Redryll? She is sending more things. More . . . beautiful things." Bredine stared into the air with wonder, her mouth open.

Sar tapped her shoulder. "Not now. Lead on."

Together they tramped into the remains of a cryo chamber where olive-skinned pirates lay among the dead. Shouts reverberated back to them from an adjacent corridor. The air grew so thin, Sar took slow, shallow breaths, each one tasting of dry cryonic exhaust and slag fumes.

"Redryll? That way. Gushing hot for Kivita, I know. That way, I said." Bredine's tone became more demanding and urgent.

"You handled yourself well back there," Sar said, as they went in the direction she'd indicated. In the next corridor, the scents of charred flesh, melted steel, and burnt hair made him gag.

"Father was selfish. I wanted all to see what Kivita has shown me. Hmm."

Walking into the next chamber, Sar realized they'd simply rounded a turn; they were heading back to Airlock Eight. He almost chided Bredine, when the clanking of magnetized boots reached his ears. He went prone with the wall, as did Bredine. Two squads of Inheritor soldiers passed. Many carried or shouldered wounded comrades. The small force entered an opposite corridor leading straight to the airlock.

A moan from the floor caught Sar's attention. One Shock Trooper, blood flowing from her cuirass, beckoned him closer.

The visage inside the faceplate shocked him. "Seul?"

"Shekelor Thal . . . took Kivita," Seul whispered. "All my Troopers . . . dead. Kivita will bring the Vim. . . . Sar, please help her."

"You're going to help me." Sar hefted her up, but Seul coughed and pushed away from him, strength still in her movements. "Can you hail one of those assault shuttles of yours?"

Seul gasped until her polyarmor compressed. Blood ceased flowing from the cut across her chest. "The Vim signal . . . The signal has blocked most communication."

"Lean on my shoulder." Sar kept the pistol aimed forward. Right now, any foe of the Inheritors became his ally.

"No, I—" Seul coughed.

"Just do it, dammit." Sar wrapped a hand around her waist, and Bredine steadied her other side.

Luccan's Wish rocked violently. His footsteps grew lighter.

"Shit. Hurry." They ran with slowing steps into another corridor. Half a platoon of Inheritor soldiers rounded the corner they'd just left.

"Thedes! Shoot them!" an Inheritor officer shouted.

Sar jerked Seul with him into a declivity between the corridor wall and an intercom panel. Bredine knelt behind a supply crate as kinetic shots dented the bulkheads around them.

The red-uniformed troops crept closer, cursing the lessening gravity. Sar poked out from the declivity and fired twice. Two soldiers bucked backward, holes in their chests, bodies floating off the floor.

"Officer . . . um, Kael, can you hear me?" Seul asked. "Sar, there's nothing but static now."

"Keep trying," Sar said.

Bredine edged forward until the pressurized door on their right hissed open. "Redryll? Go through."

Six Inheritors charged down the corridor, blades and pistols in hand.

Bredine fired, the shot snapping through one soldier's helmet. Ducking, Sar exited the corridor with Seul. Two dead Troopers barred their path. One of them still clutched a beam rifle.

"Come on!" Sar called to Bredine, and fired. An Inheritor clutched his shattered shoulder and retreated.

Seul grabbed the rifle and fired, holding down the trigger. The soldiers screamed as the concentrated beam continued on through three of them. She swept it, decapitating another before the last two fell prone and fired.

A shot ripped into Sar's left leg above the knee. He grunted and bumped against Seul, and the green beam sliced into the ceiling as she fell back. The lamps went dead, casting the corridor into darkness.

Bredine tugged him through the circular door. Seul followed, holding her chest. For a moment, the corridor's dim light revealed another charge by the Inheritors. Desperation shone on their faces, and Sar realized they might all be stranded on *Luccan's Wish*. The significance of Airlock Eight loomed larger in his mind.

"Redryll? Hold me. Not like Kivita. Redryll, Redryll," Bredine murmured as her bony frame managed to aid him from the corridor and into the airlock bay.

Inside it, a dozen pirates were boarding a ship Sar had seen too much of late: *Fanged Pauper*.

Luccan's Wish trembled as gravity decreased. The pirates tugged down several floating prisoners while ushering them toward the airlock. One prisoner had lovely red-blond hair. Straight, with a Dirr braid on the right temple.

"Kivita!" Sar shouted. All his wounds lost their pain, and he ran forward. Their past together now seemed a dream, and their future a spacer's tale without an ending.

Bredine pulled him back around the corner as two beams sliced through the metal. The heat from it warmed his face, but Sar wriggled free and aimed both pistols. Pirates kept their beam rifles trained on him while Cheseia, Rhii, Basheev, and Navon were shoved toward the airlock. Kivita kicked and struggled, her hands bound.

"Sar! Sar, I have—" Her screams sounded tinny through her helmet's exterior speaker, until a pirate crushed it with a rifle butt. Kivita mouthed words to him, but he couldn't make them out.

More beam shots kept Sar at bay as the pirates shoved Kivita, Navon, and Cheseia into *Fanged Pauper*. Shekelor pushed Rhii and Basheev aside as Sar rolled from behind the corner and fired twice. A pirate just inside the airlock clutched her chest and staggered back into the airlock bay. Another collapsed on his knees, his features red pulp.

The airlock slid shut, and *Fanged Pauper* disengaged itself from *Luccan's Wish*.

Sar cried out in rage and despair. He loved her; he needed her. These people needed her—

The sounds of more Inheritor soldiers nearing the airlock bay echoed in the corridor.

35

As *Fanged Pauper* drifted from the airlock, Kivita
cursed and shouted. She struggled with the pirate holding her, but his grip was like steel bands around her
arms. Sar had been in there. He'd come for her again—
beyond all hope, he'd come . . .

Shekelor chuckled and gestured out the viewport.
Kivita's heart jumped and her body went limp.

Through the viewport, *Aldaar* listed to starboard.
Gaping holes covered its hull. Just within eyesight, a
huge Inheritor battleship fired a kinetic barrage at the
Aldaakian cruiser. Kivita's heart sank into her stomach.

A fine data stream snapped into Kivita's thoughts, all
of it in Aldaakian code. *Aldaar*'s crew complement, its
mission around Vstrunn, Seul's genetic matrix, the Pediatric Ward . . . and a name linked to that matrix: Taeu
Jaah. All of it transmitted by Commander Baan Vuul.

"Her daughter," Kivita breathed.

The salvo slammed into *Aldaar*, gutting the cruiser.
Kivita choked as the data stream ended. All of *Aldaar*'s
viewports flashed once; then the vessel split apart. The
force of decompression flung albino bodies, cryopods,
and countless other items into space. Several Aldaakian

shuttles darted away, but debris smacked into one, crushing it. Another exploded, struck by a sabot round.

Kivita wanted to slap the smile off Shekelor's face. Seul's friends and comrades, her ship . . . all claimed by the cold darkness.

"Bastard." She glowered at Shekelor.

Navon nudged Kivita and nodded out to port. She finally recognized the battleship: *Arcuri's Glory*, flagship of Rector Thev. It veered away from the destroyed cruiser. Several rents had been cut into its 2,500-foot-long hull. Red-uniformed bodies drifted from it toward the gas giant.

Whistles, screams, and gibberish invaded her thoughts. Kivita gasped and focused her will, trying to close her mind. It was the same signal she'd received minutes ago while on *Luccan's Wish*.

"Sense something?" Shekelor smirked, then entered the cockpit and spoke with his pilot.

She shared a look with Navon as something massive filled the viewport.

A Sarrhdtuu battleship.

The vessel hovered in the void, a gray-green sentinel of death. It measured at least ten thousand feet in length, superseded in size by only Vim derelicts. Kivita swallowed as *Fanged Pauper* flew toward it. She'd been on a Sarrhdtuu ship once, after her and Sar's mission to Xeh's Crown. Then they'd visited an airlock bay and nothing else. This time she shivered at what she might see.

Port side, *Luccan's Wish* neared the gas giant's upper atmosphere, while *Frevyx* hovered near Airlock Eight. A jolt shot through her heart: someone had piloted the trawler away prior to Sar calling her name in the airlock bay. Hot, maddened hope rose in her.

Cheseia squeezed Kivita's hand for a brief moment.

"I see it, too," Navon whispered. A pirate smacked him with a rifle butt, and he fell silent.

Shekelor exited the cockpit and approached Kivita. In contrast to the empty seats she'd seen on Umiracan, *Fanged Pauper* now held dozens of pirates in dark green carapace armor. All of them had green-rigged skin, and few possessed coils or purple-slotted eyes. As one unit, they parted before Shekelor like wheat before a tread harvester. He measured her with his brown-and-purple stare.

"The Sarrhdtuu will turn this Cradle over to me once you perform your task," Shekelor said. "Yet I admire you for resisting them, Kivita. A woman of strength. Sar must not have realized what he had." One of his coils rubbed her faceplate. "Unfortunately for you, I do."

"Yeah? Then you'll just be their slave afterward."

"Ah, but I am not a threat to their designs. You are." Shekelor smiled.

Navon shook his head. "There is nothing dangerous about knowledge, only those who keep it from others. Once you are of no use to them, they will destroy you, Shekelor."

"You both disappoint me. I know you two possess great knowledge, maybe even a dash of wisdom. Sages in your own right, as it were. You assume the Sarrhdtuu will remain in the Cetturo Arm after this? How wrong you are." Shekelor smiled wider. "Yet you are correct about the Sarrhdtuu's penchant for treachery. That is why I have prepared my own defenses."

Shekelor nodded to two pirates, who turned and opened a storage locker. A tall female Ascali bustled out from it, into their arms. Attired in a translucent gown and veil, the Ascali resembled Cheseia in every detail: dark, silky mane, red-brown eyes. The same beautiful face and sinuous, athletic build.

"Zhara," Kivita breathed.

The sisters gaped at each other. Cheseia rushed forward, and four burly pirates had to restrain her. Zhara hung her head, muscles flexing in vain.

Cheseia glared at Shekelor. "What do you maliciously plan to do with us?" Raw, unrestrained violence lurked in her stance, her voice. Zhara looked up, eyes full of love and regret for her twin. Kivita's heart went out to them both.

"The Sarrhdtuu have a, shall we say, aversion to certain Ascali characteristics," Shekelor replied. "Once we are aboard Zhhl's ship and I mention the word 'Sygma,' you are both to sing in a higher register. Refuse, and one of you shall die. Cooperate, and you might live. I have nothing to gain from the death of any of you." Shekelor glanced out the viewport with a faraway gaze.

An odd look passed between the Ascali twins. Great. What did they know that Kivita didn't?

And yet Kivita knew Shekelor suffered inside. But why? What would bring him to such cruelties, drive him across the cosmos to capture her?

The teenager's portrait in Shekelor's fortress on Umiracan. That had to be it.

"What happened to your son?" she asked in a neutral tone.

Shekelor shot her a look of unabashed hatred. His muscular body flexed so much, his joints popped audibly. "Whatever Redryll may have told you, he is wrong."

"Then you tell me," Kivita said.

"My son fought alongside me years ago, against the

Inheritors on Bellerion. Byelor ambushed an Inheritor platoon on his own; he would not wait for me. When I found him . . ." He sucked in a breath. "I refused to bury him. I placed his body in cryostasis."

"He is on that Sarrhdtuu ship, isn't he?" Navon said. "Augmented by their technology as payment to you."

"Yeah, and what is this ship called?" Kivita said.

The smirk returned to Shekelor's olive features as he pointed to the bulge in Kivita's envirosuit where the Juxj Star rested in her pouch.

"Zhhl's ship is called *Juxj*." Shekelor strutted back to the cockpit.

It finally dawned on Kivita. The Juxj Star: a datacore planted by the Sarrhdtuu in preparation for this event. As her mother had sent Kivita into hiding, so the Sarrhdtuu had readied themselves for a reply to the ancient Vim signal.

A deep anger stirred in Kivita as she continued assembling the data in her brain. Her transmission would reach hundreds of ships, spaceports, and outposts. One way or another, she'd achieve the ultimate goal of the Thede organization: spreading knowledge for the freedom of all. There was no way they could stop her. Even if they killed her, her last thought would still be sent out.

Kivita shivered. If they killed her? She'd never thought about dying before, not really. There'd be no flying away in *Terredyn Narbas*. No Sar Redryll saving her.

Through the viewport, *Juxj*'s hangar bay yawned open. Unlike on human ships, no running lights or landing indicators aided *Fanged Pauper* inside.

A minor gravity flux made Kivita's stomach jump, and the pilot dimmed the overhead lamps. Diffuse gray light filtered through the viewport from the Sarrhdtuu hangar. The hatch sealed behind them, and *Fanged Pauper* touched down on a triangular landing platform. The pylons sank into the hangar floor a few inches.

"Unbind the humans," Shekelor said. "Gag the two Ascali, but not too tightly."

Pirates removed Kivita and Navon's flexi bonds, while two others placed medical tape over Cheseia and Zhara's mouths. The airlock slid open, and Shekelor herded them all out.

Kivita, at a look from Navon, turned off her air supply and opened her helmet vents. The hangar's mildewed air had a harsh lubricant taste. Gravity remained normal, and a human-friendly atmosphere allowed them to breathe, but the humid temperature made her sweat inside her suit.

Knobby protrusions and fleshlike stalk growths covered the walls. The floor was flat and unadorned. The ceiling rose fifty feet above them, with dim lamps spaced twenty feet apart. Shadows obscured the rest of the hangar, save for a twelve-foot-tall protrusion. It opened, as all Sarrhdtuu doorways, like a flower spreading its petals.

The pirates entered three abreast. Kivita forced herself to look calm. Visions of what the Sarrhdtuu had done to other Savants, as shown by the datacores, haunted her thoughts.

Juxj hummed with latent machinery as mist exhausts from high above sprinkled moisture on them. Ducts and vents pulsed with moist, slimy squishes. Kivita had to block mental whispers and mutterings from her mind, all of them unintelligible. The ship was a self-contained, living system, much like the human body.

Memories of her and Sar aboard a Sarrhdtuu ship re-

newed the combined joy and pain of their erstwhile re-
union on *Luccan's Wish*. She had so much to show him,
so much to say.

The group entered a triangular hall lined with protrusions and glowing green consoles. Pipes writhed in organic semblance along the bulkheads. Oils, jellies, and
other mixtures coursed in transparent conduits on the
walls and floor. Purple-slotted eyes stared at Kivita from
the bulkheads. In the ceiling's apex, an unbroken row of
gray light gave everything a desolate, aged sheen. The
mildew scent grew stronger.

Piles of coils lay near the walls in the next corridor.
Jelly slithered from several conduits as the coils writhed
and melded with the jelly. Heads, torsos, and arms
formed in the transparent green substance. Through
such skin, Kivita made out translucent organs pumping
with machinelike precision.

Coils and jelly morphed from the walls behind them
and formed into Sarrhdtuu warriors. These possessed a
carapace-like armor over their jelly torsos and heads.
Each wore a cylinder on its left wrist and wielded a
curved blade.

Kivita gulped, remembering what the Juxj Star had
shown her of these warriors.

"I am ready to see Zhhl now," Shekelor told one of
the warriors.

"You brought a second Savant and two Ascali," a
Sarrhdtuu said, its words ending with a thick lisp.

"The other Savant is a gift; the Ascali are mine,"
Shekelor said. "They are gagged."

As one, the Sarrhdtuu walked on their coils with intricate steps. Shekelor motioned for the pirates to follow them deeper into the ship.

Kivita blinked and shook her head. The whispers inside her mind rose in pitch.

The corridor led into a slanted chamber ringed with hundreds of oval, transparent tubes. Mist sprayed into the air at regular intervals from wall vents, while a warbling hum resounded throughout. Kivita choked on the damp, rotten stench.

The tubes made her heart skip a beat.

Each held a Kith, human, or a green-rigged figure, all more Sarrhdtuu than human. Some tubes housed cracked white exoskeletons. A few contained tall figures in yellow Rectifier uniforms. Below the tubes, Aldaakian polyarmor, Kith claws, and Ascali hides clung to jelly-covered racks.

"Atrocious," Navon muttered.

Cheseia and Zhara retched at the smell, but the pirates were unaffected.

Shekelor motioned to his followers. "Eight of you, two per captive. Follow me." They walked to a circular platform. As soon as all stepped onto it, organic stalks lifted it into the air. Kivita's head tingled and her temples burned.

"I feel it, too," Navon whispered.

Rising higher, Kivita gasped at the view. The chamber extended throughout most of *Juxj*, curving into alcoves and rounding against bulkheads. Thousands of tubes contained occupants from all over the Cetturo Arm: brawny Sutarans, thin Tahe, tall and reedy Naxans. All had undergone Sarrhdtuu Transmutation, with coils, olive flesh, and purple stares. Sarrhdtuu warriors morphed and slithered along aisles between the tubes.

Coils extended from the walls and pulled out some of the tube occupants. Lathered in green slime, the victims gurgled or tittered, their eyes glazed over. One man had transparent flesh like a Sarrhdtuu. His heart and lungs pumped and compressed, engorging his arteries with yellow-green liquid.

Kivita fought down vomit and shared a look with Navon. Cheseia and Zhara clung to each other.

The platform stopped its ascent. Green jelly poured over it while large coils wriggled up from the underside. Eyes slid right between Kivita's feet toward a growing shape. Her stomach churned and chill bumps popped along her skin. The Sarrhdtuu's sheer alienness disturbed Kivita in ways she hadn't felt before. Seeing them unearthed fears she'd never imagined, like something buried within the collective human memory.

"I have delivered her to you, Zhhl, as promised." Shekelor stepped aside. The other pirates scooted back from Kivita and her friends.

The jelly, coils, and organs coalesced into a twenty-foot-tall Sarrhdtuu. A crescent shaped, six-eyed cranium with a puckered mouth, along with a sleek torso and two humanoid arms, sat atop twelve gray-green coils.

"Child of Narbas," Zhhl said in a sibilant voice. "I have waited long. The Vim's signal must be returned."

"Why? You're not their friend. You're not mine, either." Her heart throbbed with furious abandon, contrasting her level tone.

"They abandoned you, Child of Narbas. They abandoned Children of Meh Sat, Children of Khaasis, Children of Revelas, and Children of Frevyx. You owe them nothing." Zhhl's coils rippled on either side of Kivita.

"The Vim still exist, then?" Kivita said.

Zhhl's head opened in three puckered mouths. Each made a gurgling, then a droning, noise. "Cradle after

Cradle was seeded to offset the Sarrhdtuu. Your minds, your thoughts, your voices honed to control us. We will be slaves to the Vim no longer."

Navon grumbled. Cheseia held on to Zhara, her russet eyes filled with tension.

"Slaves? But . . . but there's a Sarrhdtuu colony three thousand light years away! The Vim didn't attack it. You destroyed Meh Sat, Khaasis, and other worlds. You destroyed entire stars! You've used the Inheritors to terrorize the Cetturo Arm. You . . . you even had my mother executed. Goddamn you. What about that?" Tears dimmed Kivita's vision.

Zhhl's mouths puckered into one. "The Juxj Star shows you the past, Child of Narbas. That colony was a Vim beneficiary before our freedom. The Vim hated us for our emancipation, and hid their knowledge in rocks and crystals. They contained us in deep space with light and sound. They trapped us with thoughts from lesser creatures. No longer. Cradles will either serve us or be eliminated. Arcuri chose correctly; thus the Inheritors still live."

"You were right about us, Kivita," Navon breathed. "May the Solars preserve us, you were right."

Shekelor frowned. "You have her, Zhhl. Where is Byelor?"

Kivita stepped toward Zhhl. "Then why send the Vim a message, huh? I've seen how you tried to force other Savants to serve you. To use the Juxj Star." She wiped her eyes with trembling fingers. The burning in her temples grew.

"You will open their Portal. You will transmit the reply Terredyn Narbas refused to, but you will cut out the Vim's heart, as they created you to do to us." Zhhl rose on all twelve coils.

Kivita glowered up at Zhhl. "I won't —"

"Produce the Juxj Star!" Zhhl's voice shook the entire chamber, and Kivita stumbled to her knees. Even Shekelor backed away.

"Is this all you want? To force us to be like you?" Kivita pointed at the tubes.

"We ruled until the Vim penetrated us with you parasites and made us slaves," Zhhl replied with mucus-dripped words. "You can never be like us. Your biomass adds to our vessels. Nothing more."

Shekelor's frown deepened as he maneuvered behind the Ascali twins. "What of my son? Where is his holding tube? It is not where I saw it last time!"

"Byelor is safe, Shekelor Thal. Remain content." Zhhl's eyes formed into one giant purple ocular organ.

"Show me!" Shekelor yelled.

Two Sarrhdtuu warriors dripped from the ceiling and flanked Shekelor.

"First the Juxj Star," Zhhl said.

Kivita touched the bulge on her left hip; nothing else mattered now. She hoped Sar would escape and live to appreciate what she'd attempted in her final moments. She thought of her father, her mother. Separated by centuries and light years, both had given her what she needed for this single act.

Cheseia and Zhara nodded in encouragement.

Peace fell over Navon's countenance. "Use the gem, as only you can."

Kivita smiled at him though a tear ran down her cheek. "Damn. Some queen I turned out to be."

"I would have followed no other," Navon said.

Zhhl's coils opened her envirosuit and yanked out

the Juxj Star. It glowed a fierce red. More whispers and musical notes dug into her thoughts. As Kivita stood and resealed her suit, the whispers in her mind became screams. Her knees slammed into the platform as a million psyches touched her own.

"Open the Vim Portal!" Zhhl shouted in a voice so large it seemed to envelope the entire cosmos.

Sar aimed both pistols at the corner, while Bredine pulled him behind her. The declining gravity made him float several feet off the floor, with Bredine climbing one-handed along girders, his belt looped into hers. Seul clomped along in her magnetized polyboots, still clutching her chest. Murmurs floated to Sar's cold ears as surviving Inheritors waited just out of pistol shot.

The temperature on *Luccan's Wish* had dropped in a manner of seconds after *Fanged Pauper* flew away. All of them had sealed their helmet vents and activated oxygen supplies; Bredine had salvaged an Aldaakian helmet. Debris from the Aldaakian cruiser floated past the airlock, along with dozens of albino bodies in gray-blue uniforms.

"Kael? Please answer me." Seul's voice cracked with emotion. "Kael?"

As Bredine neared the airlock, Sar acted on impulse.

"I'll stop shooting if you do," Sar called out. "Might as well freeze with dignity. Then we'll all be the same. No Inheritor; no Thede."

Rhii and Basheev hid behind a bolted supply crate on his left, staring at him as if he were mad.

A male voice laughed with harsh heaves. "I'm still an Inheritor even after death. The Vim has prepared a place for me in the Core. You'll float in the void for eternity, you piece of shit. We're wise to the poison you Thedes spread."

"Hope you're wise to a bullet, too," Sar murmured.

Bredine pulled him right up against the transparent airlock. "Redryll? Leave them be. *Frevyx* avoiding space trash. Hmm."

Sar jerked around as his customized trawler weaved between pieces of Aldaakian hull. Small chunks and bodies still connected with it, spinning into space from the ship's movement. Corpses banged against the airlock, their white-within-blue stares accusing Sar of some unnamed trespass.

Seul closed her eyes and turned away from the scene. "Kael, please . . . ? This is Jaah, requesting pickup."

"Kivita is still sending," Bredine said.

The hum of magnetizing airlocks echoed in the cold bay as the soldiers around the corner shuffled and murmured. *Frevyx* waited mere feet away, promising hope and freedom.

"Stars burning red, Sar, they will pick us off!" Basheev cried. "Hand me a gun!"

Bredine tossed Rhii one of her pistols. The weapon floated end over end in the low-G. Basheev snatched it as Rhii pulled him back behind the crate.

"Kael?" Seul mashed buttons on her arm panel.

Despite his wounds and anxiety over Kivita, Sar kept the pistols steady. Killing his enemies no longer fed his vengeance; killing them meant his friends might live a little longer. With death so near, the simple rationale of survival provided strange comfort.

"Keep me straight," Sar said.

The airlock whooshed open. Eight Inheritors floated

around the corner, pistols raised. Sar squeezed both triggers again and again. Basheev also fired. Shots struck the airlock around Sar. One grazed Bredine's right hand, and she drifted off toward Seul. Two Inheritors floated, heads hanging down.

Light flooded the airlock bay, forcing the Inheritors to cover their eyes. Firing ceased.

"Captain Jaah?" a male Aldaakian voice came over Sar's helmet speakers.

"Kael!" Seul cried out.

An Aldaakian assault shuttle hovered near the airlock adjacent to the one *Frevyx* had just magnetized with. Bright lamps along its nose dimmed. Its airlock already stood open, with two Shock Troopers aiming beam rifles just inside.

"Seul, we'll cover you if you help us," Sar called into his mic.

A shot cracked the airlock behind him.

"I'm with you." Seul hurried toward the second airlock. Two shots whizzed near her, and one scraped her left shoulder. Three shots slammed inside the Aldaakian shuttle.

Sar emptied his left pistol. An Inheritor screamed, holding his shattered abdomen.

"Kivita . . ." Bredine staggered and bumped into the airlock. The chamber's remaining atmosphere screeched through the cracks in it.

Hands grabbed the back of Sar's ruined envirosuit and pulled him and Bredine into *Frevyx*'s airlock. Jandeel smiled down at him, then took Bredine's other pistol and covered the others.

Sar kept firing while Jandeel pushed Rhii and Basheev through the airlock hatch. Two more Inheritors jerked and floated back from the impacts. A Thede man aboard *Frevyx* cried out as a shot tore through his left side; then his corpse blocked the airlock. Three more shots burst through the man's chest.

All lights in the airlock bay went out as Sar shoved aside the floating dead man and yanked Rhii and Basheev inside. Jandeel pulled Bredine aboard, then slammed the lever while shots struck *Frevyx*'s closing airlock hatch.

Jandeel rushed into the bridge as several Thedes helped Sar and the others to the bench. Sar blinked, studying their faces. Humans, Ascali, a couple of Aldaakians. Some he knew; some he didn't. At least three dozen stood in the airlock chamber, with more in the rest of the ship. They murmured thanks, shook his hand, kissed his cheeks.

"Lots of cargo here, Jandeel," Sar called, as Rhii bandaged his leg with blue medical tape. Gasping, he leaned against the bulkhead. *Frevyx* throbbed with engine thrust.

"I managed to save fifty-eight altogether, from Airlocks Three, Five, and Six," Jandeel called back from the bridge. "I have most of our datacores, too."

Sar patted Rhii's shoulder and limped into the bridge. "They took Kiv and Navon. Cheseia, too."

Jandeel pushed on the manuals. "*Fanged Pauper* blasted from Airlock Eight and flew toward the Sarrhdtuu ship. *Arcuri's Glory* has pulled back from the planet."

"Sarrhdtuu ship?" Cold sweat ran down Sar's neck.

Jandeel just looked at him, his lips set in a grim line.

"Navon would want us to leave him, but to hell if I will," Sar said. "Fly toward that Sarrhdtuu bucket."

"We must save these people, the datacores! We are all that remains of the Thedes." Jandeel's voice quavered. "Even though Kivita is . . . We have no choice."

"Let me have the helm. Going to try something." Sar grunted. "A queen? She'll never stop reminding me of it."

Jandeel stalled the engine and eased himself into the seat. "Neither will I. They blasted apart that Aldaakian cruiser, so what can we do?"

"We have to try something. I won't give up Kiv just because they have more guns than we do. Tell everybody back there to hang on." Sar unsnapped his helmet and pushed the manuals forward.

"Sar, this is Jaah," Seul said over the console speaker. "Do you suppose three assault shuttles are enough to take on that Inheritor battleship?"

Jandeel gaped.

Sar smirked. "It'll have to be."

Frevyx sped toward the Sarrhdtuu battleship.

36

Seul slumped back into her seat as they flew away from the Thede ship. That ruffian Shekelor had sliced through both cryoports above her breasts. Though her polyarmor's inner liner had prevented her from bleeding to death, Seul still gasped and ached. Her fellow Troopers regarded her with hollow stares.

"Kael, power up the beamers. Deactivate gravity, and route all power to the engines. I don't know what Sar has planned, but we'll support him as best we—"

Kael wasn't moving. He didn't blink.

"Kael?" Cold terror dug into her heart. "Kael!"

A black, pulp-filled hole smoked in Kael's left side.

Seul jerked back, unable to breathe. The Inheritor soldiers had landed a few shots inside. . . .

"Captain Jaah?" the navigator said. The other Troopers on board watched her with solemn stares.

The coldness enveloped her heart, freezing the hopes and dreams she'd had. The future she'd wanted with Kael, finding her daughter, becoming a family—all gone.

Moisture leaked down her cheeks as she caressed Kael's chin. So handsome. Had he known she loved him? Damn everything to the void, had he? Why hadn't she spent more time with him, touched him more, told him of her feelings?

"Captain?"

Cryoports screeching open and closed, Seul rounded on the navigator. "What?"

They all continued staring at her. So what if she was crying? To the void with protocol and emotional inhibitors! For Aldaakian Shock Troopers, tears displayed weakness, lack of self-control, and a dozen other negative things. Not anymore. These tears were for Kael.

"Captain, what are your orders?" the navigator said. "*Aldaar* is gone. Commander Vuul is dead. You are our only commanding officer."

Seul grunted. Commander of what? What could they possibly do now? Three little shuttles? All her fellow Troopers, Vuul, Qaan . . . Kael. All dead for nothing. The savage fighting on the Thede ship, and—

The image of the dead Aldaakian boy floating on the Thede vessel entered her thoughts. Her jaw tightened, and then her cryoports clicked once and relaxed. The ache of her wounds became a dull throb at the back of her consciousness.

"We are all that stands between our enemies and our people in Aldaakian Space." Seul grimaced, her chest cryoports jamming shut. "We'll not survive. But we can avenge *Aldaar* and our fallen comrades. I told Sar Redryll we'd help him. Aldaakians keep their word."

"Captain Jaah, a strong signal is emitting from the Sarrhdtuu ship," the navigator said.

Seul thought of Kivita, and what the Sarrhdtuu must be doing to her. The sight of *Frevyx*, though, emboldened her. One trawler against a Sarrhdtuu vessel? Her people had always been outnumbered, but never broken.

"What is your name?" Seul asked the navigator. No more formal, impersonal military interaction. She wanted to know who would be dying with her.

"Taak, Captain."

"How well can you pilot this craft?"

Taak sat up straighter in her chair. "As well as you require, Captain Jaah."

"Captain, look," one Trooper said.

Outside the cockpit viewport, the huge Vim derelict had broken into six parts. Before their eyes, each shard flew away of its own volition, until all six formed a circle dozens of miles across.

Hope thawed Seul's chilled heart; then anger scorched it. Purpose tempered it into the hardest iron.

"Taak, alert the other surviving shuttles. We're making an attack run on that Inheritor battleship. I have fire control." She glared out the viewport. By the Vim, they would not kill her easily.

Frevyx veered toward the Sarrhdtuu battleship as warning lights blinked on the console. Sar ignored them and pushed the manuals again, then eased them to starboard. *Frevyx* dove and flew parallel with the battleship's graceful, curved hull. Voices in the chambers behind the bridge rose in anger and fright.

"Keep them calm, Jandeel!" Sar called over his shoulder. A gravity flux gave his stomach a slight tussle, while *Frevyx* flew a few yards above the other ship's hull. As long as he remained so close, *Arcuri's Glory* wouldn't dare fire on him.

Luccan's Wish, its orbit degrading, glowed red from reentry.

Jandeel entered the bridge and clutched a bulkhead

handle. "Some have gotten sick, but all are fine." He looked out the viewport and jumped. "Sar, have you gone insane? If the Sarrhdtuu were to make a light jump right now, it would dislocate our hull and rip us apart!"

"Want to scare them even more back there? Dunaar won't shoot at us, for now," Sar replied. On the scanner, three blips closed with *Arcuri's Glory*: Seul and the surviving Aldaakians.

"But what for? Sar, you are risking us all. How does this help Kivita?"

"Get Bredine up here." Sar turned the manuals. *Frevyx* rose over a mound in the craft's hull, then dipped along one of its crescent wings.

Jandeel left and returned with the bony Savant. Bredine's hand and arm had been bandaged, and her eyes had stopped darting everywhere.

"Bredine, is Kiv still sending?" Sar pulled *Frevyx* up and began the same path he'd just flown over the Sarrhdtuu vessel.

"Hmm. Redryll, Redryll. Kivita is . . . building? Yes. Building, not sending." Bredine sat beside him and pulled Jandeel close. "Hold me? But not like Redryll. Hmm."

Jandeel sighed and steadied her. "What is she building?"

Outside the viewport, the Vim derelict had split into six parts and formed a huge circle. The wreck's constituent parts shimmered with blue light.

"By the Solars," Jandeel whispered.

Bredine absently ran fingers through Jandeel's hair. "No. By Kivita Narbas."

In all his salvaging years, Sar had never heard, nor dreamt, of such a sight. The six parts winked in sequence with each other like tiny blue stars. Despite his worry over Kivita and pain at witnessing the Thedes' destruction, an old wonder crept into his heart.

Perhaps the Vim had arrived after all.

Whispers burst over the console speaker, then rose into shrieks. Passengers behind the bridge groaned and shouted, until Sar slammed the mute button.

"The Vim send!" Bredine cried. "Kivita keeps building!"

Sar gripped her hand. "Can you communicate with her? Maybe send your . . . thoughts, or whatever, to her?"

Jandeel's eyes widened in understanding. "*Frevyx*'s transmitter. Sar, focus it on the band channel Bredine says Kivita is on. Then have her send something back. Let her know we are out here and want to help."

Sar slid the transmitter terminal out to Bredine. "Do it."

Kivita gritted her teeth against the raw signal slamming into her mind. Her lungs labored to breathe, and her heart thudded with effort.

Two Sarrhdtuu warriors lifted Kivita from the platform as it floated around *Juxj*'s interior. The ship's humming grew in volume, filling her ears and vibrating her bones.

Shekelor clasped Cheseia's arm while Zhara glanced about. Navon stared at Kivita, a renewed urgency in his eyes.

"Now you will see, Child of Narbas." Zhhl's coils clamped onto the platform's edges, and the platform rose. The Juxj Star orbited her like it had when she'd first found it on Vstrunn.

The platform neared an octagonal ceiling where

glowing green terminals shone from twenty feet up. Fleshlike stalks carted large jelly capsules into wall slots. A faint gray mist hung in the air, and greenish fog roiled around their ankles.

One stalk slithered onto the platform and stopped near Kivita's feet. Its end opened up and shone a flickering light upward. Dunaar's holographic form materialized in the light.

"Greetings, my child. You have led us on a grand journey to this sacred system. Do you know that I shall build monuments to what will take place here? The destruction of the Thede leadership, the defeat of albino infidels, and you, Kivita Vondir. Your holy mission is at last fulfilled." Even through the hologram, she made out sweat running down Dunaar's chin.

"Go to hell," she replied.

Dunaar clutched a stone scepter in both hands. "Blaspheme while you still can, you filthy spacer slut. Once you have opened this Vim Portal, Zhhl will turn you over to me. Your talents must be passed on to the next generation of Inheritors. We will breed until I have one hundred Savants just like you, my child. Only they will not spread lies. They will spread the holy truth."

"Yeah? I hope these jelly-filled shit cans do turn me over to you, because then I'll—"

A coil cuffed her across the shoulders.

"You will focus now," Zhhl said. "You will unlock the sequence in the Portal."

Triangular terminals jutted from the wall, alight with yellow characters and symbols. Eight holograms projected onto the ceiling, displaying *Juxj*'s hangar, the tube chamber, and objects outside the craft. The Vim derelict had split and formed a circle, while *Frevyx* flew around the Sarrhdtuu starship. Three Aldaakian shuttles arced across the hull of *Arcuri's Glory*.

The Juxj Star stopped orbiting Kivita and hovered before her face. Its red glow bathed the platform in crimson hues. Two warriors tightened their coils on her arms. Zhhl's single eye split into two and stared at her with antediluvian maliciousness.

Still trembling, Kivita closed her eyes and tried to re-direct the overbearing signal into the Juxj Star. She had nothing else to do with it, other than absorb it.

The data stream invading her mind stopped.

Kivita opened her eyes. A wave of consciousness spread from her brain, passing through *Juxj*'s hull and into the void outside. Every nerve in her body tingled; every hair on her head quivered.

All six parts of the Vim ship blinked blue once, then went dark. Kivita felt rather than saw it. The fabric of space and time wrinkled within the circle. Stars blurred. The gas giant stopped rotating. The other vessels outside *Juxj* hovered in midflight. Navon, Cheseia, and the others stood like statues on the platform. Only Kivita could move.

Only she could see.

The Portal flickered open, and a second data stream eased into Kivita's neural pathways. She hugged herself and sighed as a comforting warmth spread through her body. All aches and bruises vanished; doubts and fears were extinguished like torches in a Susuron lagoon.

A thousand voices combined into one and spoke in her thoughts.

You have achieved what we had hoped. You have as-sembled the tools we left behind so you could find us. Yet you bring enemies.

The vista through the Portal took her breath and numbed her mind.

Dozens of yellow main-sequence stars made her squint. An undamaged, eight-mile-long Vim ship with a shimmering panel array waited. Six smaller, oblong craft flanked it. A planet with white clouds, blue seas, and green continents shone like a jewel on black velvet.

"Frevyx," she whispered.

"My children, we have found them at last!" Dunaar's hologram cried.

A violet beam shot out from *Juxj*. One of the small oblong vessels burst into shrapnel and dust.

The warm feelings terminated with Kivita's scream. Thousands of minds shrieked at being destroyed, then died away. Reality blinked back into her consciousness as the other vessels around *Juxj* moved again. Everyone on the platform wobbled and gasped.

Zhhl's coils slapped the platform. "Engage."

"What?" Dunaar asked in a distraught voice.

Juxj moved toward the Portal and a second violet beam scorched the larger Vim ship's hull.

"No!" Kivita shouted. "You're destroying life! You're—"

The two warriors almost pulled her arms out of their sockets. Pain darkened her vision, muted her scream.

"I want my son, Zhhl. Now." Shekelor morphed through the platform and appeared right before Zhhl.

Kivita's eyes fluttered back open as two more Sarrhd-tuu warriors dropped onto the platform, drew curved blades, and stalked toward Shekelor.

"He has contributed to this pair of Sentries," Zhhl said in a booming voice. "Be content."

"Zhhl, what are you doing? I demand to know! I will take action—" The hologram of Dunaar snapped off.

Juxj drew near the Portal, as did *Arcuri's Glory*.

"Where is Byelor? I have given you everything, even my own body! Where is he?" Shekelor shook with rage.

One of the Sarrhdtuu warriors flipped open its carapace armor. A thin pale human male was clamped to the creature's flesh. Tubes filled with green and yellow liquids joined human and Sarrhdtuu in symbiotic perversity.

For an instant, Kivita's eyes met Shekelor's. Though she despised him and all he'd done, sympathy and anger forced a word from her lips.

"Sygma!"

Stretching his coils, Shekelor ripped away the medical tape from the Ascalis' mouths, then the flexi around their wrists. Cheseia and Zhara both sang a high-pitched note, rising in volume and clarity. Within a second it expanded beyond human hearing.

Both warriors released Kivita and stumbled. Zhhl's coils balled up, its translucent veins clogging with green liquid. The warrior coupled with Byelor stumbled off the platform.

Throughout *Juxj*, hundreds of Sarrhdtuu warriors morphed from the walls and floor.

Shekelor grabbed a beam rifle from one of his pirates and fired, burning one warrior to green globules. Another warrior dashed aside three pirates with its coils. The sound of snapping bones and armor echoed in the chamber. Kivita and Navon ducked behind a triangular terminal as Shekelor fired again. A Sarrhdtuu flopped down, half its head sliced away. Dark jelly bubbled into the air and seeped into the platform.

"Engage!" Zhhl's voice reverberated off the walls.

Juxj blasted apart another oblong vessel on the other side of the Portal.

Kivita closed her eyes and gasped as a tingling spread through her brain. Recalling the vision of Terredyn's manipulation of Sarrhdtuu hull scrap, she focused.

Electrical impulses fired among the trillions of neurons cobbled together inside *Juxj*'s structure. All the green-rigged humans, all the biomass absorbed by the Sarrhdtuu, reacted to Kivita's invisible call. The ship's transmitter spat out all the data she'd learned from the Juxj Star and other datacores. Everything Navon, Jandeel, and the Thedes had taught her.

Juxj's bulkheads warped and bent. Every tube ringing the walls opened. The beamer stopped firing through the Portal. As the Vim had intended, and as she'd discovered over Tejuit, Kivita's mind and the ship melded into a flawless interface requiring no physical connection. Organic, biomechanical, and electrical networks fused.

She sensed every bulkhead, every rivet, every inch of hull, though a terrible weight seemed to mash her heart from the strain. All the tubes holding Kith opened. Green-rigged humans sloshed from their vats, loosing subalien moans.

With the Ascali twins continuing their song, Sarrhdtuu warriors reacted with sluggish movements. Kith, once held captive by the Sarrhdtuu, attacked with brutal strikes, splattering the walls with jelly. Green-rigged humans groaned and crawled from their tubes.

The platform rammed into the floor, tossing Cheseia and Zhara off it. Navon caught Kivita before she tumbled off. Shekelor and his pirates fought their way from the chamber, as Sarrhdtuu warriors resumed full functionality. Screams and gunfire filled the ship.

Kivita tried to hold control of the ship, but she cried out as pain stabbed into her skull. Navon held on to her. Violent, brutal movement passed in her peripheral vision.

Sar Redryll. Bredine Ov. Help them. The phrases sounded over and over in her mind. For a brief instant, Kivita visualized Sar's trawler orbiting *Juxj*. Waiting for her.

"I have control of the ship," Kivita whispered, as her brain sent the message back to *Frevyx*.

Use it to kill Dunaar Thev.

In one strike she could destroy the slayers of her mother, the Sarrhdtuu lackeys who'd used her. Through the Portal, though, the Vim didn't return fire. No one closed with *Juxj* or launched assault shuttles. The yellow suns beckoned, and the large Vim ship still waited.

As chaos and death reigned around her in the gargantuan chamber, Kivita blinked. The Vim had wanted those in the Cradles to do more than just build starships and hone Savant talents to find them.

The Vim had wanted her to eschew violence. The lack of weapon technology in the datacores now became clear. The Sarrhdtuu had been slaves of their own greed, instead of slaves to the Vim.

"This is not the answer, Sar," she mumbled. "This isn't who I am now."

Kivita rose with Navon, while the Kith ripped apart Sarrhdtuu warriors nearby. Green-rigged people limped about, gaping with childish wonder, and several walked into kinetic crossfire as Shekelor and his followers battered a path toward the hangar. Many pirate bodies lay broken or cleaved in two.

"Sar wants me to force *Juxj* to destroy the Inheritor flagship," Kivita said, as she and Navon hid behind a shattered tube.

"How can you receive such a message?" Navon said. "I do not understand."

Focusing on the code sequence, Kivita poured her will into it. The Inheritors deserved the chance to learn, as she had. Killing Dunaar would accomplish nothing. War would continue, with the Sarrhdtuu the only victors. But united, the Cetturo Arm could determine its own fate.

"I think everyone will someday," she finally whispered back.

A tearing sensation gripped her mind. All breath left Kivita's body, and her heart stopped for a moment.

Control of *Juxj* had been taken from her.

"They sharpened you well, Child of Narbas." Zhhl's sibilant voice permeated the entire ship. "Now I will use you against them."

Juxj shuddered, and a violet beam shot out from one of its crescent wings and struck *Luccan's Wish*. The Thede ship split apart, with entire decks turned into dust. The remaining sections glowed red as they plummeted into the gas giant's atmosphere.

Kivita, recalling information about Sarrhdtuu ships from the Juxj Star, inserted her hand into a triangular terminal. Mucus-filled mouths whispered in her ears; blood ran like ice in her veins. A deep warmth spread over her flesh, which made the chilled sensation painful. She had the sudden urge to urinate.

"Child of Narbas," Zhhl's thick, sinuous voice tickled her ears above the sounds of fighting. "Interface with us. You will be given honors. You will deliver our race from tyranny."

Kivita narrowed her eyes. "I've seen what you do. You stole what didn't belong to you. Your greed is so great, you've almost destroyed yourselves!"

The Juxj Star floated toward her. Its red glow hurt her eyes, as data from it stabbed her mind.

"The Vim sealed their Portals so no one but Savants could open them with a datacore," Zhhl said. Its coils lifted it onto the wall above Kivita, where it split into three smaller versions.

"Maybe I should close it," Kivita said.

The green-rigged humans all turned and glowered at Kivita. More Sarrhdtuu warriors exited the walls and ceiling. In the distance, gunfire grew faint as the last of Shekelor's force met their doom. More than twenty Kith circled Kivita and Navon in a barrier of metallic flesh and bloody claws.

"You forget that you have no hope as your stars die. Either the Prophet of Meh Sat finds the Vim or the Vim show themselves before this Cradle undergoes multiple supernovas," Zhhl said.

"So you threaten us with destruction to force your agenda? We'll find those derelicts and reverse the process!" Kivita yelled.

"You forget who planted the Juxj Star on Vstrunn. You forget we replicated Vim datacores to serve our purposes. The gem waited a thousand years. Not all of its knowledge is constructive." Zhhl's words emanated from every Sarrhdtuu mouth, every green-rigged tongue.

The Juxj Star darted at Kivita.

Glimpses of destruction seared her sanity, and Kivita cried out as the full scale of Sarrhdtuu privations became known: *beautiful worlds scorched to cinders, stars suctioned of their energy and going nova in heavily populated systems.* Over and over again. Kivita wailed and sobbed, trying to shove the millennia of predation and destruction from her mind.

The Cetturo Arm was but the latest in a long line of Cradles the Sarrhdtuu had destroyed or subjugated. Thousands of worlds; billions of lives. All because the Vim had sealed themselves in a part of the universe the Sarrhdtuu could not reach.

Kivita had led Zhhl straight to them.

The images battered her brain like spike batons. Kivita fell on her hands and knees. The floating gem neared her forehead.

"Concentrate," Navon said. "Remember the layers. Focus, attune, absorb."

"It's too awful!" she cried.

"Do not fight it!" he yelled back. Their eyes met, even as gray-green shapes rose around them.

"Wish I could have been a better student, learned more—"

Navon caressed her cheek. "You did, my queen."

Kivita swallowed and concentrated again.

Her flesh seemed to melt off. The Sarrhdtuu's complicated sequences, syntax, and alternate binary overwhelmed her mind.

"It's too much!" she shouted.

"You will not harm the Narbas line anymore," Navon said above her. Something hot passed before her face.

Navon grunted. Kivita looked up.

The Juxj Star glowed red-hot in Navon's hands as he stared into its sinister depths.

"No!" Kivita tried to knock it from his grasp, but in a

manner of seconds, he crumpled beside her. An electrical wave pushed against her brain; then she sensed Navon reverse it onto itself.

The Juxj Star shattered.

Infinitesimal crystal shards rained over her as Navon's lifeless eyes stared with the endless horrors enacted by Sarrhdtuu over the millennia.

Sarrhdtuu warriors charged the circle of Kith, their sickle blades carving away gray limbs, cleaving through squat heads. Black claws eviscerated jelly bodies and sliced away carapace armor. Black and green blood splashed Kivita's envirosuit. She wiped some off her faceplate.

Kivita tried to calm herself, tried to concentrate on *Juxj* again. Depending on the Kith to save her amounted to a fool's hope. If she gained control of the ship again, maybe she could—

Merciless coils wrapped around Kivita's legs and chest and lifted her twenty feet into the air. Zhhl's sleek, crescent-shaped head studied her with ten purple eyes.

"You humans are braver than your Vim masters. The Aldaakians, the Kith, the Ascali—all fight to cover Vim weakness. All lose because—"

Zhhl jerked back as a piercing cry echoed in the chamber. Other Sarrhdtuu stalled in their tracks, and the few remaining Kith tore through them, while one cut through Zhhl's coils. Kivita tumbled into the morass of bodies. Strong hands hefted her up.

"You definitely need to close that thing!" Cheseia hauled Kivita atop a glowing terminal. Lacerations marred her envirosuit, and a crack ran along her faceplate.

A few feet away, Zhara sang a simple, beautiful note. It soared in Kivita's ears as well as her heart. With a strong mental push, she forced the platform to rise again with all three of them on it. Among the holograms above, *Juxj* hovered near the Portal's lip with *Arcuri's Glory*.

37

Ignoring the sweat sliding down his jowls, Dunaar gaped out the viewport. The gateway had opened just for him. Never in a thousand cryo dreams had he imagined the Vim would reveal themselves this way. After all his struggles, Dunaar would finally be rewarded. His sweating disease and thyroid might be cured; he'd receive honors beyond imagining for bringing humanity from darkness into the Vim's holy light.

But Zhhl's betrayal had ruined all that.

He would not be denied! *Arcuri's Glory* drew nearer the Portal. Just a little farther, and he would be under the Vim's protection. Almost there . . .

"Rector, your orders?" Stiego asked, standing over the nav console. "Do we return fire?"

"Maintain your course, Captain."

Violet beams from *Juxj* atomized another of the Vim craft.

Dunaar dropped the Scepter and laid both trembling hands on the viewport. A catch in his throat forced him to cough. Shocked mutters and gasps filled the bridge.

"Rector, if we continue, we will collide with those

ships! We must fire on those Sarrhdtuu traitors!" Stiego's holo monocle faded in and out.

"No. We are almost there," Dunaar whispered. Sweat rolled off his nose and down the viewport. "We cannot be stopped now."

The glorious images Bredine had shown him of a Rector leading his people across time and space to safety made Dunaar smile. What were beam weapons compared to the might of the Vim? They had built the very stars themselves. Built them especially for Dunaar.

"*Juxj* has just destroyed the Thede ship and our remaining platoons! We have been betrayed, Rector!" Stiego ran over and shook Dunaar's shoulder. "We cannot fight—"

Arcuri's Glory quavered.

The security officer cleared his throat. "Rector, Aldaakian shuttles have strafed the starboard side. Sealing adjacent chambers."

Flailing bodies in red jumpsuits floated past the starboard viewport.

"Do something!" Stiego yelled in Dunaar's ear.

Why hadn't he listened to her? Bredine had warned him of enemies from the dark void. She wouldn't have done so unless she really loved him. Skeletal bitch. Why had she left?

He blinked and shook his head. He was the Rector. The guardian of humanity. The Vim would see he was their warrior, their protector. All would see now.

"Rector!" Stiego cried.

Dunaar shoved Stiego away. "Open fire on anything that moves! All batteries, now!" He grabbed the Scepter and turned back to the viewport. A second violet beam shot out, and a second Vim vessel exploded into dust.

"Tracking shuttles now," Stiego said, regaining his composure.

Zhhl's battleship neared the Portal, but Dunaar seethed. They would not take his reward from him. Too many believers had suffered; too many martyrs had died. Centuries of trust in the Sarrhdtuu had been subservience instead. This was a test from the Vim. He would not fail.

"Fire on *Juxj*." Dunaar squeezed the Scepter until the stone tore into his palms.

Stiego hesitated. "Rector, those shuttles will—"

"Fire!" Dunaar yelled.

The port-side K-gun battery loosed its sabot rounds, each projectile soaring through the void like prayers escaping Dunaar's lips. He gesticulated in blessing as the rounds penetrated *Juxj*'s starboard hull.

"Again! Fire until nothing remains!" Dunaar shoved aside the security officer and jabbed the fire button himself. Three more kinetic salvos launched at *Juxj*. Each impact made Dunaar smile wider.

Juxj's violet beams ripped away armor plating, hull, and lives. *Arcuri's Glory* shook. Warning alarms shrieked over the bridge.

"Rector, we have lost all power on Starboard Deck Two, Section C. The forward hull has been breached in three places. We must draw away!" Stiego's face pinched with fear.

"You coward. Stay on course!" Dunaar raised the Scepter and ground his teeth.

Two more violet beams darted from *Juxj* to the Vim starships.

"Damn them!" Dunaar shouted. "Can't you defeat them?" He swatted Stiego with the Scepter.

Holding his head, Stiego examined more damage readouts on the terminal. "We cannot win this!"

"Must I do all this myself?" His saliva splattered Stiego's holo monocle.

Others on the bridge stood in terrified silence. Lesser prophets cowered, eyes wide. Even the Proselytes grouped together, as if seeking protection in numbers. Dunaar feared the fools' morale would falter as more Vim ships met destruction. All they'd been taught of Vim greatness had been scorched by Sarrhdtuu treachery.

Had the Aldaakians been right in calling the Inheritor's old allies the Vim's true enemies? He leaned on the Scepter, sweat running down it from his hand. The strange gateway still lay open despite the Sarrhdtuu discharges. The Vim held it open for Dunaar, for all the frozen Rectors aboard. The promise of salvation was his if he just maintained courage and fortitude.

The means mattered little.

"Those shuttles are too small to target," Stiego said. "They are nearing the bridge itself!"

Dunaar knocked Stiego to the floor with the Scepter. "Maintain course and keep firing! Our deliverance is at hand—"

"Incoming!" Stiego yelled, hands over his face.

A single green beam flew from an Aldaakian shuttle as a violet one fired from *Juxj*. The Sarrhdtuu beam's mauve brilliance tore away armor as the Aldaakian green beam slid on through. Dunaar shoved aside prophets and Proselytes as the beam struck. He stumbled into the corridor.

The entire ship rocked, and the bulkhead on Dunaar's left collapsed as the bridge's safety hatch sealed shut. A green flash blinded him, while intense heat puckered his flesh and singed his face. The hem of his robe caught flame, and the Scepter of Office grew too hot to hold. Hundreds of slag pellets rained over Dunaar.

"Help! In the name of the Vim, I need—" Dunaar screamed as the heated slag sank into his flesh, burning as it went. Smoke billowed from the raw pink fissures. He toppled toward his personal chambers, but the entrance sealed shut. Cooled slag floated from the sandstone floor.

"Vim . . . help me . . . I pray you . . ." Dunaar pulled himself along the plush red carpet. Over the intercom speaker, Stiego ordered all cabins and chambers sealed. His sight blurred. A horrible chill blanketed his charred body, alleviating the burning agony for a fleeting moment.

He tried to pray, but the chill reached his lips.

The melted bulkhead on his left drifted into space. Dunaar sucked in his breath as an impact nearby catapulted him toward the Portal.

Vacuum cold numbed his body within seconds. The burning, the pain—all vanished. As the cold froze his lips shut and eyelids open, Dunaar turned end over end. One second he glimpsed *Arcuri's Glory* and *Juxj*; the next, the yawning Vim Portal. His last vision of yellow stars, promising warmth and life, mocked him.

Everyone cheered as the Inheritor battleship maneuvered away from the Portal. Seul patted Taak's shoulder, while the other Troopers cheered. Seul's other hand left the firing manuals, stiff and weak.

Shutting her eyes, she thought of Kael and smiled.

"An Inheritor-class ship has exited the Sarrhdtuu vessel," Taak said.

Seul studied the console readout. "That's *Fanged Pauper*." A frown pulled her smile down as the scanner revealed no Savant was aboard. Kivita remained a prisoner, then, or worse.

Optimism ended as the Sarrhdtuu vessel disintegrated the two other Aldaakian shuttles. Seul knelt beside Taak's seat, her damaged cryoports jolting with agony.

"Taak, engage the Sarrhdtuu ship. Mirror *Frevyx*'s trajectory." She keyed the mic. "Sar, Jaah here. We're tailing you in support."

The shuttle changed course and flew away from the Inheritor battleship. Every Trooper gazed along with Seul out the cockpit's starboard viewport. Archivers had never mentioned Vim wormholes or gateways. The presence of functioning Vim starships, flaring yellow stars, and a world covered in green and blue held them in awe. Ancient tales of Khaasis's glaciers, lakes, and frost groves made Seul's heart quicken.

"I want her to see this someday," she whispered. "I want my daughter to know we . . ." Seul coughed and patted Kael's lifeless hand.

"Think you can target those Sarrhdtuu beamers while I skim this heap's surface, Captain Jaah?" Taak asked.

"Of course. Troopers, it's been an honor." Seul glanced at everyone aboard. All nodded to her and touched their chest cryoports.

All her cryoports had numbed, and the muscles in her arms and shoulders grew weaker. Soon she'd perish, despite her polyarmor's sealing of her wounds. Right now, though, she didn't have time to die. Gripping the firing manuals again, she selected a target and pressed the button. The beamer fired, popping apart a Sarrhdtuu weapon like a Naxan eggshell.

The platform stopped rising as Kivita refocused on *Juxj*'s systems. Her mind delved deep into Sarrhdtuu data, a clutter of alien codes and garbled records. Thousands of coordinate sets, schematics, planetary statistics, engineering breakthroughs—knowledge stolen from countless Vim Cradles and Savants.

"Yes, Child of Narbas. Interface and destroy them." Zhhl's voice rang inside her head. Kivita covered her ears and stumbled.

The holo display above them showed a Vim craft crash into another one. The Portal's six components flashed red.

"No," Kivita mumbled.

"Fulfill your purpose. Decode and compile the destruction intended for us." Zhhl's words hummed throughout *Juxj* itself. More Sarrhdtuu warriors slid from walls and alcoves.

"No!" Kivita screamed. Cheseia and Zhara tried to steady her. Their combined voices grew weak, and their furred bosoms heaved with effort.

The humming became a roar in her ears.

All the dreams she'd had since Xeh's Crown, all the sensations she'd felt since Vstrunn, blasted open her consciousness. The impossibility of knowing each star's name, in a dictionary of a billion names, flowed through her. The location of ten thousand demolished systems beyond the Cetturo Arm made her moan with fear and pain.

"I'll . . . I'll destroy you," she gasped, her thoughts melding with *Juxj*'s weapon systems. "I'll destroy you!"

"The more you learn, the more you interface," Zhhl said.

Juxj's beamer incinerated another Vim craft on the holo display. This time, Kivita sensed the connection from her mind to the weapon placement. She'd targeted the victims; she'd activated the merciless violet light.

Coils latched onto the platform from below, and six warriors dangled from the ceiling, their coils melding into the hull itself.

Cheseia hugged Kivita and sang louder. Zhara stalked to the platform's edge, her voice ululating throughout the massive chamber.

So much knowledge, spread over a vast, infinite fabric. Kivita didn't want to see, hear, or know anymore. She wanted to purge it all from her mind and become the salvager she used to be. A simpler life, but cold and lonely. Wisdom had revealed so much, only to shackle her with slavery after all.

Dammit, she had to concentrate! She refocused her mind and screamed.

The entire ship shook. Kivita gasped, and Cheseia yanked her back from the platform's edge. Warriors clambered up after them, while more dropped from above. Below, Zhhl absorbed dozens of other Sarrhdtuu, growing into a tangle of coils, eyes, and puckering maws.

Zhara sang louder, and even Zhhl's movements slowed.

Two Sarrhdtuu warriors fired their wrist cylinders. Violet beams atomized Zhara.

Cheseia's voice faltered; then she ripped away her

helmet. Her tears splashed Kivita's faceplate. A single note stunned the warriors for a moment as the Ascali's body shivered.

Kivita's heart sank into a cesspit of fury. Thoughts raced along alien neurons; her desires merged with Sarrhdtuu brains. As she clenched her teeth, tears wet her own cheeks. So they liked to fight and kill, huh? She'd oblige them.

Eight Sarrhdtuu warriors vaporized one another with their wrist beamers.

Cheseia pulled Kivita behind a glowing terminal, while more warriors battled each other. Curved blades sliced off coils or cleaved into crescent-shaped heads. *Juxj* shook and creaked as the ship's readouts flashed in Kivita's mind: *damage from kinetic sabots and shuttle beamers. A trawler skimming the hull, its transmitter sending requests into her mind.* Arcuri's Glory, *withdrawing from the Portal.*

Gargantuan coils crushed the terminals around Kivita. Green jelly and carapace showered over her. Zhhl, now thirty feet tall, crawled along one wall toward her.

"You cannot reverse what you have initiated, Child of Narbas. A parasite cannot hold its host captive." Zhhl dashed aside battling warriors with its coils. Jelly splattered the walls, then morphed into them.

Body numb with weariness, Kivita tried to form a plan. Focusing on the ship's beamers only activated them against the Vim. C'mon, think! What else could she do? The Vim Portal's components blinked red again on the holo display. *Juxj*'s port-side hull neared one as it entered the Portal itself.

A coil whooshed over Kivita's head.

Cheseia shoved Kivita back and confronted Zhhl,

her song shrill and desperate. The huge Sarrhdtuu lurched back, coils hanging limp.

"I will always truly sing the 'Chant to Revelas' for you," Cheseia said as she turned. Russet orbs shimmered with tears, but her mouth curved into a smile. "Zhara will certainly sing, too. Tell Sar I always—"

One of Zhhl's coils wrapped around Cheseia's torso. She stood defiant as three more coils obstructed her from Kivita's sight. Zhhl's purple gaze glowered at her from twenty different eyes. The coils constricted, then squeezed.

"I'll tell him," Kivita whispered. With her remaining strength, she forced her thoughts into *Juxj*'s drive systems.

A burst of power raced throughout the starship. Warriors aimed their cylinders at her. Zhhl loomed above her, coils raised.

"Obey us, parasite! Obey—"

The ship's starboard wing collided with one of the Portal components.

A silent, concussive force rippled across *Juxj*. A million voices ordered her to change course, but Kivita, through thought alone, nudged *Juxj* into the next Portal component.

A thunderous pop crackled in the chamber. Sparks flew from bulkheads, terminals. The liquids flowing along walls and floors stopped, then burst out in sticky geysers. Sarrhdtuu tried to morph back into walls, while *Juxj*'s port-side hull snapped open. Bulkheads folded over as a blue shock wave spread into the chamber. Kivita screamed as her helmet's aural sensors shattered from the external noise. Her mental connection with *Juxj* snapped, as if someone had doubled her spine over.

Fingers and toes went numb; then her tongue stuck to her teeth. Hair stabbed into her scalp like needles. Her bladder relaxed, and a painful ripple traversed her temples.

Zhhl's coils reached for her. "You found them for us! Interface with me and understand! They must be eliminated!"

Kivita's mind lashed out with a mental storm.

The entire ship decompressed. Bodies, coils, weapons, and terminals shot out into space.

"Interface!" Zhhl's voice stabbed into her mind as a jagged bulkhead impaled its body. Though jelly globules scattered from its wound into the vacuum, Zhhl struggled toward her. Its coils lashed after Kivita. One brushed her feet.

The blue shock wave incinerated Zhhl as it continued on through the rest of *Juxj*.

The platform was yanked away, flinging Kivita from the chamber. She flew past collapsing bulkheads and writhing Sarrhdtuu. Green-rigged humans clutched at necks or chests, their atmosphere gone. Shrapnel pinged against Kivita's helmet and faceplate, joining her grunts and gasps as the only sounds. Everything else commenced in terrible silence.

A final explosion shoved Kivita from the Sarrhdtuu ship and into the void. G-forces mashed the air from her lungs, rattled the teeth in her head. She soared away in a straight line, while *Juxj* crumpled into large chunks. Particles drifted from the charred hulk like Haldon syrup bees.

The Vim Portal shimmered, and all four remaining components blinked red in rapid succession. The panorama of Vim starships, yellow suns, and the world of Frevyx became translucent.

Kivita sobbed. Her heart beat so hard, it seemed to bruise her chest. Legs and arms numbed with cold. Far away, *Arcuri's Glory* vanished as it made a light jump. She passed the wreckage of *Aldaar* and its line of floating refuse and bodies. Starlight gleamed off the black polyarmor of dead Shock Troopers.

"Cheseia," she whispered, thinking of her, Zhara, and Navon. Expecting to die, they'd saved her. Kivita hated herself for being the cause of so much destruction, so much death. The price of knowledge, the price of freedom. "Damn you all, I didn't deserve to survive."

Closer and closer, she neared the Portal. The component ring flashed quicker.

A small dot behind her arced above the gas giant, then sped toward the Portal. Questions entered her mind: *Are you alive? What happened? Can you hold on?*

Kivita smiled. Fresh tears streamed down her cheeks, then vacuum cold transformed them into painful, icy rivers. Somehow Sar had figured out how to send radio messages into her mind.

"I love you," she mumbled through chilling lips. "Can you hear me, Sar? I love you."

Ahead, two objects drew near: a body and a staff. The corpse wore a glittering outer robe and yellow inner robe. Eyes frozen open. Dunaar Thev and his Scepter of Office, now just space trash.

Kivita collided with the Scepter and spun about. Images of Arcuri kneeling and making a deal with Zhhl entered her mind. Rectifiers on colony ships. Similar data Kivita had received from other datacores followed.

One image, though, displayed a tall figure handing the Scepter to a man in a Rectifier's yellow suit. The figure stood wreathed in yellow light, with sleek physiology and

*translucent skin. The viewer in the vision looked up, but a
golden gleam hid the figure's face.*

You have seen us. You have saved us. We will wait.

As the voice in her head faded, Dunaar's body passed
into the Portal. The arrogant fool would meet the Vim,
anyway.

The entire array glimmered for an instant; then the
vista disappeared just before Kivita passed through it.
No more yellow stars, Vim starships, or Frevyx. A star-
speckled void awaited her as the Portal components exploded one by one. The blast wave jolted her onto a new
course.

Kivita groaned as she drifted into the gas giant's
planetary ring. An ice-and-debris field, perhaps a mile
deep and hundreds of miles wide, slowed her momentum. Frozen lumps battered her limbs, slowing her until
she floated in place. The system's red giant lit the ring in
glittering, pinkish shades. Beneath her, the turquoise gas
giant's storms had calmed.

To have gotten so close to the Vim, to all the answers
to her questions, only to fail, wrenched Kivita's heart.
The Thedes had placed such high hopes in her. New
tears ran chilly furrows down her cheeks. Slight vacuum
frost built up inside her faceplate.

Her sight blurred and her entire body numbed. Fighting the urge to lick her lips, Kivita swallowed. Utter silence reigned over the pink-and-turquoise gloom, while
a billion stars peeked at her through red-green nebulae.
The Vim might be orbiting any number of them. Waiting.

Kivita imagined *Terredyn Narbas* coming alongside
her, with Rhyer grinning at her through the bridge viewport. Just like he'd done in her childhood whenever he'd

return from a salvage. Grinning with the new stories he'd tell her, the exotic artifacts he'd show her before selling them to Marsque.

In one memory, Rhyer handed her a red hibiscus petal from Nax. She raised it to her nose and sniffed. Sharp sweetness mixed with fresh musk tickled her nostrils.

"It's so special, Father." Kivita smooched his cheek, still covered in stubble. *"But the prophets claim flowers from other planets might be poisonous."*

"Don't pay heed to those Inheritor prophets, Kiv. You'll find something special out there someday. Just gotta keep looking for it." Rhyer kissed her forehead.

Kivita squeezed her eyes shut and smiled as the sobs returned.

"I found something," she whispered, the cold making her tongue and gums hurt.

Rhyer had found her frozen, floating in space inside a cryopod. Placed in a secret location by Terredyn's servants, where Rhyer would "salvage" her. Now, she floated once again. Frozen. Maybe she should be allowed to freeze, forgotten so no one else would have to suffer. At least the Sarrhdtuu had failed in reaching the Vim through her.

A warmth spread from her mind to her heart as she recalled the first sugar reed Rhyer had brought her from Bellerion, or her first jiir leaf from Sygma, shining like brilliant blue glass. Places she'd only dreamt about. Places she'd wanted to see. Now Kivita had the information for an eternity of exploration.

The little girl inside her quit crying, and the woman took hold again. The salvager held up her head as a queen.

Though the frost hurt her lips, Kivita smiled. "I found it, Father. Mother. Now I want to see it."

She thought of the home she'd wanted on Susuron, with Sar at her side. Kivita didn't expect him to obey her or even bow. Just love her, give her comfort. Such fantasies loomed larger and larger in her mind, and she closed her eyes again. Her consciousness opened wide, and she focused all her will and convictions. Recalled her favorite memories, the friends she'd made: Jandeel, Rhii, Basheev, Maihh, Navon. Even Cheseia, who'd found redemption at the edge of the cosmos.

And Sar, who'd come for her on *Luccan's Wish*. He'd saved her after all. Her feelings for him were a reminder of what made life worth living.

Kivita remembered all the love she'd found while braving the chill of the void.

Her smile froze in place.

38

Sar clasped *Frevyx's* manuals as it hovered over the flotsam and jetsam from all the destroyed ships getting pulled into planetary orbit just outside the ice ring. It failed to compare with the wreckage inside his heart. A heavy coldness weighed down his stomach, chilled his tongue.

She was gone. Kivita Vondir, the flame of his heart, the burning star in his dark universe, was gone.

What would he do now? Without love or vengeance in his heart, he was nothing. Sar tried to catch his breath and gazed out the viewport. None of those stars mattered. The Inheritors didn't matter. . . .

His friends still mattered.

The console speaker popped. "Sar, this is Jaah. Our scanners are starting to come back online. Perhaps we can . . . look around."

In the chambers behind the bridge, the surviving Thedes had fallen silent. Some wept. Rhii and Basheev watched Sar from the bench, tears in their eyes.

"Sending," Bredine whispered, holding her wounded arm.

"Everything we were is gone," Jandeel said. "Gone."

"We still have the datacores. We still have each other," Sar said, voice stronger than he'd expected. "Navon would've wanted us to continue."

He said nothing of Kivita's message from the Sarrhdtuu ship via Bredine: a refusal to utilize the ship's weaponry. The chance to destroy *Arcuri's Glory* had slipped through their fingers. Part of him wanted to blame her for a missed opportunity, yet Sar knew anguish rather than wisdom ruled his thoughts. Such anger really came from his guilt at not being with Kivita in her final moments.

"Our Savants can't compare with what Kivita could do. There will be no revolution now. Our cause is dead." Jandeel slumped against a bulkhead.

Sar winced; his leg wound ached more by the minute. "Wrong. That signal from the Sarrhdtuu ship, before it disintegrated? Kiv sent it. *Frevyx*'s databanks are filled with it. It must have gone wideband, somehow."

"A Sarrhdtuu transmitter," Jandeel said, straightening. "Do you suppose it went beyond this system? How could she have managed that as their prisoner?"

"Don't know." Licking his lips, he fought back tears of his own. He'd been so close to talking to her, touching her . . . telling her.

"Redryll? Kivita is sending," Bredine said.

Sar glowered at her. "Don't."

"Sending for you. Kivita Narbas loves you." Bredine smiled.

"No way she could've survived! How can she 'send,' dammit?" He yanked off the seat restraints and half rose. "How?" His voice echoed back through the rest of *Frevyx*. The other Thedes watched him with pitying stares.

Rhii stood and touched Sar's shoulder, and Basheev hugged his leg. Shutting his eyes, Sar gritted his teeth to hide his quivering lips. How could Kivita send something and he not hear?

When he wanted nothing more than to hear from her.

Jandeel knelt beside Bredine. "You were able to track her before. Can you do it again?"

Bredine stared right through them, as if they weren't there. "Gushing hot love for Kivita. Black, cold void. I sent it to her. Hmm. Redryll? She sends it back. Gushing hot, warm. But she's cold, Kivita. So cold as she sends."

Sar, his injured heart about to burst, wanted to grab and shake the bony woman. "Where? Where does she send from?"

"In the cold. Frozen icy garbage, pink and white." Bredine narrowed her eyes and nodded.

Anxiety jolted Sar's heart, and he stared out the viewport.

Jandeel's brows rose. "You mean the planetary ring?"

Sar sat back down and activated *Frevyx*'s engines. "Bredine, man the transmitter. Focus on it like you did before." He pushed the manuals toward the gas giant's ring, weaving *Frevyx* past imploded hulls and charred engine cores.

"Sending . . . there." Bredine pointed out the viewport, then tapped keys on the transmitter console.

"Where?" Sar snapped.

"Sending." Bredine shot him an exasperated look.

The scanner beeped with a signal unlike any Sar had ever seen. Not a ship, interstellar body, or energy source, but a signal of constant, pure data.

Rhii squeezed Sar's shoulder. "Stars shining and winking, if she is alive—"

"She is," Basheev said. "Our queen lives!" His cry produced surprised shouts from the other passengers.

Hope filling the emptiness inside him, Sar pushed the manuals. The scanner detected the signal, closer now, as the ice ring's outer edges pattered against *Frevyx*'s hull. Mental oaths passed through Sar's thoughts. He hadn't saved Kivita here only to abandon her again.

He'd never leave her again.

Bredine smacked the terminal and laughed. "There! Redryll, Redryll! She sends!"

A short distance outside the viewport, a figure in an envirosuit floated among the ice and rocks. As *Frevyx* drew nearer, Sar made out a thin coating of frost all over the person's body. Easing the engines to low power, he tried to get closer. Ice impacted the viewport and hull but caused no damage. He wasn't worried about the damn ice.

Sar worried she might have already frozen to death.

"Take the helm," Sar told Jandeel, and rose. Pain shot through his left leg and he stumbled. Rhii steadied him.

"Let me retrieve her," Jandeel said. "With that injured leg you'll just—"

"Jandeel," Sar said in a low voice, "take the helm."

With a resigned nod, Jandeel grasped Sar's hand and helped him from the bridge.

The other Thedes gawked at Sar, and many talked in hushed voices. "Can he save her?" they whispered. "Our staunchest hero will rescue our queen," others mumbled. A few patted him on the back, while some prayed on his behalf. Their collective support made it easier to breathe, easier to move.

"Incoming. Redryll?" Bredine's worried query came from the bridge.

Sar slipped into an envirosuit and helmet from a storage locker. "Just get me closer. Clear the airlock chamber, everyone!"

Jandeel and the rest left the chamber, while Sar tethered himself on a dual-twine flexi cable affixed to the bay wall. All the ship's interior hatches sealed shut.

The airlock hissed open. Taking a deep breath, he stepped onto the hatch's lip.

Across from him, Shekelor Thal stood, wearing an envirosuit, in *Fanged Pauper*'s open airlock. He aimed a beam rifle at Sar. The pirate ship's starboard K-gun battery leveled at *Frevyx*.

Kivita floated facedown between them, limbs spread out. A stone staff hung in the crook of her right arm — Dunaar's Scepter of Office. Pieces of ice and small rocks drifted past. The star's reflection off the gas giant shaded everything in pink and turquoise hues.

Without a weapon, Sar was helpless. Even if he turned and closed the hatch, Shekelor could still slice him in half, but each second placed Kivita closer to death. Her envirosuit might have been compromised; her air supply might be low. The greatest fear Sar had ever known spread through his heart.

"It hurts when everything you love is stolen from you," Shekelor's voice came over Sar's helmet speaker. His index finger caressed the rifle's trigger.

"Seems the Sarrhdtuu lied to you. She's worth nothing to you now." Sar kept his gaze level, but tremors shook his body.

"You just want her for your little revolution," Shekelor said. "Do you suppose the Vim or the Aldaakians destroyed *Juxj*? Ha! Your lovely redhead here did it, Redryll. Whoever controls her has the greatest weapon at their disposal."

"And for what? Nothing will bring him back." Sar pushed off from *Frevyx*. The flexi line brushed his legs as he floated toward Kivita.

"You are wrong, Redryll—"

"Byelor's dead." Just a little closer and he'd have her.

"Zhhl told me Byelor would be reborn. My son was on *Juxj* when Kivita rammed it into that Portal. I might have saved him, damn you! Perhaps you'll enlighten me as to why I shouldn't kill you both now?"

Sar glared back at him, hands nearing Kivita's right arm. "Nothing's stopping you."

Harsh laughter came over the helmet speaker. "So, instead of dying in a climactic battle with the Inheritors, you plan to sell your life for this woman? The prophets will still desire her, Redryll." Shekelor raised the beam rifle higher.

Sar's gloved hand hung inches from Kivita's right arm.

"Redryll!" Shekelor yelled through the speaker. The rifle trembled in his grasp. "She is not yours!"

A shape blocked the red giant's glare for a moment. Sar looked up.

An Aldaakian shuttle hovered above and between *Frevyx* and *Fanged Pauper*. Seul stared at him through the cockpit viewport. Iron will gleamed in her white-within-azure eyes.

"Sar, this is Jaah. My beamer is aimed and ready," Seul said over his helmet speaker.

A long moment passed. Ice glanced off Sar's body.

He pulled Kivita to him, though a throb traveled

along his left leg. Tiny debris, frozen for epochs, drifted away from them, while the ring continued its infinitesimal rotation.

Sar embraced Kivita while eyeing Shekelor. "She belongs to everyone."

Ice drifted between them, a spackled plane of a hundred thousand frozen mirrors. Sar didn't blink. Shekelor's purple eye twitched.

Jaw tightening, Shekelor stepped back into *Fanged Pauper*'s airlock. "Make sure Kivita is worth this, Redryll. Enjoy your respite. Far worse enemies than I shall stalk you now. But I shan't be far. Not far at all."

Fanged Pauper's hatch slid shut as Shekelor smirked. The vessel drifted a few hundred feet away, shimmered into a light jump, and disappeared.

Releasing a tremendous breath, Sar tapped his wrist panel. "Jandeel, reel me in. Hurry."

While the flexi wound itself back into *Frevyx*, Sar clutched Kivita to his chest. Vacuum frost obscured all but a shadow of her face. Sar placed a hand over her heart as they both drifted from the shuttle's shadow and back into the sunlight.

The gentle beat under his hand made Sar's throat tighten.

Once inside the airlock chamber, the hatch hissed shut. Sar forced himself to wait until atmospheric pressure and air returned. *Frevyx*'s bridge and other hatches opened, and the Thedes watched with hope. Some invoked prayers to the Solars. Others beamed at Sar with admiration.

Rhii and Basheev brought medical supplies from the storage locker, while Jandeel helped Sar ease Kivita to the floor. Dunaar's Scepter clattered against a bulkhead.

"Rhyer, Rhyer, your mission is complete," Bredine whispered.

Sar knelt over Kivita. Melted frost pooled into water around her. Still wearing his gloves, he unlocked Kivita's helmet. Everyone gasped at the vacuum frost coating Kivita's nostrils and mouth. Her eyelids had almost frozen shut.

"Need some heating pads and pink mollusk extract!" Sar called.

Rhii handed him the pads, which he pressed to Kivita's face. Water ran down her cheeks and into her suit. Sar touched her neck; a weak pulse crept under his fingers.

"She's alive," Sar said in a low voice.

Everyone cheered, but he held up a hand and removed the heating pad.

Kivita didn't open her eyes.

"Stars burning, why doesn't she wake up?" Basheev asked.

"She might have frost sickness." Jandeel glanced at Sar with troubled eyes.

"Redryll? The queen has returned, gushing hot." Bredine leaned over Kivita. "Send it back to her."

Jandeel, Rhii, and the rest watched Sar with renewed hope. It seemed a new star had ignited the darkness haunting them all.

"Kiv?" Sar placed both hands on her cheeks. Their latent chill concerned him, but all the things he'd wanted to say, all the things he'd wanted to do with her, flooded the emotional pit in his soul.

Pressing his lips to hers, he imagined their short, precious months in orbit over Gontalo....Their heated, desperate moments outside the Naxan hive ship...The pain in his chest just before sending her and Cheseia away on *Frevyx*.

The pulse under his fingers beat faster and faster.

"Keep sending," Bredine whispered.

Sar kissed her again and reached deep into his heart.

The relief he'd felt upon seeing her aboard *Luccan's Wish*, then the agony when Shekelor had taken her. The pride he felt knowing she'd inspired not only him, but also his Thede friends. Inspired the entire Cetturo Arm, after sending out that wideband signal from the Sarrhdtuu vessel. Like he'd told Shekelor, Kivita and the good she could do belonged to everyone now.

A gentle, warm gasp caressed his lips.

Sar drew back. Kivita opened her eyes.

She coughed and moaned. Sar pried apart the seals on her envirosuit, still crusted with frost; then Jandeel pulled the suit away. Sar lifted her in a tight embrace as the Thedes smiled and laughed around them. Weeping again, Rhii hugged Sar and Kivita both. Basheev kissed Kivita's cheek. Everyone touched collectively for a long moment, encircling Sar and Kivita.

"You're home," Sar breathed in Kivita's ear.

She coughed, then frowned at him. "Was that supposed to be my Umiracan Kiss?"

Sar laughed and squeezed her to his chest.

39

"Stars blinking and receding, miss! Eat these thogens."
Rhii spooned the barnacle powder into Kivita's mouth.

Grimacing at the thogens' taste, Kivita stood in
Frevyx's central corridor. Though tired and aching from
her ordeal, the others wanted—maybe even needed—to
hear her speak.

Great. What could she possibly tell them after what
they'd just endured?

As the survivors from *Luccan's Wish* watched her
with anticipation, four squads of Aldaakians, fronted by
Seul, waited just inside the airlock chamber. Sar rested
in his hammock, left leg propped on a stool. A bony
woman with short dark hair and large green eyes waited
outside the bridge with Jandeel, examining Kivita with
keen interest. Every now and then, the woman tugged
Jandeel closer to her.

Kivita stared at the floor. "I don't have Navon's strong
voice or Jandeel's skillful words. I don't have all the answers. But I have some ideas on what we can do next.
First, I want to clear something up."

A lump rose in her throat. She faced everyone. "I
want you all to know that Cheseia and her twin sister,

Zhara, gave their lives on that Sarrhdtuu ship, as did Navon, so that I could be standing here now. I'll hear nothing ill of them."

Looks of surprise passed along the crowd.

Sar closed his eyes for a moment, then gave her a forlorn smile.

Kivita placed her hands on her hips. "By now you all know the Sarrhdtuu tried to use me, like they wanted to use my mother. We know the Vim still exist. Yeah, maybe not where we can easily find them, but they're out there. So are the Sarrhdtuu. And it won't take long for the prophets on Haldon Prime to select another Rector."

"War is coming between my people and the Inheritors," Seul said. "The blockade over Tejuit is just the beginning. Though I can't speak for others, I'm with you, Kivita Vondir. I don't believe the Vim will be found again without your talents. My ship and my Troopers are yours."

The Thedes all gasped and whispered. Kivita blinked, then walked over and embraced Seul.

"I swear I'll not ask you to do something I wouldn't," Kivita said.

Seul, visibly surprised by the hug, grinned. "I'll do it, anyway."

"Seul, I'm sorry about . . ." Kivita shook her head.

"Kael is with Niaaq Aldaar now. I still have my daughter to find."

A great warmth rose in Kivita's chest. "Vuul sent a transmission before *Aldaar* blew."

Seul went rigid. "What do you mean?"

"It contained *Aldaar*'s databanks," Kivita replied. "As well as your personal records."

Trembling, Seul gripped Kivita's arm. "My daughter?"

"Her name is Taeu Jaah," Kivita whispered.

Seul mouthed the name, then smiled. "Now I know who I am looking for. And who I will follow." She bowed her head.

Excited murmurs rippled through the Thedes, and expectation filled their eyes. How would she ever live up to it?

Jandeel raised his voice. "So, you'll lead us? As queen?" Numerous cheers and whistles followed his question, though Sar studied her with neutral eyes.

"No," Kivita said.

Shocked stares greeted her. Sar's brow creased.

"I'll lead you as your friend. You want me to accept my mother's throne? Yeah, then here's the rules: no bowing. No titles. I'm still Kivita. Navon told me nobility comes from within, not some silly crown."

More cheers and whoops, more hopeful smiles. But why did her throat feel so tight?

Sar sat up in the hammock. "What about a headquarters? We still have hundreds of contacts in the Cetturo Arm. How will you run the Thedes? Sutara has fallen to the Inheritors, and Tejuit will be a mess. Where can we go?"

"Redryll? Kivita Narbas can send, that's how." Bredine tugged Jandeel's sleeve and leaned on him.

"If that's what it takes," Kivita said. "The revolution isn't over, but it remains what Luccan and Navon wanted it to be: an organization of people spreading knowledge. Maybe with what I can do, our enemies will have a harder time silencing us. I won't support uprisings if we can change things in a peaceful way. But I'm not afraid to fight."

Sar's green-brown speckled eyes narrowed, and a

self-conscious anxiety overcame Kivita. What did he want?

"Tell her, Bredine," Sar said.

Kivita examined the thin woman. All she knew was that Bredine Ov had been Dunaar's most talented captive Savant.

"Rhyer slept in void cold, too," Bredine said. "Slept, and woke every few years. Kivita? Hmm. I protected Rhyer Vondir on Haldon Prime while you still slept in royal gold. Hmm. He readied you to return the Vim message. Rhyer, Rhyer. He recorded Ascali songs to mar Sarrhdtuu ears. Kivita? He saved a ship of Savants, placed them in a special system."

Sar explained Bredine's history and her relation to Rector Broujel. Upon hearing his words, all regarded the woman with awe and sympathy. Jandeel gazed at Bredine with different eyes, his exasperation at her attention vanishing.

"But where would Father have . . ." Kivita paused. "My old trawler, *Terredyn Narbas*, with all that Ascali claw graffiti. The coordinates might be in its databanks! We'll need those Savants he saved. Bredine, are you sure?"

Nodding, Bredine patted Jandeel's hand.

"Then that's our first destination," Kivita said. "Tejuit. Yeah, the blockade will be active, and war may have already broken out in the system, but we need to reestablish contact with the Tannocci nobles and Naxan merchants, anyway. Maybe the other Aldaakians, if they'll listen."

Seul and her Troopers nodded.

"What about this?" Jandeel handed Kivita the Scepter of Office. "Every Rector since Arcuri himself has carried this thing."

"A datacore," Bredine said.

With tentative steps, Kivita approached it. Her hands numbed and her temples tingled. Focusing her will, Kivita peeled away the datacore's first layer.

Her mouth fell open.

Majestic yellow suns, gorgeous blue dwarfs, and roiling-hot nebulae drifted through her thoughts. The vision transformed into a sandstone mosaic of the same image. Zhhl and a man in yellow robes stood before it. Interspersed with this was images of Meh Sat's destruction, like she'd already seen in the Juxj Star.

It was a firsthand view of Arcuri's deal with the Sarrhdtuu, when Zhhl had promised the Inheritors that they'd join the Vim in the Core—if they but followed Sarrhdtuu advice. Their whole religion was based on a lie, with every Rector a puppet in a game they hadn't understood. Hell, she barely comprehended it. Still gaping, Kivita withdrew her mind from the Scepter. What else would it reveal? She'd need time to study it, absorb everything it contained.

"What do you see?" Jandeel asked.

Concentrating, Kivita sent the information into everyone's mind. All of them blinked and inhaled.

"Sorry," she said. "But I wanted you to understand what we're really up against. We're still going to be hated, hunted. But we're going to do it anyway. First we'll salvage what cryopods we can from the wreckage outside and put them in *Frevyx's* cargo hold. There's not enough life support and food on board for everyone, so we must have them. Then we'll make a light jump to Tejuit."

"Stars flaring, then. Let's get going!" Basheev cried.

Smiling, Kivita knelt and kissed his forehead. One by

one, all the Thedes walked by and touched Kivita's shoulders. The Aldaakians drew and raised their swords.

Bredine hugged her and whispered, "Kivita? Only a true queen kneels before those she leads."

Pressing her close, Kivita whispered back, "Thank you for what you've done. For Sar."

After Kivita had spoken to everyone individually, the Aldaakians boarded their shuttle. Jandeel and several others donned envirosuits to aid Seul in finding enough cryopods for everybody. The rest waited in the main corridor, excited and talkative.

With a tight jaw, Sar limped from the hammock into the toilet.

Kivita followed him and slammed the door.

He faced her and sighed. "Look, this—"

"I know I'm guilty of promising these people a lot," Kivita whispered. "Did you see how they looked at me when I woke up in the airlock chamber? Like I was some mythical goddess or something. I don't like it. Because of me, so many—"

"Have hope," Sar said.

Kivita crossed her arms as Sar leaned on the counter. "You think I'm doing this all wrong, don't you? We don't have armies and fleets. What else can we do?"

"That signal you sent has spread across the Cetturo Arm. The Sarrhdtuu and Inheritors may think you died in the battle, but the story won't. The daughter of Queen Narbas is alive." Sar grunted and touched his left leg. "I saw some of the data you sent out on *Frevyx*'s terminal. How to replicate Vim starship engines, how to create our own fusion energy dumps. That means no more salvaging, and no more Inheritor monopoly on technology. That alone will change everything in the Arm."

Steadying him, Kivita met his eyes. "Is that all you're thinking about, smoothie?"

He plucked at his gray bodyglove, where blue medical tape and bandages had been wound around his left leg above the knee. Faint bruises covered his chin, neck, and his right brow. His eyes danced over her body, then returned to meet hers.

"No, sweetness. I'm thinking that I'm no good for you. That we'll never have enough time together. That I can't—"

"Bullshit." She placed his hand over her heart. "I felt you out there in the cold. There's a hell of a lot you can still salvage inside here, Sar Redryll."

"Greatest salvage of all," Sar said in a low voice.

She almost touched his bruised face, then grimaced. "How much will it hurt to kiss you? Looks like you got in a fight with a Bellerion swamp sloth." She didn't say he looked more handsome than ever before.

He pulled her close and kissed her lips, her cheeks, her hair, her neck. Closing her eyes, Kivita dug her fingers into his bodyglove; then something made her push away from him.

"Don't touch me unless you're staying with me," she said, tugging off her bodyglove. Clicking out of her polyboots, she undid her Dirr braid.

Sar's hands spread down her lower back. "Looks like I touched."

Dressed in nothing but her two-piece underwear, Kivita leaned close and nudged her thigh against his. "Yeah, and that chit from Tejuit is still on my trawler. I might let you cash it in. You got to find my ship first, though."

Sar jerked as she brushed his wounded left knee.

"Oh, shit. I'm sorry. I—" Kivita paused as his hands cupped her face.

"No, Kiv. I'm sorry. Bredine told me your message while you were floating out there." He stripped off his bodyglove. Larger bruises dotted his hard musculature.

"You know I love you," she breathed in his ear as he cupped her rump in one hand. "But I'm not the salvager you once knew. And I know you're not sterile."

Sar drew back. "How did you . . . ? Cheseia told you." He looked away.

"She loved you until the end. She wanted you to know that."

Sar clasped her hands. "I'll support you in this peaceful notion you have. Shekelor showed me what vengeance can do to a man. But listen. We can't take the risk of our children being mutants like me—"

Kivita silenced him with a kiss. "Life is a risk."

Pulling her close, he kissed her hair. "Moments like this will be few, Kiv. You can't stay hidden, and not just from enemies. Those people out there need to see you. Believe in you, like they did your mother."

Kivita kissed his chest. "So, you don't mind having a queen for a lover? Having the most wanted woman in the Arm . . . for your wife?"

Sar smirked. "You'll need to grow longer hair to hold two more braids, like a proper married Dirr woman."

"Picky ass." She snuggled closer to him. "How long can we stay in here before they look for us?"

Sar's hands caressed her hips. "Not long enough."

"Then I might have time to give you a Susuron Kiss," Kivita said. "It goes something like . . ."

Her words ended as their lips, hearts, and minds joined. A merger of love, a sharing of knowledge and understanding. Kivita showed him visions of Frevyx, her mother, and the secrets of their origins. All the stars uncounted and yet to be visited.

Most of all, Kivita showed him the star within herself: burning bright for him, for truth, and for the future of all.